Book 1: The Seventh of December Series

THE SEVENTH OF DECEMBER

THE CZARINA'S NECKLACE

GARRICK JONES

This is an IndieMosh book

brought to you by MoshPit Publishing
an imprint of Mosher's Business Support Pty Ltd

PO Box 4363
Penrith NSW 2750

indiemosh.com.au

 A catalogue record for this work is available from the National Library of Australia

https://www.nla.gov.au/collections

Title: The Seventh of December

Subtitle: The Czarina's Necklace

Author: Jones, Garrick (1948–)

ISBNs: 978-1-922440-74-7 (paperback)
            978-1-922440-75-4 (ebook – epub)
            978-1-922440-76-1 (ebook – mobi)

Subjects: FICTION: LGBT / Gay; Historical / World War II; Action & Adventure; Thrillers / Historical.

This story is entirely a work of fiction. No character in this story is taken from real life. Any resemblance to any person or persons living or dead is accidental and unintentional. The author, their agents and publishers cannot be held responsible for any claim otherwise and take no responsibility for any such coincidence.

Cover design by Garrick Jones.
Cover images Unsplash and Library of Congress, public domain.

Editing by Linda McQueen, Fiona Pickles.

Proofreading by Victoria Milne Professional Editing

Contents

ACKNOWLEDGEMENTS

The author wishes to thank the following people and organisations for their input, advice, and very kind and generous support, especially the archivists at the museums and the Royal institutions:

Aleksandr Voinov, Dr. David Brennan, Carol Gaskell, The Australian War Museum, The British Museum, The Imperial War Museum, The Royal Collection, The Queen's Archives.

NOTES ON THE SECOND EDITION

This new edition of The Seventh of December has been expanded and has taken into account future events from the sequel, X for Extortion, fitting them into the narrative chronologically.

There is a new lengthy prologue, which serves to introduce the reader to the action/adventure style novel that was originally intended. A deleted character has also been restored, vital to the storyline of the fourth book in the series.

Much comment was made in reviews for the first edition on the prowess of Tommy Haupner, the protagonist of this story, and his abundant talents. Readers of history and those who study the period will realise that I modelled Tommy after a true life wartime hero and spy, whose abilities make Tommy's pale by comparison.

Morris "Moe" Berg was a premier league American baseball player, who not only spoke eleven languages, but graduated from Princeton University, studied at the Sorbonne in Paris, and graduated in law from Columbia Law School. He was recruited by Billy Donovan (who you'll meet in this story) and was sent to Zürich during the war to assess the progress of the Nazi's atomic bomb development by attending a lecture by the famous physicist, Werner Heisenberg. Combat trained and licensed to kill, Berg was authorised to assassinate Heisenberg if he felt the Germans had already progressed far enough to make a viable nuclear weapon. Although there's no remaining direct evidence, many historians believe that Berg was also gay.

Thousands of classical performers fought during the Second World War, many of them famous in their homelands and many giving their lives. Equally, MI6, the SOE, and the OSS were not averse to using performers as informants, gathering information as they travelled, entertaining troops or giving morale and fund raising concerts.

Noel Coward was one such British artist, running the propaganda office in Paris at the outbreak of war, also working for the OSS to convince the American public that the war in Europe needed support.

This book is dedicated to the tens of thousands of gay servicemen on both sides of the war who fought or gave their lives to protect those they loved.

PROLOGUE

Snow?

No one had expected snow. Least of all me. Nazis, machine guns, collaborators? Yes, they were par for the course. But, of all the rotten luck, snow?

It was nine in the evening on the last day of January, 1941, and we stood smack-bang in the middle of an open field in occupied Normandy, surrounded on all sides by an expanse of unblemished snow.

"Well, here's another fine mess you've gotten me into …" my companion said with a wry grin.

"It's another *nice* mess, if you don't mind," I replied. "If you're going to quote Laurel and Hardy, make sure you get it right."

I was rewarded with a head toss and an eye-roll. I supposed I deserved both.

★★★★★

The previous day had started well. Our car trip north to St. Neots had been uneventful, although we'd been over-exuberant, considering what we were about to do.

Four of us were crammed into the back of a sequestered Bedford

OYD lorry. Crammed in because although it could hold a dozen men, most of the space was taken up by barrels of petrol and water—as if the human cargo was an afterthought. The SOE had had a sudden, urgent need of an aircraft. So, instead of their Hudson A-29 out of Biggin Hill, twelve miles southeast of London, we'd been despatched on a long journey, fifty-five miles north to RAF Tempsford in Bedfordshire, and to a specially outfitted Whitley bomber.

I'd wanted the Hudson because of the ease of getting out of the damned thing. An open doorway at the rear of the fuselage was a whole lot different from a hatch in the fuselage floor. The circular space in the floor of the Whitley had become known as the "growl hole" to many trainee parachutists at Tempsford. It was only wide enough for one man at a time, and each had to jump in an upright rigid position, otherwise there was the real danger of banging his or her nose or face against the inside of the hole. It happened so frequently it was known as "ringing the bell". It was a laborious process for us four and took valuable seconds for each procedure, unlike the Hudson, in which we'd have fastened our rip-cords to the static line that ran along the ceiling of the fuselage, and then run and jumped from the aircraft in quick succession—zip, zip, zip, zip.

That's how I'd wanted it to happen.

*****

Things had gone arse-up from the moment we'd crossed the French coast.

The lighthouse at Goury was our reference point. Once we sighted it, we headed down the coast for a few kilometres before turning inland. We were to be met by locals, who'd arranged to light a bonfire in the central square of Merquetot to celebrate the feast day of Sainte Marcelle. Once the pilot spied the fire, it was our signal to jump.

One of our jokes in the lorry on the way to Tempsford had been a variation on an old chestnut—a Scot, a Pole, a Yank, and an Aussie dropped into a bar—we hadn't dropped into a bar, but into a stupid situation, brought about by the sudden change of aircraft.

After dropping our supply canister, the Yank and the Scot successfully launched themselves through the open hole in the Whitley.

When it was the Pole's and my turn, we ran into turbulence and the aircraft lurched. The despatcher fumbled with the static line, frantically attempting to attach it to the ceiling hook, but was continuously knocked off balance. It took three attempts to get it secured before we were able to make our jumps. It cost us twenty seconds—a third of a minute. In an aircraft travelling at the best part of one hundred and fifty miles an hour, that small amount of time made an enormous difference to the distance we'd travelled between our friends' jumps and our own. From above, as I floated towards the ground, I saw them drifting in the direction of the field in which we were to be met by members of the Resistance. We landed long after them, in another field perhaps two kilometres to the north.

It certainly was a "nice mess". We were separated from our companions by the local stream, the roadway to the coast, and a dense copse of trees. The field in which we'd landed left us dangerously exposed. And then there was the snow. How we were going to get to cover without leaving footprints and the marks of our landing were a major problem.

*****

"Stop! There's a car coming."

We were about to cross the road, crouched low in a shallow ditch, just behind a straggly hedge of clipped, leafless willows. A few hundred metres to our east, the roadway on either side of a small crest was lined with trees, their branches touching over the road. I'd seen the vehicle's headlights illuminating the underside of the canopy well before it came into view. Driving at night with lights on meant it could only be Germans—there was a curfew for the locals.

Behind us was the field in which we'd landed—even at a distance and in the dim light, our footprints still showed clearly as dark tracks in the snow, making a line from the centre of the field to the bocage at its east—deliberately away from the village of Merquetot. The last thing we wanted was for Germans to tear the village apart looking for Allied spies. Once we reached the eastern edge of the field, we walked in the snow-free zone at the base of the hedgerows. No one would know which way we'd gone.

The *Kübelwagen* began to slow down as it passed by, and then came to a stop a short distance from us. There were five men in the vehicle: a uniformed corporal, two privates, and two men in civilian clothing, perched on the folded-down roof canopy of the car. The moment the vehicle drew to a stop, the two civilians jumped onto the road and immediately lit up cigarettes. They began to speak in French.

Collaborators! The word flashed across my mind at the same time the German corporal spoke. "I hate fucking collaborators," was more or less what he said, with a strong *Hessischer* accent. He heaved himself out of the car and, turning his back, began to piss into the hedges on the other side of the road, while the driver of the *Kübelwagen* began to speak to the two civilians in ragged, halting French. I was on the point of being driven crazy by the jarring, soul-destroying attempts of the three men as they tried to communicate to one another in clumsy, broken French and German. In a year of occupation, none of them seemed to have learned more than a few words of the other's language.

This whole situation was making me very nervous. The other two members of our team were waiting for us. Our orders were clear: if by chance we were separated during the drop, we should head to the rendezvous point and wait for the others. I hoped they wouldn't come looking for us and stumble into a roadside meeting of Krauts and *collabos.*

The Pole and I were trapped—there was nothing we could do. Movement of any sort, despite the darkness, would have been seen instantly. We were stuck behind a hedge in the freezing cold, metres from a car full of Jerries, and unable to move until the men on the road had finished discussing whatever had them so agitated.

Eventually, I understood before any of them did. It came from being trilingual. I'd been brought up in Australia speaking French and German—but that's another story. The local German *Kommandant* had promised a deer to the local mayor as a sweetener for the festival at Merquetot. It was a lip-service good deed. But, when the Germans had visited the gamekeeper and his wife earlier that morning, they'd taken two deer and only paid for one. They planned to have their own private party away from Merquetot.

"If you hadn't been so greedy, none of this would have happened," the driver of the wagon grumbled to his corporal.

"You won't mind tucking into a bit of free venison when we get back to barracks. How was I to know they'd complain? Anyway, this is business between *Erbfeinde*—let the French sort it out between themselves."

"Tell them we have to go," one of the Frenchmen said to his companion, the only one of the two of them who had more than a dozen words in German. "The others will already be there."

The other Frenchman mimed and pointed at his watch and then to the south, indicating the two of them were leaving. "We're off to the cottage just south of here to meet up with two pals," he said in French. "And to speak about the … deer," he added in fractured German. The Germans shook their heads. They didn't understand a word, not even his last phrase in their own language.

South? South was where our friends had landed.

"They're probably going to call in to say goodnight to the game-keeper's wife, if you ask me," the German driver mumbled. "If it weren't for our orders, I know I'd be knocking on her door for a bit of night-time fraternisation—husband or no husband."

The corporal slapped the back of the soldier's neck. No doubt he'd had the same thought himself. *"À la … sharbonyuse …?"* he asked the Frenchman.

I felt ice in my belly. Despite the man's hideous approximation of the word, I knew he meant to say *"charbonnière"*—the charcoal burner. And that was our designated rendezvous point—the charcoal burner was the wife of the local gamekeeper. I wasn't anxious about the Yank and the Scot; they could look after themselves. I was more concerned about the four local Resistance contacts who'd arranged to meet us there.

"La mitrailleuse … laquelle que vous m'avez promis?" the taller of the two Frenchmen asked.

"What did he say?"

"He's asking for a machine gun, Corporal," the driver said with disgust. "Please don't tell me you promised to give him a gun for sorting this out."

"All I did was nod before you turned up. I've no idea what any of these people are saying. French just sounds like a whole lot of mumbling with a mouth full of horse chaff to me. Give him that MP18 in the weapons locker. It's so old it'll probably blow his balls off the moment he pulls the trigger."

The driver sighed deeply and then asked his companion for the locker key. He fiddled for a moment with the antiquated machine gun. I could see he was trying to release the prominent safety catch, which seemed to be stuck. After a few unsuccessful attempts, he growled with annoyance and then threw the gun to the Frenchman, who looked very pleased with himself and slung it over his shoulder. The other collaborator already had a rifle.

After a few half-hearted farewells, the Germans leaned against their car and watched the Frenchmen disappear into the copse of trees that lined the southern edge of the roadway. The corporal spat on the ground as the men moved out of view and then flicked his cigarette butt after them.

"He forgot the ammunition," the driver said, holding the box cartridge in the air. The corporal snatched it from his hand and threw it into the tree line, at the spot where the men had disappeared into the woods.

"Fat lot of good that'll do them," the driver quipped. "And did you know the safety is fucked on that piece of shit?"

The corporal ignored him. "Did I tell you how much I hate collaborators?" he growled.

"Only a million times, Herr *Stabsgefreiter*. What with that and you stopping every five minutes to have a piss, you're going to get us all killed by one of those 'filthy collaborators', as you like to call them. Just wait until one of them learns enough German to understand you."

"You know what I hate about you, Helmut?" the corporal said as they got back into the *Kübelwagen*. "You've got a fat mouth on you and no respect for your superiors."

"Well, let me tell you, *sir*, you'll get all the respect you need in a *KZ* if I decide to tell the *Kommandant* about the black-market business you run on the side."

"Just drive the fucking car, before I shoot you and leave your body for the *Franzosen* and their pigs!"

The sounds of their squabbling became inaudible as, in a fit of anger, the driver revved the engine and then slammed the *Kübelwagen* into gear, lurching off towards Merquetot and the road north to their barracks at Saint-Germain-des-Vaux.

*****

"The tall one who got the machine gun said they were meeting *two* friends?" I asked. The men had spoken in Gascon. Although I could understand nearly all of it, there were some expressions I wasn't used to. On several occasions during sorties to occupied France last year, I'd been grateful the Pole's mother came from Bordeaux. He spoke several dialects of French faultlessly.

"Yes," he replied.

"And we've been here how long?"

"The little roadside chat took just over eleven minutes," he replied, checking his watch.

"Then we'd better shake a leg."

My companion only needed a few seconds before he raised the MP18's box magazine in the air. He had a nose for finding things, even in the dark. He put it in his backpack—better to be safe than sorry.

It was three days after the new moon—there was barely enough moonlight to see where we were going—but the well-worn trail through the stand of tall beeches was easy enough to follow. We moved silently through the dense wood, parallel with the pathway, using the trees as cover.

The Pole suddenly crouched, one hand stretched out behind him as a warning. "Shit!" he whispered. I scrambled up next to him and then saw why he'd stopped. Through the tree trunks ahead of us I saw an open field, probably about three cricket pitches across. There was no way we could follow the two collaborators over sixty metres of open ground without being seen, no matter how stealthily we moved. We had to go around the edge of the field.

About halfway down its side, I stopped and pulled out my field

7

glasses. Right at the edge, in the middle of the long side of the field, a large, roaring bonfire in front of a stone cottage threw off enough light for me to see what was going on. I counted ten figures—eight men, a boy, and a woman, who seemed to be split into two groups and were arguing. Their voices carried across the field, although not clearly enough for me to hear the words. The charcoal burner's house was hosting an impromptu party—a rowdy, dangerous-looking one.

The soft double-hoot of a barn owl made me smile with relief. In a moment, our two missing friends arrived at our side out of the dark.

"What kept you?" the American asked.

"Krauts on the road," I explained. "Those two over there, the tall one with the machine gun and the shorter one with the rifle over his shoulder, were dropped off on the road by a local patrol. They're here to meet up with two other collaborators. The man and woman must be the gamekeeper and his wife. But who's the kid?"

The Scot answered. "He's more like a half-man; you know, that in-between age—I'd say fifteen or sixteen. Boy, has he ever got a mouth on him."

"Yeah?"

"There's an argument going on about something I couldn't work out, but that kid can swear like a dock worker. It was all I could do not to piss myself with laughter."

"How did you overhear all this?" I asked.

"There's a spot not far from the house—close enough to jump in if we have intervene. Follow me, Aussie."

"Okay. But let's just let them sort it out between themselves. We don't want to get involved if we don't have to."

"You might change your mind when we get closer," the American said with a soft snort.

"Why?"

"You'll see … come on."

We threaded our way through the trees and around the edge of the field until we arrived behind a thicket of hawthorn and hazel, about fifteen metres from the loudly arguing group. The cottage was sheltered by an enormous oak, whose branches spread out over the house and the clearing in front of it. I started to wonder why the American had said he thought I might change my mind when I got here, and was about to ask, when he pointed above the group of Frenchmen, who were really going at it now.

Hell and damnation! Our supply canister was swinging in the darkness, perhaps about five metres above the heads of the quarrelsome group below. It was caught on a tree branch that had pierced one pane of its parachute. The people below seemed unaware it was dangling above them. Through my binoculars, I could see it wouldn't be long before the perilously bent tree branch gave way, or the weight of the canister tore the silk and it fell to the ground. It would sure as hell scare the living daylights out of everyone—and knock the stuffing out of anyone unlucky enough to be directly underneath.

"Speak in whatever French dialect you know," I said to the Scot and the Pole, and then, to the American, whose French was accented, "You keep quiet. Pretend you've got laryngitis if anyone asks. I think it's time we showed our faces."

We scampered quietly back down the field, about twenty metres from where we'd been observing, and then sauntered out into the field, pretend-chatting about farming and laughing every so often, as if we were sharing jokes. We'd made our drops dressed in farm worker clothing—jackets, heavy woollen trousers, flat caps or berets.

"Who are you?" the tall, machine-gun toting collaborator asked after we'd called out our various hellos—*Allô, Tiens, Salut, B'soir*—all with feigned, country, good cheer.

"Tout va bien, mes amis?" our Pole said in a thick Gascon accent, ignoring his question.

"You didn't answer my question, *salop*! Who are you?" Machine Gun said.

"I didn't answer it because I don't know who the fuck is asking it, *connard*."

"That's a stupid way of talking to the person who's holding a gun," he replied angrily.

"Steady on," I said. "We were sent here by that fat German corporal with the bladder problem."

"Oh," the man said, reluctantly backing down. "Why? Did he think we needed help?"

"I've no idea—perhaps he doesn't trust you?"

Machine Gun introduced himself as Blaise, and then offered the names of his three fellow collaborators. I noticed he didn't introduce any of the others, with whom he'd been arguing when we'd arrived, and who I assumed must be our contacts.

The boy among them didn't seem at all nervous. In fact there was a fierce gleam in his eyes—he was trying to keep his anger under control. As I caught his eye, he clasped his hands and raised them slowly to his mouth, blowing softly across the space between his thumbs. It was our call-sign—the call of the tawny owl, or *chouette hulotte*, as the French called it—the agreed signal to identify our contacts.

"Pipe down, kid! Us grown-ups are trying to talk," Blaise growled.

"It's fucking cold, you bad-tempered turd," the boy snapped. "Just warming my hands."

"You're in a friendly mood," I said to Blaise, drawing his attention away from the young man.

"I'm not here to be friendly," he replied.

"Then why are you here? And does it really matter if the kid's got cold hands?"

"What's it to you, *dandin*?"

"I'm no *dolt*, and I'm not here to make trouble. I just find it sad a grown man with a machine gun in his hands feels he has to start playing big man with a kid."

"Mind your own fucking business," the man ordered, prodding me in the chest with one forefinger. He seemed determined to provoke me.

"Why don't you put your gun down and roll your sleeves up—I'd be only too happy to rearrange your features if you're that desperate for a fight," the American said, stepping up behind me.

I groaned. I'd told him to keep quiet. His transatlantic vowels were unmistakable.

"What sort of an accent is that? Who the hell are you people?" the man snapped and then took a step backwards, raising his weapon.

A loud creak from above, following by a ripping sound, made me push the American to one side and call out at the top of my voice to get back. I cursed under my breath. I'd spoken in English. With an enormous whoosh, the canister fell directly onto the bonfire. It hit the pyre with a loud thud and an accompanying shower of sparks and a spray of flaming, broken sticks and branches.

There was a very brief moment of stunned silence, followed by an eruption of confused shouts and sounds of fighting. The collaborators had not only realised they'd fallen into the middle of a group of Resistance fighters but also they were outnumbered. My first thought was for the canister, which had sprung half-open, several of its clasps having come apart as it had hit the ground. In it was our radio and much of the equipment we'd brought for the men we were to train. But, more importantly, it held three crates of ammunition, hand grenades, and plastique—there'd be nothing much left of any of us if that lot hit the flames.

It was a heavy darned thing, as tall as me and twice the weight. With one enormous heave, my tendons straining, I pulled it from the fire and then fell backwards with a loud groan. As I sat up, I looked around. My friends had restrained three of the collaborators but were grim faced, staring intently at something behind me.

I swivelled around on my backside. Blaise stood with his back against the charcoal burner's cottage, one hand grasping the collar of the American's shirt, the other pushing the muzzle of his machine gun hard up against the Yankee's chin.

"Let them go!" Blaise yelled. "Otherwise this one loses his head."

His eyes were dark with fury, trying to stare me down as I slowly got to my feet. If he was looking at my face, it meant he wouldn't notice what I was doing with my hands. *Trust me,* I finger-spelled to the wide-eyed Yank, aggressively returning Blaise's stare and daring him to shift his gaze. "Don't do what he says," I yelled to the other members of my team in English.

"Speak in French, *fils de salaud!*" the man growled. "I won't tell you again. This one's dead if you don't do as I say."

"You haven't fired a machine gun before, have you?" I asked, wiping the dust off my trousers, but continuing to maintain eye contact.

My deliberately casual attitude made him growl. "Have you lost your mind? Of course I have … dozens of times. Get your hands in the air!"

"Then you'll know that before you fire it, you'll have to release the safety catch," I said, edging towards him, my palms upturned to show I was unarmed.

He prodded the American's neck with the muzzle of his weapon. "I won't warn you again," he said and then lifted the gun above his head to fire off a few warning shots.

Nothing happened—the trigger just clicked noisily as he repeatedly tried to fire the weapon.

The Pole shouted from behind me. "Hey, you! *Monsieur le casse-couilles!* Just in case you do manage to release the safety catch, you might need bullets!" He held up the magazine he'd retrieved from his backpack.

"What are you going to do now, Blaise?" I asked provocatively. "Shoot us with words?"

The collaborator roared in frustration and then put his knee into the American's back, sending him sprawling. He threw the machine gun at me and tore off into the darkness—I was right on his heels. He began to scream insults as he hurtled through the darkness, continually glancing over his shoulder and growling as the gap closed between us.

"Watch out for bear traps," I called out, trying to make him look at his feet instead of where he was going.

My ploy worked.

"Fils de—" he shouted. His voice cut off mid-curse as he ran head-first into the trunk of a tree. With a groan he fell back onto the ground.

I hadn't really wanted the situation to deteriorate to the point that Blaise and his three friends would have to die. However, what was done was done. I took a few deep breaths and then moved up quietly behind him and grabbed a handful of his hair. I was about to reach around to break his neck with my other arm when he sprang to his feet and jabbed at me with a knife. Instinctively, I jumped out of the way and his blade passed under my arm.

"Not so smart now are we?" Blaise spat, grinning wildly. "Ever go head-to-head with a trained knife fighter before, Englishman?"

I sighed. I'd been trained to fight with knives from the age of eleven. It was my combat speciality. This man was no trained fighter—he had no idea how to use a knife. He grasped it awkwardly, his wrist stiff and inflexible, and crouched on the soles of his feet, his heels on the ground and his knees almost touching. His balance was all wrong—a gust of wind would knock him over. By far the biggest giveaway was he couldn't stop flicking back and forth between my feet and my hands instead of maintaining eye contact, something an experienced hand-to-hand combat fighter would be certain to have as their primary focus.

"Sure I have, Blaise. But the question is, have you?"

Intent on checking my hands and my feet, he hadn't noticed I'd already retrieved my F-S knife from its holster in the belt at the back of my trousers. The knife handle was concealed in my fist, its blade tucked up tight against my wrist and pressed along the underside of my forearm.

"*Putain!* You're very arrogant for someone who's going to die. Get ready to say hello to whatever Maker it is you English have up there," he said.

"I'll yell it down to you in the special hell reserved for traitors," I replied, "over the shoulder of the demon who's up to his balls in your arsehole."

It was the provocation I'd been hoping would work. He roared angrily and rushed across the space between us with his knife hand high above his head—the fool's way of trying to stab a man.

In one swift movement, I side-stepped, punched him in the gut, and wrapped my left arm around his head as he stumbled past me, twisting his head back to expose his throat. He fell to the ground, gurgling for a few brief moments before he went limp, the handle of my knife protruding from the underside of his jaw. *Aim for the submandibular triangle*—it was a phrase I'd used endlessly while training other men. Seven inches of steel up through the tongue and the mouth and into the brain was guaranteed to kill a man—Blaise would never have known what hit him. I took small satisfaction in that knowledge. I wasn't by nature a cruel man.

"Hey!" a soft voice said in the darkness. "The cavalry's here. A bit late, but we're here …"

The American and the boy stood side by side, one with a crooked grin on his face, the other with his mouth open, eyes wide. The young man turned his head away as I placed one foot on the dead man's chin for purchase and retrieved my knife, wiping its blade in the snow.

"Your hands okay?" the tall man asked. I stretched them out to show all was well. My fingers were trembling a bit. It was never easy, taking someone else's life—despite what civilians tended to believe.

The youngster stepped forward and spat on the corpse. "Well, this piece of shit's well and truly fucked. That'll teach him to mess around with Superman and his pals." He winked at the American and then grinned broadly at me. I hadn't seen what had gone down back at the clearing, but for him to call the Yank Superman I guessed it must have been pretty impressive.

I snorted softly at the boy's bad language. "Go back to the others," I said. "Take the man who speaks Gascon to one side and tell him what happened here. When we get there, the other three will have to be dealt with. There's no way they can be allowed to go—"

"C'est déjà fait," he said calmly. *"Et à propos des cadavres, nous sommes pêcheurs…"* It sounded curiously ominous in French. *It's already done; and, as for the bodies, we are fishermen …*

He showed no distress over what he'd seen, but looked at me with steel in his eyes, as if daring me to deny he was as grown-up as we were. It was unusual for a boy in his teen years. He reminded me of myself at the same age.

"We'll bring this *collabo* in a minute," I said, gently prodding the corpse with my foot. The young man hesitated. "Shoo, *Coco!*" I said, laughing, "I need to talk business with *le grand roux.*"

"Luc," the young man said.

"What?"

"Luc, my name is Luc." To my surprise he saluted us and then, with tears in his eyes, softly sang a few bars of "God Save the King". My pal returned the young man's salute and then gently shushed him before once more encouraging him to get back to where the others were waiting.

*****

"*Superman and his pals,* huh?" I said once the boy had left us. "Either you were showing off or he reads too many comic books."

He snorted softly, his smile fading. "Tommy …" he said, his voice a whisper.

"I know. I'm sorry. I know I could've said something, but that fool had a gun at your head. He could have poked your eye out with the muzzle … or worse. I wanted him to be angry with me, not you … I did ask you to trust me."

"And I do. You know that."

"Besides, I had another reason for wanting to make him let you go."

"Which was?"

"I couldn't bear to see you get hurt. I hadn't thought about it until then. Stupid really; we're at war. But I had this image in my mind of that loony whacking you across the side of the head with the machine gun, and then you with blood on your face, and …"

He stopped me by raising one finger to my lips, and then leaned forward, his forehead against mine. "Don't you know guns and bullets bounce off Superman?" he whispered, and then rested his chin on my shoulder, his arms around my waist. With his head still on my shoulder, he raised one arm and flexed it. "See, feel the steel in my bicep."

"Save it for later, Clark Kent, when you take your suit off," I said. I laughed and then pressed my cheek against his. He chuckled against my ear and rubbed the small of my back. The gesture filled me up with "him". His smell, the warmth of his cheek against mine, the comfort of his arms holding me close, and the remarkable strength of his being that for a day less than eight weeks had lit up my soul.

"Shorty …" I said.

"Shh!"

"What?"

"Save it for later, Jimmy Olsen," he said.

"So, you're the hero and I'm the office boy am I?"

"Well, ya know … late nights alone together at the *Daily Planet*, the lights down low in the copy room, Clark and Jimmy leaning over the latest scoop …"

My laugh was smothered as he kissed me.

There was a hint of desperation in his kiss. And mine too, if I was honest. I didn't want to dwell upon what might have happened had Blaise's gun not been a dud or the ammo had gone off in our supply canister. Instead, I turned myself to returning his kiss.

"Come on, let's get back," he said eventually, taking my hands in his and rubbing my fingers. "We need to sort out this mess with the locals. I've got a few ideas how we can provide a cover for the gamekeeper and his wife. They'll need some story when the *collabos* don't resurface."

"Oh, yeah?"

"Sure, Tommy. Gamekeeper, two black eyes; his wife, ripped underwear; the house ransacked, their savings gone; an indignant visit to the local *Kommandantur.* You get the idea?"

I chuckled. It was a good cover story, one in which Blaise and his mates had turned up and confronted the gamekeeper, tried to have their way with his young and beautiful wife, beaten him up when he tried to defend her honour, stolen his valuables, and then disappeared into the night. One of us would have to sock the man in the face to provide the shiners, but it would be the least of his worries if there wasn't a plausible story when the Germans came looking for their tame Frenchies.

"It's a story Perry White would swallow," I said. "I can just see the headlines …"

"Then grab your camera, let's get going. The people of Gotham City are waiting."

He tore off into the night. All I heard before his voice faded into the blackness was "Faster than a speeding bullet …"

I hadn't read the comic books, but the radio programme had been aired, three episodes a week, for most of a year—everyone knew the lines.

I called out after him to wait—Blaise's body still lay at my feet. Oh, well, we could come back and get it. I balled my fists and rubbed my eyes with my knuckles. This was exactly what I didn't need—an operation that had nearly ended in disaster before it had even started. As I put my knife back in its sheath I thought of the boy and his excitement at seeing what I'd done. I'd bet London to a brick he wouldn't be quite so happy if ever he had to do it himself some time down the road. Right at that moment, I couldn't work out whether training the foul-mouthed young rascal was going to be testing or rewarding.

As for working on a covert operation with the first bloke in my life I'd ever fallen for ... Well, we'd cope. We were both professionals and trained soldiers, after all.

What could possibly go wrong?

The night that had changed the rest of my life had happened a hundred miles from occupied France, eight weeks beforehand …

CHAPTER 1

"Oh, for crying out loud ..." I said, stumbling for the third time.

I was in a hurry, hoping to find one of the side streets rubble-free and passable so I could take a shortcut through to Russell Square. But everything was so blasted dark. Despite there being a quarter-moon, only the glow of distant, criss-crossing searchlights lit up anything around me. I coughed. The air was thick with fog, dust, and smoke from far-away, burning buildings.

It was the seventh of December, 1940, and bombs were falling across the East End of London. There had been some damage in Bloomsbury too, but for the most part my neighbourhood had been relatively untouched.

The sudden fizz-pop and metallic clunk from somewhere in the dark gave me a start. I waited for the bright white-green of the incendiary's flare, ready to find the nearest sandbag. A few moments passed before I realised it was a dud—welcomingly frequent these days. I caught a whiff of flint and electric discharge—the bomb's mechanism had fired, but it had failed to ignite.

I took a deeper sniff, filling my lungs. We'd been bombed nigh on continuously for three months now. Although I'd got used to the blackouts, the sirens, the sudden shudders of the ground beneath my feet, the morning lists of casualties in the newspapers, there was one thing about the Blitz I couldn't get used to—the smell.

The air was very damp, foggy, and heavy with wet, burned wood and coal smoke that had drifted westward over the city from the docks in the east. Smells after raids were so varied. Sometimes there'd be hints of sulphur—but more often the air would be thick with the over-whelming gritty odour of old plaster and dust flung out from between wall cavities. There was also the all too frequent stink of burst gas and sewer pipes. The accompanying and invariable pungent hints of rat and mouse urine, released into the air from shattered hiding places, never failed to make me want to gag.

Even as a child, smells resonated in me in a way they didn't for most other people. The neurologist my parents had sent me to, worried over my preoccupation with odours, had diagnosed me with a mild form of synaesthesia. Once reassured I wasn't actually mentally unstable, my family had shelved the fact away on their bookshelf of keepsakes—another marker I wasn't an ordinary child.

I swore under my breath when I got to Bloomsbury Square Gardens—its railings had been blasted away and there was an enormous hole in the ground where a giant London plane tree had been. I'd been walking along Great Russell Street, wanting to turn up Bedford Place, but the whole north-western corner of the square was one large crater. I supposed it must have happened in a day raid. Living in nearby Coptic Street, I'd have heard a night-time explosion so close to my house, had I been at home—I was, nearly every evening.

Tonight was an exception. One of my few friends in London, Lady Tyrone, had invited me to what the British called "drinks and supper"—entertainment and finger food.

This evening, I'd been invited to play.

★★★★★

Lady Tyrone's apartment occupied the top three floors of a grand Victorian house on the square. I pushed the ground floor door open and climbed up two flights in the darkened stairwell. The tenants had been so often remiss in turning out the hallway lights that the building supervisor had disconnected them. Brief shafts of light lit up the staircase through each of the landings' tall uncurtained arched windows. The intermittent flashes were generated both by distant explosions and the pulsing glow of searchlights crossing the skies in the East End.

Thérèse had done well. Originally from Dresden, she'd married a faded aristocrat, Alistair Sinclair, Lord Tyrone, in the early 1920s. She spoke beautiful, sophisticated German. Unless I concentrated, my own still had a trace of a Bavarian accent, picked up during my four years at Munich University, where I'd worked on my PhD In 1938, just after *Kristallnacht*, I'd finally torn myself away from Germany. It was later that year, a few weeks after I'd arrived in London, I'd met Thérèse at a Christmas Eve concert at Australia House. She'd sought me out afterwards, telling me she was a musician herself and how impressed she'd been by my playing.

Tonight, I was not only her guest of honour but also her fellow performer. We were to play some Beethoven for her friends.

While I waited for her to answer her doorbell—I had to ring it four times—I could hear someone playing dance tunes on her piano, and the swell of voices from inside her apartment.

"Guten abend," I said, kissing her hand, when she finally appeared through the blackout curtains that closed off her vestibule. "You look ravishing, as usual."

"You have more charm than any man should, Tommy," she said, fondly patting the side of my face.

"It's not so hard to be charming to you, Thérèse."

She gave a little laugh. "One day you're going to surprise me and arrive with someone tall, dark, and handsome on your arm, I just know it."

As she led me into her main reception room, I felt myself blushing, and then asked who among the crowd I didn't know; most of them seemed familiar.

"That's Peter, the man I told you about—the one who's been playing with my heart." She indicated the slick, faintly tanned young man at the piano. He noticed we were looking his way and raised a glass of champagne to her with one hand, continuing to play chords with the other.

I raised an eyebrow. "Expensive?" Her intimate friends knew she "entertained" young men when her husband was absent—which seemed to be most of the time. Professional, cultured escorts could easily be passed off as visiting relatives, or nephews, or sons of other vague friends. I knew she preferred it—for a woman in her position in society, keeping a permanent lover secret was impossible.

"Very, but not financially. The cost is emotional, but he's divinely worth it," she said, somewhat wistfully, and then looked at me from under her lashes and held up a cigarette for me to light. I smiled. Her German—precise, beautifully enunciated, and rich with word choices—reminded me so very much of salon concerts in Prussian country houses, times when I'd mingled with guests after a recital and exchanged sophisticated banter.

"Darling," she added after a moment, her voice descending into a soft, mischievous purr, "I've invited a very interesting man for you to meet this evening."

I must have scowled, for she took me by the arm and led me into a small alcove near the front door of her flat. Her tone carried a hint of exasperation. "For the life of me, my sweet, I don't know how anyone gets to be twenty-eight and remain a virgin."

It was an old joke between us. She knew nothing of my private life—her jibe was an effort to get me to spill the beans. However, I'd been brought up to believe some things were not to be shared freely.

I was hardly a virgin, but I was relatively inexperienced for someone my age. My encounters had been fleeting—opportunistic. A life in the army did that to one. There'd been one or two people who'd been more than interested in repeat performances. However, it had never been at the right time, and none of them had really ignited any spark. There had been one handsome, educated, and very suave Russian—the military attaché to the consulate in Munich. But when I'd requested his file, it had arrived full of question marks—it didn't take a genius to work out he was working for the NKVD—the law enforcement agency of the Soviet Union, which was closely associated with the secret police. In the intelligence world, mixing business with pleasure invariably proved to be a double-edged sword—one with a particularly finely honed blade.

"Ah, the right person simply hasn't come along, Thérèse. And maybe it's not the right time in my life, what with the war and everything."

She pouted and then laughed when she saw me blush. I stared at my shoes. She placed one finger under my chin, so I had to look at her.

"Thomas, one doesn't need to find 'the special person', or to be in love to be intimate with someone else—although it does help. A handsome and considerate lover is surely good enough. What can you possibly be afraid of?"

"I'm not afraid of anything," I replied. "It's merely the way I was brought up. Being old-fashioned has its virtues."

She rolled her eyes and laughed, switching to English. "Come now, Tommy, let's not get so serious. We'll play our Beethoven, have a drink or two and then have something to eat. Heinrich is a great deal of fun— you could end up being friends—who knows?"

Heinrich? She'd dropped the name with a little vocal underline that hadn't escaped me. An "interesting man" with a German first name?

She led me by the arm into the main room and I started to greet the people I'd already met here before, or at other social events that involved music.

After a while, I became aware Thérèse's "companion" had been playing Gershwin and Porter for some time. I wandered over to the piano and placed my violin case against the wall behind it.

"Tommy Haupner," I said after he'd finished what he'd been playing, and held out my hand.

"Peter Farnsworth," he replied, shaking it. He waved at a waiter who seemed intent on passing us by without stopping. I took two glasses of champagne and handed him one, raising my own in a salute.

"Jerry is early tonight," he said.

"Pardon?"

"The bombs?"

"Oh yes, of course. Sorry—my mind was elsewhere."

My mind was elsewhere because I'd noticed a man standing just inside the door. I watched him stoop to kiss Thérèse's hand—he'd clearly just arrived. He was very tall—as tall as I perhaps, probably more—and looked about my age. He had a flashing, toothy grin and fair hair. His shoulders were wide and his manners appeared unaffected and smooth.

I found myself gaping. He was extraordinarily good-looking.

I looked down at my glass when Thérèse took the man's arm and began to introduce him to her guests. As they moved, I watched from under my lashes, taking in the beautifully tailored dinner jacket he wore. He moved with a casual elegance that suggested he might be continental European, were it not for his upright bearing and the tilt of his head. Aristocrat? Unlikely. Military? Perhaps.

As he passed under the bright light of the chandelier, I also noticed his hair wasn't really blond, not compared to my own straw-coloured mop. Despite the brilliantine that smoothed it to his head, it was actually very pale red, an "almost-blond". One thin, disordered strand had escaped and hung down over his right eyebrow.

I was saved the embarrassment of being caught staring by a waiter, who paused at my elbow to offer me something from his tray of exotic-looking finger foods. Rationing? Not for the rich folk, by all accounts. In fact, if one cared to travel a short distance from Piccadilly Circus, with a wink and a nod and for the right amount, anything could be purchased in Jermyn Street, and by anyone. The black market thrived all over London and was virtually impossible to police.

"Oh, hello, Tommy," said a familiar voice from my side. Damn! Thérèse was a few paces away and had been about to introduce me to the newcomer, but I was obliged to turn away and say hello. It was Lord Tempby, one of the old-school gentlemen who often attended my concerts. We chatted a little about my forthcoming recital at St. Giles, Cripplegate. It was very hard to remain attentive to his chattering, because I was partly distracted, trying to listen to what Thérèse was saying to the man I'd been admiring. Lord Tempby finally abandoned me with a soft squeeze to my forearm and a "Toodle-pip!" With relief, I turned to my hostess and the new arrival.

"I'm sorry I'm late," he was saying with a strong North American accent. "High Holborn was closed and I had to …"

His voice had trailed off as his eyes met mine. I transferred my champagne glass to my left hand, to shake hands with him, but it slipped from my grasp and shattered on the floor.

The waiter appeared quickly, and I attempted to help him retrieve the pieces.

"Let him do it, Tommy ... your hands," Thérèse said urgently.

As I was rising to my feet, the stranger whispered, under his breath, and very softly, in German to Thérèse, *"Oh my God! Is this the guy you pay to sleep with you? What a looker!"*

I didn't know who went paler, Thérèse or me. The man extended his hand and, reverting to English, introduced himself.

"Hey!" he said, grinning at me. "Captain Heinrich Reiter—from Boston, Massachusetts, in the United States. But please, everyone calls me Henry."

I took his hand and shook it coolly. "Thomas Haupner," I said, starting to feel the colour burn in my face. "From a place in a country you've probably never heard of."

I was trying to be funny, to take away the sting of his words. My voice fell out of British Received Pronunciation and into the broad Australian accent I'd grown up with. It had a habit of appearing when I least wanted it—I could hear the twangy vowels the moment they formed in my mouth.

I noticed Thérèse pulling at the American's jacket sleeve, trying to draw him away. He'd have none of it. He was bent on getting to know me. It couldn't have been more obvious.

"You're Australian?" My German surname had obviously not registered with him. He looked puzzled at my obvious discomfort—he knew something was wrong.

"Ich freue mich, Sie kennenzulernen, Herr Reiter," I said, in careful and precisely enunciated German.

He paled. I'd only said I was pleased to meet him. But, from that one sentence, and from the quick glance at Thérèse's face, he realised three things—I'd understood what he'd said to Thérèse about me, I wasn't her "paid companion", and I was the person she'd invited him to meet.

I wasn't angry. I simply felt very uncomfortable and ten times more shy and awkward than normal, as irrational as I knew those feelings to be. This man, who I'd found so attractive, had thought I was a gigolo. Perhaps he was joking, I reasoned. But I still felt affronted, despite the fact he'd said he found me attractive. The genuineness in his voice had made me doubly ill at ease—I wasn't used to flattery, and in such a guileless manner.

To cover my embarrassment, I turned to Thérèse and said, "Shall we play?"

I gave Henry Reiter a brisk nod, in the German fashion, and then moved to the piano to retrieve my violin case. I was breathing heavily and was feeling shaken.

I never suffered from nerves while performing. Sometimes I'd feel a twinge of anxiety before a major performance if I hadn't had enough time to prepare adequately, but this wasn't one of those occasions. I'd been looking forward to playing this evening and was excited to be performing with Thérèse. So, I opened the case and unwrapped my violin from the silk scarf in which it was always protected and then placed my violin under my chin. Adjusting the bow screw, I moved around the piano close to Thérèse and quietly asked her for an A.

She looked up at me, giving me the note so I could tune. She was obviously embarrassed about what had happened, but beckoned me to lean in closer and whispered, "Ignore him, Tommy. He wasn't to know you spoke German. He was only trying to be funny. You know what Americans can be like—let's just play."

She'd recognised my disappointment. It was a hurt lonely people often experienced when someone for whom they felt a strong attraction behaved inappropriately or was inadvertently rude to them. I nodded and then started to breathe deliberately and slowly, in and out through my nose. I needed to concentrate on my music, not worry about an imagined slight.

Thérèse rose from the piano stool and then clapped softly. She didn't need to do more. Her presence was enough to command the attention of everyone in the room. The American had retreated to the back of the room and was leaning against the wall, seemingly inspecting his shoes. With some wry amusement, I noted the faint redness over his cheeks and throat. The little stab of pleasure this gave me held neither malice nor satisfaction. It was simply his embarrassment revealed something of his personality that made him incredibly attractive.

Thérèse's salons always included someone who could play, sing, or recite, or a guest who could speak eloquently on a topic of interest. She was an extremely accomplished pianist herself, and it was playing together that had cemented our friendship. In early 1939, a few months after I'd returned from Germany, I'd been invited to play at a Schubert evening in St. Anne's Church, in Limehouse. I'd played the Violin Sonata in A, a piece I passionately loved. My brother Michael, who was my usual accompanist, had come down with a terrible cold, so I'd asked my new friend Thérèse to play for me. We became fast friends in record time from that day and had remained so ever since.

As her guests fell silent, she cleared her throat before speaking. I waited, violin and bow in one hand, while she introduced me.

"I think very few of you here don't already know 'Professor' Haupner, but perhaps this might be the first time you get to hear him perform. Tommy starred as the solo artist with most of the great orchestras of Europe before the war, and as you will hear, his playing is exquisite."

"Thérèse—" I began to protest, but she cut me off.

"Not only that, but to add insult to injury, while engaged in a very busy performing career, he managed to complete a PhD in European Languages from the University of Munich."

I didn't miss her quick glance at the American. Although she'd introduced me as she normally might do, the mention of my PhD was aimed at him. She'd been trying to make him feel more guilty, so he'd have to come to talk to me, to apologise. She was cunning, that was for sure—she wasn't going to let an ill-timed remark get in the way of her matchmaking.

"This evening Tommy and I will perform one of the great master-pieces of the violin repertoire—the Beethoven Romance in F," she announced and then settled on the piano stool.

Her guests applauded, and I waited until they'd settled before replacing my violin under my chin. I checked to see whether Thérèse was ready and then gently touched my bow to the string of my instrument and began to play the opening phrase of the Beethoven Romance.

At the first piano passage in which the violinist doesn't play, I was able to take my instrument from my neck for a moment.

While listening to the beautiful phrases that flowed from Thérèse's fingers, I began to reflect on the surreal nature of our performance of this sublime German work. We were performing the Romance in a country currently at war with that of its composer, and our rendition of Beethoven's masterpiece was accompanied by the distant, soft pounding of falling bombs. Bombs dropping miles away in the eastern reaches of the Thames and its crowded docklands—bombs launched by the descendants of the countrymen of the man who created the transcendental notes that fell from our instruments—and bombs that might, right at that very moment, be shredding men, women, and children as they huddled, frightened and in the dark, in their basements or shelters, a few miles from where we were making music.

The far-off explosions seemed to stop just as we came to the end of the piece.

I felt embarrassed at the amount of enthusiasm and the loud applause from the gathered guests. Murmuring quiet and sincere thanks, I turned to acknowledge Thérèse, whose eyes glistened with emotion, and then turned once more to thank the small gathering.

Straightening up from my bow, I looked again towards the lone figure leaning against the wall at the back of the room. His eyes were wide, an unlit cigarette dangling from the corner of his open mouth. There was something in his gaze. Even at a distance, I could tell it was more than surprise or shock. It was something else—something that made my stomach clench. He looked stunned, yet at the same time his eyes radiated some great, ferocious fire that I didn't recognise, nor in truth fully understood.

I slowly began to realise what it was about this man that had so disarmed me—I wanted him. I couldn't figure it out—despite his rudeness and apparent bumptiousness, something inside me was telling me to ignore those things and see past them. However, that would mean getting to know him better, and I wasn't sure I was quite up to that … yet.

"I need a cigarette and a moment alone," I muttered to Thérèse after the rounds of handshaking and promises of further conversation with each guest once I'd taken a quick *Luftpause*. I needed to escape the room for a moment.

"Go out on the landing, Tommy," she said, stroking my arm and obviously wanting to soothe me. "He's really a very nice man. Give him a chance." She led me through the blackout curtains to the door of her apartment. "At least we both know he finds you attractive—and there really is much more to him than meets the eye."

I fled to the far end of the stairwell landing and lit a cigarette and inhaled deeply, trying to settle down before I had to return to the other guests in time for supper. It was always the same, even after playing for a short amount of time—there was a need to return to the normal world, to unloosen the wound-up spring of performance.

Turning to the wall of the stairwell, I rested my face against its cool tiles. I'd never wanted to get to the age I was and not know the feeling of something more than the army, my family, and my violin. Those things should have been enough for any man, but tonight, something else had unexpectedly started to knock at a still-locked door in my breast.

I started to make excuses for his behaviour. Americans had such a strange, sometimes inappropriate sense of humour. How could he have known I spoke German? Thérèse should have warned him! I found myself wanting to blame her, rather than owning up to the fact I'd behaved like a child.

I didn't move when I heard the door to the apartment open and close. I knew who it was. I didn't turn to look. I waited for him to speak.

"I'd have punched me out," he said quietly.

"There's still time."

"Suppose sorry isn't enough?"

"Nope."

"What, then?"

As he took one step towards me, the sound of grit under his shoe echoed in the silence of the darkened stairwell. "I'm truly, truly, sorry."

Despite myself, I laughed softly against the tiled wall. How contrite he sounded. Cute, I thought, and then chuckled once more at my choice of an American word.

"Am I that funny?" he asked.

"No … *sicherlich*, you're not," I replied. I turned around to face him and leaned against the wall. Emboldened, he moved closer and rested an elbow against the wall, a foot or so away from my head. As he did so the stairwell was suddenly infused with soft, pale-blue moonlight—the clouds outside had obviously parted. Bad for the people of London underneath Heinkels looking for landmarks in order to drop their deadly loads, but strangely moving for me, standing a mere eighteen inches or so away from this stranger in a darkened stairwell in Bloomsbury.

I was no longer annoyed. There was something about his cologne, or his hair liniment, or a combination of them both, that smelled "safe" to me—anyway, that's what I told myself.

"You're forgiven, Herr Reiter," I said.

"Thank you, Herr Haupner."

"Two Krauts in a stairwell," I said. "Sounds like a book by Thomas Mann." I hoped he'd get the joke.

"Mann, oh, Mann, Thomas," he said, very softly and almost laughing, while reaching over with his free hand to brush something from the lapel of my jacket. "You sure are something."

So, we shared the same sense of humour. I moved his hand away, my fingers perhaps lingering a little too long in the doing of it. "What was that you said about a punch?" I asked.

"Go ahead, I deserve it," he said with the hint of a smile in his eyes and gravel in his voice. He was facing the windows of the landing, the bare light that filtered into the hallway illuminating his face. "You could punch me as much as you wanted, as long as I got to hear you play again."

"Are you flirting with me?" I murmured.

"If you have to ask, Aussie," he replied with a broad grin, "then I'm not trying hard enough."

I swear he was about to lean over and kiss me, when from behind us Thérèse's door swung open violently, accompanied by a gush of noise and light from inside. I was so surprised I jumped instinctively, my forehead hitting his chin with a sudden "crack".

"Sorry," a voice said from the doorway, and then whoever it was retreated back into the apartment, closing the door hastily behind them.

"Fool," I muttered. Although the door had been opened for less than a second or two, I wouldn't have been surprised if I'd heard the sound of footsteps belonging to an angry ARP warden pounding up the stairs.

"Doggone it! Ouch ..." he moaned, pretend-protesting with a "little boy" voice. "I didn't *really* mean for you to punch me when I said you could."

I laughed at his playacting and then reached for his chin and patted it. "Sorry. I didn't do that on purpose."

He rubbed the side of his mouth. "That's not what I was expecting."

"What *were* you expecting?" I asked.

His eyes flicked to my mouth and he slowly leaned forward.

That was certainly not what *I* was expecting. I drew back—pleased but tentative still. This was new territory for me—the flirting. My past encounters had been more matter-of-fact, brief, no-nonsense affairs. But this, the push-pull going on in my head, combined with the ice in my belly, had me confused. "Too fast, soldier," I explained.

He gave me a little gesture that was a quick twist of his head combined with a toothy grin. It was unmistakably "I was just seeing if I could". I was drawn to his smile; I couldn't help myself. At the corner of his mouth I noticed a small, dark stain.

"Hold still," I said.

"What?"

"I think I split your lip with my noggin."

He grinned at me in the half-light. "My mom would say 'kiss it better'."

"I doubt your 'mom' would say that, if she knew you were saying it to some bloke." His not-so-subtle attempts to land one on me were not only amusing but also quite charming.

"So, you're 'some bloke' then, are you?" he asked.

"What would you like me to be, mister?" I replied. The words were out of my mouth before I could stop them. So much for not flirting.

He didn't answer. His soft smile made me glance down to the small, dark smudge at the corner of his mouth. As I stared at it, something inside me changed. Perhaps I was finally fed up with the years of self-control and loneliness, because when he cleared his throat and I finally lifted my gaze to meet his, I saw honesty there, and I knew some barrier had come down, or at least shifted to one side.

"You're bleeding," I said.

"Will I die?"

I shook my head and chuckled, about to wipe away the smear with my thumb, when he took his handkerchief from his jacket pocket. I stopped him. "No, don't. I'll do it." I used my own, dabbing at the corner of his lip once or twice before thrusting it back into my trousers pocket.

"Thank you … Aussie," he said.

I opened my cigarette case and offered him a smoke. "I'm sorry, perhaps I shouldn't have done that," I replied, staring at his chin while I lit his cigarette.

"Done what?" he asked with unexpected humour. "Socked me in the jaw, or avoided my clumsy attempt at a smooch?"

"Smooth … Yankee," I said, trying not to laugh.

He lit my cigarette and then we stood in silence, eyes repeatedly making contact in the semi-darkness, smoking quietly. When we'd finished, he asked me if I wanted another, offering one of his, but I declined. After I'd stamped out my cigarette butt, I crouched down to pick it up and raised my face to look at him. "Maybe we should be getting back inside?"

He squatted next to me and then fished out a shallow tin from his pocket, removed the lid, and then deposited both of our butts inside it. "If you say so …" he replied with a wink, nudging my knee playfully with one of his own.

As we crossed the landing the moonlight from outside faded, and once more the stairwell was briefly illuminated with soft flashes of light, quickly followed by distant pounding. Bombs were falling again off in the east.

A few steps from the doorway, he took my elbow and turned me to face him. "Back there, a few minutes ago, you asked me what I'd like you to be … what if I asked you the same question?"

"Perhaps we could start off by being friends?"

"Where I come from, a punch in the kisser is as good as a promise."

I laughed. His sense of humour was unexpected, yet delightful.

"Friends, then?" I held out my hand.

He shook it. "It's a good start."

I nodded, and then indicated the intermittent flashes illuminating the landing window with a quick toss of my head. *"We could be dead tomorrow."*

He hadn't let go of my hand and was gently stroking my fingers with his thumb.

"Really?" I said, glancing pointedly at our hands, still clasped.

"Oops," he said. "I saw that move once in a movie; thought it might work. You can't blame me."

He let go and then leaned in to try to kiss me once more. I stopped him abruptly with one hand flat up against his chest and then, with the other, smoothed back the wayward strand of hair that still hung down over his brow. "Steady on, soldier," I said. "Hold your horses. Give me a bit of time to think about all of this."

An enormous crump from somewhere nearby shook the building and dust rained down on us from the ceiling.

"Don't take too long, mister," he said between fits of coughing. "As you said, 'we could be dead tomorrow'."

I laughed again, this time a little more heartily. "All right," I said, "how about we go out to dinner some time? I think I need to get to know you better."

"When? Where?"

I smiled at his open enthusiasm as I moved to open the door, thinking how hard it was to pretend to not be too interested in this man, and how badly I was failing. "Soon."

"How can I contact you? You know, to make arrangements?"

"For …?"

"Our date," he announced, loudly, with a very broad grin.

"You like a challenge, Seppo?"

"Seppo?"

I sighed. "It's Australian. Rhyming slang—you know, like Cockney. We have our own version."

"Ah," he said, plucking at the lapel of his tuxedo, "like whistle and flute, right? They gave us a book before we came here. But … Seppo?"

"Seppo. Septic tank, Yank—get it? You're going to need a completely different slang book, mate, if you're going to … 'date' an Aussie." The word felt odd in my mouth. I knew what it meant, but it wasn't something said where I came from.

"Some things don't need words in any language," he said, glancing at my lips.

My face burned, but I grinned so hard I thought my face might split.

He chuckled softly and then said, "So, how do I contact you after tonight?"

"You want a date, you find me … Captain."

He grabbed my arm once more and looked me straight in the eye.

"I already have … mister."

*****

Back inside, we separated and mixed with the other guests, chatting and drinking until food was served, buffet-style, from a large table in Thérèse's dining room. After a while, though, with plates in our hands, we found ourselves standing next to each other in a corner and fell into casual and easy conversation. He had a natural, genuine charm and was typically American in the way he flirted with me, more by paying attention to what I said than by dishing out compliments as men in my past had done when trying to "woo" me—a euphemism for trying to get into my pants. I wasn't ashamed of the sordid moments in my past, nor was I proud of them.

This man standing beside me, his face lit up with gentle laughter, was something altogether different.

"Army? PhD? Violin virtuoso? How did all of that come about?" he asked. I'd just confessed that I too was a military man

I sighed. "It's a long story."

"I've always thought the beginning is the best place to start …"

I'd never really liked to talk about my history, mostly because what I'd done seemed so counterproductive in so many people's eyes. But he was all smiles, gave the impression of being genuinely interested, and I had a few drinks under my belt. There was something earnest in his eyes, which seemed to say *I want to know all about you, and all at once, Tommy Haupner, but I'm finding it hard to keep the brakes on.*

I did something I'd never done before with a man who showed interested in me: I let down my guard a little and gave him a glimpse of a few of the things that mattered.

"It was a combination of things—the Depression was the main reason."

"Yeah, it hit hard in the US too."

"There was only one professional orchestra at home, so there were certainly no guaranteed careers in Australia for a solo violinist. I had scholarships behind me, and a big fundraising effort to send me overseas—that's where I was headed. But then my mother developed a serious illness. Life-threatening. The doctors said it might go on for years and we didn't know if she'd survive. I couldn't up and leave—I'm sure you understand—a man only has one mother. I was at a loss at what to do, so I chose to join the army—to be able to stay closer to home. It made a lot of people in the music world very angry, especially the fundraisers. But Officer's School looked like such an opportunity—free tertiary education, a secure job, specialised training … you know how it goes."

"But obviously, you didn't give up the violin."

I shook my head. "No, I kept playing. It was peacetime, and the army seemed happy enough to release me to play at concerts. Eventually the music world got used to the idea and forgave me, and in 1934, when I graduated from the Military Academy, I travelled to Munich to do my PhD."

"And that's where you got to be a star?"

I laughed at him. "Despite what Thérèse said earlier, we don't have stars in classical music. It's not like the motion pictures."

"I know that," he said, his gaze searching for something in mine. "I just wanted to see if I could make you smile—you sounded so serious."

I wondered if he'd realised how much I'd left out of that story. It was the bare bones. A story suitable for a stranger, or a newly met friend. For example, I didn't go into the details of what being directed to a wonderful teacher had done to my life. Konstanze Pfeiffer had not only been a player of renown, she was also a genius. She'd inspired me, drawing something out of me previously only been hinted at. She'd transformed my playing from gifted to extraordinary. My performance career had soared after she'd introduced me to her dear friend, Bruno Walter, a conductor who became enamoured of my playing and took me under his wing—under his baton I got to play everywhere, and with all the best orchestras.

"One day, I hope you'll fill me in on all the pieces you just left out," Heinrich said.

"What made you think I left pieces out?" I tried my best to sound innocent.

"You were in Germany from thirty-four and still in the army, Thomas. I'd say there was plenty you left out."

I opened my mouth, trying to find something suitable to say, when I felt, rather than saw, our hostess approach us.

"Darling, what happened?" Thérèse asked, glancing first at Heinrich's split lip and darkening bruise, and then more suspiciously glancing down to check my knuckles.

"It's nothing, Thérèse. It was merely clumsiness."

"And I suppose you have no bruises either, Tommy?" she asked, looking me up and down. "Hidden beneath your clothes?"

I felt the tall figure beside me shaking with silent laughter.

"You'll be the first to know," I said, trying to be flippant.

The tone in her voice was dry. "I doubt it," she said, before moving off to talk with some of her other guests.

*****

I wasn't the only musical one, it seemed, as later that evening, after a few more drinks, I found myself leaning on the piano as my new friend played and sang. His voice was really quite beautiful: high and light, with real charm, and a "smile" in the sound that made it irresistible.

"You want me to sing something just for you, soldier?" he asked quietly, patting the piano bench beside him. I moved around and sat next to him.

"Maybe," I said, playing a few arpeggios with my right hand.

"Don't tell me you play too?"

"My brother, Michael, is the real pianist, but yes, I can play."

"I bet you can," he said, in a smoky tone that held no other interpretation than the one he had intended.

"I can play silly buggers ..." I said with a grin.

"Hum it and I'll see if I can follow."

For some reason we both found this hysterically funny, even though I knew he must have had no idea of what the slang meant.

Once he stopped laughing, he started to play an introduction, whispering to me, "This one's for you, 'cobber'." I recognised it the moment his fingers touched the keys. At the end of the verse, as he was about to launch into the chorus, I moved over on the piano bench and nudged him with my hip, and then ostentatiously wiggled my fingers in the air before joining him in a piano-duet-style version of what he'd been about to sing—"You Do Something to Me". His voice rang through the room as many of the other guests stopped their chattering and gathered around us. For a moment, the sound of distant bombs was muffled by a room full of Thérèse's smartly dressed guests, singing loudly while swaying to the music, and then bumping their hips and shoulders together in time to the wonderfully syncopated rhythms of Cole Porter's "you do" and "voodoo" rhymes. We did a four-handed repeat of the chorus and everyone in the room joined in, right from the start, singing at the tops of their voices.

Were it not for the tuxedos and tiaras, we could just as well have been in the public bar of a boozer in the Old Kent Road.

Only I knew he'd sung that song for me. I'd never been wooed before. He'd stopped flirting ages ago. He no longer needed to. He was simply charming and attentive and he'd knocked my socks off.

Thérèse's friend Peter took over from us and started to play a few dance numbers. I was dancing with the wife of one of the merchant bankers, a talkative woman I'd met a few times at Thérèse's on previous occasions, when I became aware the balance of the sexes at the gathering was overwhelmingly male and all the women had been taken. It left most of the men standing around at a loose end, watching the few couples that had partners glide around the dance floor. Among them were two or three male couples—nothing unusual for wartime if you were in the right place. The dance floors of the service clubs were often dotted with guys dancing together if there was a shortage of girls that night.

Therefore, it was no surprise that when the banker tapped me on the shoulder to take his wife, just as Peter started to play "Ain't Misbehavin'", I found myself in Heinrich's arms, ready to dance a foxtrot.

"Would you care to dance?"

"Thought you'd never ask." I grinned.

"Who leads?" he asked as we got into the step.

I leaned him into a turn-out and said, "Let's take turns. Does one of us have to lead all the time?"

His grin and the gleam in his eyes made my feet feel light, and I found myself flicking my gaze between his eyes and his lips.

"Damn," he said, shaking his head, "you're such a fine dancer."

"You're not so bad yourself, Shorty," I answered.

"Shorty?"

"It's something in our Australian genes," I explained. "Back home, if we can find one nickname for something, we find half-a-dozen. Usually words that mean the opposite of the truth. Like a redhead is called Bluey, if it's a man. A skinny bloke is called Fatso. And, seeing you're a tall bastard …"

His smile of amusement did something to my guts—something unexpected, but something I certainly liked. He pulled me into a turn, hugging me closer to him. "Shorty, huh?"

"I can call you something else if you like."

"Nope, Shorty will do just fine."

I swung him around in my arms and began to lead. It covered our mutual chuckle.

The look in Thérèse's eyes and the smile on her face, as I saw her staring at us, was a picture in itself. Like the cat that got the cream.

"Can I walk you home, Thomas?" he asked.

"That would be nice," I said, "but Thomas sounds so formal. Only my mother calls me that."

"What does everyone else call you?"

"Tommy, usually."

"Well, grab your coat, Tommy. Where do you live?"

"Not far from here—around the corner, actually."

We made our excuses to Thérèse, who, to her credit, didn't slap us on our backs and wish us well, although I could see it in her eyes.

Halfway down the stairs, I said, "You called me 'cobber'."

"You aren't the first Aussie I've ever met, Tommy. I was trying to be cute—anything to see your pearly whites," he said, reaching from behind me in the darkness to give my shoulder a soft squeeze.

He was like a kid. He hopped on one foot along the edge of the gutter and the footpath as we wandered through the darkened streets singing snatches of Cole Porter, but changing the words on the fly. His energy and charm were infectious and endearing.

"This is my street," I said, a few minutes later, when we arrived at the corner of Great Russell Street.

He looked up at the street sign. "Coptic Street."

I nodded, waiting.

"What's that building?" he asked.

"The British Museum."

He sat on the edge of the gutter with his hands clasping his knees, looking at the heavily sandbagged building, slowly shaking his head. He patted the kerb and I plonked myself down next to him.

"After the war, I'm going to find an apartment near here and spend every day for months in that place when it's open again. It's always been my dream."

Was there no end of depth to this man?

"Say, Tommy," he asked, "were you really a professor in Germany?"

"What? Oh—no, that's a private joke between Thérèse and me."

"Explain?"

"She used to call me a professor emeritus …"

"Ah," he murmured.

"It means …"

"I know what it means," he said, kicking my ankle with the side of his shoe. "You aren't the only one with a tertiary education, you know."

I laughed, surprised and pleased at the same time. One day, I'd explain it was Goebbels himself who'd "retired" me. "Make the choice, Herr Haupner," he'd said at a reception after one of my concerts. "There is no room in the New Germany for those who sit on the wall."

I'd chosen to return to England rather than become a Party member and sport the swastika pin on my lapel.

I dragged him to his feet and down my street to the front door of my house. Now it came to the crunch, I felt inexplicably shy.

"Smoke?" I said, pulling my cigarette case from my jacket pocket and offering him one, desperate to disguise my awkwardness.

"Can I see you again?" he asked.

I laughed loudly. "How many drinks have you had? We're going out to dinner, you big dag, and I told you that you have to track me down—remember?"

"But I found you already," he pleaded in a pretend-hurt tone.

"You did indeed, mister."

"Well, we're here."

"Where?"

"My place," I said. "This is where I live. My flat is above this bookshop."

"So …?"

I put my head out into the street, checking to see we were alone. "Ah, bugger this!" I said. "Come here." I pulled him to me and wrapped him in my arms, pressing my mouth against his for what seemed a very long time.

I wanted to stay like that forever. It was only the unmistakable click of steel-tipped, hobnailed boots, signalling the approach of a patrolling policeman, made us draw apart.

"Evening, Mr. Haupner," the policeman said, touching his truncheon to his helmet as he passed by my doorway.

"Evening, Constable," I replied to my local beat-bobby.

"Have a pleasant evening, gentlemen," the man said as he continued along the street.

I waited until the footsteps faded and then pushed him back into the door recess and kissed my companion soundly once more—this time deeply.

Someone whistled from the dark on the next corner. We pulled apart again.

"Holy moly," he said softly. "I thought this was going too quick for you."

"It was. But somehow I couldn't help myself."

"Thomas Haupner, you sure are something else."

I felt as if my face would split, so broad was my grin.

"Man, your kisses ..." he said, fingering my chin gently between his thumb and forefinger.

I was slightly flustered by the whistle in the dark and the passing policeman, and wasn't quite sure what to do next. I'd only just met him—it was too soon to ask him inside for a "nightcap", as the Americans called it. So, instead, I took the coward's way out. This was all too new to me, and I needed to think about what had happened before it went any further. "As pleasant as this is," I said, "we should probably call it a night."

"I'll be in touch," he answered, throwing me a casual salute.

"Thank you for walking me home ... Shorty."

He turned and sauntered off up the street. Half-a-dozen steps away, he turned and came back to me. "I would have paid, you know ..."

"Get out of here and get to bed, you ruffian," I said, laughing. I watched him disappear into the darkness and the fog, until his whistled version of "You Do Something to Me" eventually faded away.

It was at that moment I realised he'd picked up my violin case and had walked off with it ... what was worse, I had no idea where he lived. That was no accident. What a cunning bugger he was. It would be me tracking him down now.

What the hell had I got myself into? I wondered as I put the key into my front door. Whatever it was, I knew I'd been looking for something like it for as long as I could remember.

*****

I'd barely finished undressing when I heard movement downstairs. "Cooee!"

It was Michael, my brother.

"In bed!" I yelled, pulling back the covers and getting in. It was his whistle I'd heard outside a few minutes before. I'd recognised it immediately. He'd obviously seen what was going on and had decided to walk around the block once or twice.

Michael pounded up the stairs and jumped on me from the doorway, rubbing his freezing hands on me and trying to grab my backside to annoy me while I desperately tried to keep the bed covers over me.

My fraternal twin was like a photographic negative of me. Where I was blond, he was dark. I had a broad, naturally muscular frame; his was thin and wiry. But we shared the same smile, eyes, and speech mannerisms, switching easily between Alsatian-German and Lorraine-French dialects, sometimes in the same sentence. We reserved our banter for Australian English, and when we got mushy with each other.

"Miss the train back to base?" I asked as he quickly peeled off his clothes and then jumped into bed next to me.

We had a very comfortable and close relationship, one that a lot of our British friends had at first found odd. We came from a culture of "mateship", a level of intimacy between men that existed nowhere else in the world I knew of. We were twins—intimacy came with the territory, and on top of that, we were Aussie kids at heart. The freckle-faced scallywags we'd been as children lurked just below the surface, often emerging in private in outbursts of irreverent and boisterous behaviour our British acquaintances would have found dismaying in its lack of decorum, were they to witness it. Our army mates of course, in front of whom we rarely held back, merely sighed and rolled their eyes.

"Ah, no," he said. "It was on time and would have left, had the Luftwaffe not altered the timetable."

Michael worked on an army base near Portsmouth. It had become a regular occurrence for him to arrive unannounced on my doorstep owing to the destruction of train tracks.

"Was it bad, baby brother?" I asked—he was only fifteen minutes younger than me, but I made the most of it.

"Pretty bad," he said, wrapping himself around me in an effort to warm up. "One went through the roof of the station. Lot of mess to clean up …"

Not one of us ever got used to the carnage. "Bloody oath! Your hands are cold," I said, anxious to change the subject, "and keep your frigging feet to yourself as well."

"I love you too," he said, pressing his ice-cold nose into the back of my neck. "But not as much as the tall guy in the tux …"

"I heard your whistle. Guess you saw, huh?"

"If there hadn't been an empty factory on the other side of the street, I'm sure half of London would've seen my brother locking lips with that amazing-looking man on his own front doorstep."

I groaned and put the pillow over my face. He wrestled it away. "Okay, spill the beans!" he ordered. I shook my head. He raised his hand in the air, middle two fingers together and outer fingers spread wide. "Here comes the tickle-bomber …"

He buzzed a raspberry, weaving his hand through the air, ready to descend on me and tickle the truth out of me. I wasn't ticklish, but it was a game we'd played since we were very young. At the age of nearly thirty neither of us had really grown up.

Amid tears of laughter, I held up my hands in surrender. "Okay, I give in. He's a Yank."

"My brother is dicking a Yank?"

"For God's sake, Mikey, I only met him tonight."

"But you're going to dick him, huh?" He waggled his eyebrows. I smacked his forehead with the palm of my hand.

"Ouch! Sorry," he mumbled. "I 'forgot' you were a professional virgin."

"I don't know, Michael Haupner—between you and Thérèse …"

We laughed softly together in the near-dark.

"I like him," I said, more seriously.

"I think you more than like him," he teased. "You've got a stupid look on your face."

"There's something about him …"

"Well, I bloody never …"

Our conversations were often peppered with trailing sentences. It came from being twins—there were some things we simply didn't need to say. I shushed him with one finger and then pulled him into my arms and kissed him on the temple. "I'll tell you more in the morning. I'm absolutely rooted right now …"

He nodded compliantly, and with relief I closed my eyes and began to drift off to sleep.

"Tommy, tell me the story about the handsome Yankee prince and the Aussie knight in shining armour …" he began, his voice filled with mirth.

He hit the floor with a thud as I pushed him out of bed.

CHAPTER 2

I was teetering on the edge of deep sleep and wakefulness when I thought I heard Michael speak. "It's okay, I'll get it."

I mumbled something incoherent, pulled his pillow over my head, and went back to sleep.

The next thing I remember was my brother shaking my shoulder. "Come on, soldier—up and at 'em!"

"Wha …?"

"Come on, Tommy, quickly. Downstairs. There's something you need to see."

He pulled me out of bed by one arm, so I staggered after him, down to my living room, yawning and stretching as I followed. The house was warm. He'd obviously lit the gas fire in the living room some time before.

As I reached the bottom of the stairs, I turned into the living room, scratching my belly with one hand and rubbing my eyes with the other. "This better be good …" I started to say, when Michael, who was standing behind me, in the doorway to the kitchen, grabbed my arms and held them behind my back.

My words caught in my throat when I saw Heinrich sitting in an armchair under one of the windows of my living room. The look on his face was a combination of confusion, embarrassment, delight, and, well … admiration.

"Michael," I said between gritted teeth, "I'm going to kill you …"

I knew what was going to happen. It was like watching two automobiles collide, knowing no matter what you did, there was no way of stopping the inevitable smash.

"Just let him check out your muscles and hairy chest before you go running off," my brother said in German. "No use hiding all that prime Australian beef under layers of clothing."

To his credit, Heinrich didn't miss a beat, nor move a muscle in his face. He kept his gaze fixed on mine and said, "Good morning, Thomas. This is all your brother's doing. I told him to let you sleep a while longer."

His German was impeccable, of course.

"Oops," Michael said quietly.

I was wearing only my identity discs and a pair of too-small white cotton skivvies, the buttons of which I hadn't had time to fasten before being dragged out of bed. The way Michael held me had obviously stretched the shorts tightly across my hips and couldn't have left much to the imagination. I twisted around and grabbed my brother in a headlock, punching his bicep with the knuckle of my free hand. He was hysterical with laughter.

"You're dead meat, Michael Haupner," I said.

"You'll have to catch me first," he said, breaking free from my grip. Before I could react, he pulled my shorts down to my ankles.

"See, Henry, hair all the way to his ankles too," he called out over his shoulder as he bounded up the stairs, whooping like a fourteen-year-old. I nearly tripped over my shorts as I tried to grab him before he reached the bottom of the stairs, and I hastily pulled them up as I hurtled up the stairs after him.

I caught him in my bedroom, trying to dodge around my bed. I tackled him and held him face-down on the bed, one arm twisted up behind his back, and whispered in his ear, "You bastard! Just you wait, I'm going to get you one day when you least expect it "

"Help! Henry! He called me a bastard!" he screamed between yelps of laughter.

"Fight your own battles, Michael!" was the reply from downstairs.

I fell onto my back next to him, put my hands over my eyes, and groaned.

"You let this guy get away, Thomas, and I'm cutting the twin-tie. For good!" He poked me in the ribs. "Get down there!"

Never one to let a good opportunity pass him by, Michael jumped off the bed and hoicked my skivvies off before I could stop him. He ran onto the landing outside my bedroom door and waved them at me, like a matador with a red cape at a bull. God knows what our visitor must have been thinking as I leaped from the bed to retrieve my underwear. Just as I reached him, my brother threw them down the stairs, and then quickly ran behind me back into the bedroom and slammed the door behind him, locking it.

I rattled the doorknob and then turned to the bathroom door. It was locked too. My brother had set this up.

Not quite sure what to do, standing naked and embarrassed on the landing between my bedroom and bathroom, I heard a soft humming from downstairs, followed by a few equally softly sung words of "You Do Something to Me".

I moved hesitantly to the top of the staircase and peered down over the edge of the top stair. Heinrich was standing out of sight in the kitchen, one hand protruding into the living room, twirling my skivvies on one finger.

I grinned.

"I'm not looking," he sang, using Cole Porter's tune, and then continued his humming.

I clumped down the stairs, one at a time, and then stood against the wall outside the door to the kitchen, took my underpants from his finger and slipped them on. I leaned against the wall and then reached out and took his hand in mine, lacing my fingers through his. "Thank you, Heinrich, you're a true gentleman," I said.

He poked his head around the doorframe and grinned at me. "I aim to please."

The kiss was merely a soft touch of lips, nothing more, but I felt the heat rushing to my face. I was about to lean in for some heavier-duty action when we were interrupted by a familiar voice behind me.

"Aw! *So süß*," Michael said in a semi-mocking tone.

I growled at my brother and then pointed back and forth between my brother and me. "Father German, mother French."

Heinrich's eyebrows lifted with an unspoken "ah!". "Father German, mother Italian-Polish," he said, pointing to himself. "My grandparents were from …"

And then he said a word that sounded like *Vrotswoff.*

"Pardon?" Michael asked.

"Sorry. Breslau—*Vrotswoff* is how we pronounce the name of the town—it's *Wrocław* in Polish."

"How does the Polish-Italian thing work?" I asked.

"My grandmother was the only daughter of a *Junker*—a member of the old Prussian landed gentry. She disgraced herself by eloping with their Italian gardener. They ran away to Breslau, where my mom was born, and where she grew up. That's also where she met my pop—he worked for the Silesian Railway."

"That's why you speak German with such a perfect Prussian accent?"

He nodded. "Okay then, you guys," he said. "German father, French mother? Let me guess …"

"Strasbourg," Michael blurted out, without allowing him to finish. My brother was terrible at letting people guess. "Our father and mother emigrated to Australia around the turn of the century. On our father's side, the family's been farmers in Alsace-Lorraine for centuries—"

"But our grandpa was anxious to break the chain. He wanted something better for his sons, so he indentured our father and his brother, our uncle Otto, to a cabinet maker," I added, interrupting him.

Heinrich laughed. Michael and I found it impossible to let each other actually finish a sentence when we were speaking on the same topic.

My brother draped his arm around my shoulder and chuckled, before finishing what I'd been about to say. "Papa didn't have the patience for woodwork. He went back to farming—sheep and cattle. Uncle Otto, who taught the violin to this long streak of misery here, is the cabinet maker."

"Then it's him we have to thank," Heinrich said.

I felt myself blushing again.

"He does that a lot—the blushing, I mean," Michael said, squeezing my shoulder. "You said your father worked for the railways?"

"*Vati* was a locomotive designer and engineer. When he came to America, no one would employ him in the workshops, despite his experience, because he spoke no English. So, he founded a dynasty of shopkeepers—we have a family grocery store."

It was only then I noticed my violin case on the living room table.

"You brought it back? Thanks, Shorty," I said, smiling at him. "Clever move! I wondered how long it would take you to 'accidentally' find your way back here."

"I try," he said. He stood and then gave me a small bow, before retrieving my violin case, which he ceremoniously presented to me with both hands, as if it were on a silver platter.

I returned his bow with a soft, "Thank you."

"Shorty?" Michael gave me a shifty look. I smacked him playfully across the ear.

"I dropped it in the first time I came around," Heinrich said, ignoring us. "Michael let me in."

I wasn't sure this was good news. "The first time?"

"Yup, about seven thirty. We chatted for a while, and then I decided to head out to grab a few things. Your brother invited me for breakfast."

He was beaming. I was suspicious. "You chatted for a while?"

I glared at Michael. He held up both hands in surrender. "I said nothing," he replied, feigning innocence. But I knew what that look meant. I couldn't wait to get him alone and torture the truth out of him.

I was about to excuse myself, to go upstairs and put some clothes on, when I caught the tall American's very quick glance up and down my body.

"Well, blow me down!" Michael commented drily. "Even your back is blushing now."

"That's nothing," Heinrich said. "He was red right down to his ankles when you pulled down his underwear."

My mock-outrage didn't fool anyone, and after a heartbeat we all began to chuckle.

"Brothers!" I said.

"You don't need to tell me. I'm the youngest of five—all boys!" He glanced at my identity discs before asking, "So what part of the service do you guys work in? You obviously don't sit behind a desk all day." He gave my chest and upper arms a once-over.

Michael and I simultaneously gave the same polite but enigmatic smile—one known to servicemen all over the world. The smile that was always followed by a white lie.

"Um, we work in lots of different areas … mainly administrative," Michael said and then avoided any further involvement in the conversation by announcing that he'd go upstairs to find me a T-shirt.

"You work *'in lots of different areas'*?" Shorty laughed very loudly and then shook his head. "That's a decoy phrase if I ever heard one. Good try, Michael," he called out up the stairs after my brother.

"How about you?" I asked, rather too cheerfully, trying to avoid another, more penetrating question about our line of work.

"Well, you're going to find out sooner or later, so I may as well tell you," he said, patently ignoring my obviously failed attempt to bring the conversation to a halt. "I've been here for a bit over a month now. I'm the new ADC to the military attaché at the embassy."

I swear you would have heard my jaw click out of place, had not the phone rung at that precise moment. The telephones worked infrequently. It gave me a shock.

"I'll get it," my brother shouted as he thundered down the stairs. He threw a T-shirt at me and then answered the phone. He held the receiver out to me. "It's for you."

"Hello?" I said.

"I'm missing my ADC, half a pound of butter, a pound of bacon, a dozen eggs, an unknown quantity of bread rolls, and a large tin of coffee, plus some impossible-to-find fresh tomatoes. Have you any idea where any of these items might be?"

I looked around. A leather Gladstone bag sat near the living room door.

"All are present and correct, by the looks of things," I said to my old friend Colonel Steve Smith. "Which would you like returned?"

"The ADC I'd prefer returned in one piece—if that's possible."

I laughed. "I guess Thérèse rang you?"

"Maybe," was the evasive response.

Things began to click into place. "So, I imagine you two planned this …?"

"No comment, Tommy. Just be gentle with my nephew, you great galoot!" I could hear the grin in his voice. "Or I'll give you such a kick in the keyster, you won't poop for a week."

I wasn't quite sure what a keyster was, but had a pretty good idea. The "nephew" thing made my brain hurt, though. Really? I tried to get my head around the concept.

"Isn't this rather complicated, Steve?"

"It's only as complicated as you want to make it. It's about time you made some new pals."

The slight underlining on the word "pals" was unmissable. Was everyone in London obsessed with my love life, or perceived lack of it?

"Come over about six thirty, Tommy, and have a bite to eat, if you're free."

"I might have Mikey with me, Steve, if that's okay? He got caught up in some stoush at Waterloo station last night and stayed over."

"That would be the icing on the cake," he said. "See you then."

I hung up. Michael and Heinrich were chatting in the kitchen. I hadn't noticed them move in there while I was on the phone.

As I got to the door, I heard the end of Michael's whispered conversation. "Just go slow with him, okay? He's shy and old-fashioned. I was the wild one growing up. He was too busy being the prodigy of the age. I've never known him to invite anyone home before. You're the first."

"Well, then, Michael, I'm very honoured," my American replied.

I could feel my ears burning, this time with embarrassment. Was I really so old-fashioned? I had to admit that I was. But to tell Shorty I hadn't invited anyone home before …

"Who was that on the phone?" Michael asked when he noticed me standing in the doorway glaring at him.

"Steve," I said, and then switched to French. "I'll kill you later on.

But, first things first, you're never going to believe this, but this is his nephew."

"What?" Michael and Heinrich both said.

"You two know my uncle?" the tall American asked in French.

"Oh God, you speak French too?" I spluttered.

"We do languages at West Point, you know." He slapped his forehead. "I'm so dumb! I should have put two and two together. Tommy … you're the 'Spanish Tommy'? My Uncle Steve's best friend?"

*****

It was two years after arriving in Munich, in March, 1936, I'd got my first call to go to Spain. The country had been in the middle of a civil war, but under the guise of searching out manuscripts for my doctoral thesis, I went for short periods to work into conflict areas, training mercenaries and volunteers. My contact there back then was Steve Smith, the current military attaché at the US embassy, and as I'd learned a moment ago, Heinrich's uncle.

I watched in wonder as I saw the clouds parting in Shorty's eyes. Our visitor had worked things out.

It was Michael who eventually broke the silence. "American SIS?" he postulated, hesitantly.

Heinrich had told us he was an aide-de-camp to a military attaché, a position universally understood to be a front for an intelligence officer, and the Signals Intelligence Service was the American equivalent of MI5.

"MI5? MI6? The SOE?" Heinrich asked, countering Michael's question with one of his own.

The Special Operations Executive had only been formed in July earlier this year and Michael and I'd been transferred over from MI6, where we'd both been working. I'd been appointed as a counter-intelligence officer and co-ordinator of part of F section, a subdivision of the SOE that organised infiltration and sabotage in occupied France. My bailiwick was the Alsace-Lorraine area—I also co-ordinated local Resistance groups in Normandy and Brittany. Michael ran the training school of a hands-on physical discipline. He taught guerrilla tactics at

Hayling Island, one of the main centres of the "commando" specialisation for the British Army.

"Colonel Steve Smith is your uncle?" Michael asked, again deflecting with a question instead of answering the American.

"He sure is … and my godfather."

Michael raised his eyebrows and moved to the cupboard behind me, patting my arm. "Boy, oh boy!" he said, "I can just hear the 'make sure he's home by eleven' speeches."

"Can we talk about this later, please?" I pleaded. "In case you haven't noticed, I'm still in my underwear and I need to clean up and get dressed."

"Then I suggest you go do it!" Michael said and then gave me a cheeky grin.

I became aware I was standing very close to Heinrich, the little fingers of our hands barely brushing each other.

"Go get washed up. You have twenty minutes," Shorty said.

"Twenty minutes for what?"

"I'm cooking breakfast, courtesy of the American embassy icebox."

Michael pushed me towards the staircase. "Go! Make yourself presentable. He'll still be here when you get back downstairs."

I fled up the stairs to the accompaniment of quiet laughter from the kitchen.

*****

Standing in my bathroom, the shower running behind me, I gave myself a once-over in the mirror that hung on the back of the bathroom door.

As yet uncombed, my hair hung over my forehead, almost covering my right eye. I certainly had that Aussie larrikin look. Years of combat training in the defence academy at Duntroon, followed by championship Mensur fencing during my university years in Munich, and then clandestine involvement, both as a fighter and as a trainer in the Spanish Civil War, had left me with a strongly defined body.

Michael and I had both excelled at what was broadly called "hand-to-hand combat". He used his fists. I used my feet, knees, and elbows. As children, we'd both been taught to look after ourselves by one of our farm workers. Klaus was a former Great War guerrilla fighter, who'd spent all of his time fighting in German New Guinea—the north-eastern part of that country that was now a protectorate of Australia. He'd taught both Michael and me the Indonesian martial arts form of hand-to-hand combat known as Silat. There were dozens of variations within the discipline, and Klaus tailored our lessons around our strengths, or in my case, weaknesses. Michael was brave with his hands. I was overprotective with mine. As a result, my brother's practice was more ju-jitsu-like, while mine depended on kicks, joint manipulations, throws, and the use of bladed weapons.

I stepped under the shower, my mind turning over what had happened downstairs. The merest brushing of my little finger against Heinrich's, a few minutes ago, had made my gut clench in an unmistakable way. My body certainly seemed ready to proceed, something I found very hard to believe. No one had ever made me react quite like that—not ever. It was my mind that wasn't moving as fast. I truly was old-fashioned. I couldn't help it.

I'd towelled off and was halfway through shaving when Michael barged into the bathroom. "Five minutes to breakfast." He stood behind me, wrapped his arms around my chest, and leaned his head on the back of my shoulder. I kept on shaving and waited for him to say what was on his mind.

"Tommy?"

I grunted a "go on".

"I'm going to lose a part of you, you know."

"What do you mean, Mikey? I'm not going anywhere …"

"But, you're going to fall for that man downstairs," he said, squeezing me. "And when you do, a big part of you will belong to him and not to me anymore."

I rinsed my razor and chuckled, trying to make light of the situation. "You've already put me through that same situation twice now, Michael—first with Catherine and then with Rhys. Maybe it's payback time?"

He was way too quiet. Maybe he thought I was being serious? I'd used his full name. "Hey," I said gently, "Mikey, I only met him last night! Don't you think it's too early to be talking like this?"

He shook his head. "Nope. I can see it in your eyes. Both of you have that same look, even if you can't see it yourselves. It's inevitable, you know—I saw it every time I looked in the mirror when I first met Rhys." His face fell and he looked away.

"Ah, Jesus, Mikey, don't do this to yourself." I wiped my face clean and pulled him into my arms.

Michael had been an early bloomer, not like me. He'd got serious with Catherine Dunstone when he was only eighteen, just as we'd both entered officer training school at Duntroon. Their relationship had lasted until he was about twenty-four. She'd dumped him because he didn't want to get married. He'd asked for a transfer to England, arriving in 1935. I'd already been in Germany by then, up to my neck in books, writing the literature review of my doctorate. I'd always known gender was never a priority with Michael, but it had still been a surprise when he came to visit me in Germany in 1937 on the arm of a very handsome Welsh RAF pilot. It had been about eighteen months before war broke out. He and Rhys were made for each other. I'd never seen him happier—nor more devastated when Rhys had failed to return from a mission during the latter stages of the Battle of Britain early in September, three months ago. His plane had last been seen chasing a Messerschmitt over the Channel, heading towards France. However, quite a number of pilots had successfully crash-landed either in France, Belgium, or the Netherlands, or into the sea off the coast. Getting information from the Continent was still pretty tricky, and I knew Michael still hoped deep in his heart that somehow Rhys was either a POW or was being hidden by the Resistance in one of the occupied countries.

I was keeping all my fingers and toes crossed for him. He still felt like half of me—even fraternal twins could be more like one person, rather than two.

"We'll find him, Mikey," I said, rocking him in my arms, "and we'll get him back—you'll see."

"Just make sure *you* don't bugger things up by being too coy."

"What do you mean?" I asked.

He pointed in the direction of the kitchen downstairs and then gave a long, luxurious sniff. The smell of bacon, toast, and coffee percolated under the bathroom door.

"Those types don't grow on trees, Tommy. Grab him while you can. Life is shorter than you think."

As he was about to close the door, he stopped me as I started to pour brilliantine into the palm of my hand. "Leave it hanging over your eyes. It makes you look cute."

*****

About an hour later, I stretched back in my chair with my hands clasped behind my neck, my tummy groaning, full from the heartiest breakfast I'd eaten in months.

Michael had begged off, saying he had to go into the office to arrange alternative transportation—he had to get back to Hayling Island. He could easily have used my telephone. He was just giving us an hour or two without him hanging around.

"Had enough to eat?" Heinrich asked.

"Sure have. Thank you very much."

"I like your brother. I can tell he loves you a lot."

"You like him because he loves me?"

"Shows what good taste he has," he said.

"West Point obviously gives degrees in flirting too."

"Comes with the American heritage. I already told you that," he said. "You've obviously never dated an American before."

I looked at him from under my forelock. "I've never dated anyone before. So … that's what we're doing, is it? Dating?"

"Well, I suppose it is. You did kiss me on the first night we met."

"What makes me think you just made that rule up?"

He leaned across the table and ran his fingers through my hair. "At home we're brought up to believe if we want something, we should go get it. There are 'dating rules' in the States, you know?"

"I'm not interested in rules, Shorty, only intentions."

He snorted. "Man, you're something else."

"I'm hoping you are too." I took his hand. "All right then, Yankee. How does this dating thing work, now we seem to be doing it?"

He laughed and then pointed to my couch. "Sit!" he said. I did. He sat next to me and then swung his body around to lay his head in my lap, dangling his feet over the armrest. "Dating? Well, we go out, we smooch, we go out more, you put out, everyone is happy!"

It was my turn to laugh. "I suppose my putting out is the point of the exercise?"

"Nah," he said, "it's seeing whether you can get me to put out when you try."

"Arrogant bugger," I said. "Are you ticklish?" I didn't wait for an answer. I attacked him instead. We ended up on the floor, a bit breathless, but laughing. Boy, did this ever feel good, especially when I took a few cushions from the couch and put them under our heads, weaving one arm under his neck, spooning up close behind him, and holding him with my other arm, across his chest.

"Mmm," he murmured.

"So tell me all about you, handsome," I said.

"Well, I come from Boston …"

"I guessed that, being Steve's nephew, but your accent sounds like 'movie mid-Atlantic'."

"That's the accent I put on when I want to impress. I already told you I'm the youngest of five boys, so I know and understand the crap that goes on between you and Michael. My mother's sister married Uncle Steve's brother—that's how we're related. He encouraged me to apply to West Point. After I graduated, I was posted to Fort Monroe in Virginia to train …"

He paused and I understood why. We were all the same—military people who worked in Intelligence. Censoring our speech was so ingrained we often did it with people we trusted, and sometimes even when talking about things that weren't even classified. I teased his earlobe gently between my thumb and forefinger. "I could simply request your file if I really needed to," I said. "But I was hoping you might tell me yourself."

He turned in my arms, so we were face to face. "But you still haven't told me what *you* do," he said. There was no hint of complaint, nor of pressing me to answer.

"Later …" I replied.

He nodded and then continued his own story. "So—I went to Virginia to help set up a training course for counter-intelligence."

This was interesting, but I put it out of my mind for the moment and let him speak.

"Everyone with half a brain knew that even in thirty-six the situation in Europe was already getting very hairy—way before the Nazis invaded Poland—and, despite the official not-getting-involved policy, there were a lot of powerful people who knew sooner or later, if it came to war, we'd be dragged into a European conflict. Even now, everyone thinks it's only a matter of time before the US gets in on the act."

I began to play with the buttons on his shirt with my free hand.

"What are you doing?"

"Exploring," I said. "Go on …"

"For about a year, I travelled around the States to work with veterans of the Great War. I wanted to find out what close-combat techniques they'd used. At the same time, I was researching the possibility of using refined sign language in the field. What we call 'hand/arm signals' is fairly restrictive. I wanted to find out if what deaf people used could be more effective in combat situations—at least when the line of sight is clear."

Something clicked in my brain. "Hang on … so, it's you who's coming to talk to us on Tuesday afternoon then?"

"I am," he said and then chuckled. "Which means even if I hadn't turned up at Thérèse's shindig I'd have met you anyway."

I gently touched his bruised lip with the tip of my finger. "But then I wouldn't have had the pleasure of giving you this keepsake."

"And, Mr. Spy," he said with a wink, "you've just given away where you work, and therefore what you do."

I laughed. I'd been about to tell him part of it anyway. There was no harm done. Steve would have filled him in.

I'd written the time of the lecture in my diary last week. Tuesday afternoon had been pencilled in as "United States embassy lecture—all training officers to attend. Hand Signals in the Field."

"You know, we probably do the same sort of thing." I started to play with his dog tags.

"Seems like it. But yours is more field-based, I imagine?"

I gave him the "button-my-lips" gesture, before returning to trace the skin of his chest along the line of his singlet. I'd surreptitiously opened his shirt to the second button from the neck. The Yanks called them A-shirts, I remembered, but to me the Australian icon was a singlet, plain and simple.

"If you come a bit early," I said, "you can catch one of the knife-skills classes I run for the Polish army exiles, and I can show you around. Maybe we could have a beer with the guys after the class? "

"I'd like that," he said.

His eyes were inches from mine; his lips even closer. My mind flew back to our goodnight kiss at the front door last night. We both knew we wanted more. I gave him a very quick peck and then sat upright— I'd felt the blood rising up my neck and didn't want him to see how deeply I knew I was going to blush. I'd been aiming for sophisticate, not bumpkin. As it turned out, he couldn't have cared less. There was something in his tiny chuckle told me he liked the fact I'd coloured up— I'd often been told by my friends it was one of my more endearing traits.

He raised one arm languidly, rubbing it over my back. "I don't bite, you know," he said.

"I bet you do," I replied.

I stared at my hands, trying to twist something invisible between my fingers.

"Tommy, can I tell you something?" he asked, after a moment's silence.

"Sure," I said. "What?"

"I think we were set up last night."

"Oh, really? You think so?"

He laughed and then sat up beside me and leaned his head on my shoulder. "I think they did a good thing," he said softly.

"I'm inclined to think that too, Heinrich."

He pulled my head to his and kissed me. It was a luscious, warm kiss. One without urgency or need. But it made my heart pound in my chest.

He mumbled something.

"What was that?" I asked.

60

"Please, don't call me Heinrich. I sorta like 'Shorty'—even though it sounds like it belongs to a gangster—one of Capone's mob, for example."

"Have you got a nickname at home? What do other people call you?"

"Henry, mostly. My brothers call me ... Sunny."

I noticed the slight hesitation. "Because you're so good-natured?"

"Nup," he said, squeezing my knee. "Because they all reckoned my mom thinks the sun shines out of my ass."

I lowered my back onto the floor and laughed loudly, rubbing my eyes. I felt his mouth against mine.

"Was there a reason for that?" I asked, after I'd wound my arms around him.

"Yeah," he said, his face inches from mine. "If you're going to call me a gangster, then I thought I should behave like one and steal something from you."

I still couldn't believe the light in his eyes; it mesmerised me. I pulled his head down onto my chest and my heart thumped against his ear. His words had overwhelmed me. Had it been a line in a corny motion picture, I might have chuckled. But the warmth and the desire in his voice were too much to bear—I didn't have the strength to hold his gaze.

"Too fast?" he asked.

"Yes ... no ... no. Definitely no!" I replied. "It's only that I've never done this before."

"What?"

"You know," I said, "what we've just been doing." I didn't have a word for it, other than a few quaint, old-fashioned ones.

He laughed. "Oh, you mean, making out?"

"Is that what you call it?"

"You, me, kissing? Making out, necking ... you name it, we have lots of words for it."

"And let me guess, Yankee, you have a degree in that too?"

He chuckled softly. "I'd be lying, Tommy, if I told you I hadn't been around the block once, or maybe even twice before ... but this? This is my first ride in a limousine."

I didn't care if it was the most hackneyed phrase I'd never heard before—I kissed him. It was he who eventually broke the moment by smacking his lips loudly as we moved apart, like a cartoon kiss. He waggled his eyebrows, trying to make me laugh. "We can take this at your pace, Tommy, if that's what you want. There's no hurry."

An air-raid siren started off in the distance. He groaned. "Or maybe there is. Any chance of another coffee?"

"Can do," I replied. I untangled myself from his arms and went to the kitchen. I was grateful for the chance to collect my thoughts and sort out my feelings. As I moved to the stove, I said to myself, "Come on, Haupner! Pull yourself together! Isn't this what you've been waiting for?" I leaned my bum against the stove, closed my eyes, and tilted my head back, grinning at the ceiling.

"Need a hand?"

"No, I'm fine, thank you," I replied.

I filled the bottom half of the Moka pot with cold water and then packed the small perforated container with coffee from the tin he'd brought with him earlier. He began to whistle more Cole Porter, and I soon felt myself joining in with a quiet hum. I did a few carefree dance steps around my kitchen—the broom my hastily gathered and improvised partner.

"This flat is amazing," he called out.

"Come in here and talk to me while the coffee brews."

"In a minute," he replied, "I want to have a quick look around, if that's okay."

"Knock yourself out."

A small ceramic kangaroo, which was sitting on the kitchen window sill, caught my eye. I supposed I noticed it because it had been sitting on my kitchen bench for only a few days. Less than a week ago, I'd been sorting through some private papers left behind by an agent I'd sent to Nantes, who'd tragically been shot, not fifteen metres from the ground, after parachuting from his drop-off aircraft. A farmer, out looking for a lost cow in the middle of the night, had seen him floating down from the sky and had mistaken him for a German invader. The enclosed letter to his brother—to be delivered only if something happened to him—was full of brave thoughts and only one regret—that he'd probably die a virgin and never to know what it would be like to be loved and to love someone in return.

I, too, had once confessed similar feelings to someone else—Heinrich's uncle, Steve.

I'd given the kangaroo to my agent when he'd set off on his mission—his brother had returned it, as a keepsake.

"Why don't you do something with the floors downstairs?" Shorty's voice interrupted my thoughts.

"I will do … after the war," I called out.

The internal layout of my house felt as if it had been designed by a committee of people who couldn't concur. The staircase changed positions on each floor, dividing the space into unequal-sized rooms, which, as one ascended through the building, were not in the same place as on the floor below. Everyone agreed it was eccentric, but I'd felt drawn to it the moment I'd first seen it—its quirkiness was part of its bohemian charm.

"This floor was originally an artist's gallery during the twenties," I said as he came into the kitchen. "One of the lesser-known members of the Bloomsbury Set lived here. She took down a partition wall in the living room to open it up for a gallery. The kitchen was the preparation and storage room for her oils and pastels. I had it converted when I moved in about eighteen months ago."

"And upstairs?" he asked, leaning against the doorframe. He put a lit cigarette in my mouth. My hands were wet—I had my hands in the sink, washing up cups and saucers.

"Go look, if you like. It's just my bedroom and the bathroom."

I heard him clumping up the stairs, feeling both confused and happy about what was going on. There was something about him made my blood run hot, despite my protestations of shyness.

"Wow!" I heard him say. "Nice! A shower!"

"That's the reason I got the place," I called out.

"Bedroom is a mess!"

"Not my fault!"

Michael rarely stayed over. He did have his own life. He still kept the small flat he and Rhys had shared behind the Gaumont Film Studio in Shepherd's Bush. He'd sometimes arrive here unexpectedly if the Underground wasn't running—my flat in Bloomsbury was way closer than the trudge out to the west. Some of the time it was an obvious excuse to avoid feeling lonely. I could understand that.

"So how long have you known my uncle?" Shorty asked. He'd returned from his foray upstairs and was leaning against the doorframe.

"As a friend? Since the end of thirty-six, or thereabouts," I said. "We got to know each other properly as 'observers' during the Civil War in Spain."

"I'm confused—I thought you were in Munich then?"

I looked at him under my eyebrows.

"I see," he said. He understood that look. I guessed he'd used it himself on numerous occasions.

It had been quite a dangerous time for me, mainly because the Nazis supported the Nationalists, yet so many intellectuals from Britain and the US had come to fight fascism on the side of the Republicans. As I was well-known in Munich and in some circles in Berlin, if I'd been recognised by someone I knew from Germany, things would have become very messy, very quickly—I wasn't supposed to have been there.

My PhD and my violin playing were, as he'd already worked out, smokescreens for my intelligence work. I'd been sent to Germany to make influential friends, hopefully to perform in rarefied circles, and to gather information on the new and alarmingly prominent National Socialist German Workers' Party—the Nazis.

"Is that where you got this? In Spain?" He lifted my shirt to show the puckered scar above my right hip. I nodded. He rubbed it gently with the palm of his hand. "I did notice a bit more than your manly physique, you know."

"No you didn't," I said, grinning broadly. "I was watching where you looked."

"Well, in my defence, you could have poked my eye out."

I felt myself blushing again, so poured him a coffee.

"To get back to Steve," I said, changing the subject. "We originally met here in London in thirty-four, a few days after I got off the ship from Australia. My colonel at home had written to the Home Office in London, telling them about my language skills, intelligence training, and combat expertise. No need to tell you how quickly news gets around in the intelligence world—your uncle introduced himself at the pub one night. We got on like a house on fire, although I did think at first he was trying to pick me up."

"Maybe he was? I have no idea what his thing is."

"I have no real idea either. He's always behaved as a gentleman should."

I went into the living room to turn down the gas of the fire—it was getting a little too warm.

"We worked together for the first time at Toledo. I showed him a few hand-to-hand strategies and trained his guys with some knife moves for a week or two. Writing a PhD is not like classwork. No one cared if I wasn't around in Munich for months at a time, you can write anywhere. Anyway, we struck up a friendship and he came to Germany every so often—you know how it goes. But I expect he's already told you all of this."

"Not really," he replied. "I know you're best friends, and some-thing went down at Badajoz made you very close. That's all."

I nodded, but said no more.

"You passed on information to him?" he asked.

"I still do."

"But you work for the British now."

"The Brits keep stuff from the Aussies too, you know. I believe in the free trade of important information … You know if you tell anyone any of this I'm going to have to shoot you?"

He smiled at me over the rim of his cup.

I went back to sit on the couch and beckoned him to join me. "Now, where were we before the tickling began?" I asked.

He stretched out at my feet and then pulled me down onto the floor. "Cushions, Haupner," he said.

They went under our heads as he spooned up close behind, his arms around me.

"Tommy?"

"Yes?"

"When's your next big concert? I looked through the invitation register at the embassy last night to make sure I was free, but couldn't see your name on any of the programme details."

"I don't get to play in London with the big orchestras," I said with a sigh. "Only recitals, private performances, like last night, and lunchtime concerts at places like the National Gallery."

He sat up. "What? But why?"

I pulled him back down on the floor next to me. "I don't fit," I explained. "Oh, I get to play with all the best conductors with all of the regional orchestras—Manchester, Birmingham, Edinburgh, and the rest. But you have to understand what some British people think of us colonials."

I knew I sounded bitter, disappointed at the way things had turned out when I came back to England, but there was little I could do about it.

"But Thérèse told me about how famous you were in Germany," he said. "While you were outside in the stairwell—before I came looking for you."

"Have you heard of a conductor called Bruno Walter?" I asked.

"Sure I have," he said. "He comes to Boston all the time. Even I know he's one of the most famous conductors in the world."

"Well," I explained, "he took me under his wing in Europe, long before he left for the United States. I had a great deal of success in Germany because of his support—he introduced me to his colleagues. I found myself engaged to play under those extraordinary men—men like Klemperer and Furtwängler—and with all the major orchestras. When I wrote to Bruno and told him that I, too, felt it was time to leave, and I was coming here, he wrote a letter of introduction to Sir Thomas Beecham, who was kind enough to give me a concert in Leeds, on the strength of his recommendation."

"And?"

"Oh, Sir Thomas was very, very kind. He, in turn, introduced me to Malcolm Sargent, the other great British conductor, and between the two of them I get to play with all of the big orchestras around the country."

"But not in London," he said.

"But not in London," I replied. "Maybe, one day ..."

Being a musician from one of the colonies of the Empire, I believed unless something extraordinarily untoward happened, some people would always consider me a second-class citizen, an amusement, and an outsider. We expatriates often joked that many British snobs thought Australians had only recently been granted freedom from our convict chains.

I knew I was exaggerating. It wasn't the case in all areas of society or professional expertise in the capital. But, in the case of Geoffrey Alders, the manager of the Royal Philharmonic Orchestra, the land of my birth was an insurmountable obstacle, no matter how talented I might be, or how frequently famous conductors pushed for me as their soloist, as long as he was in charge of bookings I'd never play with the major orchestras either in Queen's Hall or in the Royal Albert Hall.

"Leave it to me," he said. "I'll fix it, Tommy."

I laughed loudly once more. "And exactly how are you going to fix it, Mr. Superman?"

"Just point me at the obstacle and I'll take care of it," he said, folding himself against my back. "With my Winchester at my shoulder, nothing is unassailable."

He was a trained sniper? That was another piece of interesting information.

"They can't ignore the heaven that comes out of your hands—not if a heart beats in their chests. My mom says, *good comes to all those who have love in their hearts*'. No one could play like you, Tommy, and have no good come from it. It's only a matter of time—you'll see."

"Thank you ... Shorty," I said.

He wasn't just spouting homilies, I could hear the genuineness in his voice and felt a moment of panic, that this man was way too good for me, that it would all end in grief; but then, in the next instant, I thought what he'd said was something my own mother might have said. Those sentiments were so ingrained in me and in my brother that I took them for a truth, despite the war proving us wrong at every moment.

He wound his arms tighter around me and let out a long, soft hum of contentment. "Wake me in half an hour," he whispered into my ear, and then kissed the back of my neck.

Who was I to argue with such a proposition?

*****

A little before six that evening, I changed into my uniform. I knew what I'd really liked to have worn, but it was completely inappropriate for dinner at the US embassy.

Maybe I'd get a chance at some other time to show off my dark brown slacks, a white shirt, my favourite shoes of the moment—two-toned brown and cream brogues—and a trophied Luftwaffe leather flight jacket that had cost me a bottle of Glenfiddich and two cartons of cigarettes. Part of my job at the SOE was the routine questioning of captured enemies, so it wasn't so hard to arrange a swap or trade for some of the more desirable German trophies. It wasn't strictly above board, but I was senior enough for no one to make a fuss.

I checked myself in the mirror on the back of the bathroom door and fiddled with my forelock, wondering if I could really get used to the lack of hair tonic. I did a quick pose and a cheeky grin. "Good enough for a Yank," I said to myself.

There was no official curfew in central London, but in case I was challenged in the street I donned my army greatcoat and cap, wound a heavy woollen scarf around my neck, and then headed off to Grosvenor Square. At the last moment, before leaving, I retrieved the handkerchief from my sock drawer where I'd placed it last night while getting undressed. I held it to my nose and inhaled. It had the smell of him on it—his cologne, his brilliantine, and a vague whiff of Lucky Strikes. In one corner there was a brown bloodstain, about the size of a two-bob piece.

I folded the handkerchief carefully and put it in the pocket of my trousers for luck.

At the corner of Regent Street, a few Pommy soldiers stopped and saluted me. I threw a salute back, knowing I must have been in a good mood, as more often than not, senior officers merely nodded at enlisted men. Michael, had he been with me, would have ignored them and continued on his way.

My brother had come home briefly earlier to collect his duffle, as he'd finally arranged transport to get to Portsmouth. Once he got there, he'd make his own way to Hayling Island. I wasn't sure when I'd see him next, but was past the stage of worrying needlessly about him. He'd walked in on us, curled up on the floor, a large package of fish and chips rolled in newspaper under his arm for lunch. I'd smiled to myself after he'd woken me with the sound of clumping up the stairs, as the first thing I'd noticed was the man behind me trying to bayonet my rear end in his sleep.

After Michael, and then Shorty, had gone, the rest of my afternoon had been an unstructured, lazy one—a precious hour or two of violin practice; reading for a while … even some paperwork; all interspersed with recurring thoughts of bright-green eyes and soft, almost-blond hair.

*****

The guard outside the embassy saluted and then checked my papers before opening the door. I couldn't help thinking how stupidly placed the main door was for Macdonald House, opening into Grosvenor Street instead of into the square itself.

Dinner was in the senior-staff dining room in the basement of the embassy. The meal was delicious and over-abundant, as it always was at one of the embassies, leaving me with a slightly guilty feeling when I considered the millions of Londoners around us trying to make do on the supper they could cobble together from rations. I was really spoiled in comparison, for, should I really want to, I could take advantage of the free meals for senior officers at Baker Street, at the Ministry of Defence, or indeed, at the Australian High Commission building. There was no real need for me to either cook for myself or buy food. Strictly speaking, an army major was field grade officer, not a senior officer, but it was a good enough rank to allow me access to those dining areas, as long as there wasn't some stuffy, retired brigadier-general with a broom up his arse who wanted to lord his status over us "lower" ranks.

After dinner we were joined by John McQueen, who was visiting as assistant naval attaché—a title that was nearly always a euphemism for an intelligence officer. He was a nice enough guy and always ready for a good story.

"So, Aussie," he said, lighting up his pipe and sitting back in his armchair. We'd retreated to the sitting room adjacent to Steve's office, "I read somewhere you got an Order of Valour from the Spanish?"

"You did?" Shorty raised his eyebrows.

I nodded.

"So you must have been in Spain, then!" John playfully kicked the sole of my shoe. "Come on, out with the story."

"Maybe not that story," I said, not wanting to relive the horror of Badajoz. The whole episode was something I'd rather not remember: the piles of bodies, men and women, civilians and soldiers; the smoke and stench; the recovery of one of our comrades just as he was about to be executed; and my own shooting, as we tried to escape—these were things I wanted to forget. It wasn't the sort of tale one told to pass the time.

"Another time, John," Steve said, his voice brooking no argument.

There was a moment's silence.

"I can tell you about Steve's fart at Brihuega, though, if you like?" I said.

"Shut up, you!" Steve reached over and gently punched my shoulder.

"This one I really want to hear!" Shorty said.

"If anyone tells that story, it's going to be me," Steve said.

But I ignored him and started to relate what had happened.

"We were holed up about two miles out of town, Steve, me, and an Italian colonel, when the shelling began—"

"My fart, my story!" Steve interrupted. "Well, the Italian colonel says to me in really, really bad English, 'we are-a really safe-a here, you theenk?' I see Tommy roll his eyes, just as a shell hits the wall behind our dugout and knocks us every which way."

I started to snigger.

"When we get up and dust ourselves off," Steve continued, "we see the Italian's butt and legs sticking out of a big oil barrel that's been blown into the wall of the dugout. The explosion had obviously hurled him into the open barrel and he was stuck in it. I go over, grab his legs, and try to pull him out, but I couldn't, so I say to Tommy, 'give me a hand here'. Tommy comes over, puts his hands around me, and I say, 'don't grab my guts, you'll make me fart'."

I was trying not to laugh, vividly remembering the story as Steve told it to the others.

"So, trying to be a silly ass-crack, Tommy squeezes my stomach, and I let rip the biggest fart in the world—sounds louder than the shell explosion. The colonel pops free, we all fall down in a heap, and then the colonel says to me, real serious, 'how come-a squeezing your-a stomach will make-a you fat?'"

The four of us laughed loudly, causing a few of the other men in the room to turn to see what the fuss was about. What was it with men and fart stories?

About nine thirty, more members of the embassy staff began to come down to the basement. Bombs were falling not too far away. From the sounds of the explosions, I thought probably somewhere around Hyde Park and Marble Arch. Even inside, one could often tell. I felt a pang of concern. This part of London rarely got bombed so heavily. It was usually the industrial areas in the east that copped a pounding. I hoped it wasn't a sign of things to come. The shuddering, even in the basement, was quite violent, so Steve and I decided to go up and fetch the guards to safety too.

The two men guarding the front door didn't seem too anxious to leave when we got there, so we all lit up and chatted for a while, Steve drawing me away to lean on the iron railings along the front of the building—there were so few left in the streets anymore. One hoped they were reborn as cladding for battleships, or barrels of long-range, heavy guns, as the War Office told us they would be.

"So?" he asked me.

I grinned. "Thank you, Steve."

He nudged me with his elbow.

"Okay, I owe you," I said.

"I figured you two could be pretty good for each other, Tommy. He's so like you in so many ways."

I was about to ask what he meant when I heard the unmistakable whistle of a bomb, and then, immediately after, felt a massive explosion to the north of us. The blast wave rocketed down Duke Street, smashing windows and blowing off roof slates. We were nearly knocked off our feet and instantly crouched, but no one ran. We'd been bombed nightly since early in September and most of us were fairly blasé, unless a bomb fell almost right on top of us.

Broken glass from upper windows rained down from above, covering the street in shiny, ice-like shards. A moment later, the front door of the embassy flew open, and Shorty burst onto the street. "Everyone all right?" he shouted.

"All good," I said. My ears were still ringing, but not loudly enough to mask the sound of someone screaming, north of us, in Duke Street.

Instinctively, I began to run towards the sound, to see if there was anything I could do, but was stopped after about fifty yards by a group of air-raid wardens and a few policemen who appeared out of the darkness and ordered me back. Shorty and Steve were behind me, pulling me back and telling me to leave it to the experts. I could still hear screams and shouts for help—a second woman's voice began to wail.

"Go back, sir," one of the bobbies said to me. "We have this under control."

Over his shoulder I could see billowing dark smoke rising from the roadway, illuminated from behind by tongues of red and yellow flames from a broken gas pipe. Even from where I stood, I could clearly see the front of a terrace house had collapsed into the roadway, and several injured people sat in the rubble, already attended by Red Cross workers.

"There's an ambulance station just up there," Steve said. "Come on, Tommy, you know the drill. Leave it to the experts, unless invited to help."

Even though providing assistance was the first order of the day before police and specialist service members arrived, once they were in place the general public was more likely to be asked to stand aside, mainly due to the abhorrent amount of looting that took place.

"We're servicemen," I tried to explain to the patient, but determined bobby. "We're trained to help."

"I understand, sir," he said, ushering us back gently, but unwaveringly. "But, as I said, everything's in hand."

"Well, we're at the American embassy, down on the corner, if you need extra hands," Steve offered, trying to pull me away.

"Thank you, sir. We'll certainly come looking for you if it's needed. Now if you'd be so kind, please clear the street."

Although they were a few streets away yet, I could hear ambulances and a fire appliance approaching—the sounds of their sirens and bells were distinctly different. Reluctantly, I followed Steve and Shorty back to the embassy as three vehicles whizzed past us.

"It sounded like a Herman," one of the embassy guards said. The "Herman" was the nickname Londoners gave to the fat, one-thousand-kilogram bombs the Germans had started dropping. I'd read reports of a newer, eighteen-hundred-kilogram bomb, nicknamed "the Satan", but rather hoped it was a rumour—nearly two tonnes of high explosive in a densely populated city didn't bear thinking about.

Two more explosions echoed through the streets, one closer than the big one, and one a bit farther to the west.

"All right, everyone, downstairs!" Steve ordered. He locked the embassy door after we were all inside and we filed down to the basement.

Over the next few hours we chatted and played cards. There were only one or two more big explosions, and then the target area seemed to shift somewhere off to the east. Poor bastards in the docks, I thought to myself, they were the ones who seemed to get it every night.

By midnight, only three of us remained in the sitting room—Steve, Shorty, and me.

"You're staying here tonight, Tommy," Steve said.

I wasn't going to argue. I didn't fancy the thought of weaving through the streets while a heavy raid was still under way. Bombs might still be falling where I lived, and the possibility of parachute mines was also quite high. It wouldn't be until morning that patrols would sort those out. Until then, it was probably safer to stay put.

"You run along to bed, Henry," Steve said, hugging his nephew. "I'll show this Aussie where he can sleep."

I smiled at the "Henry". Although he'd told me everyone called him by that name, it now sounded odd, because I'd christened him "Shorty" in my mind.

"Thanks for the great day, Tommy," he said against my shoulder, briefly holding me in a hug. "Night, buddy," he said with a wink, and then was gone, out the door.

Steve lit a cigarette and held out the pack to me. I took one and lit it. He picked a thread of tobacco from the corner of his mouth and then snorted softly.

"Remember the night after Badajoz, Tommy? What you said to me?"

I knew where this conversation was leading. How could I forget that night? I'd been scared out of my wits, had missed a third guard in the dark, the one who'd shot me, and we'd fallen into a pile of dead women and children while trying to get away. And then, later that night, when I'd broken down as Steve had cleaned my gunshot wound by firelight, I'd spilled my guts to him, afraid I might bleed to death, confessing my loneliness, my frustration at not ever seeming to meet anyone who I liked, and at never having known what love was.

I knew exactly what he was going to say now.

"You told me that night, when you thought you were dying, your one regret was never to have been lucky enough to meet the right person."

"I said a whole lot of things."

"You did. But that was the one that made you cry."

"I never did such a thing," I protested, albeit feebly.

He ignored me. "And look, here we are again. I was just thinking we could have had our asses handed to us on a plate a few hours ago if that bomb had dropped a bit farther to the south."

I stared at him, but said nothing.

"This war is a shit-fight, Tommy. You could get blown into a thousand pieces while you walk in the street, or be turned into a smear of raspberry jelly in your sleep if a bomb hit your house. Not to mention that crap you get up to in France."

I started to object, but he held up a hand to silence me.

"I know what you do over there on your mysterious weeks of absence. You really think the US has no idea what the SOE really does and what you did before at MI6? I worry my guts into an ulcer every time I hear you and Michael are, how do they say it … unavailable?"

"Steve—"

"Life is so terribly fucking short, Tommy. You're still a young man. You deserve something good in this fucked-up war!"

I didn't understand why he sounded so choked up. Perhaps it was another story for another time.

He pulled me to my feet. "Come with me," he said.

I followed him through a maze of corridors into what was obviously the living area of the embassy staff. We stopped outside a door with a small brass plate at eye level. It held a card with Heinrich's name on it.

"What's in here, Steve?" I knew, but I wanted him to tell me.

"Henry is in here, Tommy."

I bit my lip and hung my head. I was really getting embarrassed.

He shook my hand then gave me a small battery-powered flashlight, which he retrieved from a holder next to the door. "Goodnight, my friend. I hope you sleep well."

He slapped my shoulder and then disappeared down the corridor.

I stood in the dimly lit passageway, my mind racing at a thousand miles an hour and my heart pounding in my chest. I was afraid, but not sure what there was to be afraid of. There was nothing at risk, no danger behind the closed door—there was only opportunity.

For some inexplicable reason, Steve's words made me feel as if I had been handed a book, a book of empty pages.

I gently laid my fist against the door and rested my forehead on it while I tried to clear my thoughts. But, as hard as I tried, nothing worked—all I saw in my mind was the first blank page of the book, and my hand hovering over it, ready to write the first words.

Well, if this was to be the first chapter in the book of the rest of my life, I'd better get on with it. I swallowed hard, took a few deep breaths, and then opened the door.

Shorty was in bed, lying on his side, his shoulder and arm over the top of the blankets, one eye open, watching me.

"Hi," I whispered.

"Hi yourself," he answered.

I put the flashlight on the bedside table, its lens nearly touching the wall. It suffused the room with a dull glow.

"What are you doing here?" he asked quietly.

"Um … I got lost?"

He laughed and then folded back a corner of the blanket.

"And now, Tommy?"

There was another brief moment of silence, a moment in which I saw only uncertainty and vulnerability in his eyes. Something massive gave way inside me. I dropped my arms to my sides and took two steps towards him.

"I guess I found what I've been looking for."

CHAPTER 3

It took me a while to work out where I was.

While checking the luminous dial of my wristwatch in the dark, I slowly remembered. It was five thirty in the morning and I could hear the all-clear alert. It must have been a bitch of a night out there. All-night raids were not unknown of late, but infrequent. The siren had woken me.

I felt extraordinarily relaxed. A heavy head rested on my shoulder, threads of hair tickled my cheek and my ear, one arm lay on my chest, fingers spread through my chest hair.

I took a long, slow lungful of his smell and then drifted off into a half-sleep again. Images played over in my mind: elbows and knees; hastily ripped off undershorts and bumping heads; the awkwardness of bodies that had never touched before; and the sweet, urgent release brought about by proximity rather than manipulation.

It was a miracle. A miracle another human being could evoke such a strong physical response by the mere presence of someone who stood out from all the others. Did other men think the same thoughts, have the same feelings while making love with a person who was special? Or did they merely experience the physical release and think no more about it? The feel of his breath on my chest made me aware of him once more.

My first truly intimate experience had been made extraordinary by who he was rather than what we'd done.

I was roused from my half-sleep by a gentle scratching of my chest.

"You awake?" I whispered.

"Nope," he said and then chuckled. "You're a funny man, Thomas Haupner."

"I try," I said. "But what have I done?"

"Nothing, really," he replied, and then after a pause, asked, "What made you change your mind last night?"

"About?"

"You know …"

"Ah, that!" I said. "I got escorted in here at gunpoint. Your uncle said he'd shoot me if I didn't make an honest man of you, so what could I do but comply? Who's going to argue with a jarhead holding a Luger?"

Shorty laughed. "Technically he's a grunt," he said. "A jarhead is a marine, and Americans don't have Lugers."

"I know that, but I still wasn't going to argue."

He rolled onto his back, curling me into his arms. I was already starting to formulate and recognise the "smell of Shorty" in my mind. It was a heady combination of his skin, the soap and the cologne he used, the brilliantine in his hair, the subtle lingering odour of American cigarettes, and the residual, pleasant whiff of leather from his jacket.

It smelled like something I wanted to eat rather than inhale.

"How are we going to manage this?" I asked him after a while.

"What?"

"You know, this you and me thing."

"We have a thing, do we?"

"I'm not sure," I replied. "Do we?"

"I'm ready to put my shoulder behind the wheel if you are." His voice was soft and gentle. "But I guess what you're wondering is more about how we're going to manage outside, in the world we live and work in?"

"Yes, I suppose I am."

I fumbled at the bedside table for the flashlight and then turned it on. I found my cigarettes and an ashtray, lit one smoke for each of us and gave him one, resting the ashtray on the sheet between my knees.

He coughed after the first drag—the one every smoker enjoyed the most: the first puff of the first fag of the day. "What the hell are these?"

"Sorry—Players. It was all I could get. Senior Service was sold out."

He laughed and then told me he'd keep me supplied with Marlboros or Luckies from the PX store.

"If you're worried about what people might say," he continued, "then folks where I come from are taught it's very bad manners to discuss other people's personal life in public ... or in private, when it comes down to the wire. That's nothing more than plain old gossip, and the crowd I mixed with at home and at work would be more upset someone had said something out of place than by what was said."

I thought about it. It was true, of course. These days we weren't as bad as the Victorians, but our manners didn't encourage people to make observations on private matters in social situations. It was considered vulgar.

"I think we just keep calm, keep our heads down, and go about our lives. It's no one's business but our own, Tommy," he added. "After all, I'm sure we both know plenty of guys who are hooked up together, with no one but their pals any the wiser."

I'd often wondered about what would happen, should I eventually meet someone. Where I worked, no one could give a hoot. Loose-lipped types and bigots were filtered out well before the final selection process. We had our ways of discerning who could keep their mouths shut and who couldn't—security depended on it. My workplace was a whirlpool of differing races, religions, social classes, and special abilities, all drawn into the vortex that was the Special Operations Executive. We employed law-breakers both current and reformed, scientists, medical experts, and even plain old thugs. We were too busy trying to win a war and to do our jobs, the major part of which revolved around secrecy. No one cared what anyone did behind closed doors, as long as they were discreet about it and didn't discuss their work when they were between the sheets.

As for music circles and the upper-class folk I mixed with on a regular basis, homosexuality was an understood variant of human behaviour. One still behaved with propriety, but the atmosphere was much more relaxed on such matters. Relationships between members of the same sex were not only often acknowledged, but usually accepted with no value judgement. Of course, it all depended on the amount of discretion homosexual men and women exercised.

There were exceptions. However, we all learned to steer clear of those people and perhaps gather a little useful information about them, to keep up our sleeves, should the need arise. No one's dossier was squeaky-clean, except for we lucky few who had access to our own Government files and who could erase, or rewrite, the information kept in them.

"But if you're asking how we're going to manage what's happening between us, I can only say we're two grown men—we'll sort things out as we go along. If it was meant to be, then it'll happen just as naturally as it should."

I gave a small murmur of agreement as I stubbed out my cigarette and then slipped down in the bed, snuggling my head on his thigh, like a cat who'd found a warm place to curl up against.

"Where's that wheel I have to put my shoulder behind?" I asked.

He slipped down beside me in the bed and wrapped his arms around my shoulders, our foreheads touching.

"I think the cart is already doing just fine, Aussie," he said, very softly, and then kissed me gently on the tip of my nose. "I don't think anyone is going to need to give it any help at all."

*****

Brook Street was cordoned off, as were most of the streets to the east of the embassy, so I decided not to go home first, but directly to work. I kept a spare shirt and a few pairs of skivvies in the locker room and would find time to change during the morning.

There was a spring in my step as I turned north, intending to head up Duke Street, but it was still closed off from last night. The lightness in my heart slowly turned leaden as I stopped to chat with the policeman who was monitoring the cordon.

Over his shoulder, I could see several "sleepwalkers"—it was the name we gave to those who were dispossessed after a raid. Those whose houses were gone, whose belongings were strewn in full view over heaps of smashed bricks and splintered timbers, and whose parents, children, lovers, or spouses were perhaps dead or missing. They wandered around aimlessly, like ghosts, picking up small items from the edges of the debris, turning them over in their hands, and then dropping them without really looking at what they'd retrieved.

It was heart-wrenching.

After several detours, I finally got as far as Selfridges, which had clearly taken several big hits last night. Parts of the rooftop garden were exposed—a large portion of the corner of the building had crashed down into Oxford Street. A double-decker bus lay on its side, the entire top peeled back like a sardine tin. Rescue crews were still at work, trying to retrieve bodies. I recognised their canvas bags and specialised cutting equipment. I'd been there too, helping, more than once.

"The shelter?" I asked of an older, careworn policeman who sat, dirty and dishevelled, on the edge of the gutter.

"Empty," he said and then smiled wanly at me.

I breathed a sigh of relief. Only recently, in September, John Lewis's had been hit while over two hundred people had sheltered in its basement.

It was after I turned the corner into Baker Street I realised something really terrible had happened. The street was cordoned off at All Souls' Place, so I asked one of the bobbies on duty. Apparently, a high-explosive bomb had fallen at the edge of the open area ahead, where several streets converged, demolishing a large number of buildings along either side of the central garden area, and gouging a twenty-foot hole in the middle of the road—it must have been the Herman we'd heard last night.

However, worse was to come. When I finally reached my office, my boss, Brigadier Mark Harris, was already at work—a thing unheard of for eight thirty in the morning, especially on a Monday. I was called into his office immediately and told the terrible news. Four of my specialist field officers had been killed last night in the devastation I'd stopped to look at not half an hour ago. The Langham Hotel, in which the four men had gathered to play cards and to have a few drinks, had been badly damaged by the blast. It was a freak accident. By mere chance, a stick of five-hundred-kilogram bombs from another aircraft had fallen in an arc up Regent Street, hitting the side of the hotel at exactly the same time the Herman had demolished the nearby crossroads. The bar in which they'd been seated had been completely obliterated by both explosions.

I called a hurried meeting with both my chief-of-staff and staff captain to discuss the implications. We were now hopelessly stuck for fluent German-speakers with actual hands-on experience. Should the need arise to send trained operatives into Germany in the near future to pose as enemy officers, the loss of the four men left us with only two men capable of doing the job—my brother and myself. This was very serious.

I drafted a coded telegraph message to Michael and to Stuart McGillivray at Lochailort, in Scotland, to see if they had any potential replacements. Our best hopes were Jewish refugees from Germany, Austria, or the Sudetenland. We had one Polish army officer in the SOE at the moment whose German was fluent, although he spoke with a very slight Polish accent. He could be used in an emergency.

My staff captain and I had fought with our superiors about this situation for months. We'd already been undermanned in this specialist group, even before the loss of my four friends. But Mark Harris was as obstinate as he was lazy. As he spoke no languages, other than "what ho, the hounds!", he thought that good-enough was good enough. Other than Michael and me, there were only two other fully trained "impersonation" agents, and they were already deployed in the field, organising resistance groups in Norway—no great help if anything needed to be done in occupied France in the immediate future, for example.

Knowing I'd get no help from Harris, I got on the blower to Whitehall. I decided I'd make our predicament known to friends in the MOD, mainly to see whether any of the co-ordinators had contacts with any native German-speakers in the Navy or Air Force who we could appropriate and who could be trained up swiftly.

After the meeting, there was nothing to do but to get back to business. Every morning after the raids, dozens of bombed-out milliners, grocers, and butchers who'd lost their premises did the same thing—cleaned themselves up and got on with their lives.

On Mondays, if we'd managed to get the latest *Deutsche Wochenschau*, we'd watch it frame by frame, analysing who was in each section, trying to piece together where they were, which was actual current footage and which were older shots edited in for visual effect. Our team this morning would be sadly depleted, as two of the men who were killed last night in the bomb blast were regulars in the review group, each specialising in two or three specific high-ranking officers who frequently appeared in the newsreels.

I had no idea who was going to go through the latest *Signal* or *Der Stürmer* magazines. We trawled through them both to find information, not from the text, but from the reproduced photos. The backgrounds of photos often revealed a lot of information—locations, weapons, vehicle number plates, and so forth. I guessed it would have to be me. My sigh of resignation wasn't because I didn't like that particular type of work, it was because I'd hoped to leave a little early today and to do a bit of practice before dinner. I also wanted some time to myself to dwell on what had happened last night—it had left me elated, but also a little confused.

It was nearly seven before I started to pack up my desk for the day. I was still locked in a dark space in my head, preoccupied with the death of my friends who made up my "Number One Kraut Squad", as I liked to call them. Hans, Pieter, Karl, and Jean, all gone in a flash of light and a bang while I'd stood smoking my cigarette in front of the American embassy.

I'd finished writing the last of my notes when my phone rang. There was a visitor from the US embassy waiting downstairs. I told the guard to send him up and then went down the corridor to the lift, willing my mood to shift—I could deal with my dark thoughts later.

"Hey," he said.

"Hey yourself."

He held out a parcel. "Got something for you."

"Can I eat it? Because I'm starved," I said.

"Six of the latest *Rheinische Landeszeitung* and two copies of the *Berliner Börsen-Zeitung* ..."

"How the hell did you get these?" I was astonished. Fresh German newspapers were a pretty rare find for us. Ours were usually a week or two old by the time we got them.

"It's called a diplomatic bag—we're not at war with the Nazis. Remember?"

I smiled. "Well, buddy, I think I owe you something in return. Have you eaten yet?"

"I'm an American, Tommy—I'm always hungry."

I smiled at him. "Quick supper in the officers' dining room suit you?"

"Sure thing—lead on!"

I showed him around my office, introducing him to a few of my colleagues who were still working, and finally depositing the newspapers with Gladys, my secretary, who was packing up for the day. I told her they should go for analysis the following morning and then introduced Captain Heinrich Reiter.

Gladys Gleeson, my secretary, had been waiting for me outside my office door on my first day at the SOE. As she proved to be incredibly efficient, spoke good German and French and could type and take dictation in those languages, I accepted she'd been assigned to keep an eye on me. Spying on spies—our organisation thrived on that mentality.

Gladys was extremely beautiful. I liked to describe her as looking like Rita Hayworth, with the brain of Albert Einstein, and the cutting wit of Dorothy Parker—she was never short of an appropriate one-liner. She'd gone from being a secretary who'd been assigned to keep tabs on her boss to my pal in a matter of weeks. We looked out for each other's backs and enjoyed each other's company out on the town. She was also very happy to accompany me to parties and social functions when I needed to attend with a woman of a certain social level on my arm. Sometimes a pretty face wasn't enough—in certain situations, breeding and culture in a companion were considered the hallmark of a gentleman.

As I handed the newspapers to Gladys, she gave Shorty a slow up-and-down and then whistled under her breath. "I hope this is pleasure, not business," she said to me, in German, while smiling warmly at my guest.

"Es ist mein Geschäft Freude zu bereiten, Gladys. Ich freue mich Sie kennen zu lernen," he said, returning her smile. He took her hand and kissed it.

It is my business—giving pleasure, he'd replied.

To her credit, Gladys barely reacted. Only the merest widening of her eyes, and the slightest blush over her impressive cleavage, indicated any surprise. "I hope we'll be seeing more of you, Captain Reiter," she replied just before I steered him away from her desk towards the stairwell that led down to the dining room.

As we turned the corner at the top of the stairway, I glanced back at Gladys over my shoulder. She gave me a brief shrug, and a look at Shorty that could only have been interpreted as a facial wolf-whistle.

The food was always very ordinary, even in the officers' "dining room", as it was euphemistically called. I contributed some food stamps for his dinner, trying to imagine what he must think of what was on our plates, compared to what they got at the American embassy. Still, he tucked in and didn't seem to mind. How anyone could smile while eating tripe in white sauce with turnips and mashed potatoes was beyond me. Had he not been there, and me trying to be polite, I might have marched into the kitchen to look for the chef's private stash.

"So," he was saying, "what time is the training class tomorrow?"

We'd arranged for him to work out with my Polish group the following afternoon, before he gave us his talk about hand signals.

"We start at one. That okay with you?"

"Sure," he said. "I really appreciate it, Tommy. My muscles are going to forget what to do if I don't keep up training. It's the combat readiness, you know, not muscular strength. I never want to lose that co-ordination."

He was right. Strength had nothing to do with combat fighting. It came in handy, but it was more about dexterity, quick reflexes, and snap judgements. The ability to weigh up outcomes and to react instinctively was a developmental skill requiring constant reinforcement.

"Why don't you turn up at about twelve thirty? You and I can work out together for a bit. I don't want to either throw you in at the deep end or make you feel uncomfortable if I put you in a group that's below your level. If you and I spend thirty minutes beforehand, I'll see where you best fit."

"You guys wear a special outfit or anything?"

"Wear whatever you feel comfortable in. I wear a singlet and an old one-piece swimsuit I roll down to my waist over a belt."

"Mmm," he mumbled appreciatively, with a mouthful of steamed pudding and custard.

"You must be starved," I said, "Mine tastes like wallpaper paste."

He almost choked. "I was thinking of what you wear in training, not the food. Maybe it's better I get a good look before the class. I wouldn't want to embarrass myself."

I grinned and then looked around as a voice said, "Mind if I join you?" It was Andrzej Godowsky, the most experienced of the exiled Polish guerrilla fighters we had at the SOE. He trained newcomers.

"Of course," I said in German. "This will be a good opportunity for you to practise *auf Deutsch*."

I introduced the two men to each other, and then the three of us fell into an easy, comfortable conversation, only interrupted when the waiter arrived to take Andrzej's order.

In all the time I'd been working with the trainers from varying European countries, Andrzej had stood out among them all. He was intelligent, quick on his feet, and a very fast learner—very nearly unique among the men I'd worked with. Not all people who were clever could listen to instructions and then translate them immediately into an accomplished physical activity as easily as he did. Most men had to practise a new task at least a few times before they got it right. He mostly did it right the first time and then repeated it until it became second nature.

When war had broken out, he'd been in England for his best friend's wedding. He'd travelled alone, his wife staying behind in Poland to look after their child, who had croup. He'd kissed them goodbye and then the following week had found himself stranded in London, prevented from returning home by the Nazi invasion of his country. I'd never heard a human being wail as miserably as he did when he was told his wife and child had been killed during the bombing of Warsaw.

Andrzej had become one of the very few friends I'd cultivated within my workplace, apart from Gladys, and my friend Andrew McGillivray in Scotland. Andrzej had an easy, happy disposition, and despite his personal losses had never let his heart rule his head in tough situations. I'd taken him to France several times, where his maternally inherited Breton French had smoothed our way when dealing with some of the more awkward locals.

I sat back and stretched my feet out under the table, taking a great deal of pleasure in Shorty's impeccable, precise use of the German language. Once or twice he laughed at some of my Bavarian slang, suggesting I should concentrate on either Berliner or Prussian pronunciation and expressions, so Andrzej could have a proper reminder of what to emulate. It made perfect sense, and I censured myself a bit for not thinking of it earlier.

As he related his experiences in the US to Andrzej, I learned a great deal about Shorty's training and background. Unlike me, he hadn't specialised in one form of hand-to-hand combat, but in a type of fighting we called "silent killing"—a no-holds-barred combat style that followed no precise rules, but which combined brutality and violence from all sorts of disciplines. It was energetic, aggressive, and ugly—and it worked.

I also learned he was an expert marksman, as I'd suspected, having trained as a sniper while at Fort Monroe.

"Have you ever done much shooting with a suppressor, Heinrich?" I asked. In the back of my mind I was thinking it could be something worth remembering if he ever got into the field.

"What's that word—a *Schalldämpfer*?" Andrzej interrupted, pulling out a notebook and pencil from his jacket to write it down.

"Silencer," I said, using the American term, and then added *un silencieux*, in case he didn't know what it was called in French either.

"On a rifle, sure. Very little with a pistol," Shorty replied.

"You should come practice with us some time, Yankee-boy," Andrzej said, punching Shorty's arm. It was good to see them hit it off.

"Sounds like fun, *Andreas*," Shorty said.

"My name sounds funny in German, *Rudzielec*."

Then Shorty switched to what I guessed was Polish and rattled off a long speech, leaving my Polish friend open-mouthed.

I folded my arms, sat back, and waited. Andrzej's eyes were moist. Finally, I asked, *"Rudzielec?"*

"Redhead," Andrzej explained to me, switching to French. "He told me his mother had said anyone who was brave enough to call him a redhead to his face on the first meeting was sure to become his friend, and would be someone he could trust to have his back in a fight."

There was no way I could have stopped what Andrzej said next. It was in French, because even today, in 1940, men still didn't pass compliments to each other in public.

"Tommy, this man is one hell of a fellow. I trust him already, and that's saying something."

*****

It was eight thirty by the time we three went our separate ways, and my thirty-five-minute walk home from Baker Street gave me ample opportunity to reflect on the extraordinary things that had happened since Saturday night at Thérèse's apartment.

Was I truly the same person? I couldn't be. There now appeared to be someone else who was constantly on my mind. I was more than attracted to him, and it was way too soon to think of what it could become, despite my mind running through the possibilities. I'd missed out on a normal social life in my teen years, never having had a sweetheart when I was at the age I should have been feeling the things I was now. Maybe that was the reason I seemed to be thinking about him all of the time?

But, despite the unfamiliarity, it felt so right.

I turned on the gas fire in my bedroom when I got in and then went down to the kitchen to make myself a cup of tea, which I took back up to my bedroom. I lay on the bed and looked over some notes I'd brought home about the western desert offensive against the Italians in North Africa, which had started earlier that morning.

Eventually exhausted, my teacup empty and my eyes aching, I jumped into the shower to get ready for bed. Quite by accident, I caught the edge of my foot on the tap at the end of the bathtub. I cursed and then sat on the edge of the bath with my foot in my hand, inspecting the tiny nick and the small, spreading stain of blood that covered my little toe. The insignificance of that small wound made my heart break.

Four of my friends, bloodied and broken, lay dead in the morgue of the military hospital in Brook Street. Three days ago they'd invited me to their card game. I'd backed off, telling them I was tired after playing at Thérèse's soirée and had office work to catch up on. Had I been at that game with them …

The air-raid siren sounded faintly in the distance. Gradually it grew in intensity, as other warning stations closer to where I lived took up its howl. One could judge the predicted path of the nightly bombers by the locations of the sirens.

I wrapped a towel around my waist and ran down the stairs to the ground floor to turn off the gas main.

The soft crump of the first, far-away explosions had come by the time I checked the stove in the kitchen, releasing the last of the gas in its pipes before heading up to bed. As I picked up my coffee pot, placing it in its usual place on the shelf, I thought of Shorty and me standing right where I was now, but the day before—side by side, our little fingers barely touching. It made me smile.

The flat felt empty when I finally got into bed. I thought it odd I felt that way, for unless Michael was on one of his rare visits, it had always been so.

✶✶✶✶✶

Standing in the doorway of our training exercise room, I tried to unravel the knot in my stomach.

I'd known he'd already arrived and must have been warming up in the gymnasium, as I'd noticed his uniform, neatly folded and on top of a leather Gladstone bag in the officers' changing room.

I stood for a few minutes and watched him stretch. He wore a pair of woollen exercise tights, cut off at mid-thigh and held up by a broad leather belt at his waist. His torso was bare, although a T-shirt was tucked into the waistband of his tights, under the belt. He was standing with his back to me, legs apart, as he stretched with both hands to alternately touch the toes of either foot. The muscles in his back rippled with each broad sideways movement. The outline of those in his buttocks and upper thighs, accentuated by the pale grey of the woollen tights, was what was making my stomach clench. I'd imagined from the moment I met him he'd have a defined musculature underneath his clothes, but the dim light in his bedroom, two mornings ago, had not shown what this man was made of. This was the first time I could explore him visually at my leisure. And I liked what I saw. He wasn't as broad across the shoulders as I was, but his thighs and calf muscles were more developed. I couldn't help but notice he was also very light on his feet for such a tall man.

In my hand was a fan of training knives—they were heavy-handled, blunt-tipped, and had filed-down blades, which gave them the weight and feel of a real knife but without sharp edges. I called out to him and then threw one of the knives to a point about ten feet to his right, watching to check his reflexes. Impressively, he did a quick dive-roll to the side, grabbed the knife by the handle in mid-air, and then returned the throw to me, finally settling into a kneeling position on one leg with a *voilà* gesture.

""Good catch," I said.

"Yes, I think I am," he said with a smile. His eyes were serious.

I wanted to hold that picture in my mind forever—that handsome, flirtatious man with the picture-perfect smile he was beaming just for me. His skin and hair together made up a colour palette that reminded me of milky coffee—not tan, not cream, but close to the colour of a pale calfskin jacket. It was a colour combination I almost wanted to taste.

"You Yanks certainly have the gift of the gab," I said, chuckling softly as I moved to him, holding out my hand to shake his.

"I told you. When we want something, we go for it."

"Meaning the knife?" I asked, holding one up.

"Yeah," he said with a wink, "the knife … too."

We spent the next half-hour talking about and demonstrating our various unarmed combat skills to each other. He was surprised when I told him that although I'd mostly trained with knives and handguns, my expertise laid in Silat. He'd never even heard of it and was truly impressed when I showed him one of the more difficult moves—a quick swivel of the body over the hips, the torso leaning back, and then one foot flung upwards quickly, crushing the larynx of the victim and snapping his neck at the same time. It was done in the blink of an eye and from a standing position.

"What the …?" he started to say.

"Want a quick lesson?" I asked.

He nodded enthusiastically, so I took him through some leg stretches, promising he'd be able to kick higher than the waist with regular practice.

Out of the corner of my eye, I noticed the Polish training class had begun to filter in. I'd been showing him how I used my knees, elbows, and forearms in combination, so I never had to use my fists and therefore risk injury to my hands.

"I was wondering how you could do it," he said, taking one of my hands, turning it back and forth in his own as he inspected it. "So risky, Tommy," he added.

"Everything in war is risky, soldier," I replied as Andrzej arrived at our side. "But some things are worth the risk."

He gulped and blushed softly. Andrzej was unaware of what had just passed between us.

"Are all of the class Polish?" he asked. Andrzej nodded. "May I talk to them?" he asked me.

"Be my guest," I said and then beckoned the men over to join us.

He addressed them in Polish, and it was a while before we could start, as they flocked around him, slapping his back and laughing with him in a way they'd never done with me. I was way more impressed than envious.

"What did he say?" I whispered to Andrzej, while he was busy with the other soldiers.

"I'll tell you later, Tommy. Your head is big enough as it is," he replied with a broad grin. "He speaks Polish with a German accent," he continued, "but I like him."

"He's a good man, Andrzej," I answered. "And you speak German with a Polish accent, guess that makes you equal. Get the men into teams of two and we'll do some shoulder-throwing to start off with."

He gave me a casual salute and headed off to organise the groupings.

I asked Shorty to roam between the couples to help them, because incorrect shoulder-throwing could hurt both the thrower and the one thrown. The theory was that if correctly placed against the body of the opponent, the shoulder could be used as a fulcrum to throw the antagonist over one's own shoulder and onto the floor. The placement of feet and hands was very important, as was the momentum of moving into position for the throw.

We both moved among the groups, Shorty calmly and carefully helping each pair he stopped at. He had a natural ability to explain and switched between English and Polish.

After about half an hour, I asked him quietly if there was anything he'd like to teach the group. He thought for a moment and then asked me, "Have you done bone-breaking yet?"

"Only forearm and mandible at this point."

"You want me to run through collarbone and eye socket?"

"Do your worst," I replied and then clapped my hands for attention. "Captain Reiter will now take the class for a revision of bone fractures. We will do a quick recapitulation on the fracturing we've already worked on, but then he'll show you collarbone and zygomatic arch fractures—and why and when we should and should not try them."

As Shorty moved over to start the demonstration, I noticed Steve standing at the back of the room with a familiar-looking man, both glancing back and forth into the room, talking softly to each other. Steve waved me over.

"What are you doing here, Colonel?" I asked, shaking Steve's hand.

"Hiya, Tommy. This is an old friend of mine, Billy Donovan."

I shook hands with the stylish sixtyish-year-old, remembering this was Donovan's second visit to Britain.

"Colonel," I said to him. "Nice to see you again."

"You know each other?"

"Tommy can't work for the SOE and be in bed with MI6 at the

same time without knowing who I am and why I'm here, Steve," Donovan said, patting me on the shoulder but not bothering to return my salute.

"Are you staying at the embassy this time, sir?"

He laughed loudly. "You already know I'm not, soldier."

His wink and smile accompanied his handshake.

Donovan was generally known in intelligence circles as "Wild Bill". I'd already heard he was in the country, staying at Claridge's hotel—Gladys always kept me up-to-date on visiting VIPs that were relevant to our business. He'd never stay at the US embassy—he'd fallen out with the former ambassador. It was fairly common knowledge he'd recommended that Joseph Kennedy, the previous ambassador to Britain, should be sacked, because Wild Bill believed him to be both a defeatist and a pro-Nazi.

I kept my opinions to myself on that subject. Kennedy had barely talked to Donovan after an explosive argument. And even now, two months after Joe Kennedy had returned to the USA, Donovan had declined the invitation to stay at the embassy. He didn't like to be kept under eternal vigilance—especially as several of the staff were still loyal to the previous ambassador.

Wild Bill liked to do exactly what he wanted, and that didn't always fit in with the embassy's plans or surveillance staff. Neither did he want there to be a chance for tittle-tattle about his comings and goings sent across the Atlantic to Kennedy, who could be malicious with very little reason other than his bruised ego.

"So, Colonel," I said. "I suppose you aren't here for the training class?"

"Well, you're wrong there, son," he replied. "Is that him?" he asked Steve, nodding at Shorty. Steve grunted affirmatively. "I think you and Reiter should have supper with me tonight, Tommy—Claridge's at seven thirty?"

It wasn't an invitation, it was an order, and I could tell Steve wasn't included.

"Gladys will arrange transport and I want her there too," he said, turning to leave. "No need for a girl on your arm, Tommy. It isn't strictly a social occasion—Reiter can be your date. Right now I'm going to discuss a few matters with Colin Gubbins."

Colin Gubbins was the head of the SOE. Donovan's announcement was a complete surprise.

"Don't look at me," Steve said. "Henry being your date was simply a turn of phrase, I'm sure. Why is Donovan going to talk to Gubbins? All he said to me, when I told him Henry was training here, was that he wanted to come watch. What the hell is going on, Tommy?"

"Buggered if I know, Steve, but I bet London to a brick it has to have something to do with the OSS thing. It must be gathering momentum."

The Office of Strategic Services was the holding name given to the Americans' mooted new international intelligence organisation, equal to our MI6.

"The moment your country gets sick enough of having its shipping torpedoed off the East Coast and declares war, there'll have to be some intelligence system already in place. One with strong ties to us as well," I said. "You guys can't simply create a new organisation from the start, that wouldn't make sense."

"But why is he so interested in Henry?"

I gave him a look from under my eyebrows. He got it. Shorty was perfect for the new organisation. He'd trained in intelligence at West Point, and had gone on to specialise at Fort Monroe. I didn't need to mention a third thing—he now had a new, personal connection with both the SOE and MI6—me. I guess Shorty's visit to my office had been the hottest news on the gossip wire, and the Americans had fingers, or should I say dollars, in every pie.

One thing was clear, however, I'd have to find an opportunity to talk with Shorty before dinner. There was a lot he needed to know. Steve said he'd stick around to listen to his nephew's talk on hand signals, so I told him I'd give Shorty a quick heads-up while we showered after we'd finished the class with the Poles.

When I rejoined the group, Shorty was finishing his eye socket fracture routines, so I added on a few moves that could also break the cheekbone and nose. These weren't fatal injuries, but incapacitating enough to make capture easier. I finished off the class by asking them to thank our guest for his enthusiasm and knowledge.

Instead of the usual grins and sporadic handclaps I normally got, he was surrounded by loud, gregarious Poles, slapping his back and shaking his hand. There was a lot of mention of *piwo*, which I knew, since becoming friends with Andrzej, meant *beer*.

"Shower?" he asked me, after bidding farewell to the last of my class.

"I'll join you in a moment," I said. "I have to lock up the equipment from the class."

"Okay. See you there," he replied and then smiled over his shoulder when he reached the officers' change room door.

He was already under the water by the time I joined him, and he talked to me from behind the dividing wall that separated the showers from the changing area while I got out of my gymnasium clothes. He chatted about some of the guys in the group, where he thought their strengths were and who needed more work in other areas. It was nothing I didn't already know, but his perceptions were spot on.

By the time I walked into the shower area, he was no longer under the water, but waiting for me, leaning against the tiles with his hands behind his back. Damn, he was so beautiful.

Tiny drops of spray were sprinkled densely over the coffee-coloured canvas of his body—exactly like dew on the grass on an early, outback morning. I could see he was shaking slightly, so I reached out with one hand and touched his shoulder with a forefinger.

"Cold?" I asked.

He shook his head. "It's you," he said. "You do this to me, you son-of-a-bitch." He pulled me into his arms and kissed me quickly.

"Not here," I managed to say.

"I know. I simply couldn't help myself." He peeped around the edge of the shower room partition. "All clear," he said, running his hand across the back of my neck. "Maybe tonight ...?"

"Ah," I said. "About tonight ..."

As we scrubbed down, I told him about our invitation to Claridge's with Bill Donovan, saying I'd share my suspicions about the purpose of dinner after Shorty's lecture.

Gladys was waiting when we reached the lecture room, to let us know what time we'd be picked up for dinner—American colonels didn't have to worry about British petrol rationing the way we did. It was a surprise, however, when she mentioned the dress was white tie, and then snapped at me for complaining, as *I* didn't have to find "a suitable evening gown".

Dinner at Claridge's in tails suggested there were sure to be more guests than us four. It was quite puzzling. Bill Donovan had said *"it isn't strictly a social occasion"*, and yet we were to wear formal attire rather than the usual black tie for dinner.

"Decorations?" I wisecracked, only to be silenced with a glare from my secretary, who I secretly suspected was better at unarmed combat than me.

Despite her griping, I could tell she was pleased. Now we were at war, not every girl in London was invited to dine on excellent food in the company of well-placed gentlemen, and at a ritzy hotel. The food wouldn't be rationed, neither would the booze—only the conversation would probably prove to be dry, until Bill Donovan eventually excused himself and shuffled off upstairs to bed.

Well, forewarned was forearmed. I excused myself for a moment and rang my old friend at MI6, Charlie Evans, whose job was to look after, and at the same time spy on the VIPs in the services. After a bit of chitchat, I had the information I wanted, and so passed a few snippets of harmless gossip back to Charlie—tit-for-tat was expected, even between professionals.

"You have your own tails, Shorty?" I whispered when I returned to the lecture room. I was delighted with the grin he returned me. He liked his newly bestowed nickname.

"Of course I do. What do you think we are in America, savages?"

He laughed when I blushed. I hadn't meant it to sound the way it had come out. I was merely concerned he hadn't brought everything across the pond with him.

The officers were slowly trickling in for his talk, so I gestured for Gladys, Steve, and Shorty to join me in the corner of the room. "I've been on the blower," I explained. "Best behaviour tonight, everyone. It's the *other* George."

Gladys nearly had a heart attack. "The Duke of Kent?"

"The very same," I said, "and Harrogate will be there as well, so I was told."

"Well, you two will be in good company," Gladys said saucily, giving Shorty and me a quick glance. Everyone knew the rumours about the duke and the marquis, even though I'd found out they were merely that—rumours.

"Rumours, Gladys, rumours," Steve said, tutting, but smiling at the same time.

"Qui s'excuse, s'accuse ..."

If the shoe fits, wear it. It made us all laugh.

Shorty's talk turned out to be more than informative—it was actually inspirational. He'd worked intensively in the US with combat groups, training them in the use of American Sign Language to augment their use of hand and arm signals in the field. He demonstrated how precise, articulate information could be transmitted between group members when silence was imperative.

Of course, we'd all heard of sign language used by deaf people, but to my knowledge the practical application hadn't been explored by our armed forces. The more I thought about it, the more it made perfect logical sense. It really was something I'd like to see our groups adopt, mainly because we were frequently in situations in the field where we couldn't communicate by voice, and plans had to be changed at a moment's notice.

Shorty was eloquent, succinct, and an extremely competent communicator. It gave me a great deal of pleasure to see him in professional mode—in charge and relaxed, but confident and charming in his delivery. There were dozens of questions after his presentation, and I was happy to see my colleagues were as interested as I was. All of us could see the value. Sign language training would be something that I'd push for.

*****

It was getting close to four thirty by the time everyone started to wander back to their workstations, so I suggested Shorty and I talk in my office.

I invited Steve along, not only for the pleasure of his company but also because I felt it was high time I came clean with him on some issues.

I kept a bottle of reasonable whisky in my office and poured us all a drink while we settled down to talk. Gladys marched in with a spare glass and sat on the edge of my desk. After all, my business was her business.

"He leaves things out, you know," she said, raising an eyebrow at me, as a way of explaining her presence.

"There are parts of my job you don't know about, Steve, nor would I normally tell you. But, if tonight's meeting turns out to be about what I think it will be about, it might be best for you to know part of what I actually do."

I explained my dual role: being "nested" within the British army structure, while still a member of the Australian army. It wasn't an unknown situation, but it really meant my orders came from Whitehall rather than Canberra. I also explained that although I was head of a particular sub-branch within the SOE, I was also responsible for setting up Resistance cells and the in-situ training of members of the Resistance and other *maquisards*. It was the reason I'd frequently been "out of contact"—I'd been behind enemy lines in occupied France, first for MI6 and then, more recently, for the SOE.

Shorty nodded every so often and occasionally asked a few questions to clarify some aspects of my field work, but Steve appeared to take it all on board in silence, despite the grumpy look on his face. Before I'd started to explain, he hadn't known exactly what I did, but I could see he was angry with me now he was wiser.

"Can I venture to tell you what I think is going to happen tonight?" Gladys asked.

"Go ahead, Gladys," I said.

"My feeling is Bill Donovan will want Captain Reiter to find out how we operate in Britain, and then report it on to him. Not the administrative stuff, the operational areas."

"Really?" Shorty said.

She held out her hand for one of his cigarettes. He lit it for her, and then she explained. "I bet he'll want you to attend our classes, visit some of the other training bases, and then help set up a similar scheme at home, in the USA."

"Why wouldn't he simply merge an existing US intelligence service with one you have already, instead of reinventing the wheel?" Shorty asked.

"What makes you think your administration 'merges' anything with anyone else?" I said. "It's all about control. And when your country eventually gets involved in this war it's going to be the USA who thinks it's going to run the whole shebang. The British and the rest of us will just be pawns to be moved around the battlefields of the great American chessboard called war."

"That sounds a bit cynical, Tommy," Shorty said.

"I think he's right, Heinrich," Gladys said. "It's all conjecture, but I bet you a dinner at the Savoy this is what we'll hear tonight," Gladys said.

"Keep your pennies, Gladys. If we go to the Savoy it will be on me."

I knew she struggled financially and didn't want to embarrass her. She smiled at me a little coyly as she held out her glass for a refill. That's why I liked her. Underneath her quips and smart, businesslike behaviour she was kind and affectionate. I liked to have people like that in my life.

Steve had been pacing around the room during our conversation, looking like thunder. Eventually, he stopped. "So you and Michael parachute or fly into occupied areas of France and Belgium and train Resistance groups and set up their operations?"

"That, and other things, yes," I replied. "Sometimes together, sometimes alone … every now and then we also get rid of sticky situations."

"Like … people?"

I nodded.

"Of all the …"

"What are you, Steve—my mother?"

I glared at him until he eventually softened. "I'm sorry, Tommy," he said. "I was way out of line." He held out his glass and I filled it up. "I had no idea."

"You're welcome to come along anytime yourself, Steve."

His eyebrow raise and accompanying smile indicated that although he was worried about the danger Michael and I put ourselves in, he'd be up for it like a shot. Steve was as brave as any man I'd ever known.

"You're in line, next after me," Gladys quipped.

"What about me?" Shorty asked

"Too young and too handsome," I said, despite the gnawing feeling that it's just what he might be doing, if Donovan wanted him to learn everything we did.

CHAPTER 4

There was something about white tie and tails that brought out the best in every man.

Perhaps it was the cut of the coat and the line of the tie and wing collar that accentuated jaw lines, or the white of the shirt and tie that contrasted with flesh and hair tones. At any rate, in my opinion, men always looked more handsome in either uniform or in formal evening wear.

Shorty was no exception—he looked amazing in his tails. I was about to comment when he sidled up to me and said, "Can I have three servings of you daily? Morning, noon, and night? Man, you look so handsome, Tommy."

Damn! How could I return the compliment without it sounding as if I was repaying his? I'd worn my best tails, with my Spanish Medal of Valour decoration around my neck—the red and yellow stripes of its ribbon fell well against my white shirt.

We ordered drinks at the bar—an old-fashioned for me, and a martini for Shorty. We moved to the far end of the bar to chat privately while we waited for Gladys and Bill Donovan to arrive. We'd just taken the first sip of our drinks when a young man approached us, introducing himself as Charles Simpson, private secretary of His Royal Highness, the Duke of Kent.

"Please, gentlemen, a small gesture from the Duke of Kent," he said, as he proceeded to pin a boutonnière on each of our lapels. "His Highness will join you for dinner in about half an hour—I'll come to find you and show you to the room then. The duke has also asked me to inform you he has invited his brother, the Duke of Gloucester, and Brigadier Mark Harris."

"Gloucester," Shorty said, after the man had left us. "He's the brother who runs the British army, isn't he?"

"Well, he doesn't run the army, but he's all but second-in-command. I suppose you know he and the Duke of Kent worked in the Intelligence Division of the navy?"

"Do I detect some common thread this evening?"

"With my boss turning up unexpectedly, I think there's a fair chance." We clinked glasses in a silent toast. It was certainly not good manners in polite society, but Shorty had held out his glass in invitation and who was I to resist? It reminded me of how different our cultural backgrounds were—I liked it.

"Say, Tommy …?"

"Yes, Shorty?"

"There's something I need to know before we meet … you know …"

"The Duke of Kent?"

"Yes. What do I call him? I've never said hi to a duke before."

I smiled at his American pronunciation—"dook".

"Well, his name is George, but no one except close friends call him that. You call both of the royal dukes 'Your Royal Highness' when you first greet them, after that you simply call them sir."

He nodded, mulling over the information, while sucking thoughtfully on the large green olive from his cocktail. With the toothpick still hanging from the corner of his mouth, he said, "I'm still confused."

"About what?"

"You said his name was George. I thought that was the King's name."

I removed the offending toothpick from his teeth, chuckling at the same time. "You're a Roman Catholic, Shorty. Did you think that the Pope's real name is actually Pius?"

"Of course not," he said, pretend-offended I might have thought him so stupid. It made my heart warm to see the penny drop.

"It's the same thing, my friend. The current King's name is actually Albert—they call him 'Bertie' in the family. He chose George for his title—George the Sixth. Coincidentally, the last King, Edward the Eighth's first name actually was Edward, but the family call him David."

"That's really confusing. Why would they do that?"

"The whole family was full of Edwards. He was named after his great-uncle … and the extended family is full of men with the same name, and has been for generations."

"Uh huh," he said, in the particular tone most foreigners that came from countries that didn't have a monarchy used when trying to work out titles, the aristocracy, and protocol.

"Another drink, sir?" The barman had noticed our empty glasses and had been hovering at a discreet distance, waiting for a break in our conversation.

"Yes, please. One more round of the same," I said.

When I turned back to Shorty, he was looking over my shoulder into the hotel's large, beautifully appointed, formal dining room. "I've always wanted to eat in there," he said. "I'd like to take you to dinner soon. What do you think, babe?"

"I think I'd be happy sharing a packet of fish and chips on the Embankment with you, Shorty. But, thank you—I'd love to have dinner here with you some time."

Oblivious to English propriety, he moved in to sniff my white carnation. His head was so close to my nose I could smell the brilliantine in his hair. "Why are you smiling like that?" he asked.

"Babe?" I said under my breath. "Really?"

"Well, now we're going steady …" he said with a gleam in his eye.

"We're going steady? Since when? What happened to dating?"

"Dating is over-rated," he replied. A light shone in his eyes that made me feel warm, right through to the soles of my feet.

He offered me a cigarette—I leaned in to light it from his, our eyes fencing with playful thoughts.

"Evening, fellows!"

I turned to find Peter Farnsworth, Thérèse's companion from Saturday night, standing behind us. He was in mess dress—a blue-grey cutaway evening jacket with twin bands of gold on the sleeves.

"Peter," I said, holding out my hand. "Nice to see you again. I wouldn't have taken you for a fly boy?"

"Flight Lieutenant Peter Farnsworth at your service," he said. "Yes, fly boy all the way—worked as a pilot before the war."

We shook hands.

"Is Thérèse joining you here for dinner?" Shorty asked.

"No, Henry, I came here tonight to catch up with a friend I haven't seen in quite a while. You must know him, Tommy, he's an Aussie too—Frank Goyen, he's Kent's private pilot."

It still astounded me people automatically assumed all Australians were either related to each other or knew one another, no matter how often one explained the vastness of my country.

"No, I'm sorry, I don't. But somehow I believe we may be dining with him this evening," I replied. Things were starting to click into place.

He was about to reply when we were interrupted by the arrival of Gladys, on the arm of "Wild Bill" Donovan. She looked very glamorous in a long, sequined black gown. Pinned to her left shoulder was a corsage almost the size of a dinner plate. Shorty introduced Peter to them and I was somewhat amazed to find Gladys already knew him. "You must get out more often, Tommy," she whispered, in French, as she leaned in to me so I could light her cigarette. "He's one of our best Ravens."

What she'd said was so unexpected I nearly burned her eyebrow off. A Raven was an undercover agent whose job was to sleep with persons of interest in order to get information. It was a name we used primarily for men who slept with other men—although some of the more versatile young men did double-duty. I suppose I'd been too busy in my own department to get to know every person who worked in Baker Street. I glanced at him again—he didn't seem the type. But then again, in this stupid war nothing surprised me.

I surreptitiously passed on that interesting piece of information to Shorty, softly, in German, as Gladys, Bill, and Peter chatted.

"Well, I'll be darned," he said. "You don't think he's spying on Thérèse, or using her to find out stuff about her husband …?"

"I think I'd have heard something if we were using an agent to sleep with her. What sort of information could she or her obnoxious husband have of interest to the Crown?"

"I guess …" he said.

Although I'd heard that turn of phrase once or twice since returning to England from Germany, the American expression still had me waiting for the rest of a sentence to follow. Although we shared the same language, we came from different places. To me, he was something exotic. He spoke like Clark Gable, or Spencer Tracy. Movie stars were the only Americans I'd ever seen or heard before I'd arrived in Europe in 1934.

"Just what do you guess, young man?"

He laughed softly at me and then cocked his head to one side. "Listen, Tommy."

A far-away jazz band was playing Irving Berlin—"Top Hat, White Tie, and Tails". The words of the song couldn't have been more appropriate for us two, dressed to the nines, and indeed invited to step out this evening in our smart formal wear.

"Have I told you how good you look in your evening clothes?" I asked.

"You just wait until I get out of them," he said, and then began to sing along with the band under his breath. Gladys appeared at our side. Peter Farnsworth seemed deep in conversation with Bill Donovan.

"Shh, this isn't Manhattan, Mr. Reiter. What will people think?"

"Let them think what they want, Miss Gleeson. I'm one of the few men here who is dressed *properly* for dinner."

Most of the other male guests at the bar wore tuxedos.

He slipped his hand around her waist, as if to dance with her. She laughed and then playfully slapped his shoulder.

"Why did Donovan ask me to come tonight?" she asked, as she glanced at the barman, who was giving her an old-fashioned—look that was, not cocktail. "Surely he won't be expecting me to take notes?"

"I think our American friend is merely guarding his reputation," I said. "Couldn't have it known at home he was dining in a room full of men with no ladies present, could he?"

We were interrupted by the arrival of Peter Farnsworth's Australian friend, Frank Goyen. He was introduced around the circle, and he and I chatted briefly about missing home. It didn't take long for me to find out he came from Shepparton in Victoria, and from a sheep station, so we had a lot in common, even if our families lived about five hundred miles apart—near neighbours in the Great Brown Land. He was very charming, complimenting Gladys on her dress and corsage, which I learned, in the course of their conversation, had been delivered to her home.

A few moments later, the Duke of Kent's private secretary reappeared to inform us we should proceed upstairs.

"It was nice to see you again, Peter," I said. "Please pass on my best to Thérèse when next you see her."

"I wish I saw her more frequently, but alas, her husband has returned—it's time for me to move on." Did I detect a note of sadness? "Anyway, I'll see you upstairs later on," he added, "when the dancing begins."

Dancing? I wondered what sort of evening was planned. As we reached a large vestibule at the top of Claridge's main staircase, my immediate superior, Brigadier Harris, called out. He hurried up the stairs from behind us, somewhat out of breath. I was relieved to see he was alone. His wife, Cynthia, had the unfortunate habit of having a lot to say about herself, and, more often than not, chose the most inappropriate moments to share her misfortunes.

"Sorry I'm late," he said, "I had to go back—left this on my desk." He handed me a flat brown leather-covered box. "Go on, it's for you … the main stairs of Claridge's isn't the best place for this, but it needs to be done before we get inside."

I became aware Gladys was giving me the brightest of smiles. Puzzled, I opened the box. Inside were new uniform insignia and two pairs of epaulettes, each with a single gold star and crown. One pair was for my normal uniform, and the other for my mess dress.

"Congratulations, Colonel," he said, shaking my hand. "I certainly hope you'll put this promotion to good use."

I wasn't expecting this. Not here, not now, but accepted his congratulations with a handshake and a smile. I knew a promotion had been in the pipeline, but had been led to believe it was at least a year off. I wondered how the timing of his rather hasty presentation played in the great scheme of things.

A small part of me was irritated. Ordinarily, there would have been some ceremony—something more formal than a quick passing-over of insignia on the stairs of a public venue. It seemed once more the fact I'd gone to neither Eton nor Oxbridge was rearing its ugly head. I could almost hear the "Oh, well, needs must—he's only a colonial."

"Forget him," Gladys hissed in my ear, drawing me back from the others. "He's a heartless old fart at the best of times."

"Gladys!" I exclaimed in mock-indignation. She kissed me on the cheek.

"Well, maybe not old," she said with a gleam in her eye.

Over her shoulder, I could see one very excited and broadly grinning American waiting to speak. A moment before we entered the private dining room, he pulled gently at my sleeve. "So, I get to go steady with a big-wig now, do I?" he whispered in my ear, as he put one arm around my shoulder, and then slapped me on the back. "Congratulations, Tommy. I really mean it—Lieutenant Colonel! Wow!"

I could tell he wanted to do more than slap me on the back, but it was neither the time nor the place.

*****

Dinner rolled past in a relaxed and comfortable fashion.

The Duke of Kent was charming, articulate, and spontaneous. His comfortable and affable behaviour made everyone feel at ease. He possessed the rare but wonderful gift of making whoever he was speaking with feel what they had to say was the most important thing in the world.

William Stanfield, the Marquess of Harrogate, was, like the duke, also witty and charming. He was very handsome, but gave the impression of being quite unaware of it. Some of his asides were quite risqué, but he was so amiable none of us could take offence. I was surprised how quickly I warmed to his schoolboy-like charisma.

After dessert, and before coffee, the duke settled back in his chair and gave a signal over his shoulder to the butler who'd been supervising the dinner service. Without a word, the room emptied, leaving the two dukes, Bill Donovan, Mark Harris, Gladys, Shorty, and me alone to talk.

The Duke of Gloucester waited until the doors were closed before speaking. "Well, Colonel Donovan, I suspect you'd like to get down to 'brass tacks'?"

"Wild Bill" cleared his throat before replying.

"Indeed, sir. As you may be aware, the President is convinced the United States will enter the war, one way or the other, in the next year or so. It's only the moderates in the Senate, and on his staff, and the influence of isolationists and those who misunderstand the Monroe Doctrine, who are keeping us at arm's length, so to speak. I can tell you President Roosevelt is very keen to help Britain in a material way, and I have it on good authority that before long, the United States will help the European war with the supply of foodstuffs, armaments, and materiel."

"I can't tell you how much that will be appreciated by His Majesty's government," Gloucester said, smoothly.

Donovan continued. "I, too, believe we will be drawn into this cataclysmic event. When we do, both the President and I believe we should have a well-structured intelligence agency already in place to help our efforts towards an early victory. So, he's ordered me to come to Britain to make contacts and to see how your operations work, in view of setting up a similar agency at home at the present time, so we're already well-prepared when war becomes an eventuality."

Even though Bill Donovan spoke as if he were reading text from a training manual, everyone at the table understood from what he'd said the Americans would never willingly put themselves under the authority of another country's national intelligence service, so would be compelled to create their own. It was as I'd suspected.

"I'm presuming this has something to do with Heinrich ... I mean Captain Reiter?" I asked.

"I've spoken with the Duke of Gloucester about Henry," Donovan replied, "and we feel it might be helpful to our joint causes, were he to have a more formal association with the Special Operations Executive, and with MI6 of course."

"And that would be why I'm here, sir?"

I tried hard to sound neutral, but the irony hadn't escaped me. I looked sternly at Mark Harris, now realising the reason for the why and when of the unexpected presentation of my insignia on the stairs. He was oblivious—basking in the reflected glow of the presences of two of the princes of the realm.

"Of course," Gloucester said. "Who else would be a better liaison?"

"The Empire would be very grateful to you for showing Captain Reiter the way we do things, Thomas," the Duke of Kent said. "And may I add my congratulations on your promotion and your new area of command."

New area of command? My ears pricked up. "Thank you, Your Royal Highness. Brigadier Harris was kind enough to inform me about my promotion on the stairs, just before we came in to dine. I was delighted and surprised when I opened the presentation case but ninety minutes ago, to find my epaulettes and uniform insignia."

Gladys nearly choked on her wine.

The Duke of Kent supressed a smile and then glanced at my boss with a blank expression. "On the stairs, Harris?" he said neutrally. "How quaint."

"I beg your pardon, sir … you mentioned a new area of command?" Although it had been announced almost as an afterthought, I was anxious to find out what else was in store for me.

"All will be revealed, Thomas, and in good time." As he was seated facing me, and in profile to Mark Harris, he winked at me with his "upstage" eye—it was a signal I should be patient.

I knew all negotiation was strongest at the start, when one party needed something more than the other. I also knew I'd never get this opportunity again, and if I played my cards correctly I could gain the upper hand here.

"I'm extremely honoured, sir," I said, noticing Gladys looking at me over the top of her glass. She knew me well enough to know I had something up my sleeve. "But, with the recent loss of four of my senior field officers, the extremely busy nature of our organisation, and always having to ask up the chain for what I need …?"

It had become apparent that although the Duke of Gloucester was the man Donovan constantly referred to, his brother the Duke of Kent was in control of the meeting. He smiled and then said, "I assume what you are politely trying to say is with your promotion, and your new area of command that comes with it, you'd like to have complete control? I know how irksome all that red-tape can be. I think it perfectly reasonable you run your own show. You can report directly to Colin Gubbins, the director of the SOE—I see no problems there, do you, Harris?"

Mark Harris looked as if he'd swallowed a tennis ball. Me, Thomas Haupner, being autonomous? And reporting to the head of our organisation, and not to him?

However, suddenly things clicked into place. I understood the reason for my promotion. Someone had something they wanted me to do for them. Something that would bear no unwanted attention in my organisation, nor interference from above. Were I my own boss, I could do things that would normally need approval. The whole sequence of events so far this evening had been carefully planned, and presented in a manner that couldn't be challenged. It was a public showing for Mark Harris—one that would enable me to stay within my organisation, yet provide me with a cover if I were required to do anything on the Q.T.

"Thank you, sir," I said. "Captain Reiter will be seconded in what capacity, may I ask?"

"It will be up to Colonel Donovan to work out the details of how Captain Reiter will be fitted in. But I expect it will be you who works out and supervises his training schedules. Do you see any problems, Thomas?"

"A minor one, sir … if I may?"

The Duke of Kent indicated I should go on.

"If Captain Reiter is to work alongside me, then I think it only fair he gets a kick up the ladder. Simply to make things run a bit more smoothly within the team—he'll need to be at least a major, to fill out the chain of command."

It was Shorty's turn to look as though he'd swallowed a tennis ball.

"Of course—that goes without saying," Bill Donovan said. "I'll sort it out—major it is then. Congratulations, Reiter."

"Thank you, sir," Shorty said and then stood to salute him. The two royal princes also got to their feet to shake hands with Shorty.

I noticed that as we all stood, Gladys seemed to be studying the dukes carefully. Now they were standing next to each other, she seemed to be comparing them. Prince Henry, the Duke of Gloucester, was a pair with his brother, the Duke of Kent, in that they'd both missed out on the stern, drawn angles of the faces of their two older brothers, the King and the Duke of Windsor. Their faces were somewhat softer, their eyes rounder—two features that made them both very attractive. They had a pin-up quality to their looks. The type of handsome the King possessed had something more to do with inner strength and bearing—the Duke of Windsor, on the other hand, had always looked to my mind like a forlorn spaniel.

Gladys winked at me and then gave me one of her smiles. I could read her thoughts. My promotion—the jump from major to lieutenant-colonel—and the autonomy the duke had promised, meant a very different level of operation. So many decisions that had been dependant on orders from above would now be mine, and mine alone, to make. It would be understood I'd make my own staff. I'd have a real chance to gather my war-ducklings around me.

It never ceased to amaze me that in Britain, decisions about field work were sometimes made by mostly inexperienced, untrained commanders who came to their position by virtue of the schools and universities they'd attended. There were, obviously, very good commanders who rose through the ranks without having attended Eton, Marlborough College, or Oxbridge, but some of the disastrous lessons of World War One had still not been learned.

I was about to have a word with Shorty when the Duke of Kent spoke softly to me, drawing me away from the others. "Thomas," he said, "I'd like to give you a quick heads-up that sometime later this evening my brother, Gloucester, will draw you aside to have a little tête-à-tête. I know you must be itching to know what we've got planned for you, but trust me—all in good time."

I was about to thank him, but he stopped me with a smile, and the offer of one of his cigarettes from a beautiful gold case. "Before that happens, I'd like to get you on your own and have a private chat—one that's far from the madding crowd."

Puzzled, I raised an eyebrow.

"I suppose you've read the book?"

"Indeed I have, sir."

"What would you say its themes were?" His eyes were bright with mischief. "Come on … play along with me."

I couldn't help but warm to his banter, even though I had no idea what was going on. "Love, honour, and betrayal are the first words that come to mind," I replied after a moment.

"Just so, Thomas. Just so." For the briefest moment, his eyes were immensely serious, and then, as if someone had flipped a switch, he chuckled at what seemed to be some private joke, while patting me on the shoulder. "Press that small white button on the wall behind you, if you please." I did as he asked, and then, as if by magic, the doors of the room opened and the Duke of Kent's personal assistant appeared, followed by the coffee service. A very attractive young woman trailed behind and then drew apart sliding doors at the far end of the room to reveal a large, open drawing room with a grand piano, at which she sat and began to play.

*****

"Cat got your tongue, Seppo?" I whispered in Shorty's ear as I took a glass of champagne from him. He'd been standing at the other end of the room, watching my interaction with the duke.

"I'll be darned, Tommy," he said. "They didn't know what hit them. As a matter of fact, neither did I."

"Stick by me, my friend. It might be a bumpy ride, but I guarantee it will be fun."

"I intend to stick around, Tommy. That's if you want me to."

"What do you reckon, handsome?" I gave him a look that indicated precisely what I wanted.

"You two need to get a room," Gladys said, interrupting us, obviously tired of waiting for me to come over to her. She looked relieved to have escaped a three-way natter with Bill Donovan and Mark Harris.

My companion offered her a cigarette, before lighting two and then passing one of them to me.

"Well, well, well," she said, puffing out a long, studied cloud of smoke, "and you're going to tell me you hadn't worked all of this out hours before you got here?"

"You know me, Gladys, spontaneity is my middle name."

"Maybe in your dreams it is."

"You were certainly on the money. Heinrich is on the team now, just as you thought he'd be. It does make a lot of sense, now I think about it."

"You played the situation well, Tommy," Gladys said. "Our own operation? And two promotions in one evening? I was busting to tell you about yours, but didn't want to spoil the surprise."

"I have to say I *was* surprised," I replied.

"Congratulations, Tommy." She threw her arms around my neck, careful not to crush her corsage. "It's well overdue."

"Yes, congratulations, *Colonel*," Shorty said, pumping my hand.

"My pleasure, *Major.*"

"You two can spend as long as you like, shaking whatever you like, later on," Gladys quipped, "but just think, Tommy—no more stupid in-house requisitions, no more stalling for equipment or for training approvals."

"That means you'll become a personal assistant, with your own secretary, Gladys." I couldn't help but feel sorry for the poor person in that job. A personal assistant was the top of the rank as far as secretarial assistants went in our organisation. The next step would be private secretary. However, I didn't see myself becoming a brigadier-general any time soon. "Big pay rise, too," I added, "for both of us."

Her eyes gleamed, and she touched me lightly on the arm. I'd never understood how women managed to survive on the pitiful salaries they were paid, especially in comparison to men who performed the same duties.

"I figured out another reason Mark Harris was invited here tonight," she said.

"To hand Tommy his promotion before the meeting?" Heinrich asked.

Gladys shook her head and then smiled at him. The malicious gleam in her eyes was impossible not to notice. "No, you sweet man," she said. "Tommy's already worked it out. I can see it from the look on his face. Harris was invited to be told that Tommy is his own boss from now on and Brigadier Mark Harris is to keep his nose out of our business."

"I wonder how Bill Donovan got to know our beloved leader was an interfering pain-in-the-you-know-what?" I asked.

Gladys merely smiled and batted her eyelashes at me.

"Mark Harris is obviously not your favourite person," Shorty said to her.

"He may look like a walrus, but he has more hands than an octopus."

"Really?" I was outraged.

She patted my hand. "No need to be offended on my behalf, Tommy. I can look after myself. I stabbed him in the arse with my hatpin last time he tried to pinch me."

I chortled. "His arse, Gladys? Don't you mean his *posterior*?"

She grimaced. "Yours is a posterior, Tommy, so is Heinrich's. Something as unseemly as the thing *he* sits on is an arse."

As we laughed, I noticed the Duke of Kent's private secretary motioning to me from the other side of the room. I excused myself and made my way over to him

"His Royal Highness was wondering if you had a moment to speak with him in private, Colonel."

"Yes, of course," I said, following the man to a pair of French doors that led to an outside terrace.

*****

The night was clear and quiet.

114

There had been no sirens as yet. The moon was half-full. Its soft light illuminated one side of the dozens of barrage balloons that floated quietly above the city. It felt very odd, standing in the serenity of that silver light, to think with very little warning the peaceful gleam that shone over us could be interrupted by death from above.

As soon as I felt the doors close behind me, I saw the duke, who was leaning on the parapet at the far end of the broad balcony. He'd lit two cigarettes and held one out to me. "Hello, Thomas," he said. His smile was slight and seemed a little wistful.

"Your Royal Highness," I replied, taking the cigarette after inclining my head in what passed for a bow these days.

"Do you have your new epaulettes?" he asked, holding out his hand for them. "The pair meant for your uniform?"

"Not about my person, sir. They're inside, Gladys has the box in her handbag. Shall I fetch it?"

"If you please, Thomas."

I ran back into the main room and asked an astonished Gladys if I might retrieve my presentation case. When I returned to the duke, I handed it to him. He opened it and then asked, "May I?"

Caught between the automatic response to salute and the confusion as to what was appropriate, I merely grinned. I felt the heat running up my face but hoped he wouldn't notice it in the dark.

"Please relax," he said, draping the epaulettes over the shoulders of my tails jacket, in the position they'd eventually be once they were on my uniform. "I'd prefer it if you didn't treat me like some fragile creature, Thomas. I'm a military man too, like you, and I've always wanted to do this."

He stood back and inspected me, chuckling. I couldn't help but smile along with him, as nervous as it made me feel. I'd never interacted with a member of the Royal Family before. What did one do? I suppose I'd find out, and most likely out here on the terrace.

I laughed. "Always? Really, sir?"

"Really," he said. "It's very satisfying to have more of a hands-on experience when bestowing an award, something more than simply pinning on a medal. It seemed to me you deserved more of a ceremony than a quick 'here-you-go' on the stairs. Now you can tell your family the Duke of Kent awarded your promotion with his own hands."

I saluted him, and as a result one of the epaulettes fell from my shoulders. He caught it mid-air, with a snappy "Voilà" and then winked.

"During my time in the Intelligence Division, I heard all about you. You're a bit of a celebrity. Did you know?"

I shook my head.

"What, you think every Tom, Dick, and Harry in the armed forces who is an accomplished musician, *and* who has a doctorate, *and* who was a hero in the Spanish Civil War, can work as an intelligence agent for Britain without anyone taking notice?"

"I've only been doing my duty, sir."

"Only doing my duty—what a meaningful phrase, Thomas, don't you think? I spend my life doing my duty by representing my brother officially, and yet am not allowed to get my hands dirty. Don't you think that makes me a little envious?"

"To be frank, sir, I have absolutely no idea why you should be envious of someone like me." It was an unsophisticated thing to say and I should have waited for him to continue, instead of speaking.

"Look at me, Thomas," he said and then replaced the fallen epaulette on my shoulder, waiting for me to raise my eyes. "I'm sorry. I didn't mean to embarrass you. What I was going to say is you're a real warrior, and I'm merely a token warrior."

I was about to object, but he stopped me. "Did you know my ancestor, Henry the Seventh, was the last English king to bear arms on the battlefield? Both my brother Henry and I are 'token' warriors. Don't think I wouldn't lay down my life for my country, for I would. But, unlike you, I'd never be allowed to—my brother and I must command from the rear. It makes me feel dreadfully sick when I think about it."

"I think what you just said, sir, is the bravest thing I've ever heard from someone in your position."

"Well," he continued, "the one thing I have learned about studying you—and yes, I've asked a lot of questions and double-checked my facts—is you're not stupid. You must suspect there's more to this evening than meets the eye. Why a sudden promotion? Why dinner at

Claridge's with two princes of the realm? And why your new area of command?"

"I'm sure you're about to tell me, sir."

"Indeed, I am. We're going to win this war, Tommy. I know it will be a bloody hard fight, but I'm convinced we have right on our side. However, we do need the Americans to help us win—you've no idea how much we need them. That's one of the reasons Bill Donovan is here. Isn't it obvious we're buttering him up? Not many Americans get to have a private meeting with two princes of England."

"You think he has that much sway with President Roosevelt?"

I saw one of my own smiles reflected back at me—the one I used when I was being an intelligence officer and wanted to say, "What do you think?"

The French doors slowly opened a smidgeon, and the duke's private secretary peeped though them. Inside, the piano player started into "Tea for Two".

The duke offered me his arm. "Foxtrot?"

"Out here?"

"No of course not. Do you know John?" he indicated his private secretary and then nodded at him. The man came out onto the terrace, closing the French doors behind him.

"I've met Mr. Lowther once or twice, sir. Why do you ask?"

"You see those doors at the right-hand side of where he's standing, the pair next to the room we came from? That's where you and I might attempt to 'trip the light fantastic'."

After replacing my epaulettes back into their box, I handed it to Lowther and then followed the duke into an empty room, through the walls of which we could clearly hear the piano next door. It seemed to be an annexe to the room in which our friends were partying, separated by cleverly constructed panelled doors, which I'm sure opened to create one very large space, most probably for a ball.

"Shall we?" he asked, opening his arms.

As he led me into the dance, I started to laugh at the madness of what we were doing. "We can change the lead halfway through," he whispered into my ear, almost conspiratorially. "In that way, if there are peep holes in the walls, no one will be any the wiser who's the boy and who's the girl."

I couldn't help but laugh, and it was then I decided I really liked His Royal Highness, Prince George, the Duke of Kent.

"You're a very fine dancer, Thomas," he said, as he expertly moved me around the room. "Has anyone ever told you so?"

"One or two, sir."

"But gentlemen?"

"What sort of gentleman would *I* be if I were to discuss other men I've danced with?"

His laugh was light and gay, and very friendly. We changed arms and I began to lead.

"Have you ever thought about how rare it is for me to do this? Just to enjoy a simple dance with an extremely nice person? A person who's starting to relax in my company and beginning to see me for whom I am?"

As he said this, the look in his eyes demolished a few of my own barriers. I slowly became aware I'd indeed begun to see the man, not the prince. I'd been too in awe of his station to realise he'd been flirting with me—the type of flirting that was done for fun, not to lead anywhere. I'd heard the rumours about his male and female lovers. His earlier remark about not being able to get his hands dirty resonated in a new way now.

When the music stopped, he released me from his arms. "You know, Tommy, I truly think we could become friends. That surprises me and delights me. I hope it doesn't offend you."

"Offend me? Why on earth would you think it would offend me, sir? I can't tell you how pleasant it's been for me too, to see the man behind the title." He wasn't the only one who could flirt for fun.

He gave a small, soft laugh and squeezed my forearm. "I really hope we get a chance to do this again, Thomas," he said.

"The evening is still young … what should I call you, Your Royal Highness? Saying 'sir' all the time makes me feel like a young American talking to his father."

"Oh, I have an idea it won't be long, Colonel, before you're calling me George," he said with wry amusement.

I waited. I could tell he was ready to tell me why I'd been summoned to the outside balcony.

"Thomas … there's something I might like you to do for me."

"Your wish is my command," I said, bowing to him in an exaggerated fashion. He laughed at my gesture.

"One moment. You don't know what it is yet. It could mean you might be placed in considerable danger."

I was no whizz-bang boffin, but I could put two and two together. "You want me to go to France—most probably behind enemy lines."

He chuckled softly, before replying. "It would require someone who could speak more than passable French, yes, that's true. And, it would need to be someone I trust—someone my family and I could trust, actually."

I had no words—the moment he'd mentioned his family, the gears in my mind had begun to whirl.

"It's a little complicated, but in a nutshell, I need to have a letter delivered to a special friend who lives in occupied France. It needs to get there quite soon. I'm sure you can arrange it, especially since you are running agents in Normandy?"

"I can't foresee any problem. If it were extremely sensitive, either my brother or I could make sure it could be delivered in person."

"I wish it could be otherwise, but I don't think I can risk this letter going any other way … let's talk of this outside on the terrace."

I'm not sure we could be overheard in this room, but it was a good indication of how sensitive the information was going to be, so we returned to the parapet against which he'd been leaning when I'd first come out to meet him. I offered him a cigarette, which he took and I lit for him.

"I know that the Comte de Villiers-Fossard is a good friend of yours, Thomas," he said, tipping his head to the sky and then blowing a perfect smoke ring into the air. It was very still tonight.

The mention of the Comte de Villiers-Fossard really startled me. Édouard Dubois was indeed an old friend of mine. He was one of the quartet of pals who'd fought together in Spain—Steve, Édouard, Édouard's lover Elizabeth Petersen, and me. Earlier this year, in June,

I'd helped him set up a Resistance cell in Saint-Lô. He lived in a few rooms in his large, mostly closed-up château, a few miles outside the town. I had no idea how he was connected to the Duke of Kent.

"As I've mentioned his name, I'm sure you'll understand the need for complete discretion—and I can't stress highly enough how very confidential this conversation must be. Whatever I tell you must remain between us. You mustn't speak of it to anyone. Not to Miss Gleeson, in fact not to anyone you work with, and not to your American—for the time being, at least."

"I understand, sir." I was curious and not a little alarmed at the hint of urgency in his voice. It was as if he were trying to conceal how important the matter truly was.

"Thomas … call me George, if you please. Once—to see if I like it or not."

"Very well, as long as you call me Tommy … George." I was surprised at how shy I was to use his name. The true colonial boy was still in hiding, just under my skin.

He extended his arm and rested it on my shoulder, inspecting my face. His request had been a momentary diversion to gather courage before continuing. We all had them—small moments of hesitation before leaping into some unpleasant task, or divulging uncomfortable facts.

"It is a simple task, but one of national importance—the reason the Prime Minister isn't talking to you is that he too must be kept in the dark until the whole mess is a fait accompli. Do I make myself clear?"

I nodded. I couldn't begin to imagine what could be so important the Prime Minister should not know of it, yet be of seemingly vital significance to the duke and the Royal Family. And he'd said "simple task" and "mess" in the same breath. My intelligence agent sense began to kick in. Perhaps there was more to this venture than the delivery of a letter to France, which could have been done by anyone trustworthy. I was intrigued.

"We'll talk more about this quite soon—this is neither the time nor the place. But I did want to get a chance to chat with you alone, mainly to see whether I liked you enough to trust you. I'm sorry if that sounds blunt, but the truth in these situations is more important than flattery."

"I'm honoured, sir."

I was more than honoured—I actually felt quite humbled. I was also intrigued about the nature of the task. I was an intelligence officer after all—puzzles and mysteries were part of my daily craft. One of national importance would gnaw at my insides until it was shared with me. However, he was right about two things—this was neither the right time nor the right place, and he was wise to first find out whether I was the right person for the job.

"Now," he said, "there are two other, totally different things I really want. First of all, I want to hear you play. When is your next concert? Everyone tells me how wonderful you are, but you never seem to play at the places I'm invited to. Secondly, I want to watch you dance with Heinrich."

I bit my lip before replying. "I was to perform a concert tomorrow night at St. Giles, Cripplegate. But, regrettably, I heard this morning it was really badly hit last Saturday."

The duke's piercing stare lasted but for a second or two before he took an imaginary partner in his arms and danced a few steps of a tango. He grinned at me while he did it—the gesture was spontaneous and quite charming to watch, as crazy as it seemed.

"He called you 'The Great White Hope of Australian Classical Music'," he said, stopping abruptly, and then coming over to sit next to me.

"Who?"

"Stonehaven."

For a moment I was nonplussed. "Stonehaven?"

He laughed softly at me. "Then you haven't heard? Don't you keep up with your former governors-general—ones who have been kind to you?"

"Oh, how stupid of me, of course—Sir John Baird." I remembered reading he'd recently been made the first Viscount of Stonehaven.

"Well, Thomas, he returned from Australia shortly before war broke out, and he'd be sad to know you didn't recognise his new name immediately. Although he is quite unwell, he is still very fond of you."

"He is?"

"He is—and remains a great fan of your playing. He told me of an occasion when he'd been invited to speak about you after one of your performances—one to raise money for your studies abroad. In his speech, he'd said not only did you hold the promise of being the next important violinist of our era, but you carried the hopes of your country on your shoulders, and everyone in your homeland was expecting you to catapult your nation's musical aspirations onto the international stage."

I began to feel very uncomfortable. I remembered that particular speech, in which he referred to me as "that rare bird, the virtuosic male violinist" only too well. It had come at the end of a gala in the Melbourne Town Hall. My Uncle Otto had travelled to hear me play the Mendelssohn concerto—it was the first time I'd stood on the concert platform with a major orchestra and had seen my beloved uncle, the man who'd taught me to play the violin, sitting in the audience.

"In the course of finding out more about you, I spoke with Sir John not a few weeks ago. What happened, Thomas?"

"Life happened, Your Royal Highness."

"Please call me George. You say my name so carefully and it sounds so well when you speak it. Sir John told me you had scholarships coming out of your ears, and you had nearly a thousand pounds in subscriptions to send you overseas to make a name for yourself …"

I swallowed and then bit my tongue—I could taste bitterness and frustration in the back of my throat. Life had indeed gotten in the way.

"Yes all of that's only too true. Everyone had so much hope for me, and all I did was to make them angry and to disappoint them."

"By joining the army."

"Yes, George. You see, it was the Depression, and …"

"Thomas. Let me speak plainly. As I've already said, if we're to be friends, I'd like you to be completely honest with me. Let me ask again. What happened?"

I felt so tormented I could hardly get the words out.

"My mother was diagnosed with ovarian cancer."

"Dear heavens! Now I understand—you joined the army in order to stay at home and be close to her."

"Yes, I did. Ultimately it was disappointing, but there was a silver lining—serving my country also meant a great deal to my brother and me."

"Because your father and your uncle had been interned during the Great War?"

I nodded. "My brother, Michael, and I felt we needed to prove something on their behalf—the family honour had been called into question in 1914."

"But you'd also have accomplished that had you gone on to become a great performer on the world stage. Instead, you gave it all up."

"It seemed the right thing to do."

"Your mother recovered?"

"Yes, she did."

"And you told no one of her illness."

I shook my head.

"So, not one of those dowagers who invested in your future, and then subsequently disowned you, knew of your sacrifice?"

"They thought I'd lost my mind—that I was capricious and ungrateful. People were so dreadfully angry. But, I simply couldn't do it—it was beyond me to abandon my mother in the time of her greatest need. She'd given all she had to my brother and me. I did what I felt was right."

"Shame upon them, Thomas. Did no one at least ask you why you'd joined up?"

"Had they done so, they would've been none the wiser—I felt it was a private matter, sir."

His smile was barely a smile, but accompanied with a slight nod, as if confirming something about me he'd suspected. "The great pity was such a heavy burden of expectation should have been placed upon your shoulders in the first place. It was inhuman to then add humiliation when you didn't 'make them proud'."

We sat, side by side, our shoulders touching, in silence. For a brief moment, I wondered what he was thinking, but then assumed he was most probably weighing up what I'd said tonight, comparing it to what he'd read about me, and what others might have told him. I'd have done the same in his position. I wondered if I'd passed his test.

"You'll do, Thomas, you'll do just fine," he said, quite suddenly, squeezing the back of my neck in the most affectionate manner.

It was as if he'd read my mind—I'd been found acceptable.

"Well then, seeing St. Giles, Cripplegate has fallen victim to the *'rain of terror'* from above, when can I next hear you perform?"

"I'd be happy to play for you, when and wherever you wish," I said, thankful to change the subject. Even though I'd eventually been forgiven by my countrymen, thoughts of those early days still hurt and bewildered me. "My brother and I could give you a private recital at your home, or—"

"And, I'd love that very much. But what about the Albert Hall? Queen's Hall? No concerts at either of those places?"

"I'm not one of the soloists who is invited to play at those venues."

"Hmm," he murmured. "I can't imagine why not, especially after reading the reviews of your recent outstanding successes in Ireland, and then of your concerts in Leeds, Manchester, and Edinburgh. There is obviously more to your current situation than meets the eye ... however, my other request: dancing with Heinrich?"

"With your private room so convenient, I'm sure we can fulfil your wish—shall I fetch him?"

He shook his head. "In a moment, Thomas. He'll join us momentarily."

I didn't question him, merely raised an eyebrow.

"Tommy ... I meant what I said about becoming friends, and I'd also like to get to know your charming American. Perhaps you'd both like to come to Belgrave Square soon for dinner?"

"I'd be delighted, sir. In fact, I know we both would be honoured."

Perhaps you'd both like to come to Belgrave Square soon for dinner, he'd said. We both knew dinner would be the cover for a private conversation away from the other guests. I was fairly sure the invitation would arrive in the very near future—sooner, rather than later. Until we went to dine at the duke's London residence, I could only wonder what this mission was all about, and what I'd be getting myself into.

Once more the French doors opened a crack, and the duke gestured to his private secretary, who nodded and then disappeared again. A few moments later, Heinrich sidled out through the French doors and onto the terrace, juggling three glasses of champagne. I smiled to myself, watching him manipulating the glasses as he tried to pass one to the duke and bow to him at the same time.

"Thank you, Heinrich," the duke said, and then moved away from us, instantly deep in conversation with his private secretary, who'd followed Shorty out onto the terrace and who waited outside the doors. "Wow!" I said quietly, gulping down the entire glass. "That man sure is something!"

"Do I need to be worried?" he asked, teasingly.

"You'll never have to be worried on that account, Shorty. I'm a one-person sort of man."

As I said it, I became aware I'd finally lost the parenthesis around his nickname in my mind. I knew it was what I'd always call him when we were alone.

He laughed softly and then began to hum along with the pianist, who we could hear through the closed French doors. She was playing "It Had to Be You".

"Boy, oh boy!" Shorty said, breaking off his soft hum. His eyes gleamed in the light of the half-moon. "Could these words ever be more suitable? I knew right from the start too, Tommy …"

He leaned closer for a kiss, but I laughed, embarrassed. The duke, who'd turned away from his secretary, was now looking at us with a bright smile. Bugger this, I thought, and then gave him a quick peck on the cheek. "Care to?" I asked, offering him my arm.

"Out here?"

"No, silly, follow me." I led him into the room in which I'd danced with the Duke of Kent.

He directed me into a quickstep. "My first dance with a colonel—have I ever told what a great dancer you are?"

I told him he had, on the night we'd met, but still it was nice to hear him say it again. We did a spin and changed arms, so I could lead for a while.

"And you got me a promotion. Damn you, Thomas Haupner, you know how to get around a guy."

"I was only taking advantage of the situation. Let's talk about it tomorrow. There are things, like worrying about you, that I'm not happy about if we're going to be working together, but for tonight I just want it to be about you and me having fun and not being too serious."

"Hey, you! Worry all you like, but you don't get to protect me, understood? I'm a big grown-up boy, and fighting is my job. We make a pact right now we look out for each other, but when we're on the job it's all business."

"Or what?"

"Or you aren't getting into my pants for at least ... um, until tomorrow."

We laughed as we cantered along the diagonal of the room. I loved the quickstep.

A tap on the shoulder interrupted our tripping of the light fantastic. It was the Marquess of Harrogate, who'd slipped out into the darkness and had discovered us in the private room. He led me off into the next dance. Ironically, it was a slow balboa, and the music was "Stompin' at the Savoy".

"Well, it's not the Savoy, but needs must, Tommy," the Marquess said. "Claridge's will have to do."

He was an excellent dancer and I hoped to keep up, mainly because I hadn't danced the balboa for ages.

Over his shoulder, I noticed Heinrich expertly weaving and twirling around with the Duke of Kent, both of them chatting amiably. The surreal nature of the situation was somewhat heightened by the sound of the first air-raid sirens of the night and the sight of the Duke's private secretary, who was keeping guard at the doors out onto the terrace, preserving our privacy.

★★★★★

A bit later, once we were back inside with the other guests, I found myself talking to Frank Goyen in a corner of the room about the lateness of the air-raid sirens. It was ten o'clock. Sometimes they started bombing a little after it got dark; at other times it wasn't until after midnight.

After a few minutes, He glanced over my shoulder. He touched the tip of his finger to the side of his nose—someone seemed to have signalled him.

"The Duke of Gloucester wants to speak with you in a few minutes, Tommy," he said. "I need to confess something—I'm here under false pretences. I knew you were an Aussie, and I've wanted to meet you ever since I heard you play at Australia House, months ago. When His Royal Highness said he was meeting you tonight, I sort of put the screws on, and here I am. I just had to say hello. I mean … gidday!"

His Aussie hello broke the ice, well and truly. We chatted a bit more about missing home, and then he ushered me to a quiet corner, where the Duke of Kent's brother was waiting for us.

"George asked me to chat with you, Thomas. I suppose you've been wondering what this is all about?"

I had a feeling it had nothing to do with what I'd discussed outside with his brother. This was another matter altogether. I waited for him to speak.

"As you know, the Nazis have had the Channel Islands under their control since the middle of the year," the duke said. "Someone has whispered in my ear we need to set up a cell somewhere on the coast, to keep an eye on movements to and from Alderney."

"We do?" This was an area I controlled at the SOE, but knew nothing about the need for a new cell there. "I beg your pardon, Your Royal Highness—why Alderney?"

"It's really to do with the concentration camps on the island. I've received information that indicates the *Bewaffnung und Munition* are using forced labour to construct fortifications."

That was impossible—I'd heard nothing of the sort. Besides, the German Ministry of Weapons and Munitions didn't do engineering works. I wondered what his source was. We'd gone through mountains of files and endless meetings, trying to work out what the four prisoner-of-war camps on the island actually did—not a whisper had been heard about fortifications.

"So, we need a cell in Auderville to keep an eye on things," he continued. "There's no airstrip on the island, so most likely they're delivering and receiving goods sent by boat from Alderney, Goury, or La Roche on the Normandy coast. Perhaps two cells would be better? I'll leave the final decision up to you."

"Well, if you're certain, sir. I'll spend a bit of time deciding who to choose, but I'm sure I can assemble the perfect team to set it up."

"No, Thomas," he said, shaking his head. "That's what tonight is all about—you're going to take our American friend over there to show him the ropes while you set up the cells yourself—to show him how we do things. My brother and I agreed it will be the perfect opportunity to show Reiter the nitty-gritty of setting up a Resistance group. He can report back to the Americans when he gets back."

I groaned internally. Working with Shorty in the field could be complicated, especially with our relationship so new. But things were quite different from the way they'd been before the war. In those days, had we met then, our relationship might have progressed in quite a different way—it would have been more leisurely, for certain.

As these thoughts were going through my mind, I heard the first, distant explosions of the raid. There was no time for unhurried courting anymore. Unexpected and unprepared weddings, the couple knowing each other for merely a week, were not uncommon—engagements were practically unheard of. No one wanted to "wait until after the war".

Shorty was dancing with Gladys. He winked at me. I caught it over the Duke of Gloucester's shoulder as he was shaking my hand and telling me he'd be in touch.

Heinrich and I'd only known each other for a matter of days, yet it didn't feel to me what we had was going to be a flash in the pan. If it were to turn out to be a "marriage", or the nearest thing like it two men could have, it would survive and prosper if it was meant to be, despite what the world threw at us.

Maybe it was naïve to think those thoughts, but what did I have in my life to judge it on, or compare it to? All I knew was what I already felt in my heart and what I saw in Shorty's eyes.

"After all," I said to myself, as I glanced across the room at the wondrous man who'd turned my life upside down, "we could be dead tomorrow."

CHAPTER 5

"So, you still think you're friskier than me?" I asked.

He'd actually said "horny" to me earlier that morning. But, as it was a word I hadn't heard before, I found it too quaint as yet to use in conversation.

Last night, after Claridge's, he'd walked me home, and then had stayed over. Now, we were walking along Oxford Street on our way to work, he to Grosvenor Square and me to Baker Street. We could walk together most of the way, only having to part at Orchard Street.

"Yup," he said, doing one of those little sideways jumps, with a mid-air click of the heels one saw in Vaudeville, or in American cinema comedies. "Got time for another before work?"

He waggled his eyebrows. It made me laugh. Despite the cold of the December morning, my heart thought it was springtime.

"You weren't kidding when you said morning, noon, and night."

"Been saving it up for you for twenty-nine years, babe."

We'd arrived at Orchard Street. "Get on with you," I said, pretending to be shocked. "If the phones are up, I'll call you around lunchtime, to say hello. If I don't get through, I'll see you later tonight. You're coming to the pub, I hope?" Promotions were a cause for drinks all round. It would be my shout, and no doubt a costly one.

"I'll be there. Have a good day, Aussie—I'll talk to you later."

We saluted each other formally in the street and headed off on our separate ways. After a few moments, I glanced back at him and caught him looking at me over his shoulder as he strode off down the street.

There was a lot of back-slapping and some soft applause as I made my way through to my office. Word had obviously got around. I'd barely got my coat off and hung my cap on the coat-rack in my room, when Gladys appeared.

"New office is down the hallway," she said.

"Already?"

I followed her. A line of young women were standing outside the new rooms. It was apparent they'd been press-ganged into helping move our effects into the new office.

"If you're finished, you can get about your business," she snapped.

One by one they smiled as they passed us on their way back to the typing pool. One or two of them made "goo-goo" eyes at me as they moved by, murmuring, "Congratulations ... Colonel."

I swear Gladys growled like a Rottweiler. They scampered away.

"Gladys, you're so mean," I said. She tossed her hair and gave me her very best "who me?" look.

The new office was excellent. Much larger than my old one. It had a separate ante-room, exactly like that of my now-former boss, Mark Harris. I couldn't help but wonder which poor bugger had been moved sideways to vacate this suite of rooms for me. I'd never ventured into this part of the building before now. It was very convenient indeed, as the staircase that led to counter-intelligence and imagery analysis was a short way down the corridor. On the floor below that was combat intelligence and linguistics. But the crowning glory of our new nest was a small room off to one side, in its corner a sink, a preparation bench, and a gas outlet from the wall.

I pointed at it. "We can make coffee and tea here?" She nodded. "Gladys, I love you!"

"You won't love me when I tell you Colonel Smith has rung at least a dozen times this morning."

"Did you tell him anything?"

"No. I thought I'd leave that up to you."

I checked my watch. "Better get him on the line, then."

"I'll put him through and then retrieve your hat and coat, shall I?" she said.

"No, I'll fetch them in a bit—" But she'd gone before I could stop her.

I plonked myself in my wheeled library chair, put my feet up on the desk, and then crossed my hands on my stomach, only lifting them to pick up the telephone when the call came through.

"You fucking son-of-a-bitch" and *"taking him to France?"* were some of the first sentences I heard him say. It was followed by a diatribe of *"looking after my nephew"* and *"having your balls tied around your neck"*. Steve, it seemed, had stayed up waiting for Shorty to get back to the embassy to find out what had happened at Claridge's. I held the phone away from my ear for a while during the blah-de-blah, until I heard him stop to take breath.

"I'll make sure that next time I have him home by eleven o'clock, and no strong liquor, and I won't go past first base, *Dad!*" I growled into the phone. That was stupid of me, in retrospect, as I started him off all over again.

"For heaven's sake, Steve," I said eventually, "this is good for him. He'll have a foot so far up the bloody ladder, by the time you guys get into the war, he'll be pissing on everyone else's head!"

No doubt, Bill Donovan had already mentioned the "F" word to Steve that morning—the reason he'd been yelling down the phone. It was the first time I'd heard "France" used as a *cuss-word*, as the Americans called it.

He calmed down after a while, finally accepting it wasn't my doing. He told me to have a good day and then get myself back to work. Just before he hung up, he did have the courtesy to throw a quick "Congratulations," and a promise to turn up at the pub.

As soon as I hung up the phone, a cup appeared in front of me. "Coffee?" I asked, amazed.

"New kitchenette is quite handy, don't you think, *Colonel?*" Gladys's imitation of the girls from the typing pool was outstanding. She pulled up a chair, crossed her legs, and got out her shorthand notebook. "And next time you're speaking with Colonel Smith, will you remind him we're running out of coffee. A carton of six tins wouldn't go amiss. One each for us for home use, and the rest locked in the safe here." She winked at me.

"I suppose you'd like a pint of the white stuff too?"

"Well, of course that would be lovely, but by now I'm quite used to my tea and my coffee black. Thank heavens neither of us have ever taken sugar."

After last night's euphoria, in the cold, hard light of day, I was feeling overwhelmed. We both knew there'd be a mountain of work to be done. With my promotion, things had changed completely. First of all, my new rank and her new position as my personal assistant needed to be circulated to all the relevant departments, so when requisitions for goods or services were put through, there'd be no hold-ups or questions. The chain of command would have to be made aware I should be contacted directly, and no longer through Mark Harris's office.

Gladys passed me a large box file.

"What's this?" I asked.

"It's a dossier on your new responsibilities. That new position they were so vague about last night? Seems you're being moved out of F Section."

"Oh, really?" I growled. "We'll see about that."

Gladys smirked. Everyone knew Mark Harris thought I was obsessive over the details of our undercover work in France. He always aimed to spend the least time possible at his desk. Onerous details, like making sure our operatives were safe, were not high on his agenda. There was no way, even if I were moved away from the responsibility, I'd not keep an eye on how it was administered.

The sheaf of documents was thick. I sighed, realising the cover report had been drawn up a long time ago for someone else and then shelved out of inertia. I checked the date on the cover: 4th February, 1940. It was just shy of a year old.

I smiled when I opened the dossier. The title clearly said *Partial Occupational Responsibility*. The words were underlined in pale lavender ink. There was only one person I knew who used that special colour as a flag to me—my new personal assistant.

"I thought you might find the job description rather interesting," she said, over her shoulder, as she went to refill our cups. *Partial Occupational Responsibility* meant it wasn't a full-time focus. It was meant to be an adjunct area of command. It gave me a great deal of leverage to argue I could continue to control my area of F Section.

"Well, then, fellow conspirator," I said to her when she came back into the room, "what's this new position all about?" I tapped the outside of the dossier, which I'd thrown onto my desktop.

"It's about reorganising covert ops training all over the country and how best to achieve it." She retrieved a manila folder from the box file and handed it to me. She'd already affixed a précis to its inside cover, together with a list of my other new responsibilities.

Reading it, I let out a long groan. "Holy cow! And they want me to do all of this? This is a job for four people, not just for one. How on earth am I going to manage this, along with—"

It was at that moment I saw the smile on Gladys's face. The one she used to signal *"it's all under control—Gladys is at the helm"*.

"I have four words," she said.

"And they are?"

"Thomas, Gladys, Andrew, and Michael. It's call a TEAM," she said, spelling out the word, as if I were a backward eight-year-old. "A team is a group of people who share responsibilities."

"I know that, Gladys. I'm not totally stupid."

"You're anything but, Tommy. However, your shoulders are only so wide. Delegate your responsibilities. Farm out the work. Share it with the three brightest people you know. You have the authority now—it's about time you used it and stopped trying to win the war single-handedly."

She was right, of course. I knew I'd find it hard to relinquish control, but if I didn't there was no way I could manage all of the new areas of responsibility—I was already stretched as it was. The only way would be to do as they wanted—abandon my control of my area of F Section—and I certainly wasn't going to do that. I'd worked too hard to place agents safely and monitor their well-being. It wasn't merely about me.

"I suppose you've already thought about how this could work?" I asked.

"Tommy 'rhetorical question' Haupner ... how sweet of you to ask. Be a love and fill up our coffee cups while I sort out the documents that will make you think you'd come up with the ideas yourself."

I found myself in the kitchenette, cleaning out our cups, before I knew where I was. Gladys the superwoman—what had I done in my life to deserve someone like her? Had she stopped quipping, I'd have been seriously worried—it was part of her modus operandi.

"Here you are," she said, handing me a neatly handwritten précis of her ideas for the management of my life, while at the same time taking her coffee cup from me. I kissed her cheek.

"Thank you. I mean it, Gladys. Thank you."

"Aw," she said. "Thanks mean nothing if they aren't in diamonds, Tommy. Every girl knows that." We both laughed. "Go on, read it," she said.

I read her notes, realising she must have been working on them since early this morning and knowing I'd ask for her advice.

"Let's get transport arranged for Michael and Andrew," I said. "They need to be involved in this conversation right from the start. Let's see if we can get them here by, say, eleven tomorrow morning? Andrew can get the overnight train down, or hitch a lift with the fly boys. If there's a problem, call the duke's office. He promised to help."

"No need to bother him unless you want to, Tommy. You can issue a D.5 now." A D.5 was a direct transport requisition, one that could be ordered over the telephone to the right department, without accompanying paperwork.

"Wow! I hadn't thought of that. Okay, get Andrew onto a flight this afternoon. I want to talk this through with him and Michael before we meet with the regional training officers."

"Of course. Now, here, look at this," she said, leaning over my shoulder and leafing through the documents I was reading. She tapped on a file marked with a red tab. "I think you'll have to lose your Monday reviews and pass along the supervision of combat training courses here in Baker Street to someone else. Neither of these two things will be any loss—I know you find them time-consuming. But last night, while you were outside making pals with his brother, the Duke of Gloucester told me you'll be spending 'more time out of the office', so I got here early and tried to work out what would be vital to your new position and what could be sacrificed in order to manage your new responsibilities."

"Thank you, Gladys," I said. "You're a miracle worker."

"These are merely my ideas, Tommy. You don't have to agree," she replied.

I walked to the window and looked down on the street below. Even with wartime petrol rationing there were still an amazing number of vehicles travelling along the street. I was sure the "out of the office" was also referring to the task the Duke of Kent had alluded to last night—his brother would be bound to know—but I couldn't discuss that possibility with Gladys. I thought for a minute.

"Andrzej will have to take over the training of the Polish soldiers," I said. "And I think we should also write a recommendation for his promotion to captain and send it over to General Sikorski, with my added endorsement. I'd also like to try to get a promotion for both Michael and Andrew. I don't know if the army board will agree, but now's the time, while things are new and I have everyone's goodwill."

Gladys smiled at me. I recognised her look—I'd done something she approved of.

"What?" I asked. I could feel the colour in my cheeks.

"I get to jump several grades in the public service, your friends get promotions ... what about you, Tommy?"

"Lieutenant-Colonel will do just fine for now," I said.

"Strike while the iron is hot, that's what you should do. Give yourself a little treat. Go out to lunch, have a day off, do something that's solely for you."

"Too much to do, Gladys," I said.

"But most importantly, weigh up your options, think of something you'd really love for yourself. Now's the time to call in some favours ..."

I pretended not to know what she was talking about.

Miss Gladys Gleeson could spot a deal going down from a mile off. She'd worked out wheels were turning in secret rooms, and I was somehow going to be asked to do something in reward for what I—or rather, we—had been given.

"I'd hold out for the Albert Hall," she said perceptively, as she began to close the door between our offices, "or the Queen's Hall, at least."

*****

An hour or so later, after moving the furniture around in the room several times to suit me, I put my head outside the door and smiled. Gladys had placed her desk strategically so she could stop anyone from bypassing her and walking directly into my office.

"Gladys," I asked, "would you mind booking a table for two at Charlie's at twelve thirty, and then ring Heinrich and ask him to meet me there for lunch?"

She looked at me over the top of her glasses.

"It's business," I said firmly.

"Is that what it's called where you come from?"

I smiled at her with as much sarcasm as I could muster. "And get Andrzej up here right now, could you? I'd like to discuss a few other things with him."

I found a phone book in the bottom drawer of my new desk and looked up the phone number of the florist near Charlie's. I rang them and asked them what was the biggest bunch of flowers they could make. When they informed me, I told them I wanted one twice the size and that it should be delivered to Gladys—I'd call in and pay for it on my way to lunch. Diamonds I couldn't do—I hoped she'd be happy with dahlias.

Then I rang Northney Training Station, asking to be put through to Michael.

"Captain Haupner," my brother said, answering the phone.

"Colonel Haupner speaking," I said, the tone in my voice telling him it was no joke.

"You rotten bastard!" he yelled into the phone, laughing and whooping at the same time. I wished I could have been there to tell him in person. I'd have given anything to see the look on his face.

"Damn, you, Tommy," he said softly, once he'd calmed down. "I'm so bloody happy for you. How the hell did that come about?"

"They've been giving them away in cornflake packets, and I guess I bought the lucky box." I waited for him to finish laughing. "No, I'll fill you in on all the gossip tomorrow up here. Gladys will ring you and arrange transport to London, and then I'll tell you everything. There's a reorganisation of my responsibilities that goes with the promotion, which will affect you too. Andrew is coming down from Scotland so we three can discuss it together with Gladys. We're meeting at eleven, I think I said."

"Andrew is coming down?"

I sighed. "Lots to talk about, little brother … and, by the way, you get to stay in a nice hotel from now on when you can't be bothered going home to Shepherd's Bush."

"Oh?"

"Yeah," I said, a little more shyly than I wanted to.

"Good for you. Nice to hear your bed is booked out—you two done 'it' yet?"

"Michael, loose lips sink ships."

"Ah, so you have done everything except put the ship in the harbour."

I laughed very hard. "See you tomorrow, brother. I love you very much."

"You too, and congrats again," he said, before hanging up.

I leaned back in my chair, my feet stretched out in front of me. If I swivelled, I could see out the new office window, over London, towards the west.

This was the sweet-spot before the real, hard-knuckled part of the business truly began. Taking Shorty behind enemy lines wasn't something I was looking forward to. Not that I thought he couldn't take care of himself, but I even worried when Michael was with me after several operations together.

If I was to be honest, I was also a bit concerned about how fast things were going with the handsome man who had me thinking of him almost constantly. But, I couldn't help what I felt, and it seemed reciprocal.

What did I feel? I wasn't quite sure, but the attraction was very compelling.

Well, if he was to be initiated into our "spy world" over the next few weeks, we would be spending quite a bit of time apart while he was off undergoing training and induction into the world that was the SOE. With some distance between us, I was sure things would become clearer.

In the meantime, though, I had lunch with him to look forward to and then drinks at the pub and then perhaps the night together …

Andrzej's knock at my door interrupted my thoughts, so I rose from my chair and went to the door to let him in.

CHAPTER 6

It was Friday the twentieth, five days before Christmas, and eight days since I'd last seen him.

I'd come into work early, to exercise by myself in the deserted gymnasium in the basement of our Baker Street headquarters. I'd been grumpy for the past few days, to the point that yesterday morning Gladys had picked up the phone and handed it to me. "Phone him!" she'd ordered.

I'd told her to bugger off in sign language—she'd told me to get knotted in the same. Sign language had become one of the most attended classes at Baker Street since I'd instituted it into the training programme. Our teacher, Nathan Cooke, was a very charming adolescent—tall and willowy. A metal brace on his right leg was the only indication of a bout of poliomyelitis. Together with his profound deafness, it explained the reason an otherwise healthy nineteen-year-old wasn't in uniform.

Of course, when I'd tried, I couldn't reach Shorty, because he'd been travelling at the time. That had made my mood worse, so I'd grumped off to Henley to do some pistol shooting, dragging poor Andrzej along with me. I'd taken out my ill humour on the targets—mostly.

Okay, I was forced to admit to myself I wasn't doing so well without Shorty around.

It worried me on one hand, but also made me feel warm inside on the other. The worry was over what was going to happen in future when we were separated for longer periods of time. I'd come to realise he felt part of me, even after two weeks. Stupid really, I admitted, but I'd always known there would only be one person for me. Now I'd found him, what should I do, run away?

I reached for the circular rings. I knew I was overworking my upper body, but it seemed to help with my bad mood. I'd smiled to myself a little earlier—such was my grouchiness—that I'd wound the bandages around my wrists and palms so tightly I'd almost cut off circulation to my fingers.

I found myself doing handstands in the rings, all the while wondering when his train would arrive at King's Cross. He'd been due to arrive last night, but a raid had disrupted services, and I'd been told he'd be getting here this morning. That was the main reason for my current bout of crankiness. I'd spent a lot of ration coupons on the ingredients for a special dinner last night and had been looking forward to a whole day together before he headed off again.

It had been decided it would be best to start his specialist training shortly after after the evening at Claridge's. We'd met for lunch at Charlie's and actually had spent nearly all of our time throwing ideas back and forth about his strengths versus his needs. He needed no combat training at all, that was obvious—he simply needed practice with someone of his own standard. So, after three days at Ringway undergoing parachute training, he was to go north, to Lochailort, to teach commando classes for Andrew, who'd remained with me in London to help organise the new areas in the restructure we'd devised.

The level at the facility in Scotland was very high. So many of the men up there were Poles who had a fierce and special hatred for the race that had devastated their nation—by all accounts, they trained until they dropped. There were also squads made up of Dutchmen and Norwegians, expert and ready for deployment. It would provide Shorty with men of a very high standard to fight and train with.

He'd sent me a very funny letter, written during the course of his journey from the Midlands to Scotland, in which he'd described his parachute training and the obligatory nine jumps he'd needed to complete to qualify. It had been hand-delivered by one of the Poles who'd returned not long after Shorty had arrived in Lochailort. I'd read that particular section so many times now I knew it by heart:

> *... the guys here are wonderful, but all so very young-looking. I feel a great lump in my throat to see these youngsters so full of beans and really anxious to start jumping down on top of the enemy. If they only knew the Germans aren't going to stand there like the sandbag dummies these boys train with and take a bayonet in the guts without protest. Most of them have that look a lot of skinny adolescents have—pimples on their cheeks and Adam's apples that stick out as far as the points of their chins. Did we ever look like that when we were their age?*
>
> *I never did get around to telling you how much I love animals. It's one of the many things you'll find out about me—critters and me are like bees and honey. If there's a stray dog about, he's my friend quicker than you can say Jack Robinson. Hey! Maybe that's why you and me have become such good pals so quickly. Ha ha!*
>
> *Anyways, at the airbase they have this "paradog" unit. They train pooches to sniff out explosives and gunpowder—they even teach them to chase and pull down anything wearing Feldgrau, and to bark at guys who are sporting a swastika armband. A big part of their training is to get them accustomed to jumping out of planes. They have their own parachutes and special harnesses. My first jump here was preceded by a German Shepherd (what they call an Alsatian here on base), a Border collie, and a bulldog! They all had their ripcords fastened to the static line by the training sergeant and jumped out without help. The collie, whose name is Meg,*

141

even stopped at the fuselage door and barked at me, as if she was saying, "Come on, slowcoach, this is how it's done."

Boy, oh, boy, Tommy! What a story. My mom is going to love it when I get the chance to tell her …

He continued, telling me he'd been able to hitch a ride in an aircraft to Dalcross airfield, in Scotland, piloted by the leader of the Second Commando Unit. Subsequently, the man had telephoned me, asking if by any chance this "new Yankee trainee" could be seconded to his command—I'd responded with a terse "no".

His letter had been a joy to read. He'd continued writing it after he'd got off the aircraft and then once he'd boarded the "quaint Scottish train" that took him from Inverness to Lochailort. *Quaint* was the word he'd written to describe it—my impression, having done the journey more than once, was it was more like a cattle truck with seats.

He wrote in such a casual yet informative style, it was like reading a good book: the touches of humour, references to small things we'd shared, made the letter feel more like a conversation he'd already had with me, and which he'd then put down on paper. Underneath his signature, in tiny letters, was written *hier schnüffeln*. I'd smelled that tiny spot of his cologne until I'd made a shiny patch on the paper with my nose.

His trip back to London had not been so easy to organise, and I'd grimaced when I'd signed the travel permits, noting that, although he'd be taking the same "quaint" train trip back to Inverness, he'd then be put on an overnight bus ride to Edinburgh, after which another train to King's Cross. That was bad enough, but last night's news, that off-target bombs had taken out the railway lines outside Coventry, now meant he'd have to bus it to Peterborough and then catch another train to be able to get back to London this morning. I also knew he'd be exhausted when he got in and was due to leave again tonight to go to Station XVII at Brickendon.

I went to the telephone at the corner of the room in the gymnasium and asked to speak to Gladys.

"I want a car for the next two days, Gladys, and somewhere very nice to stay near Brickendonbury—for two. One room will suffice. Have the driver pick me up at home tomorrow morning."

"A car?" she asked, as if I'd asked for a trip to the moon.

"Yes, Gladys, a car! I've decided to have a look at the new Nobel 808 plastic explosive they're using there. Cancel everything on my agenda over the weekend."

I'd hung up before she could say anything else. Afterwards, I didn't feel quite as cross as I'd been all morning. I'd worked every day and well into the night over the past eight days, and I was buggered if I was going to miss out on the special meal I'd planned to have with him. I reasoned I could cook it tonight, and we could travel by car to Hertford in the morning. He could do his training course and I'd have a look around the facility. We could drive back on Sunday night and then have a few days together before we went to the STS3 facility for foreign weapons training. I'd booked time there for him, Andrew, Michael, Andrzej and me, because we'd recently "obtained" a crate of new German weapons from North Africa I thought we should all have a look at. There had been a huge surprise in the crate—a Maschinenpistole 40, or a Schmeisser, as we were calling it, after its designer, Hugo Schmeisser. It was the Germans' latest top-of-the-range sub-machine gun.

I checked my leather-reinforced cotton gloves were tied securely and then did some handsprings across the floor mats. After that, I began some leg work on the balance beam. I'd had the gloves made especially for me to protect my hands while doing physical exercise. I always avoided anything that might compromise the flexibility of my fingers and wrists. Years of careful selection had led to a routine that built strength in my arms and shoulders, yet didn't adversely affect my hands for my playing.

I was feeling very tired. The nightly bombings hadn't eased since Shorty had gone away and last night an enormous explosion had nearly thrown me out of bed. The bomb had fallen in Oxford Street, just down the corner from my house, closing off the intersection of Museum Street with a large crater and mounds of debris. Nothing had been broken in my flat, but the sudden noise in my sleep and the shuddering of the house had made me leap out of bed ready for action.

I reckoned it must have been a "straggler"—the name we were giving to the lazy or fear-filled bomber crews, those who simply wanted to drop their loads and quickly get away from our anti-aircraft guns, Hurricanes, and Spitfires. The stragglers didn't even try for the main targets—they usually unloaded well away from the main air-fights, opening their bomb bays on random parts of London. I was fairly sure some of our own pilots did exactly the same over Berlin, Frankfurt, or Hamburg.

The balance beam was proving a challenge. I'd been doing squats on it to hone my balance and could already feel the pain in my legs. My body was telling me I needed to work harder, so I spent about fifteen minutes repeating mounting and dismounting exercises.

It would be a fun Christmas, I hoped, unless the Germans stuffed things up by bombing everything flat. The Duke of Kent's invitation had arrived yesterday. Shorty and I were to dine in a few days' time, on Monday, at Belgrave Square. The invitation said it would be informal, which meant black tie, and the duke's private secretary had written a personal note accompanying the card, informing us it would be a quiet gathering—Gladys had told me this could mean anything from four to twenty guests.

On Christmas Eve, we were to have a more formal dinner at the private residence of the American embassy. All the staff and their companions had been invited. As John McQueen and Steve were basically holding the fort until the arrival of the next ambassador, the evening was promised to be far more relaxed than under Joe Kennedy's disapproving eye.

I was strangely proud Shorty had asked me to accompany him. Everyone who knew either of us was aware we'd become good friends. However, not everyone was aware how good that friendship had become. After war broke out, it wasn't in the least bit unusual to see military men teaming up in pairs, as they'd done twenty or so years before. The re-emergence of the buddy system, highlight of the trenches in the Great War, was once more universally acknowledged and accepted. I knew no one would think anything of our close friendship, except to laud it and to exemplify it as a norm between true fighting men who looked out for each other.

The evening at the embassy would also give me a chance to show off the new black mess dress that had just been delivered. The army would only provide one dress uniform for my new rank, so I'd chosen my British regiment's version, and had to pay for the Australian summer and winter mess dress myself. Who would have thought promotion would prove to be so expensive?

I'd shifted to the newly installed asymmetrical parallel bars and had begun to feel quite hot, so stripped off my singlet and began to run a few routines, trying to figure out how best to take advantage of these American imports—I'd been told they worked wonders for upper body strength and eye-hand co-ordination.

Michael and I had decided to hold Christmas Day at my flat. He'd arranged to get a goose on the weekend while visiting Rhys's parents at Alton, not far out of London. They ran a poultry farm, and, although all of their stock was requisitioned for the armed forces, they'd kept a goose for us. I missed their kindness and their lilting Welsh accents. I must take Shorty there for a visit soon, I promised myself.

Goose had been the bird of choice in both of our families. After all, it was the German celebratory feast bird—Shorty, Steve, Michael, and I were all from Teutonic backgrounds—despite Steve's distinctive British surname, his mother's maiden name was Grosskopf. I'd also invited Gladys and a companion—she'd declined the companion part, but had offered to bring a small wheel of stilton she'd hidden in the basement of her ground-floor Holland Park flat.

Finished on the bars, I moved to the centre of the room and stood with my legs wide apart to begin some slow stretching. I'd just bent over, to touch my right foot with my left hand, when I felt warm arms around my stomach and a head pressed into the middle of my back.

"Thank the Lord you're back!" I yelled. "Crikey, you're a sight for sore eyes …"

He picked me up and twirled me around the room, before unceremoniously dragging me into the broom cupboard. He closed the door behind us and then kissed me, squeezing me in his arms. "Oh, babe, I missed you so much," he said when we came up for air, his face pressed against mine. I wound my arms around the back of his neck.

"My staff missed you more," I mumbled.

"Huh?"

"If you hadn't come back soon they were all about to go AWOL. Seems I've been a bastard to work with for the past eight days."

"Aw … did you miss me then?"

Damn, I was a sucker for his puppy-dog look and the "little kid" voice that went with it. "Maybe."

"Only maybe?" he asked. I could have eaten the sound of his voice.

"Okay I give up. I know when I'm beaten. The Nazis will never break me, no matter how hard or bad the torture, but you, sweetheart … yeah, I confess; I missed you a lot."

"Sweetheart?" he asked, in a whisper. "You going all gooey on me, Tommy?"

"Nah," I said. "I'm letting you have your way until your defences are down."

"And then what?" he whispered, breathily, into my ear.

"Then, when your defences are down, I'm going to let you do whatever you want with me." I pulled him to me by the lapels of his overcoat and then kissed him back, long and hard.

*****

Dinner at the Duke of Kent's London house, a few days before Christmas, was a memorable evening, for more reasons than one.

There were nine other guests apart from us two. I was so relaxed it was some time before I realised all of his guests were men—military men. One or two of them I already knew. It was only after Shorty whispered to me I became aware of something more.

"Do you realise apart from that guy over there," he asked, indicating a tall, Canadian air force pilot officer who was laughing with George, "the rest are couples?"

"What do you mean?" I asked.

"I mean couples … like you and me."

I blinked for a moment as I took in what he'd said.

"Did you really think we were the only men in the world to hook up like we have?" He smiled at me over his martini.

"Of course not, you big dag. Michael and Rhys were together for two years, and I suppose there were one or two other guys who I suspected ..."

He shook his head at me slowly, as if I were seriously retarded. "'One or two other guys? Honestly, Haupner, how do you ever find your clothes in the morning to get dressed?"

I grinned at him. "Simple—I just stand in the middle of my room, hold my arms out, and you put my shirts on for me, and tie my tie, and—"

My sentence was terminated by a well-concealed pinch to my behind.

We were interrupted by the Duke of Kent, with whom we chatted for a while until his butler apologised for the intrusion and handed him a note.

"Excuse me, gentlemen," he said then turned away to read it. He whispered something to his butler before turning back to us. "It seems my last guest has been unavoidably detained. But, never fear, there will never be an empty chair at *my* dining table if I can help it. A replacement is on his way. Shall we ...?"

We were summoned to the dining room.

After the soup, Charles Simpson, the duke's private secretary, arrived, somewhat out of breath, obviously having been abruptly summoned away from whatever he'd been doing to make up the party.

Shorty sat opposite me. On my right sat the Conde João do Braga, the son of the Portuguese Duke of Farrabo, and opposite me, on Shorty's left, his lover—a tall, dark-haired lieutenant commander of the New Zealand navy, Lindsay Evans, whose name I recognised, but who was someone I'd never met. They seemed a very unlikely couple, until I learned they'd met in the Philippines in 1935 while the Kiwis had been taking part in naval exercises and the count had been sailing his yacht around the world. There had been a near collision, an exchange of abuse, a slow reconciliation and now a comfortable, five-year-long relationship.

Both men were delightful company and we exchanged cards. I had many other contacts in Lisbon, where João normally lived, and it was a city through which we often funnelled operatives into occupied France or returned them home.

Lisbon was a very important city. It was the hub of what commercial air travel still functioned in Europe. Daily direct flights to London, Zürich, and Madrid allowed us to shuffle our agents around the southern parts of Europe, to gain access to Germany, Italy, and indirectly to Malta, and then on to Egypt and India. Seaplane services still ran from Lisbon to South America, via the Azores, to the Caribbean, and to Western Africa. It wasn't unknown for agents from different sides to be seated on the same aircraft. Portugal was a neutral country.

As I looked around the table, all I saw was fighting men. Not merely men who loved other men—but warriors, like Shorty and me. The thought gave me a great deal of comfort—the comfort of belonging to a group of men with specific common interests, yet who were not so dissimilar from every other serving man.

★★★★★

After dessert, the duke indicated I should follow him, so I excused myself to Shorty and the Canadian pilot with whom we'd been speaking. George led me out of the back of the house into a dark, enclosed garden, which was shielded on one side by a very high brick wall and on the other by a row of leafless elms.

"So, young man, are you having fun yet?" he asked with a wide smile, offering me a cigarette.

"Yes, I am, sir, the meal was delicious—"

He interrupted what I was about to say by patting me gently on the side of the face. "Thomas, I promise you I'm not interested in you in any other way than as a friend. I hope you understand. I loved the way you called me George at Claridge's when we were out on the balcony. Can we continue that from now on, when we're not in public?"

I lit his cigarette and then my own. "Of course ... George."

"I don't stick my nose where it doesn't belong ... or anything else," he added with a naughty chuckle. "I live my love life vicariously through a few of my acquaintances. Right now, you and Heinrich are my warriors. You must understand all the male couples in my life have something I can see and experience from a distance, but cannot touch. I'm now a very happily married man."

I nodded—I did understand.

"You're so tall; you and he both. It must be a nightmare finding a bed long enough."

I chortled. "One learns to make do, George."

We laughed at the same time. "Thank you, Tommy. I've met so few people I take to. In your case it was something rather instant that made me know we could become pals … and you do make me laugh for all the right reasons. It was something I didn't expect, did you know that? I thought you'd be all semiquavers and seriousness."

"Who, me?"

"There is something quite extraordinary about you. One moment you seem to be all hardness and steel—the next you're like a small child at an exhibition, all eyes and wonder. No wonder Heinrich is so in love with you."

I must have twitched, for he continued, his voice broken with soft laughter, "What, you aren't aware of that?"

I shook my head.

"I saw it in his eyes the first time I met you at Claridge's. And you're in love with him, do you at least know that?"

Things finally began to make sense in my head. I'd embraced the start of my feelings when he'd come back from Scotland and knew I felt more and more part of an "us" since then. Now that George had stated the blatantly obvious, I couldn't deny I'd been aware of Heinrich's feelings for me for some time.

"Maybe I haven't accepted it yet because I'm not sure I feel worthy of what he has to offer," I said, even though I couldn't quite believe I'd actually given word to those thoughts.

"You're a perfect foil for him, and he for you, Tommy. It's so refreshing to hear men speak from their hearts to me, rather than from what etiquette dictates … and that's precisely why I like people like you around me—you're honest. My father was fond of quoting *'Why, brothers, look you out among you seven men of honest report, full of the Holy Ghost and wisdom, whom we may appoint over this business.'*"

"*Acts*, verse six, chapter three," I said.

"Bravo!" he replied. "How extraordinary it is you know that quote. Seeing you do, you'll understand that honesty, for us princes, is the most valuable of commodities of all, in our friends and advisors."

He sat on one of the garden benches and patted the seat next to him as an indication I should join him. I knew the time had come to talk turkey.

"The note I want you to take to Saint-Lô contains nothing that could be thought of as scandalous."

I nodded, but I'd already worked that out—I knew Édouard very well.

"If I had any indiscretions nowadays—and I don't—they'd stay closer to home. What I'm about to tell you must remain a secret for the time being—a secret from everyone, and that includes Heinrich."

"You have my word," I said.

"Our mutual friend, Édouard, has many important contacts in the German High Command and at the *Reichskanzlei*, but I suppose you already know that."

I nodded.

"But maybe what you don't know is there are a few of them—major figures in the Nazi hierarchy—who are still in regular, inappropriate contact with my brother, the Duke of Windsor."

I was aghast. "Still? Even now he's in Nassau?"

"Even now."

This wasn't good news—it was totally unfitting for our former king to be in contact with leaders of the German regime. God knows what he thought he was doing. If George's brother was still corresponding with the Germans, this news would have to be passed on to the Americans—we had tabs on everything that went through normal channels because he had a reputation for indiscreet talk. Letters to and from Germany must be being delivered by visitors from the United States. I could only assume Wallis Simpson's cronies were the couriers.

What I feared most, however, was one of the correspondents still in contact with the Windsors was their former "pal" Joachim von Ribbentrop, the German ambassador in London before the war. Despite Wallis having broken off an affair with him to commit herself to our former King, it wouldn't have surprised me to find out they were still writing to each other. Both were duplicitous.

I decided to see if I could draw George out more on the topic, without asking directly—something one did not do with princes, even if they professed to be one's friend.

"I've not had a chance to tell you this," I said, "but I saw first-hand how cosy your brother was with the Nazis before the war. I met him in thirty-five, while he was still the Prince of Wales. It was at Hermann Göring's birthday party—I'd been invited to play. They were courting him quite assiduously even then."

"Then you do know David? I'd no idea."

"If you can call *knowing* him a glance over my shoulder at a pretty woman while he shook my hand, then yes, I suppose I do."

George laughed softly. Perhaps I'd been a little out of line, but he seemed to find what I'd said entirely typical of our previous king's behaviour. "I saw what you did," he said.

"What did I do?"

"You wanted to know more, but thought it impolite to ask, so you gave me some information you hoped might draw me out. Am I correct?"

"Am I that transparent?"

"No, not at all. You're sensitive, well-mannered, and you have my trust. I give you permission to speak to me as you wish—when we're in private, of course. I can't tell you how tedious it is to spend an age pussy-footing around something important, because of protocol and court etiquette."

"Then ... George, as you're urging me to speak as I wish ..."

"Go on."

"I have a nose for these things—and you've just told me you trust me. The letter to Édouard is only part of something much larger you'd like me to do. Am I right?"

I couldn't get parts of our conversation at Claridge's out of my mind—national importance, the Royal Family, the "whole mess"—these things didn't add up to being about a bit of indiscreet correspondence between his brother and someone well-placed in the Nazi zoo.

Although his smile was barely there, he nodded, showing he was pleased I'd put two and two together. Once again, I sensed I'd passed some test.

"You are, of course, correct. I'm trying to summon up the courage to tell you about it. Where on earth to start …?"

"Heinrich continually tells me the beginning is always a good place."

"The beginning's far too long ago," he said. "Light me another cigarette, would you?"

I did so and passed it to him. He unbuttoned his tuxedo jacket, dusted off the garden bench with his handkerchief, and then stretched out on his back, crossing his ankles and resting them on top of my knees. He puffed away in silence, and I waited for him to talk. When he did speak, it came out like the release of a stubborn cork from bottle—with a sudden rush.

"Hitler has promised to restore my brother to the Crown after he invades us."

I couldn't believe my ears. Depose the present king and replace him with twopence-worth of wet wool and a twice-divorced American woman, both of whose husbands were still alive? I must have gasped out loud.

"No, this can't be true …"

"It's most definitely true, Thomas. It's hideous, devious, treacherous, and unbelievable."

I took a moment to think carefully before replying. The letter I was to take to Édouard, correspondence between Germans at the Kanzlei and the Windsors, and the plan to overthrow the British Government and Crown were all somehow linked—yet I didn't have enough information to connect the dots.

Even though George remained flat on his back, the way he furiously puffed at his cigarette showed how upset he was.

I was furious too, on his behalf. "Your brother will never return to the throne, because Operation Sealion will never come to pass," I said. "I promise you there will *never* be an invasion of England. That fat-arse Göring has really put paid to any possibility—he promised Hitler he'd have air supremacy over our skies, but has failed miserably at the task.

The Germans won't risk a full-scale invasion unless they own the air over our country, and you and I both know that's not likely at this point in the war, or in the near future."

George sat up slowly and then rested his arm over my shoulders. "I can't tell you how much it hurts me to think of my brother's betrayal—he was privy to this plan to put him back on the throne," he said, somewhat sadly.

"Which betrayal?" I asked quietly and with as much concern as I could put into my voice. "The betrayal of his country or of his brothers?" The fact he'd said the Duke of Windsor was aware of the proposal had not escaped me.

He didn't reply immediately. I could see the turmoil in his eyes and was about to apologise—I'd hit a raw nerve—when he spoke. "Tommy, of course you're right. The note I want you to take to Édouard is indeed only a small part of what I'd like you to do for me … for us."

He swallowed twice and then wiped his lips on his pocket handkerchief. I recognised the gesture for what it was—a way of gathering thoughts before he continued. I guessed I was about to hear my unspoken questions answered.

"Dear God, how to put this …?"

"Please, George, it's best to be forthright. I respond well to plain speech."

"Very well, Thomas," he blurted suddenly. "Someone has stolen a valuable piece of jewellery from the Duke of Windsor, one which belongs to my mother. It's a necklace of great sentimental value, a well-known piece, and an important part of the Royal inheritance."

"And you want me to get it back," I said.

He nodded.

"And?"

"How do you know there is an 'and'?" he asked.

I waited. His face was ruddy, even in the moonlight.

"The same person has stolen private letters from my brother, sent to him by Hitler, in which the Führer's intentions to restore my brother to the throne are clearly spelled out."

"Oh!" I said. Such was my shock, I jumped to my feet, clasping my hands over my ears, as if to block out what I'd heard. This was disastrous and not what I'd expected. There could only be one explanation. "Blackmail?"

The Duke of Kent quickly wiped his eyes and then replaced his handkerchief.

"Indeed, Tommy. There's been no demand as yet, only a letter revealing the blackmailer is in possession of both the correspondence and the necklace. I doubt it will be long before another letter arrives asking for an extortionate sum. If we don't pay up, it will be the end of everything. I need you to retrieve both items for me, for my family, and for the sake of the Kingdom."

"I see," I said quietly. The blackmailer who had these letters must either be in Germany or France. That's why I'd been chosen. I could easily pass muster for a citizen of either country and had the ability and the resources at my disposal to get there. The person who had the letters and the necklace would also presumably not give them up freely of his or her own accord. I was trained to kill—it was all starting to make sense now.

"The letters are recent?"

"Yes, Thomas. As you most likely know, David and his wife fled France earlier this year, in July. The letters must have been stolen from their home in Paris while they were packing up—I can tell you, however, they were all written *after* the outbreak of war."

A cold shiver ran up the side of my neck and over the top of my head. I felt afraid—not of the danger of retrieving what had been stolen, but of the damage to the reputation of the Royal Family and to the morale of the British people were it revealed, in our current state of war, our former king had turned traitor. People would ask what they were fighting for, if a man for whom many still showed great respect thought so little of his country he'd collude with and then surrender it up to the enemy.

It might not cost us the war, but it would shake the nation to its very foundations.

"George … I'm so sorry," I said and then opened my arms. He stood to accept my embrace. "So very, very sorry," I continued, as I hugged him.

His question at Claridge's, about *Far from the Madding Crowd*, now made a great deal of sense. *Love, honour, and betrayal,* I'd replied—those were the themes of the story, and most probably the feelings running through my friend right at this moment. However, unlike Hardy's novel—played out in bucolic Victorian England—unless stopped, the Royal Family's story would be performed on a larger stage, in a world that was conflicted by war, where the costs could be catastrophic and perhaps affect millions of people.

I looked at my friend's face. I could see the pain in his eyes. Despite everything, he loved his brother. I couldn't help but put myself in his shoes. What would I have done, had Michael betrayed me in such a heartless, selfish, and callous manner? I'd have been devastated too. How could I say no to him? This whole affair was far bigger than Thomas Haupner and his cosy little life.

"You will do it?" he asked.

"Of course I'll do it—should you find there is no other way."

"My God, Thomas. I know what I'm asking, and I couldn't live with myself if anything happens to you. Let's just hope we can find some other solution."

"Let's hope, George. By God, let's hope so."

★★★★★

By the time we'd composed ourselves and returned to the party, several new arrivals had swelled the number of men inside. It was no surprise to find Flight Lieutenant Peter Farnsworth seated at the grand piano playing dance music, but it was a surprise to see my giant man dancing with his uncle.

I cut in.

"Evening, Colonel," I said to Steve, sliding into Shorty's arms.

"Evening yourself, Colonel," Steve replied. "Drink?"

"I need one—badly," I said.

"So how was your time with His Royal Highness?" Shorty asked.

"Interesting, Heinrich—he's a delightful person. Such a shame he wasn't next in line for the throne …"

"Hmm," he said, gently rubbing the small of my back as we danced.

"The word 'interesting', and using my real name, instead of Shorty, in the same sentence can only mean there's trouble brewing. I guess you aren't going to tell me what it was all about?"

I shook my head. "I can't—I want to, but I can't. Not until he gives me the go-ahead."

He squeezed my waist. "Man, I'm so lucky to have you, Tommy. Charm, good looks, talent, and integrity. What else could a fella wish for in his buddy?"

My man felt warm and mellow, he kissed me behind the ear.

"Hey, you're making me blush. Everyone will stare!"

"Too late, babe," he said, "everyone in the room is staring at you anyway—they all only have eyes for you."

"Shorty—"

He kissed me deeply as we danced. We were given a few cheerful wolf-whistles, a glare from his uncle, and a small round of applause from George.

It wasn't too long before we were dancing with other men, glancing at each other over the shoulders of newly made friends. I soon found myself in Steve's arms.

"You arrived late," I said, "and where's that drink you said you'd get for me?"

"Probably warm by now," he said, "and His Royal Highness entertains in shifts, didn't you know? He has special guests first and then the riff-raff later on."

The music suddenly changed.

"Ivor Novello is part of the riff-raff?" I nodded towards the famous British composer who'd clearly arrived while I was outside with the duke, and who'd replaced Peter at the piano. "Why are you so protective of Heinrich, Steve?" I asked. "You glared at us, don't deny it. You must know by now this isn't a fly-by-night type of thing between us. I care for him—I've never felt like this for anyone before."

Steve sighed. "I know you think I'm an overprotective fusspot, Tommy, but I made a promise to his mother to look after him."

"What, and you think I'm bad for him, or leading him astray?"

"No, wait. Keep your shirt on, Tommy! That's not what I mean.

I'm worried something will happen to you out there, and it will be me who'll have to pick up the pieces of what's left of him."

It felt as if I'd been slapped—I hadn't thought of it like that. However, what he'd said was based on an assumption—something would happen to me. I was hell-bent on making sure that nothing would.

"Steve, look around you. The room is full of guys who have made a commitment to each other, no matter how much or how little time they will have to enjoy it. It's what people do during a war. Lighten up a little will you, and cut us some slack? Be part of us, have fun with us, and enjoy the fact that I love him."

He snorted. "Does he know that?"

"Look at his face, Steve," I said, catching Shorty's eyes.

"But the words, Tommy?"

I looked at him very seriously as the music finished and I moved out of his arms.

"You'd think me a fool if I told you I'd said those three words already, Steve. It's far too soon yet. But there's something about him I can't put my finger on. What he and I have, well, it's like playing with a pair of magnets. Switch them around the right way, and if they're strong enough it's damned near impossible to pull them apart. I live, eat, breathe, sweat, and dream your nephew, Steve ... isn't that enough for the time being?"

*****

Shorty and I were a couple of the last to leave, both kissed goodnight on the cheek by George, who was very mellow by the time we left. I hadn't expected to be chauffeur-driven home, and it was a pleasant surprise not to have to traipse through the darkened streets with a load of booze under my belt.

That night, in bed, just before I drifted off to sleep, his head resting on my shoulder, and his gentle snoring telling me he'd already drifted off, I whispered quietly, merely to see what it felt like, "I love you, Heinrich ... I really think I do."

He snored back at me; but I knew, in the saying of the words, I really did.

CHAPTER 7

It was Sunday, the twenty-ninth of December, and Michael's and my twenty-ninth birthday.

I glanced at my wristwatch. It was quarter past seven. Shorty would be here soon. I wandered along the Embankment, listening to the sounds from the Thames while I waited for him. The sky was a tower of orange in the east and northeast—the German bombers were dropping incendiaries again. We'd long been afraid they'd try to create a fire storm, and with the river at very low tide tonight it seemed like the perfect opportunity for them—fire crews would have a hard time pumping enough water with the river so low and so far away from its normal high-tide mark.

This hadn't been my idea—a birthday party at the Savoy. But Shorty and Steve had organised it, and here we were. At home, the family tradition had always been that Michael and I perform for our parents and our family friends on our birthday. So, we'd found some time to practise together after Christmas while Shorty had been busy studying codes with the MI6 Cipher Division, conveniently located in St. Erwin's Hotel, not far from Whitehall.

He'd left to go to work at half past eight this morning, with a kiss on my cheek, making me promise I wouldn't eat too much lunch, to leave room for dinner. I'd kissed him back and crossed my heart, and then, hearing my front door close, leaned out of my living room window to watch him walk up the street. After that, I'd practised my scales for an hour or so, starting every scale a position up on the fingerboard if possible, to finely hone my finger placements close to the bridge. Eventually I'd stopped, sweat on my forehead, despite the cold of the flat, knowing I'd done as well as I possibly could and any more practice would have been futile. My day had flown past.

Now, later that evening, leaning on the Embankment wall, watching the glowing reflection of the conflagrations to the east on the river, I heard a familiar, very beautiful soft voice from someone who was moving up behind me, singing one of the latest hits, "When You Wish Upon a Star".

Before I could turn around, he'd run both his hands around my body and into the pockets of my trousers. I must admit I liked it a lot. I looked up above us into the night.

"Did you wish upon a star?" he asked softly.

"No stars tonight, Shorty."

"There are in my eyes, gorgeous."

"Looking for my lighter?" I asked, feeling his hands rummaging in my trouser pockets.

"Nope," he said in German, "merely minding my own business, singing a little song …"

"Then, what are you doing down—" My words were cut off as his hands found their target. It was very dark where we stood and no one could have seen us. Smothering a laugh, I turned around and kissed him. "You're a madman!" I said, switching to English. "Kissing a strange man and copping a feel in public, *and* speaking in German will not only get us in gaol, but probably in a *KZ*!"

"They have those here?"

My answer was stopped as he kissed me again, very passionately. "What's with you?" I asked, laughing into his eyes.

"It's all your fault."

"Glad to hear it," I said.

159

"It must be the moonlight."

"There is no damn moon either, Shorty." I rested my forehead against his. "How is it you're always so darned happy and ... what was it—horny?"

"Ha! Ask anyone at MI6. They think I'm Mr. Grumpy Boots. But I only need to look at you and I feel horny and happy at the same time."

"Aw. *Süß*." I licked the tip of his nose.

"Hey, babe, what's this?"

While rummaging in my pocket, he'd found my handkerchief, the one I'd used to blot his lip on the night I'd met him. "Nothing," I said. My reply sounded lame, even to me.

"You kept it," he said. The look in his eyes was ferocious in its intensity.

"It's for luck."

"Or another word starting with the same letter ...?"

"Laundry?"

He laughed, but ran his fingers through my hair, above my ear, and then pulled my face to his. The kiss was but a light touch of our lips. "Come on, let's go meet everyone." He took my hand and led me up the side lane of the Savoy, only letting it go when we reached the street outside the front door. "I'd forgotten how smashing you look in your tails," he said, after the doorman had taken our overcoats, and as we walked into the Savoy Grill.

"Smashing?" It was unlike him to use a British expression when he could make me smile at some new, as yet unheard, Yankee one.

"When in Rome ..."

Who'd have known it was wartime? The room was filled with smoke and people drinking cocktails, behaving as if it was 1928, before the crash, when everything had been hunky-dory, and all was right with the world.

Shorty looked wonderful, as usual, but not nearly as handsome as he did in the ADC dress uniform he'd worn on Christmas Eve at the embassy. He'd looked like Prince Charming that night in his dark blue cutaway coat, masses of cascading gold braid falling over his right shoulder. On that evening, I'd decided to wear my new, black, high-collared regimental mess dress, as it contrasted very well with my red and gold Order of Valour sash and medal. The medal was enormous and hung suspended under my campaign medals and bars.

But, tonight, for my birthday party, I wore my best set of tails.

"Well, well, what's this?"

I turned to see our host of the previous Monday, the Duke of Kent, arriving with a tall, slender man whose face, although exceedingly familiar, I couldn't place at the moment.

"Am I finally going to get to hear you play, Thomas? I thought it was a birthday celebration." He'd given a quick glance at my violin case.

"It's a family tradition, Your Royal Highness. At home, Michael and I have always had to perform on our birthday, to show how we've progressed over the previous year."

"Musically, that is," Shorty added, with unmistakable innuendo.

I kicked his shin. We both grinned stupidly.

"As you can see, George," I said, leaning in to speak privately, "despite the formality of the dress, my companion seems determined to be anything but."

The gentleman with the Duke of Kent, obviously having heard my aside, also leaned over and whispered, "Best keep your pants on tonight then, George."

The duke sighed and rolled his eyes, a little theatrically, but with great humour, before introducing his companion. "Heinrich Reiter, Thomas Haupner, may I present my cousin, Louis Mountbatten?"

We both shook hands, with the head-nod that had replaced the formal bow at the waist.

"I'm very pleased to meet you," he said, "and I'm so sorry to invade your private celebrations, but George was kind enough to invite me. I'm sailing first thing in the morning and he said a night out would do me good."

"You're back as Commander of the Fifth, on HMS *Kelly*, I believe, sir?" It was small talk, as I knew all about Lord Mountbatten. From the way he looked at Shorty and me, I gathered George had filled him in on a few details about us as well.

"I am indeed, Colonel. It's no great secret." His smile became genuine rather than "interested".

Over Mountbatten's shoulder, I caught a glimpse of another familiar face. My friend Thérèse was waiting patiently behind us. It was such a surprise to see her, as I'd expected her to still be away at her husband's seat for the Christmas season.

"Do you know Lady Tyrone, George?" I whispered.

"No, but I should jolly well like to," he whispered back. "I hear she throws the best parties."

"Then let me make sure you're always on the guest list."

Thérèse's curtsey was one of those that were rarely seen these days. She sank almost to the ground, her splendid royal-blue gown billowing around her like a drop of ink falling through a tall glass of water.

"Your Royal Highness," she murmured. George and his cousin were captivated, and within the space of a few minutes had accepted an invitation to her next soirée, at the end of January. We chatted for a short while, until Michael joined us and I introduced him.

The small ballroom, in which our other guests were waiting, and in which Michael and I were to perform, was crowded by the time we entered. I estimated nearly everyone we'd invited had turned up—there must have been at least seventy guests. I wasn't in the least surprised to see Peter Farnsworth again at the piano, placed on a low rostrum across the back of the room. The room shook gently, resonating to a distant roll of explosions.

"I think we may be in for it tonight," I whispered to Shorty as we stood in the doorway.

"Why do you say that?"

"They don't usually drop large explosives at the same time as incendiaries," I replied. "The incendiaries are meant to be markers for the following waves of bombers. They don't want anyone to put these flames out."

I had no stomach for food. The unusual pattern of the bombing had me worried. I did my best to circulate, trying to chat briefly with everyone in the room, finally sighing when I found Shorty and George in a quiet corner.

"Now you know what I have to go through," George said.

"I'm no stranger to working the floor, George—I'm unused to it, that's all."

"Well, we'll have to do something about that, won't we, Tommy?"

I was about to ask him what on earth he meant, when Shorty spoke. "George? You're allowed to call His Royal Highness, the Duke of Kent, by his first name?"

"In good time you may get to call me George, too, Heinrich. The scandal would be quite delicious—an American on first-name terms with the brother of the King? I bet Wallis would pee herself in anger. She only ever gets to call me 'sir', even *en famille*."

We both gaped. George had spoken in excellent, fluent German. How easy it was to forget his mother, Queen Mary, had been a Princess of Teck. Even though she'd been born in Kensington Palace, it was common knowledge she spoke German as effortlessly as she did English.

Before I could say anything further, Michael moved onto the rostrum. He clapped to gather everyone's attention and then spoke when the room had quietened.

"Your Royal Highness, lords, ladies, and gentlemen," he began, "welcome to a celebration of the birthday of my beloved brother and myself—two Australians, far from home, who are here in England to give our all to our Motherland."

There was a loud cheer and round of applause.

"Every year on our birthday, from a very early age, we dressed in our best and performed for our family and close friends. Except for a few years before the war, we kept up the tradition. Sadly, we missed last year too—Tommy was away on His Majesty's business in other parts of the country. However, tonight is something we've both been looking forward to. We don't get enough opportunity to perform together these days.

"At home, our concerts were always dedicated to our mother and father, and our uncle Otto. As they obviously can't be with us tonight, I'd like to play a little something in honour of the newest member of our 'overseas' family."

He bowed to the applause and then sat at the piano.

As he played the first bar of tremolos and then the sweeping arpeggios that followed, I recognised the piece immediately. It was Gottschalk's "Union Fantasy". Louis Moreau Gottschalk had written this virtuosic fantasy for piano in the 1860s, during the American Civil War.

My heart swelled. The dedication was for the man who stood beside me. I watched the tears form in Shorty's eyes when, after the introduction, Michael started to play the piece's first theme—"The Star-Spangled Banner". I couldn't possibly have loved my brother more at that moment. Not only was this piece one requiring great pianistic bravura, but it was about war and warriors, using traditional tunes of the Civil War in Shorty's and Steve's own country.

There was rapturous applause when he finished, and when pushed, he played his own paraphrase of "Waltzing Matilda" as an encore.

When it came to my turn, I followed my usual ritual while I spoke, unpacking my violin, wiping it over with a silk scarf, and then tuning it.

"It's always been a thankless task, having to play straight after my brother," I said. "However, having said that, there's always been healthy competition between us, to keep each other on our toes. So, thinking I might have got away with "Mary Had a Little Lamb" tonight, I now have to think seriously about what to play. Michael and I had prepared the Violin Sonata by Richard Strauss, but after hearing that, I've changed my mind."

Everyone laughed at Michael's loud groan as I produced a slim volume of music from my violin case. "Michael may never speak to me again after this, as he hasn't played it in nearly ten years."

My brother took the folio from me and pretended to hit me over the head with it. "I need to tell you before we start this," he announced, "there are very few violin players I know of who'd either be able to or be brave enough to play this piece ad hoc, in the impromptu way he seems compelled to. Tommy's famous for being way too modest about his playing—I'll let the results speak for themselves. He's one of the very few people who really does hide his light underneath his blond bushel."

It was with no small amount of excitement I announced what I'd decided to play. "Thank you, Michael. This 'blond bushel' would like to play for you the third movement of the Paganini Violin Concerto, no. 2, in B minor—'La Campanella'."

There was an audible gasp from Thérèse, and not a few sounds of surprise from others in the room. The duke actually looked startled— he obviously knew the work. This made me incredibly nervous for a moment. But once I lifted my bow and placed it on my violin strings, all thoughts of nervousness fled. It had always been the same—with my instrument in my hands, I was its master. Nothing and no one had been able to make me feel otherwise.

The first section, with its Italian tarantella, was relatively easy, despite its multitude of acciaccaturas. It wasn't until I'd finished the first bow jetés that I really relaxed into the work and started to enjoy playing. For me, it was always those particular bow strokes that predicted the quality of my rendition of the rest of the piece. If they were clear, then somehow I knew the rest of the work would go well. It was a tour-de-force piece, but when I'd practised enough, was well within my technique. Once I got to the awkward double-stopping later in the work, I began to show off. Michael's confident accompaniment pushed me to play as well as I possibly could. The piece was quite difficult, but not the hardest in the repertoire—it was one of those works that sounded harder than it actually was.

Gradually, I became aware I'd begun to invest "love" into the sound of my playing. It was a special sound, one that came from the heart, and which fed into my fingers, carrying me into another world and on to another, higher level of performance. It was something I hadn't experienced more than two or three times since leaving Germany. Perhaps it had reappeared tonight because of the new feelings I had, now Shorty had come into my life.

Despite myself, I glanced into the room and saw my beautiful man, his mouth open and his eyes glistening as he journeyed with me through Paganini's fantastical opus.

As I got close to the end of the piece, I closed my eyes to concentrate— it was technically quite tricky. However, the last few bars were a wonderful relief, written beautifully, allowing the violinist to coast to the end after a nine-minute rollercoaster ride of technical exertion. After the last chord, I lifted my bow from my violin with a large, showy flourish, feeling my very soul overflowing with the joy of completion and achievement.

I didn't hear the applause, because at the very moment I dropped my instrument from my shoulder, Michael leaped from the piano seat and engulfed me, hugging me tight and kissing my ear. I knew I'd played it better than ever before. Perhaps it was the occasion? Or perhaps it was the presence of the tall, almost-blond man furiously clapping his hands off at the back of the room.

Michael finally released me and I was able to take his hand to bow, while our small audience continued to thunder out their applause and stamp their feet. I even heard a loud American whistle.

Eventually, Steve bounded onto the rostrum with us and held up his hands for silence. When the room had quietened, he said, "How can the Nazis win with a pair like this to beat?" This caused another round of clapping. "But we do have another musical treat this evening, and this time not from one of the birthday boys." He gestured into the audience, and to my surprise both Shorty and the Duke of Kent came onto the platform, shooing Michael and me down onto the floor with the rest of our guests.

"Good evening, everyone," the duke said. "Before tonight, I'd heard these two soldiers could play 'a little', therefore, you can imagine my surprise at what we've just heard. I've only recently met Michael, so forgive me if I'm sparing in my praise of anything but his wonderful piano-playing. This other rascal I do know somewhat better." He pointed to the star of my Medal of Valour. "I find it rather sad one doesn't get a medal like that for playing the violin. If it were the case, we might have had to drag him here this evening with a very large magnet."

Michael put his arm around my shoulders and kissed the side of my head while I packed up my instrument.

"I'm sure most of you here will already know Heinrich Reiter, also known to one person in this room as 'Shorty'."

Everyone laughed at the absurdity of this nickname, apart from me. I had a curious presentiment.

"Although I do not have the piano skills of the younger Mr. Haupner, the late king, my father, was insistent his children have a sound musical upbringing. So, when I say I can play 'a little', you'd better believe me."

He sat at the piano.

Shorty retrieved a microphone from the side of the rostrum. "I feel whatever thanks I should offer this evening should be not only for the magnificent music we have heard tonight, but also to thank whoever up there gave us these two wonderful young men."

Michael's arm slipped around my waist at the same time I felt Steve arrive at my side. As the duke put his fingers to the keyboard to begin a series of arpeggios, I saw Gladys at the corner of the room—she blew a kiss to me.

Shorty began to sing in his beautiful, clear voice, and, as he did, my heart started to pound in my chest. I knew this song: "All the Things You Are".

At the end of the verse, Jerome Kern had written three slow chords that modulated to the new key of the chorus. On these chords, Shorty gradually turned his head and sang straight into my eyes. The words of the song were about promise turned into fulfilment—things longed for in the soul, and which were then realised. As he sang, I found my heart clenching.

I stood like a huge galah for what seemed an eternity, staring back into his eyes as he continually caught mine between bows. The impact of what he'd sung and to whom he'd sung it couldn't have been clearer. I'd been serenaded by a Yank and a duke, one of whom had publicly told half of London he was in love with me.

"Out on the balcony! I'll send him to join you." Steve grabbed my arm and pushed me through double doors at the end of the room and onto an outside balcony.

I leaned against the wall of the Savoy, watching the searchlights in the east, their beams accentuated by flashes of exploding bombs. The distant sound of ack-acks matched the pounding of my heart.

I heard the door open and then smelled him standing next to me. "I'd have punched me out," he said quietly.

"There's still time."

"Suppose sorry isn't enough?"

"Nope," I replied.

"What then?"

I said nothing for a moment, and then, "So, you remembered?" It was part of our conversation in the hallway outside Thérèse's apartment, on the night we'd first met.

"Line for line," he said. He passed me a cigarette and then leaned in, with his cigarette in his mouth, to light them both. There was no way I could avoid looking into his eyes. He reached up with one hand and caressed the side of my mouth with his thumb. "Do I get to sock you now?"

I nodded. He kissed me hard and deep instead. "Heinrich Reiter, what the hell am I going to do now?"

"As compared to when?"

"It seems we're an 'us' …"

"Seems like it, Aussie. Tommy, I—"

I put my finger up to close his lips and then rested my head against his chest. At that moment, I couldn't help but think about the task George had asked me to undertake for him in France.

"Tommy, what I said in there, or rather, what I sang in there … I meant it, you know."

"I know, Shorty," I said, "I know." I was about to say more when George and his cousin came bursting through the door.

"I'm so sorry to interrupt," George said. "I'm still somewhat in shock over what I heard inside from *both* of you."

I started to say he was too kind, but he interrupted me. "I know this is terribly bad timing, and I'm sorry, but I've just been informed the Guildhall and St. Paul's have been hit—the Germans are mass-bombing with incendiaries, and a second wave has been spotted by radar. Mountbatten and I must go. I do apologise, but I have duties I must attend to. I'll be in touch."

There was a sudden loud explosion not far away and we four looked to the east. Although the skyline was obscured by other buildings, we could see the entire eastern part of the city was glowing in red and yellow. George grabbed me in a hug and then left, turning as he got to the door to wish me happy birthday and congratulate me on my playing.

"Should we join our friends?" I asked Shorty, as I leaned my head against his shoulder.

"Finished blushing yet?" he asked.

"Oh, I'm sure there is going to be plenty more this evening," I replied. "The night is still young."

He laughed, deep in his throat. "I like it when you call me Shorty," he murmured.

"I like it when you call me Tommy," I said.

"But that's your name," he said, puzzled.

"It's something else altogether when you say it, Yankee," I explained.

He kissed my forehead and then took me by the hand, leading me to the doors that led back inside.

"That's because it means something else to me too, my friend," he said, as he opened them and gestured for me to return to the noise and the light.

CHAPTER 8

It was past ten o'clock by the time the management of the Savoy told us it would be wise to find shelter—another wave of aircraft had been spotted on the coast, heading towards the capital.

The bombing had become sporadic, more like stragglers dropping and running than carpet-bombing. Some of the hits had sounded quite near, and although the Savoy hadn't taken any damage, there'd been a few stray bombs in the Strand, to its west.

When we stepped out into the street, I noticed a few buses still seemed to be running. During raids it was up to the individual driver's discretion whether to continue to service his bus route or not. But, as there were no buses from Aldwych to Oxford Street tonight, and my house was perhaps not quite a mile away, we decided to walk.

There was not only a lot of smoke in the air but also gritty, dense fog, making it hard to see more than about twenty yards in any direction. As we reached the corner of Drury Lane, I heard a muffled "pop, pop, pop". Incendiaries were raining down on the street ahead of us. It sounded like they'd fallen near the corner of Kingsway—the dull, metallic sound as they hit the ground was unmistakeable. Incendiary bombs looked more like long tubes than high-explosive bombs. Once triggered, they flared up into a brightly burning, hot, greenish-white flame that ignited everything flammable it touched.

Instinctively, we both crouched close to the ground, in one swift motion pulling our overcoat collars up around our ears and folding the lapels over our mouths. It was done in a trice—every military man did it by instinct these days.

"Come on, big fella," I said to Shorty, "let's see if we can't do something about those."

He took off like a rabbit, disappearing into the fog ahead of us towards the blurred patches of flame glowing through the haze.

I found him pulling down sandbags from the façade of the Aldwych Theatre. Its walls were piled high with them. I looked around for somewhere to put my violin—behind a head-high stack of sandbags that half-covered the doors into the theatre vestibule looked safest—and then began to haul bags down from the top of another pile. We started to run a relay, heaving a sandbag on top of each of the incendiaries we could find.

After about the fourth trip to the front of the theatre, someone called out. A young copper appeared out of the smoke, fumbling with his whistle, his face streaked with black, and his helmet askew. The white cotton face protector underneath his gas mask was blackened with smoke and grime; it hung loosely around his neck. "Oi! What the fuck are you two up to?" he yelled, and then, noticing my medals under my gaping overcoat, apologised for his coarse language.

"We were on our way for tea with the King, but decided to have a go at the bloody incendiaries instead." I knew I was being cheeky, but somehow knew he'd laugh. "Give us a hand, copper," I added.

"Sorry, sir," he said. "Thought you was a pair of looters. It's a bastard of a thing when you can't see squat in the fucking dark."

Ten minutes or so later, after we'd smothered the last of the incendiaries we could find, I retrieved my violin and, with a satisfied sigh, plonked myself down between Shorty and the young man on the edge of the pile of sandbags outside the theatre. Both of them offered me a cigarette at the same time.

"Tommy," I said, offering the policeman my hand.

171

"Alfred—Alfred Heath. First night on the fucking job and I get a load of fucking incendiaries."

Under the grime, he couldn't have been more than about eighteen. "Wanted so bad to join up and see some action," he said. "Would have, but for bad fucking eyes." He pulled his glasses out of his jacket pocket and held them up. One lens was shattered and one earpiece entirely gone. "Trod on the fuckers," he added, by way of explanation.

"I can hear you love to swear, Al-fucking-fred," I said, causing us all to hoot with laughter.

Shorty nudged my knee. Apart from private, spectacular bursts of profanity with my brother, I didn't normally use coarse language. As an Australian in London, I knew it was expected my turn of phrase would naturally be colourful. Weeding out swear words, except in select company, was something I'd worked hard to change—mostly to deny those who expected it the pleasure of confirming their preconceptions.

"Sorry, your highness," Alfred said, glancing at my ribbon bars, "misspent youth. Anyway, as well as being beat policeman here, I'm also the air-raid warden, and I suggest you two gentlemen get your arses into a shelter."

As if to reinforce his words, the long, loud whistle of a falling bomb, followed by a nearby explosion, told us the stragglers were still dropping high-explosives from four miles above us.

"Very well, Constable, which way?" I had no idea where the nearest shelter might be.

"Either Lincoln's Inn Fields or Covent Garden?" he suggested. "Take your pick. Both are fairly close."

From the throbbing drone of bombers, I knew another wave of planes was passing overhead. If anyone were to ask me, I'd have said incendiaries were far scarier than bombs. I'd rather be torn into a thousand fragments in a fraction of a second than be covered in phosphorus and die, screaming in agony.

"Covent Garden," I said, thinking it was marginally closer. "What do you reckon, Shorty?"

"Shorty?" Our companion asked, with a grin, looking up at the man who loomed a good twelve inches over the top of his head.

172

"Righty-ho, this way to Covent Garden tube station, chaps, follow me!"
He took off up the street with us hard on his heels.

Public bomb shelters were scattered everywhere over London, but
you could never know exactly where they were unless you knew the
area well, or could see the signs in the blackout. Some bright spark in
the Ministry had decided, for the oddest of reasons, to place a white "S"
on a black, enamelled sign. Barely two feet high and sixteen inches wide,
they were next to impossible to see in the dark, especially when the
streets were thick with smoke or fog and the signs were smeared with
grime and soot.

We'd barely got as far as the corner of Floral Street when I heard a
loud whistle from above. It was going to be close—too close. We
jumped into the nearest doorway and squatted on our haunches,
wrapping our arms around each other.

The whistling sound stopped ... it was then my stomach turned to
ice and I squeezed Shorty protectively. It had been drilled into us that if
the whistling seemed to stop before the bomb hit the ground, then it
was almost on top of you.

There was an enormous explosion and we were flung against the
stout wooden door of the shop entrance in which we'd crouched.
Fortunately, the bomb must have landed a little south of our doorway,
so the majority of the shrapnel shredded through shopfronts and
buildings around us, but missed our little niche.

"Damn! My violin!" I cursed softly. I'd dropped it when we'd dived
into the doorway and couldn't see it through the cloud of ash, smoke,
and dust billowing thickly around us.

Bricks and dust rained down outside, and I was about to ask Shorty
if he was hurt, when I heard another bomb whistling above our heads.
The whistle was louder—it meant the bomb would be even closer.

The blast was so violent it threw the three of us through the
remains of the heavy wooden door we'd huddled against.

Most people thought bomb explosions would be like punches—
until they felt one. The shock wave pummelled your guts from the
inside. The blast wave could rip the clothes from your back, the hair
from your head, and even the shoes and socks from your feet. However,

it was the stinging behind your forehead that was the worst—it felt the same as falling backwards and hitting the back of your head hard on the ground. There was no other description for it—it was an acid, electric, burning sensation that centred over the bridge of your nose.

The world went black, although only for a moment. I could hear Shorty calling my name, but faintly, as my ears were ringing loudly. Flames were rising behind him, burning fiercely in the wreckage. The panic on his face subsided after I blinked a few times and then smiled at him. We were both alive.

The person clinging to my back unfolded awkwardly, stood up, and then helped us to our feet. "Everyone all right?" the young bobby asked, using hand gestures. His mouth was moving, but the sound of his words was too indistinct to make out what he'd actually said.

A sudden crash and an avalanche of bricks and plaster dust behind us made Shorty grab us both by the arms and drag us out of the building. Once in the street, carefully protecting my face with my forearm, I turned and looked up, to see what had happened. The façade of the building above us was three-quarters gone.

The young constable opened his mouth and shouted something. I didn't have time to react, for he grabbed the back of my coat and pulled me towards him. I tripped and fell on my arse, just as another landslide of burning beams and broken bricks hurtled down into the space in which we'd been standing but a moment before. Had we not moved when we did, we would have been crushed by the collapse of the building above us. Alfred had most probably saved our lives.

As I raised myself up on my elbows, my hands slid through slivers of lacquered wood and twisted, thin wires. My violin and its case were a tortured mess of matchsticks. A square block, made up of half-a-dozen bricks, had smashed it to pieces. A curious lump of marble was leaning against the clump of bricks, not far from my head—it was the top three-quarters of a life-sized statue of Queen Victoria, which had also plummeted down from somewhere above us.

There was no point lamenting, or trying to retrieve the pieces. My instrument was beyond repair. I sighed and ran my fingers through the fragments.

Shorty squatted next to me, his face pained. He, too, recognised the pieces for what they were. Over his shoulder, Alfred was stumbling about, pulling at his earlobe, trying to clear his ear. They were both nigh on unrecognisable, faces and hair black, thickly coated with soot and dust. The bobby had lost his helmet.

"You okay, Tommy?" Shorty yelled into my ear, his mouth right up against my head. "Your violin ..."

I smiled, to tell him I was fine. I mimed playing my violin while making a sad face. I could see the sympathetic pain in his eyes. I shrugged. It could have been one of us, not a replaceable musical instrument. But, there was something that did have me worried—I pointed to my right arm.

The sleeve of my greatcoat was in tatters and my arm was numb. I ran my left hand over it, checking to see if anything was broken. I nearly cried with relief when I flexed my hand and my fingers rippled easily, responding as they always did. Shorty pulled me to my feet and then pushed up what was left of the sleeve of my overcoat, carefully removing the cufflink from the shirt to check my forearm. The cuff was no longer white. It was red with blood.

After a quick inspection, he patted my shoulder and gave me a thumbs up. I interpreted it as a sign that it wasn't too bad. His lopsided grin was meant to reassure me, but it couldn't hide his concern over our situation.

It had been drilled into us to stay put for a few minutes if it wasn't dangerous and if there were fires close by. The updraught from burning buildings cleared the air of dust and smoke—made it less treacherous when trying to find shelter. The light from the burning shopfront opposite began to reveal the wider extent of the wreckage around us. I turned my arm into the light. There were a few long lacerations along my forearm—they didn't gape when I pried at them with my fingers, so I assumed they were only shallow cuts. But, when I stood and then dropped my arm to my side, I could feel blood dripping down over my fingers. Thank God my hands were all right, I said to myself for a second time in as many minutes.

Alfred appeared at Shorty's side, clutched his shoulder, and then said something I couldn't quite work out. He put his whistle to his mouth as if to blow it, but then suddenly fell in a heap at our feet. We both scrambled onto our knees at his side. The young policeman's mouth was moving, but I couldn't hear what he was saying. His words were indistinct and jumbled. I pointed at my ears and shook my head to indicate I couldn't understand what he was trying to tell me. He reached around to the back of his head and showed me his palm—it was covered in blood.

I nearly jumped out of my skin when I gently ran my hand around the back of his head—it felt spongy. I couldn't understand why he was still conscious, or able to talk. He must have really banged his head hard when we were blown about by the explosion.

Shorty grabbed my hand and then, using simple hand signs, indicated I should let him see what could be done. Through the ringing in my ears, I started to hear loud cracking sounds above us—it was the sound of exploding window panes. He helped Alfred to his feet and then yelled, "Fireman's chair," close to my ear—we called it an "arm carry", but I knew what he meant. We were about to link arms when Alfred started writhing—not gently, but in spasmodic violent jerks, as if he was fitting. I guessed Shorty recognised this was something extremely serious, because he quickly gathered the young man into his arms and lurched off towards the tube station, jumping over burning debris and piles of rubble. I held my breath as I ran after them, dodging bricks and pieces of masonry, which continued to thud down sporadically and without warning around us.

He carefully put the constable down when we got inside the ticket office vestibule. The station entrance was undamaged, as was the brown-arched building above it.

"Will you be all right with him?" I shouted. "I'll run down to the platform and see if there's a doctor or an ambulance worker down there."

Shorty didn't reply for a moment. Alfred had stopped fitting. I knew it couldn't be a good sign.

"I pissed myself," Shorty eventually said and then laughed quietly, despite the seriousness of our situation. A dark wet patch spread over his thighs and down one leg. Shock did strange things to us all. Dignity was one of the first things to go in war, and humour the first to revive.

"If it really bothers you, rub a handful of dust into it and over the rest of your pants, no one will be any the wiser—it could be so much worse, Shorty."

His laugh stopped abruptly. He knew I meant blood. He pressed his forehead against mine and whispered, "Be quick! I'll look after him."

I ran down the darkened circular stairwell, "Anybody there? Hello?" I called out into the gloom, my words echoing back at me. When I was about halfway down, a faint voice answered, so I jumped down the stairs three at a time, using the handrail to steady myself, until I nearly knocked over a pair of bobbies and an air-raid warden who must have heard my yelling, and were coming up in my direction.

"One of yours up top," I said, "and it doesn't look good."

"I'll get Ethel," the warden said, before disappearing once more down the stairs in the direction of the station platform.

The two policemen hurtled up the stairway in front of me. When we emerged at the top, the young man was still lying on the floor of the ticket office, where I'd left him with Shorty a few minutes before. I knew instantly Alfred was dead. I recognised that special stillness—I'd seen it so many times in the war in Spain. Shorty was on one knee, holding one of the bobby's hands, his head raised to us, shaking it slowly. "Too late, I'm afraid," he said.

"Jesus Christ, it's Alfie," one of the policemen said and then fell to his knees.

At that moment, another bomb whistle was quickly followed by a nearby, deafening explosion, which drove thick, choking clouds of dust through the half-opened grille of the station entrance, engulfing us all, and once more plunging us into utter darkness. In the silence that followed, all I could hear, over the occasional thud of falling bricks, was the sobbing of the policeman. As the dust cleared a bit, I saw him, illuminated by the flames from outside, spread over Alfred's body, as if protecting him.

After a while, the other policeman said to me, "It's his boy."

Not long after, I heard more voices on the stairway. The air-raid warden had returned with a large, florid-faced woman in a make-do nurse's uniform. The startled look on her face told me she'd assessed the situation quickly. There was nothing to be done for Alfred, so she made a beeline for me. "I'm Ethel," she said. "I'm a Friends Ambulance Unit worker." Quakers worked as medical aides in most shelters during a raid.

She'd barely asked Shorty whether he was injured too when firemen began to arrive. A few of them were calling out to see if anyone might be trapped in the buildings around the tube entrance. One of them covered Alfred's body with a blanket, while another led his father to one side. The man took a mug of hot tea from a smartly uniformed but harried-looking young woman, who patted his shoulder, and then left him to see what else she could do.

Funny, I thought, that in the middle of carnage the first thing to arrive after the firemen and rescue workers was the tea van.

"I'm sorry I dragged you up those stairs for nothing," I said to the woman who'd laboured up the stairway. She still hadn't caught her breath. "I didn't know the ambulance people would be here so soon."

She was rummaging in her first-aid bag and had managed to find her torch. "That's all right, ducks," she said, patting my hand. "Don't you worry about me. There's always plenty to do in a raid. Let's have a look at you, sweetheart."

"I think I'm all right," I said. "Most of the blood on my hands is his." I nodded at Alfred's body. "But, I'd be grateful if you could have a quick squiz at this." I showed her my arm.

She smiled at my slang, but pulled out her torch, pushed up my sleeve, and then gave it a once-over.

"Just a scratch, you'll be fine, my love." She smiled at me, her gaze on Alfred's father. "Charlie?" she yelled to an ambulance man who'd arrived with a stretcher strapped to his back. "Have a look at this gentleman's arm; there's a dear."

She bustled off to other business, so I sat on the ground next to Shorty, who already had a blanket around his shoulders and who was sipping a mug of tea.

"Squiz?" he asked.

"Take a gander," I explained. "Care to share your cuppa?"

He looked up from his mug. On his face was written the awful awareness that it could have been one of us lying under the blanket not far from where we sat.

"Fucking war!" I muttered, not quietly enough, my head still ringing.

"There, there, darling," Ethel said. I hadn't noticed, but she'd returned with a mug of tea for me. She patted my head absentmindedly. "But, you're right—war is a bitch!"

I smiled at that word, coming from this Quaker woman. She seemed to be, at that moment, the epitome of what I imagined the famous British "spirit" to be. She was all smiles, worrying about Shorty and me—two blackened foreigners squatting in the rubble and ruins of her city—while still not having repeated a single endearment as she bustled around, seeing to everyone's needs.

I leaned closer to Shorty, my hip touching his, as a fireman tucked a blanket around my shoulders. "That's why the Nazis will never win the war," I said, indicating Ethel with a toss of my head.

The fireman snickered. "Churchill should send our Ethel in with her rolling pin. That'd sort out Hitler and his cronies in five minutes!"

He shook my shoulder as we laughed, and then he disappeared with a bright, "Cheerio!"

To our surprise, not long before midnight, the all-clear siren sounded. What had happened to the third wave? I wondered. The Nazis' usual bombing strategy was to send in a first wave, primarily to start fires, and then to follow it up with a second wave, which used those fires as their target for further intensive bombing. The two waves of bombers would follow each other back to France to refuel, and then come back for a third run, to add maximum damage to those areas already hit, plus the added "bonus" of killing firefighters and rescue crews.

Just after the siren sounded, I found Shorty a little way down the street, sitting on what I'd assumed was a large box. It was only when I got closer I realised it was a harmonium, fallen from someone's flat, lying on its face on the street. I sat on it, next to him.

"It's an organ," I said. "Reminds me of weddings in small churches in the outback."

He began to sing softly:

"Oh promise me that someday you and I,
Will take our love together to some sky …"

His voice petered-out, breaking on the last word. He shook his head and then wiped away a small portion of the grime next to his mouth with his thumb.

"Do go on, darls," a voice said from behind us. Ethel had appeared out of the gloom, followed by a few of the firemen. She was carrying a tray with mugs of tea. "You sound so lovely in the middle of all this." She glanced around at the devastation that surrounded us.

He took a sip from the mug she'd given him and then cleared his throat and continued the song from where he'd stopped.

"… Where we may be alone and faith renew,
And find the hollows where those flowers grew.
Those first sweet violets of early spring
Which come in whispers, thrill us both, and sing
Of love unspeakable that is to be;
Oh, promise me! Oh, promise me!

"Oh, promise me that you will take my hand,
The most unworthy in this lonely land,
And let me sit beside you in your eyes,
Seeing the vision of our paradise …"

"I'm sorry, I can't go on."

He stopped singing. I'd heard the lump in his throat for some time, wondering how long he'd last before the tears started. It was very emotive—singing about violets and spring, while we sat on a ruined harmonium in blackened, smoking ruins and piles of shattered masonry and broken bricks.

His soft, hesitant song was rewarded by a light smattering of applause and back thumping.

"No matter what they do," Ethel said, her voice thick with emotion, "whether we're here to see it or not, there will still be violets in the spring somewhere. Even they can't stop that."

We finished our tea, asking if there was anything more to be done—if we could help in any way. We were answered by good-humoured men and women asking Shorty to get his fellow Yanks to join the fray—to bring American bombers over to help win the day, like they did in the last war, by repaying Schicklgruber with some of his own medicine. We were told to go home and thanked profusely for our help. "I never knew you toffs could grub in like what you did," one fireman said, shaking my hand with an admiring grin.

"What did he say?" Shorty asked, after the man had left us. I smiled and then explained to him in French, guessing that German wouldn't be the best choice at that particular moment.

"He thinks I was born with a silver spoon in my mouth?" he exclaimed.

"Well, you're wearing ... or rather, were wearing, your best tail suit," I said, grinning at him. "Although I rather think you look like the dustman right now." He was blackened from head to foot, his clothes tattered, and his beautiful patent-leather shoes slashed and ruined.

We gave our victory signs and then took off our overcoats to drape them over the shoulders of two young women, dressed only in their nightclothes, who'd been pulled out of a destroyed terraced house just up the street from the tube station. The firemen had run out of blankets and we'd already used the ones we'd been given to cover two bodies, among the dozen or so now lined up along the wall of the ticket office. The two women thanked us and we comforted them for a few minutes, deciding we should head for home to see whether my house was still standing, or if it was only another crater in the ground like so many around us.

Just before we left, Shorty squatted down next to Alfred's dad. He explained he was at the American embassy and asked whether there was anything he could do. Alfred's father told us to call around and have a cup of tea with him and "the missus", giving Shorty the address in Paddington.

We both nodded and said we would call in to check on them.

"Tommy?" he asked, not more than a minute after we left the tube station entrance.

"Yes, Shorty?"

"What's a dustman?"

"I think what you Yanks call it is a trash-collector," I said.

He smiled, looked down at his ruined suit, and then laughed—finally squatting down to guffaw. It was a release of tension. I couldn't help joining in, despite the fact it wasn't really funny at all. We ended up leaning against a wooden hoarding that covered a shopfront, with tears in our eyes, holding our sides.

"Come on, you," I said. "My arm hurts, and I ache all over, and I need to have a tub."

"Have a tub?"

"Oh, for God's sake …"

I was stopped mid-sentence by the sound of pounding footsteps coming closer. It was Alfred's father. The man grabbed Shorty's hand fiercely, threw his arms around him and sobbed.

I had to turn away when I heard him say, "Thank you for not leaving him there to burn! Thank you, son, thank you. God bless you!"

*****

It took us the best part of an hour to get back to Coptic Street. Neal Street had been relatively clear, but when we reached Shorts Gardens, we were sent on a detour up Endell Street and into High Holborn. The corner of Grape Street was unrecognisable. My heart was heavy in my chest when we finally turned out of Oxford Street and into Coptic Street. I breathed a sigh of relief as we turned the corner and I saw my house was still there.

The local beat policemen had been waving traffic onto the other side of Oxford Street and told me a bomb had hit in Streatham Street, just around the corner from where I lived. Mrs. Margolis, the local midwife, had gone to visit her sister in Manchester for Christmas. She'd return to find her house, and those of her neighbours on either side, piles of rubble.

We stood at my front door for a moment, looking across the road. There was a ragged gap at the upper corner of the factory opposite and a pile of bricks on the footpath. "I bet all my crockery is broken …" I started to say and then slowly shook my head. It was a stupid thought, worrying about plates and cups after what we'd been through.

"I was singing for you, you know," Shorty said, leaning against the wall while I fumbled for my keys.

"I know you were, sweetheart. That makes it twice tonight." I knew he meant the Jerome Kern at the Savoy, as well as the song he'd sung while we'd been sitting on the harmonium. I put my key in the lock and said, "So much for another year older."

He gently rubbed my bum.

Opening the front door, I said to him, "Don't go upstairs before taking your pants off, handsome." He reeked of piss.

He took them off once I'd closed the door, but stopped when we got up to the first landing. "You haven't carried me over the threshold, even after I sang you a wedding song." He was only half-joking, I knew it. He tried to disguise it with his "little kid" voice, the one that made me feel very warm inside. I grabbed his hand and pulled him back downstairs to the short corridor inside the front door. We laughed like a couple of ten-year-olds. I picked him up and carried him in my arms up the stairs to my living room. My cut forearm hurt like a bitch, but I was so overcome with emotion I barely noticed it.

"Let me down," he murmured in my ear as we stood in the middle of the living room. I shook my head. "Tommy, we could have died …"

"But we didn't," I said. I knew what he'd been going to say, even before he'd said it. "I'm not going anywhere without you," I said, kissing his cheek.

He laughed.

"What?" I asked.

"You have black lips now."

I gave him a serious, tender kiss, in reaction to which he pretend-spluttered and wiped his mouth on the sleeve of his jacket. I put him down then, finally, and pulled him into my arms. "If we'd died tonight, Shorty, I'd only have one regret."

"What's that?" he asked, his voice muffled in the shoulder of my jacket.

"That I didn't get to tell you I loved you." He stood quite still for an inordinate length of time, holding me so tightly I could feel the constant clench and release of his chest as he fought the urge to say something.

"You didn't need to, Tommy. I know you do," he eventually said. His voice was choked.

"Shut up, you fool," I said, gently pushing him into a foxtrot.

"You are certifiable." His laugh was soft and tender.

"No fool like a fool in love."

I led him around the room for a moment, humming "You Do Something to Me".

*****

There wasn't enough length in the average English bathtub, I realised, for two six-foot-something men to lie down in it together.

But we tried. I found myself lying in the bath, my head hitting the back of the tub, while my feet were under the running showerhead. My freshly bandaged arm rested on the edge of the bath, and Shorty lay beside me, gently trying to get the worst of the grime off with a soapy flannel. I could feel his heart pounding against my chest and knew he was upset. It was obvious what he'd been thinking about.

"But we didn't," I whispered, answering his unspoken thoughts.

"I know, but we could have …"

I tried to make light of the situation, but remembered the sight of my violin smashed into tiny fragments under that gleaming white statue, which could easily have hit either of us. I started to chuckle.

"What?" he asked, after kissing my chin.

"Queen Victoria killed my violin."

We both laughed so hard I couldn't get my breath for several moments.

"Tommy?"

"Yes?"

"I want it," he said, his voice quiet and serious. "What you said before. The you and me thing … I want it. Seriously. I'm not joking—"

I kissed him and then pressed the side of my face to his. "I told your uncle the other night I felt you and I were like a pair of the strongest possible magnets."

"Meaning?"

"Meaning, no one can pull us apart, Shorty. It's forever as far as I'm concerned."

"Damn you, Tommy Haupner …"

Much later on, as we lay in bed, his head in its usual place on my shoulder, my arm around him, I thought back on the whole evening: the concert, his singing to me, the bombs, Alfred … but mostly the look of wonder on his face when I'd held him in my arms when we'd finally got back home and told him I loved him.

*****

In the morning, I untangled myself from his arms and went downstairs to put the kettle on.

"Good morning," I said from the doorway a few minutes later, a steaming cup of tea in each hand. He sat up in bed and we both stared at each other. His chest and right arm and shoulder were blue with bruises. I must have looked equally as bad.

"Damn, Tommy … you look like you got hit by a combine-harvester!"

"Pull the cover back," I said, putting our cups down on the bedside table. He wasn't as bruised as me on the lower body, but I pushed him over on his side to look at his back. "Don't you hurt? Your back is bruised all over," I asked, running a finger down his spine.

He nodded. "I ache, but I thought it was from what you put me through last night in the bathtub."

"What *I* put *you* through? That'll be the day!"

He kissed the tip of my nose. "We should get checked over. We can call in at the embassy on our way. If Dr. Harper is on duty, he can have a look at us, and then, after that, I think we should call in to see how that young copper's folks are doing."

I jumped into bed and snuggled up behind him, drawing the coverlet over us both. He handed me my cup from the bedside table. "You know, I feel very sore and stiff, now I come to think of it," I said.

"Now, the stiffness I can help you with."

Our tea was about to be forgotten, either that or spilled over the bed, when there was a loud, persistent knocking on the front door. I groaned. "If that's the gas warden to tell me they're turning the gas off, I may well be on the point of committing my first civilian murder!"

The banging got more demanding as I stumbled down the stairs, while throwing on my dressing gown.

Steve nearly knocked me over as I opened the door. His face was white. "Thank Christ you're all right," he yelled, pulling me to him and holding me fiercely. "Did you know your phone is out?" He pulled my dressing gown open, despite my protests. After all, we were standing in the street and I was naked under it. "Jesus Christ, Tommy, you're black and blue!"

Dragging my dressing gown closed, to cover myself, I noticed Michael standing behind him, holding up our overcoats, one in each hand, with a grin on his face.

"Someone found a letter addressed to Henry at the embassy inside the pocket of his coat. It was dug out of a pile of rubble, along with yours, when they were cleaning up the rubble of a building that collapsed over the entrance to Covent-fucking-Garden tube station this morning," Steve yelled at me.

He was pretty upset, I could tell.

"Get inside, up the stairs, you two," I ordered. "It's bloody freezing out here and you're letting all the warm air out."

"Actually, Tommy, hot air rises, so it's unlikely—"

I shut up Michael with a look. I'd seen the worry and then the relief on his face when I'd opened the door.

A building had collapsed over the entrance to the tube? I thought of Ethel and the others, still hard at work when we'd left them last night.

"The police rang about thirty minutes ago saying they'd found the coats. Jesus, I was frantic with worry. Just as well your brother was already at work. I don't know what the hell I'd have done if I wasn't able to get hold of him! Tommy, they're still pulling bodies out from around the area, you know. Please tell me Henry is okay …"

"We're all right, Steve. A bit bruised, that's all," Shorty called out. He'd heard the voices and was already in the kitchen by the time we reached the top of the stairs. He was filling up the Moka pot, preparing to make coffee—he only drank tea under protest if I made it first without asking him—dressed only in a pair of my pyjama bottoms.

"What happened to you two, anyway?" Steve asked.

"Coffee first, and then I'll feel up to letting you know," I said.

Shorty sat with them in the living room while I got things ready in the kitchen, asking his uncle if he knew the extent of last night's damage in the east of the city. I put the pot on the gas and then went into my living room and pulled back the curtains to look out over the roof of the factory on the other side of the street. The sky was uniformly black with smoke. The relentlessness of the colour only broken by a few long trails of white and dirt-grey. I had a new vista—with part of the factory collapsed, I could see as far as the back of the Bloomsbury Ballroom.

"… it was the worst bombing so far," Steve was saying, as I watched large smuts, the size of two-shilling pieces, rain down over the street outside my house. "Half the city's been flattened, and if it hadn't been for the quick thinking and action of a few men, we would have lost St. Paul's."

"It must have been pretty terrible," my brother said. I hadn't missed his glance at the gathered tension in my shoulders.

"You have no idea, Michael," Shorty replied. "If the folks back home really knew what it was like here, and the same thing could happen to New York, or to Boston—"

"Coffee sounds like it's ready," I said, a little too loudly, wanting to change the subject. I needed to steel myself before we began to recount the events of the evening. Alfred's death had affected me greatly. I'd warmed in an instant to the cheeky young constable, with his broken eyeglasses and his speech peppered with coarse words.

"I did bring home one positive thing from last night," I said from the kitchen.

"What's that?" Shorty asked.

"The value of having a special mate beside you—one who thinks the same way, has a cool head, and can muck in with the best of them."

"Muck in?" he said.

"You know what I mean. You and me, we're a born team. If it hadn't been for us working so smoothly together, we might not have made it …"

"What do you mean, you might not have made it?" Michael said, standing in the kitchen doorway, his eyes bright with anger mixed with concern.

"You know me, Mikey—coffee or tea immediately precedes the ability to speak clearly. Go! Sit with Steve and Shorty. I'll bring it in."

A few minutes later, I brought the tea tray in and placed it on the carpet in front of the gas fire. Once we all had a cup in our hands, I smiled at Shorty and then we related what had happened after we'd left Michael and Steve at the Savoy.

We left nothing out.

*****

It took us about an hour to get dressed and get to the embassy to see if Dr. Harper was there. He checked us both, re-dressed my arm, and gave each of us a large tub of ointment for our bruises. We were given orders to take it easy for a few days and to come back if we felt any stiffness in our necks or developed headaches. He returned our smiles and our avowals we'd follow orders with a look of resigned acceptance. He knew we wouldn't.

I was following Shorty up the staircase that led to the entrance of the embassy when he grabbed my arm, opened a door on our left, and led me through it.

"Where's this go?" I asked him.

"Kitchen," he said. I could hear a grin in his voice. "I thought I might grab something to take to Alfred's parents."

"Uh huh," I mumbled, and then bumped right into him, as he'd stopped abruptly in the middle of the corridor. He indicated a door with a quick tilt of his head.

"What's in there?" I asked.

He whispered against my ear, "That's the janitor's cupboard, into which you're about to be kidnapped."

He led me into the small closet, closing the door behind us. It was pitch black, but he took me in his arms and kissed me.

"What's this for?" I asked, smiling against his mouth.

"I was thinking …" he said.

"About?"

"Luck," he replied.

"Luck?"

"Yes, Tommy, luck. When I saw the bruises on your chest and arms while the doctor was examining you, it made me realise yet again how lucky we are to still be alive." I tried to interrupt but he stopped me by placing a finger against my lips. "But what I feel most of all is I'm the luckiest dumb Yankee in the world to have you in my life. That's the real luck in this whole goddamned awful mess …"

I rested my forehead against his, too moved to say anything. Anything I could have said would have been trite compared to his spare, sincere words. *"Merçi, mon amour,"* I said softly. I said it in French, because it was the language in which my mother spoke to Michael and me. It was the language I identified with strong feelings—care, encouragement, and, of course, love. "Thank you", in English, wouldn't have meant quite the same to me.

"De rien, mon brave," he replied, taking my hand and squeezing it. "Shall we?"

He opened the closet door a crack and peeped out to check the corridor was empty, patting my backside as I walked out into the hallway.

*****

Almost an hour later, we were sitting in the parlour, or front room, of Alfred's parents, Lionel and Dorothy Heath, quietly sipping cups of tea.

I was feeling quite uneasy and annoyed with myself, realising that after not quite two years in London, I'd had no real direct exposure to the ordinary man's life or culture. Even the word "ordinary" felt condescending. It made me realise I was from a comfortable, middle-class colonial background and had lived here in a cocooned existence, only mixing with wealthy, or middle- and-upper class, Britons. I knew nothing about the working classes that teemed around me in the streets of London.

It made me feel ashamed.

The house was one of many in a row of blackened mid-Victorian cinder-block terraces at the Marylebone edge of Paddington. The parlour was the special room, reserved for visitors—cluttered with bric-a-brac, stuffed with over-large armchairs each dripping with antimacassars, and hidden from the street outside by dark, heavy curtains.

Alfred's mother had nearly fallen to her knees when Shorty had handed her a small basket containing a bottle of Scotch whisky from the officers' liquor cabinet, a pound of butter, a tin of coffee, several rashers of bacon, and a dozen eggs. In reality, it was a meagre gift, although I could see how much it was appreciated. She'd cut into her precious Christmas cake and presented each of us with a small wedge, to have with our "cuppa". Never had I felt so humbled, especially in view of the fact her son had been killed the night before, and here she was, trying so hard to be the perfect hostess.

Neither of us had offered the customary platitudes. Instead, I'd tried to concentrate on talking about how brave Alfred had been—a hero in the flames. His parents deserved to have the last memory of him a bright, positive one. It would help keep them going. I told them we'd met while he was putting out incendiaries—I left out all the swearing, although I knew it was something I'd always associate with him whenever I thought of him. Without contradicting them, I let them believe it was his idea to use the sandbags outside the Aldwych Theatre. I finished by telling them I believed that by pulling us out of the way of the collapsing building, he'd saved both of our lives.

My eyes felt very scratchy when I saw the look of pride on his mother's face.

"That's our Alfred," she said, "always looking out for everyone else but hisself."

Amid farewells, and promises to keep in touch, I stood at the front door and caught a glimpse of the rest of the ground floor of their house—a long dark corridor, at the end of which I could see the kitchen with its coal-fired stove, and opposite it, in the same room, a white claw-footed bath. One could have stood in the bath and stirred the gravy, I thought, with some sadness.

We waved goodbye and were perhaps a dozen yards down Praed Street when someone clutched my arm. It was Mrs. Heath. She looked painfully embarrassed and kept glancing around her. I guessed it was expected that her grief remain behind her closed front door.

"I'm sorry to bother you again, Colonel Haupner," she said, screwing her handkerchief in her clenched hands. "You have been so kind."

"Please, Mrs. Heath," I replied, taking her hands in mine. "Please, it's not kindness. Our visit was to share our sadness at Alfred's passing, and to honour your brave son."

The dam of her grief burst. "Promise me he was in no pain?" she pleaded. I shook my head and held her for a moment while she sobbed against my chest.

Shorty walked her back to her front door while I lit a cigarette. She collapsed into her husband's arms, and I watched as he led her back into their house.

*****

Later that day, before lunch, Shorty, Gladys, and I were sitting in my office, going through a list of candidates to decide exactly who we were going to take to Auderville.

The spectacular bruise that had formed over the left side of my neck, and which also almost covered my jaw, seemed to be the hit of the morning with everyone at work when we'd eventually walked into the building. I'd grimaced at Gladys' "tsk-tsk" when she'd seen us arrive.

"What in heaven's name are you doing here after what happened last night?" she'd said crossly.

"How did you find out what happened last night?"

"How do you think, Thomas?" she'd asked, casting a glance at Shorty.

"My uncle?" he'd asked hesitantly.

"He rang to tell me you'd both be late and you'd been pulling bodies out of that awful mess at Covent Garden. He also told me he'd ordered you to stay home and rest."

"Did he now?" I'd asked, a little annoyed to hear Steve's thoughts on what we should do.

Gladys had glared at us, seemingly exasperated at what we'd done, despite the look of admiration that occasionally escaped through her steely gaze.

"Well, we're here now! Can we please get on with it?" I'd said, braving her disapproval.

"I can only offer you black tea. I suppose you'd like a cup now you're here?"

"Yes, please, Miss Gleeson, if you'd be so kind," Shorty had said, his hat in his hands, looking as cute as a button.

She'd harrumphed and had then smiled at him before disappearing into the closet off my office to put the kettle on the gas ring.

"I wish I had that knack," I'd whispered to him. "Her bite is far worse than her bark."

"I heard that!" she'd yelled from the room. "But, then again, I expect I was meant to," she'd added, poking her head around the doorjamb and scowling at me. Shorty, though, got a wink.

Once tea had been made and Gladys had summoned one of her "heavies" to sit at her desk and guard my office door, she'd said, after closing it behind her, "Now, let's get on with this little tête-à-tête. We need to get the Auderville team chosen and assembled and then you two need to go home and get some rest."

I kissed her cheek and then took the cup she was holding out to me. "Thank you, Gladys," I said.

"Honestly, Tommy …" she began to say, the worry clear in her face.

"We're fine. I promise you. And you can stop looking so cross. We didn't go looking for trouble, you know. We just didn't run away from helping when we came across it."

She sighed and then sat on the edge of my desk, leaning forward with a cigarette in her hand so Shorty could light it for her.

To limit the amount of time we'd need to stay in occupied France, we'd already decided we should take two teams of two people each—four of us would have to parachute into Normandy. I rather hoped one of our female trainees, Aimée, would be up to the job, but Gladys informed me she'd already spoken with her supervisor in Bristol, who'd advised us Aimée was still not ready.

The perfect team would be Michael, Andrew, Heinrich, and me. However, if I could find another solution, I didn't want to take my brother and my lover on the same mission. I couldn't afford the distraction of worrying about the two of them. It would be bad enough having Shorty with me for his first time in enemy territory.

"What about Andrzej?" Shorty asked.

"His German is accented, but at least his French is fluent. We could get away with it. I'm more worried about your French accent, mister," I said.

"My accent?" he asked, pretend-offended. "I have an accent?"

"You speak French like a turnip," I said, throwing a crumpled ball of paper at him, and then wincing at the pain I felt along my arm.

"Do you two want to have lunch downstairs?" Gladys asked, grinning.

"Food?" Shorty asked. "Sure thing, Gladys. I'm so hungry I could even eat here."

"Then you're a braver man than I, Gunga Din," she quipped.

"That movie is ancient," Shorty replied.

"1939 is ancient?"

"Sure is," he replied.

"You two go ahead, I'll join you in a minute," I said.

Shorty held out his arm and she threaded hers through it. "Have you seen *Night Train to Munich* yet?" he asked as they left the room. "Boy, is that ever one swell movie ..."

I waited until their voices faded and then rang the florist near Charlie's and asked to place an order.

"Two dozen yellow roses, Colonel?" the florist asked.

"Yes, please," I said. "I'll call over in about an hour, after lunch, and give you a card to go with them and an address for their delivery."

I fished out the printed card for yellow roses I'd bought a week ago and had kept for a special occasion. I'd chosen it from a rack of cards that had been titled "The Language of Flowers". There had been one card for each flower commonly stocked by the florist. The SOE often used flowers to deliver hidden messages—no one would think twice about who they were sent by, or to. Even if someone somehow managed to open the envelope and read the card, they'd spend the rest of their lives trying to decipher some hidden, non-existent code in the message. Neither would anyone at the American embassy bat an eyelid when an extravagant bunch of roses arrived for Shorty with an unsigned, printed card. He was a man-about-town. No one would know they'd come from me—only he would.

Before sealing the envelope, I read the card one last time. There was no need for any code—what it said was exactly what I meant.

CHAPTER 9

I didn't know which was colder—the icy, westerly winds off the Atlantic or the barrel of the binoculars resting against my cheek.

Shorty and I sat in a small hollow, on the southern headland, overlooking the half-circle that was Goury harbour. The ground around us was sparsely spotted with snow, but we were too close to the coast for there to be anything like the heavy falls that had been blocking the roads farther inland for the past week.

It was the end of February and the last days of our three-week incursion into occupied Normandy. Shorty was still preoccupied—I'd only told him a few hours ago I wouldn't be returning with him, Andrew and Andrzej to England. It wasn't really the fact I'd deliberately not mentioned it until the last minute that had surprised him, it was more the fact I couldn't tell him why.

We sat spooned together—him behind, his binoculars resting on my shoulder, his knees up on either side of me. He held me around the chest with his free arm. "I tell you everything," he said. I heard a smidgen of "little kid" voice

I laughed. I was already used to his games. "Well, seeing you do, how many boxes have they unloaded so far?" He was supposed to be

195

counting the number of grey boxes the German patrol had been unloading onto the quayside.

"You know what I mean."

I sighed. "Yes, I do, but as I told you before, there are some secrets I have to keep—even from you."

"I'm only asking because I know I'm going to worry myself sick unless I know what you're up to."

"Do we have to have this conversation right now?" I asked. "The one about 'can we really expect to work together like this if you're going to be so protective'."

"Thirty-seven," he said.

"Well, your grumpiness, even I can't follow the logic here …"

He kicked my shin with his heel. "That's the number of boxes they've unloaded so far. The *Stabsgefreiter* is having a piss on the tyre of his truck, and the others look like they're about to settle down for a chinwag and a smoke."

"Corporal Löwe pissing on the truck … again?"

He nodded.

"That man has a bladder problem, I tell you."

"I hate secrets, even though it's our job to keep them," he said. There was no judgement in his voice, or any sense of being peeved. It was a statement of fact. All members of our organisation found it irksome, at some times more so than at others. "Orders is orders," he added in his George Raft gangster voice. It made me laugh.

"I'd love to tell you what I have to do, Shorty. But you and I both know there are things that can't be discussed, even between us. But if you feel like chancing your arm, when you get back to London, you could always ask George."

"George, as in the Duke of Kent, George?"

"That's the one. Remember the night we went to dinner? George asked me out into the garden for a private chat. When I got back inside, you asked me what it was all about. And what did I say …?"

"That you couldn't tell me."

"There's your answer. Nothing's changed."

I leaned my head back on his shoulder and kissed his cheek.

He chuckled. "You know I'm only messing with you, don't you."

"Of course I do. All I can tell you is I'm going to Saint-Lô, and if things go well, I'll be back in a few days … and yes, I promise to be careful, for heaven's sake."

"You better. I'm looking forward to an evening with QV when you get home."

QV stood for Queen Victoria. It had been the top threequarters of her statue that had smashed my violin on the night our blossoming relationship had changed into a firm and committed one. We'd escaped either death or serious injury that night and had both realised life was too short to hold back our as then unspoken feelings for each other.

QV was also the name he'd bestowed on my new instrument.

A few days after the air raid, he'd come home with a present for me—a violin from a pawnshop in Islington. I hadn't wanted to hurt his feelings, but it was a bloody terrible mass-produced instrument. Although he'd christened it QV, I'd named it my "steam-powered violin" in honour of the era in which the murderess of its predecessor had lived. It was a bitch of a thing to play—it buzzed on some notes and didn't resonate on others, but I'd smiled and had thanked him for his kind gesture.

"Can't I come with you?" he pleaded, playfully squeezing my thighs with his knees.

"Sweetheart, you're an American. If something went wrong and you got captured, what do you think would happen when the Germans found out? It would cause an international incident."

"That logic doesn't make sense," he argued. "I could get captured here and I'm still an American. And we're a team, Tommy. Surely you know I'd be useful—whatever this task is. It does sound important …"

I wanted to explain, but I couldn't. If George chose to fill him in one day that would be fine, but I couldn't, no matter how much I'd have liked to. I had to admit he was a born field operative. I'd never worked with anyone who'd taken to it so naturally. He was all business when we were about our work. Sometimes, his sternness and concentration made him seem like someone I didn't know. I'd come to appreciate his easy manner with people, having seen it in our training sessions at the gymnasium with the Poles, at Stodham Park, and now here, working with the French Resistance. The local agents we'd recruited would do anything for him.

He'd never crossed the line with me, unless we were alone. I couldn't have wished for anyone more professional to work with, and that included my brother. I'd begun to think I'd give my life for him, and more recently that I trusted him with my own.

He was right. We were a team and there was no doubt he'd certainly be an asset to the operation. But I couldn't break my promise, especially since I'd basically been ordered to keep stumm.

"Psst!" he whispered and then handed me the binoculars. It seemed as though the Germans on the quay had finished pissing and smoking and were packing up their military vehicle, ready to head back to their field headquarters in Auderville. The *Lastwagen*, laden with grey boxes, had already left and had passed by us on the road below our vantage point.

I took the opportunity to scan across the ocean. The air was clear, but we weren't quite high enough to see Alderney to our west. Even though it was only about an hour before sunset, there was still no sign of the small local fishing fleet.

"What's for dinner tonight?" he asked.

"Not sure. Depends on the catch—unless you want to bag a couple of rabbits?"

The locals we'd recruited were fishermen. The majority of their catch went first to the small German garrison in Auderville and then whatever they didn't take was sold in the markets at controlled, cheap prices—only a few fish kept by the fishermen for their own meals. I'd been surprised at the level of non-interference after the best part of a year of occupation. I'd expected the Germans to exercise a far stricter control over the local French population.

The Germans were, on the whole, happy to be in France. They had a saying: *"Leben wie Gott in Frankreich"*. In English, it meant something like, "Live like a king in France". Good food and wine was still abundant for the occupiers—especially compared to the austerity they'd faced at home since 1938.

"How much time have we got?" he asked.

I checked my watch and then used the binoculars to scan the roadway to the north until I found Corporal Löwe's car turning off the coastal road on its way back to Auderville. "If you wait five minutes, the last patrol of the day is due to come past."

The Germans' coastal patrol was as punctual as their country's prewar train timetables. At first, it had amused me to see the three men driving along, sitting up ramrod-straight in their *Kübelwagen*, their rifles held upright and pressed to the chests, ready for deployment. There seemed to be no banter or friendly chatter between them. It was as if their patrol duty was a chore and they couldn't wait to get back to their barracks to put their feet up.

"How's the new rifle?" I asked.

Shorty had brought a new weapon along with him—a test piece. A lightweight, portable version of the M1 Garand. It had been designed with paratrooper use in mind, with a foldable stock and a modified, screw-on barrel.

"Piece of crap, really. It needs some serious rejigging. But, ya know, in the hands of a professional …"

I nudged his foot with mine and was rewarded with a soft chortle. He reached into his backpack and retrieved the weapon, and as he inspected the bore of the barrel, while holding it over my shoulder, he began to sing softly and I knew I was forgiven—for the time being, at least.

"Bunnies in the morning, bunnies in the evening, bunnies for supper-time …"

I laughed, of course.

"Gotta make sure this barrel is screwed on tight," he said to me. "I tell you, if a guy wasn't serious about really tightening it, he could blow his eye out."

"Don't do that," I said. "I like your eyes."

He grunted. "Once the patrol's gone past, I'll give them five minutes before I start bagging the bunnies. That'll give them time to get to the bar in Saint-Germain-des-Vaux and start on their first stein of that rubbish they call beer."

*****

Shorty's accurate shooting had given us more than a few unexpected meals. By the time we'd returned to the farmhouse, in which we'd been hiding out, we had three hares and a *marcassin* in our backpacks. I didn't know if there was a special name for baby wild boars in English, but the French thought them a delicacy. I set about to skinning the hares and singeing the piglet ready for roasting.

Our French hosts were envious of Shorty's accuracy and pestered him continually for sniper training, especially Luc, the fifteen-year-old son of one of our new field agents. Jean-Baptiste and his son made up the two-man cell Shorty and I had trained. We slept in the hayloft of Jean-Baptiste's barn, usually getting to sleep about three in the morning after training sessions and staying in bed until about ten. It was warm up there in the hay, and we didn't have to worry about being too quiet at the times we wanted not to be.

The two Andrews had set up in Laye, a few kilometres to the south, where they were training another two-man cell. We four got together every night to share food, and to discuss the business of the day. "Oh, my God, this is delicious," Andrew said, chomping into a sandwich he'd made with a torn-off hunk of baguette and some roast pork.

"Well, as of tomorrow night you're back to rations, so eat up," I said and then wiped my chin. I couldn't remember the last time I'd even seen pork crackling.

"Don't think every oppo is as easy as this, *Rudzielec*," Andrzej said to Shorty. "This one is a doddle, set up just for you so you don't get your dainty little fingies dirty."

He was rewarded with a slap across the back of the head, followed by a friendly tussle and a lot of what sounded like cursing in Polish.

From outside the barn, I heard the call of a *chouette hulotte*—a tawny owl. "That'll be Luc," I said to the others. I returned the call.

A few moments later, the young fisherman stuck his head around the door and said, "Gidday." It came out in a curious mix of Australian accent and French vowels. It was all I could do not to burst out laughing.

"*Bonsoir, Coco,*" I replied, grinning. I knew I should never have told him about Australia. "*As-tu envie de manger quelque chose?*"

"*Ah, putain!* Your French is still too posh for this part of the world. *Ton mari le parle mieux que toi.*"

He jumped down next to me and then stole the piece of pork from my fingers I was about to eat myself. I thumped him. Shorty laughed, and as Luc had joined us, we continued our conversation in French. As hard as he'd tried, Luc's English, learned from American popular songs and comic books, was rudimentary to say the least. Of necessity, we always spoke French when he was around—except on the odd occasion when he pestered Shorty and me to teach him more English.

"He's not my husband, and he speaks French like a turnip," I said, also giving Shorty a whack, to shut him up. The French were so much more relaxed about men being together. Under the Napoleonic Code, it had never been illegal, since as far back as 1810. Besides, Luc's godfather, Jean, who'd fled once the Germans had invaded, had taken his 'special friend' Bernard with him. Luc had grown up with their relationship as nothing unusual.

Once the others had finished laughing, Shorty asked Luc if he had any news on the contents of the crates the Germans had been unloading from Alderney.

"Here you are, *Ricain*, this is what they've been up to." Luc reached into his backpack and pulled out a handgun and then threw it to Shorty, who caught it and then whistled softly.

"Browning High Power," he said, turning the weapon in his hands. "They were making these BHPs in Belgium until a few years ago. What do you think, Luc? Are they casting them on Alderney or only assembling them there?"

Luc shook his head. "Foundries aren't like candles, you know. You can't light them up and then blow them out. They have to be kept going all day and night. If they were casting parts, we'd see the chimney flares when it got dark, even this far away. I think they're probably just assembling them there and using slave labour from the camps to do it."

"So this is what the *Bewaffnung und Munition* are up to on Alderney," Shorty mumbled. It came out like a thought, spoken out loud. "Are you sure this is all they're shipping from the island in those grey crates?"

"Yep," Luc replied. "I swapped this one for three hares and four turbot, and I'm convinced my information is correct. I can tell you one thing though—they're being assembled as a special paratrooper issue."

"Are you sure, Luc? Specialist *Fallschirmjäger* weapons? How did you find that out?"

He pulled a pencil and piece of paper from his shirt pocket and then began to sketch out a design. "This is stamped on the top of every box," he said. He'd drawn a pretty good picture of a diving eagle with a swastika in its claws.

"This information needs to get to Brigadier Harris as soon as you get back," I said to Andrew in English. "If these guns are being assembled on Alderney, specifically for paratroopers, then he needs to get some people on to it as a matter of urgency. We're packing up tomorrow, so we can't do anything about it now. Maybe the Jerries have some other airborne attack planned we haven't heard of yet ..."

"Do you think Harris will do anything?" Andrew asked.

"I have no bloody idea, Andrew, and that's the sad truth of it."

"Well, I might drop into MI6 and 'accidentally' let it drop to Stewart Menzies while I'm there," he replied.

My former boss, Mark Harris had always been the biggest obstructionist I'd ever run across. He seemed to think the war was something that disrupted his weekend shooting parties and interrupted dinners with his upper-class pals. Once I'd been moved from under his command, he had, of course, moaned to his cronies that he "didn't know what was going on in his own organisation anymore". I'd subsequently been issued with a directive to keep him informed. Happily, Gladys could write "I'm going to lunch" in such complex administrative-speak it would fill five pages and could make an expert cryptologist none the wiser.

Early on, I'd discovered there'd been fifteen of us in the same situation within the SOE, spread out all over the country, all trying to do what was best for the training of new operatives. Once I finally got my promotion and access to the relevant files, I'd also discovered we'd each been kept in the dark about what the others were doing. Were it not for a few progressives within the group, who called us together for unofficial and informal meetings, the left hand would never have found out what the right was doing. It was Harris's way of holding onto control, even though his inactions were terribly counterproductive.

We'd all agreed on one thing: we desperately needed one strong administrator to look after all training operations, and because of my recent promotion, they'd all voted I should be that person. Promotions were two-edged swords during wartime, and I hoped I wouldn't get another one until after the war, because it would mean I'd never have a chance of hands-on work again. As a full colonel, I'd be stuck behind a desk for the rest of my army career.

As it was, I had my hands full looking after operations and training for the northern and middle areas of France. Even with my new "TEAM", as Gladys had christened it, my recent promotion and all the other areas of responsibility that came with it were really too much for one person— I desperately needed an offsider. Usually, an officer, at my new rank, would have been allocated an adjutant. However, as none had been forthcoming, I'd come to the conclusion that squabbles were going on in circles above me over whose "boy" would be sent to spy on me.

I thanked God on a daily basis Gladys was so capable and efficient. Since we'd advanced up the ladder, she'd got things done in a way that would never have been possible before. I secretly suspected she bribed some of her friends who worked on the floor we'd moved from, using the hidden stock of nylons, coffee, and chocolate Shorty gave her.

One day, a woman might be a man's offsider, or at least his equal. In this stupid war it would have made perfect sense to be able to abrogate a lot of my work to Gladys officially, rather than under the counter, as a pact between friends, as we had done.

I rather hoped I lived to see that day in my lifetime.

*****

About ten o'clock that night, we were standing in a field north of Laye, handing out rabbit and pork leftovers to our small band of local Resistance members. As Shorty, Andrzej, and Andrew were due to return to Britain the following night, we were there to demonstrate how to mark up a field for an RAF pickup.

Tomorrow night's trip back for my three friends would be very uncomfortable. Fields in this area were rarely more than five or six hundred metres in length. The one in which we were standing was a little over seven hundred, only allowing a Lysander Mark IIIA to land— a plane designed for the pilot and only one passenger. However, all three would have to squeeze into the passenger space tomorrow night. It would be tight, but with the rear seat removed and a paillasse on the floor, they'd fit—even though the ninety-minute flight would feel like an eternity, and with the extra weight the engines would be at full throttle, making a hell of a noise. But we were far away enough from the Germans that no one would hear it.

My train of thought was abruptly brought to a halt when Shorty, who'd been horsing around with Luc, tripped and fell flat on his face. I bent over double and bit my scarf in an effort not to laugh. For, as he pushed himself up on his elbows, I saw the sandwich he'd been clutching between his teeth was now squashed over his face. "Yuk!" he said, rolling over and sitting up. He brushed the sandwich free of debris and then devoured it in one enormous gulp. "Can't waste it!"

"What am I going to do with you?" I said, squatting down next to him in the darkened field.

"Ten-second rule, babe!"

"You and your ten-second rules," I replied. "Just make sure you keep them out of the bedroom, thank you."

"How about ten lots of 'seconds', then, Tommy?" He waggled his eyebrows and smirked.

"Braggart!" I said under my breath as Luc had headed back in our direction, his arms outstretched, pretending to be an aeroplane.

"A smoke and a glass of wine between each … why not?"

I laughed. "I'm game, if you are."

"Game? As in baseball, or cricket?" Luc asked. He was omnivorous when it came to English words.

I explained what the expression meant.

"Ah," he said after a moment. "I understand. Well, I'm ready for anything too!"

"Well, I don't think you're quite ready for what we were talking about," Shorty said, getting to his feet and then ruffling Luc's hair.

"Filthy buggers," Luc said. He couldn't have looked cheekier if he'd tried.

"What did I tell you about swearing?" Shorty asked and then gave chase, as Luc had pre-empted his reaction and had already started to head off across the field at a brisk run. I shook my head. *Boys!* I heard my mother's voice say. That word was always muttered with an accompanying deep sigh and a smile. Michael and I had been a handful. The feeling that washed over me was warm and enveloping, like my mother's hugs.

Luc was an explosion waiting to happen. Not only physically, for his voice had started to break, but metaphorically as well. He was too big inside to be contained in a small French fishing village. Something inside him was ready to burst into the wider world. He was clever, inquisitive, and capable—voracious for anything that was outside his sphere of experience. He loved movies, music, and serious books—not only the comic books he seemed to constantly have rolled up in the pockets of his jackets. He'd pestered Shorty endlessly to help him with his pronunciation of American songs—Bing Crosby was his favourite. As a result, Shorty, Andrew, and I'd been driven crazy by Luc's engaging but purposely error-riddled—and peppered with swear words— renditions of "Somebody Loves Me" and "You Must Have Been A Beautiful Baby".

The two of them were currently helpless with laughter, Luc having rendered a breathless version of "You Must Have Been a Beautiful Asshole". He had ears for swear words like no one I'd ever known— even more so than Al-fucking-fred.

What Luc had sung wasn't that funny really. But it was indicative of who he was right now—an adolescent boy with universal adolescent boys' humour. We'd all done it—the inappropriate, stupid toilet humour, pissing in public places, fart jokes and the like. No wonder girls of the same age had shaken their heads and muttered. As grown-ups, most women seemed happy to have left their turbulent teen years behind them, but men never really grew up, not inside that is. All it took was the right opportunity for the fifteen-year-old inside each of us to poke his tongue out at the world, let go a corker and smirk, or to dissolve into uncontrollable mirth at a substituted swear-word in a song title. The nostalgia for those mildly offensive moments was almost inescapable. Shorty's inner adolescent was having a ball with Luc, and for a moment I felt myself falling into their fun.

"Penny for them, Aussie," Shorty said, arriving at my side panting. He held a writhing fifteen-year-old under one arm, the two of them struggling to catch their breaths between barks of laughter. His face radiated happiness.

I didn't reply for a moment, instead squeezed his knee and smiled. My thoughts were too grim to share right now.

Between this part of France and the island of Great Britain the SOE had air routes pretty tightly worked out. Thankfully, the Germans hadn't developed radar to the same level as we had, and flying out over the sea, between the Channel Islands and the coast, allowed planes to cross over between the continent and the United Kingdom at a very low altitude. There were risks of course, usually German gunboats, but I didn't want to think about that right now. I brushed aside the fleeting thought of what might happen to me after he'd flown home. When I'd left to come to France, George had still not heard anything more from the blackmailer, other than the initial letter informing him that he or she was in possession of the correspondence and the necklace. As a contingency measure, we'd tossed around a few plans. The best of them was that when a letter of demand arrived, I'd pose as a negotiator on George's behalf. We didn't even know where the blackmailer was. If he or she was in Germany, the operation would be significantly more dangerous than if they were in occupied France.

For a brief moment, I felt very uneasy. I wasn't afraid of the Germans, I was afraid something else could happen to me, and I'd never see my handsome American again.

Penny for them, Aussie, Shorty had asked.

Penny for them, Haupner—they were the same words my training sergeant had often growled at me during classes at the academy. I'd never been inattentive—it was only because in those days, until I'd learned to consciously change my behaviour, my eyes had gone blank when I concentrated.

The motto of the Intelligence Corps crossed my mind, summoned by Shorty's simple, gentle question. Forewarned is forearmed—*praemonitus, praemunitus*—that was the official version. However, the same growling sergeant had instilled the unofficial version in all of us. *Vitam praecogita, mortem praepara*—plan to survive, but be prepared to die.

Tired of waiting for a reply, Shorty nudged my knee with his own. "Come on, babe," he whispered. "What were you thinking?"

"Nothing, Shorty," I said. "Nothing, at all, Yankee."

*****

The following day, Heinrich's last before he went back to England, was spent on Jean-Baptiste's fishing boat.

I sat in the trawler's cabin, watching Shorty running around on the deck outside, thinking he was born to the sea. In the cold, his skin was no longer the same milky-coffee colour I remembered when I'd seen him in the gym for the very first time without his shirt on, but almost white, except for his cheeks, which were ruddy from the icy wind. His hair whipped around his face, and I could sense his excitement. He really loved the ocean.

I'd been thinking about "us" and had finally accepted he was right—I couldn't protect him all the time—that wasn't my role as his lover, or as his partner. I could try to be there for him when he needed it, but he wasn't a child to be sheltered from every misfortune life threw up. 1941 was a bad time to be our age and to be fighting men. I promised myself when he was around I'd treasure every moment and to try to stop being so cranky.

As we headed back into the harbour, shortly after lunch, I caught his eye and signed to him, "How are you?"

"Cold," he signed back.

"I can warm you up," I replied, forgetting the British Sign Language gesture for what I then suggested as remedy was universal, consisting of a ring made from the thumb and finger in one hand and the insertion of an index finger from the other hand. A soft clucking from outside the deck cabin made me realise that Luc had seen what I'd done.

"Enough! You've got such a dirty mind, *mon capitain*," he said in gutter French, laughing at me, and then gestured I should get out into the spray and the wind to help ready the boat for its return to harbour.

"He's right you know," Shorty whispered when I got close to him. "Although butter wouldn't melt in your mouth, Thomas Haupner, you do have a dirty mind."

I blushed.

"Didn't say I didn't like it," he added with his lopsided grin.

*****

Corporal Löwe and a private were lounging around on the jetty when we arrived, sitting casually on the mooring bollards at the dockside with their rifles resting across their knees. They didn't even glance up when the fisherman unloaded their few boxes of fish and began to gut them. The Germans weren't normally still on the dock at this time of day, so it meant Shorty and I had to stay on board, hidden from sight until they left. There wasn't a lot of hiding space, but I put down a few planks and we stowed ourselves on top of them, underneath a tarpaulin in the bilge-well.

After about thirty minutes, we heard the Germans talking as they walked off up the small hill, away from the docks, to their *Kübelwagen*. I kissed him when I heard them drive off.

"I could get used to this face-fuzz," I said, nuzzling his three-week-old growth.

"You only say that because you like it when I rub it on your ass," he replied.

"You two going to stop jabbering in English and get out of there?" Jean-Baptiste's voice interrupted us.

We managed to get an hour alone before it was time to pack up to leave.

*****

The night-time take-off went very well, the Lysander landing easily, guided by our small group of torch-holders. Shorty stayed with me for a moment while the rest of the group ran over to the aircraft to help turn it around for departure.

"Hey, you," he said, "be careful, please."

"I will, sweetheart, don't worry. I should be home in a few days."

He reached into his inside coat pocket and took out a small, flat object and pressed it into my hand. "Tommy ... *wo du bist, da bin ich auch,*" he whispered. His voice was so choked up he could hardly get the words out. He turned away quickly, so I couldn't see his face, and then ran to the plane. I saw him scrunch down with the other two men in the area behind the pilot. He waved to me, pulled the cockpit cover over his head, and then, in a matter of thirty seconds, the plane lifted off over the stone walls that surrounded the fields. I watched it heave sluggishly into the air and fly off over the sea until it finally disappeared into the darkness. I crossed my fingers that all those aboard the overladen plane would arrive safely. Due to the extra weight, the trip would be longer than normal, and I hoped the fuel would last long enough to get them as far as either Croydon or Northolt. If not, there were plenty of landing strips closer to the coast.

"Goodbye, Shorty," I said to myself. "Yes, *'wherever you are, I will be with you too'.*"

I was still clutching whatever it was he'd pressed into my hand. I held it under my torch. It was a dried yellow rose.

CHAPTER 10

It was one-hundred-odd kilometres from Goury to Saint-Lô. A matter of hours by car or train. However, as I only had a battered bicycle, I reckoned it would take the best part of the day—perhaps a bit longer if I stuck to side roads. I'd allowed myself nine hours. Fortunately, the snow had stopped and a warmer south-westerly had sprung up in the early hours of the morning, melting most of the ice on the road.

The smaller lanes and byways in Normandy were bordered by tall hedgerows, which I remembered as being an amazing sight in the spring and summer, but which were now bare-branched. Oak, beech, wild cherry, hazelnut, and apple trees were interspersed with blackberry, elder, and cotoneaster. It was a place I vowed to return to after the war, to bring my man for some sightseeing and a holiday. In the back of my mind, I still clung to the hope the war would be over within a year of the Yanks getting into the fray. I'd daydreamed of Shorty and me, either on my family's front veranda in New South Wales, watching the cattle, or in the United States, eating lobsters in a seaside restaurant somewhere near Boston.

As an afterthought, I couldn't help but imagine what sort of a bitch these hedgerows and the local *bocages* would be if the Allies ever decided to invade Europe through Normandy.

I'd only got as far as Sainte-Croix-Hague when I heard the sound of a truck tearing up the narrow lane behind me. I dismounted and pushed my bicycle and myself into the hedge at the side of the road to let it pass. With a squeal of brakes it stopped, discharged a passenger, and then roared off again.

"Quelqu'un nous a trahi, Koala, mais j'ai sauvé la radio!"

Luc's French gushed out, the words nearly all joined together. "Hey," I said, pulling him into my arms, trying to calm him down. "Take a few deep breaths, settle yourself and tell me what's going on. What are you doing here, and what do you mean? Who betrayed you?"

It took him a few attempts to get out what had happened. One of the townsfolk had got drunk and set fire to Corporal Löwe's house in Auderville. As no one would own up, they'd rounded up all the men in Goury and put them into prison.

There'd been no betrayal, I explained. It seemed to be a disciplinary measure, and as no one seemed to have been injured, I also believed the men would be freed before too long.

"Corporal Löwe's house?" I asked. "It's a wonder he didn't unbutton his pants and piss the fire out." Luc didn't smile, but his grim expression softened a little. "But you saved the radio, *Coco?*" He nodded. I chucked him under the chin. He was a great kid, so full of energy and trust. I'd come to like the fact he'd "adopted" me.

"So I can't go home, there's no one there. I'll have to come with you," he announced, emphatically crossing his arms.

I sighed at the thought of travelling across the countryside with a fifteen-year-old carrying a heavy radio hidden in his brown leather suitcase.

"Very well, but once we get to Saint-Lô I'm sending you back. Your father will only spend a day or so in jail and then they'll let them all out. The Germans are like that. If someone had died, that'd be a different thing. But a fire … phht!"

Actually, the two of us on one bike wasn't as bad as I'd imagined it would be. Luc was a fisherman. A lad who was not only tall for his age but also very strong. We took turns. While one of us stood upright on the pedals, using his body weight to propel the bicycle, the other sat back on the seat, clutching the radio to his chest. I'd strung my duffle across my back like a haversack.

It had turned out to be a glorious day. The sun was out, but the air was cold. Normally, I'd have thought it a beautiful day for a bicycle ride, had not Luc's sudden arrival made me uneasy over what might happen.

"What?" I asked.

"That's the third time I've asked you about the place we're going to."

"Sorry, Luc, my mind was elsewhere."

"I wish you'd stop worrying. Guess what, *mon capitain*? I know every stone, every tree, and every place to have a piss in the whole of Normandy. You're my uncle, and you're taking me to Saint-Lô to see my father's cousin, who's a dentist. That's what we'll tell the Boches if they stop us."

"I wasn't worrying," I lied.

"You'll see *him* soon enough," he added and then playfully admonished me with a familiar proverb in his most "careful" French. A real turnaround from his usual coarse Normand dialect. *"Quand on n'a pas ce que l'on aime, il faut aimer ce que l'on à ... regardez autour, quelle belle journée!"*

I laughed. He'd mistaken my preoccupation. For once, I wasn't thinking about Shorty. What he'd said, however, rang true. It was a beautiful French saying. I wasn't entirely sure there was an equivalent in English. However, roughly translated it meant, *When we don't have what we love, we must love what we have.* He'd also advised me to look around us—it truly was a beautiful day.

I decided to do just what he'd suggested. Despite his shushing, and laughter at my unseemly madness, I began to sing loudly as our bicycle rattled down the pot-holed country lane.

"Somebody loves me ..."

I only managed to get three words into the song when Luc joined in, uproariously out of tune, but with a very good American accent. To an onlooker, had there been one, it must have seemed either outrageous or foolhardy—a fully grown man and an adolescent haring down the steep incline, shrieking an American popular song. Halfway down our steep incline, we ran over a small hole and immediately careened out of control into the hedgerow, helpless with mirth.

Sharing the bike was very tiring, but the problem was solved around three in the afternoon when we stopped by the side of the road to have a bite to eat. I'd packed some cheese and bread, barely enough for one. But we shared what I had and it stopped our stomachs growling. We were on the outskirts of La Haye-du-Puits, and I'd gone into the bushes to relieve myself. It was less than a minute later I discovered Luc had disappeared, leaving the radio suitcase next to the bike. I hadn't heard any car come past, so assumed he'd gone behind the bushes on the other side of the road. After a while, I became anxious and called out his name.

I could see the roofs of the village houses behind a row of poplars at the end of the lane where I waited. I hoped he hadn't done anything too stupid, and decided to start to walk slowly towards the village. It was then I saw him bicycling quickly towards me. He gestured I should get on my bike and follow him.

He grinned at me. "They'll never notice it's gone until later on."

I groaned. The bicycle belonged to the local *gendarmerie*. He pedalled off furiously down the lane, so I had no option but to follow.

With the second bike we made good time, switching to winding, very narrow country lanes once it got dark. There was enough moonlight to see where we were going, and at about eight in the evening we stopped underneath a bridge, about half a kilometre from Hébécrevon, to light up. I'd long given up trying to get Luc to stop smoking.

"You should be in school, you know," I said to him.

"You're not my father, Koala. You're supposed to be my war chief."

I laughed. "War chief? You read too many American comic books, and you should stop calling me Koala, by the way. I've been telling you that all day."

"But you look like a koala bear!" He ducked too quickly for me to box his ears.

I stretched out on my back and closed my eyes for a moment. One hand found its way into my pocket, and I gently moved the dried yellow rosebud between my fingers. Apparently, I hadn't sung "Somebody

Loves Me" at random. Somebody did love me, and I did know who. The thought had made me happier than I'd ever remembered being. It glowed inside me. I knew my life had begun to change. It was an odd realisation. The one that said: *you are finally growing up, Haupner.*

"What are you smiling at?" Luc asked with a smirk. I winked at him.

"Nothing you want to hear, *mon vieux*. Now, let's get the radio set up."

He'd turned out to be the most proficient radio operator I'd come across in years. A combination of playing secret codes with his friends before the war, together with a keen mind, had led to him picking it up exceedingly quickly when he was still a child. His father had told me Luc had been obsessed with Morse code since he was eight, when he'd read about it in one of Georges Simenon's *Commissar Maigret* stories.

I put the bicycle up on its stand and attached the drive belt over its rear wheel to the generator in the radio suitcase. The battery needed to be kept at full charge so I pedalled while he transmitted.

I asked him to send two messages. The first was *Gardenias are in bloom again*. He sent it twice and waited for a received call. Once it had been acknowledged, he sent the second—*The wombat is good*. The first message was for the Duke of Kent. I'd chosen *Gardenia* as his code name for my messages. What Luc had transmitted was to tell him I'd reached Saint-Lô. The second message, of course, was for Shorty. *Good* was our agreed code that I loved him and missed him. We waited for a moment for the received signal, and then one word came through for me. *Coptic*, it said—the name of my street. He'd left it for when I contacted the office to let me know that he'd arrived home safely.

We waited in silence for the end code, not worried, as Germans could only trace radio signals while they were being transmitted. They couldn't triangulate our position merely by our having the receiver turned on. Just as we were about to give up, one more word came through— *Babel*. It meant to call back in a few hours. Something was up.

Luc and I walked our bicycles the few kilometres that remained, going through fields and staying close to hedgerows until I recognised the back gates of Édouard's house.

"Wait here, Luc," I whispered. "If I'm not back in twenty minutes or so, come over to the house. But be careful!" I wasn't expecting any trouble, but pulled out my Beretta and screwed on its silencer.

I left Luc near the gate and moved towards the back of the house. It was very dark, but a light shone in a downstairs room at the rear, which I knew was the kitchen. As I got close to the back door, I could hear voices speaking in German.

A tall statue of Diana the Huntress stood on the terrace, a few metres from the kitchen window. I angled myself behind it so I could see into the room. Édouard was drinking wine, seated in front of his large cooking range, and in front of him, their backs turned to me, were two German soldiers, an *Obersturmbannführer* and a *Stabsunteroffizier.* Interesting. Why would an SS lieutenant-colonel be accompanied by a Wehrmacht sergeant, and what were they doing in Édouard's kitchen?

There was only one way to find out, and it was to assume another identity. I quickly closed my eyes for a moment while I slipped into my most favourite *nom de guerre*. As my aristocrat was someone who'd not be armed, I stashed my gun behind the boot-scraper next to the back door and then knocked.

Édouard's eyes nearly popped out of his head when he saw me standing there.

"Hello, Édouard," I said in German, using my best Berlin accent. "I'm sorry to call in so unexpectedly, but my car has boiled over, and I wonder if I could grab some water for the radiator? I'd have sent my driver, but he's trying to change a flat tyre. *Ein Unglück kommt selten allein."*

He was so flabbergasted he didn't speak, so I looked around him into the room and then spoke to the two Germans, who were slowly getting to their feet. "Von Plettenberg," I said, introducing myself.

"Obersturmbannführer Leonard Alberbach," the colonel said, giving me a *Heil* with an accompanying heel-click. "And you are right. *It never rains but it pours.*" I returned his *Heil* with a lazy hand-gesture—the type that the diffident but socially obedient aristocracy used in the salons and ballrooms of Berlin and Leipzig.

Édouard was still somewhat in shock, and as it became apparent he wasn't going to speak, Alberbach made a stab at small talk, as one did when a situation felt awkward. "You live locally, Herr von Plettenberg?"

"No," I replied and then added a convenient, believable lie. "I'm on my way to Cherbourg, and ... I'm sorry to be so pedantic, but let me introduce myself correctly. My first name is Ernst, and perhaps you might know me better as the Prince von Plettenberg."

He gave a second salute—one that was vigorous and accompanied by a very snappy heel-click. "I'm dreadfully sorry, *Hoheit*, I had no idea," he stammered. "I beg your pardon, this is my adjutant, *Stabsunteroffizier* Wilhelm."

"*Stabsunteroffizier*," I murmured. He clicked his heels and gave me an overly enthusiastic *Heil*.

"Let's not be formal, please. You may call me Ernst," I said, smiling at Alberbach.

"Hello? Édouard? This is your house. What on earth is wrong with you?" I said, turning from the Germans and raising my eyebrows. His silence was beginning to feel uncomfortable.

"Oh yes, of course. I'm sorry, Ernst," Édouard said as he pulled up a chair for me. "As you'd begun to introduce yourselves to each other, I felt it rude to interrupt."

"That would be a first time," I said with a smile.

Both he and Alberbach chuckled.

"Your arrival was quite unexpected," Édouard explained hastily. "I feel so foolish gawping for what must have seemed like an age. The *Obersturmbannführer* is on his way south, and when he contacted me last week I told him I'd be delighted to put him and his men up for the night." The subtle emphasis on "men" wasn't lost on me. There were more Germans around. I started to worry about Luc outside.

Schutzstaffel officers of a certain type were often overly obsequious. The way the colonel had reacted when he thought he was in the company of a prince had told me straight off that this particular colonel was a bum-licker of the first degree.

Despite his rank, and the odd situation, I wouldn't have risked coming inside had I not noticed the milky-green piping around his epaulettes when I'd been looking through the window. It indicated he was in the *Sicherheitsdienst*—Security and Intelligence Corps. What I wouldn't give to get this bastard back to England for interrogation.

But first of all, I needed to know what he was doing here and where the rest of his men were.

Prinz Ernst von Plettenberg had been a long-established alias of mine. I'd invented him when I'd first trained in Section D at MI6, not long before going to Germany in 1934. The main line of the von Plettenbergs had died out in the late nineteenth century, but the name lived on through gossip of the "would-be-if-they-could-be" minor German aristocrats during the Hindenburg regime. The title was familiar in certain circles, but no one ever seemed to be able to put a face to the man who used it. A prince was about as good as you could get in Nazi Germany, now the SS had become the new aristocracy.

"Perhaps I could get my sergeant to take some water out to your car?" the colonel suggested. "There are only three of us, and my driver also seems to have gone missing for the moment."

I waved off his offer with one hand. "My *chauffeur* will eventually come here once he's managed to change the tyre—did I mention the spare was also flat? However, while I wait, it gives me a chance to chat with my old friend."

"Are you staying overnight nearby … Ernst?" the *Obersturm-bannführer* asked me. It wasn't hard to see he was confused. If Édouard and I were such great pals, why wasn't I a guest in his château?

"You haven't told me how you know my friend Édouard, Colonel," I replied, avoiding his question with one of my own.

"We're acquaintances of relatively new standing," he said. "We have mutual friends in Berlin who introduced us by letter when I told them I was coming to France."

Out of the corner of my eye, I thought I saw a shadow pass by the window. A short moment later, an owl hooted in the darkness. Luc had come looking for me.

"Excuse me," I said and then opened the kitchen door, standing in the doorway, blocking those inside from seeing who I was talking to. I abused my "driver" in the filthiest French I could muster. Luc's cheeky grin and pretend *chauffeur* grunt told me he'd seen my gun on the ground outside the door. I finished by telling him to keep his eye out for a German driver, who was outside somewhere. Perhaps the driver could help Luc with the flat tyre on "our car".

I'd visited Édouard's house twice before the war. The first occasion had been before I'd gone to Spain for the first time, the second when I'd needed to recuperate after Badajoz, and before I'd returned to Munich. I knew the house well. I knew where Édouard stashed his weapons. I also knew where the Huguenot priest hole was in the corridor between the kitchen and the main hallway. I began to make plans.

Just after I closed the door, I heard another quiet tawny owl call. Luc had spotted the third German.

"You must be very well thought of, Obersturmbannführer Alberbach," I said, inspecting the man's Iron Cross and North Africa medal and bars, "to be sent on some errand at this time during the war. I can see you've recently returned from Africa. I'm sure you must have been there on a special task for the Führer himself?"

I heard a distant yet resonating "thwack" from the garden. It was the unmistakable sound of a heavy object hitting the back of someone's head. The "wet crunch" was unlike any other sound on earth. Those of us who'd heard it more than once could never mistake it for anything else.

I was standing next to the credenza near the back door of the kitchen and quickly took a glass from one of the shelves, at the same time assessing how many steps it would take me to get to the door, to open it and to retrieve my pistol.

"May I have some wine please, Édouard?" I asked, rather more loudly than I perhaps should have, to draw attention away from the sound from outside.

"*Aber natürlich, Hoheit,*" Édouard replied. His slightly widened eyes told me he'd also heard the muffled *smack*.

"What was that?" the colonel asked. His sergeant had half-risen from his chair.

"What? That cracking sound? Probably Eva," Édouard explained, "my brown cow. She often gets restless at night and kicks the door of her stable."

Let neither of them have either grown up on a farm or spent much time fighting hand-to-hand, I prayed, holding my breath. I playfully cocked my head to one side, as if waiting for another thump from the stable. The others in the room chuckled at the gesture. In truth I'd been preparing myself in case I'd heard Alberbach's man yelling in the garden. Something inside me was convinced it had been Luc who'd been the one doing the hitting, and not the other way around.

It remained quiet, and then, as I held out my glass for it to be filled, I heard two short, successive owl calls. It was all I could do not to collapse with a loud sigh of relief. "Does either of you have a cigarette?" I asked. "I seem to have left mine in the car."

Distracted by my request, and obviously satisfied with Édouard's explanation, the sergeant stood from his chair and took out his cigarette case, which he opened to me. I took one and then waited for him to light it. I was somewhat surprised to see it was a Lucky Strike.

"Belgium," he explained when he saw me raise an eyebrow. "We liberated many cases of American cigarettes."

My own cigarette case felt cold against my chest. It was stowed in my jacket pocket, full of Gauloises, a brand a German prince would never smoke.

"You were saying, Colonel? The Führer ...?" I asked.

"Well, I have met the Führer, of course ... in a strictly official capacity. You must have met him socially quite often, I suppose?" he replied.

I'd purposely not given the colonel the opportunity to lead the conversation. I'd tried to keep him off-balance since I'd arrived, to give myself a chance to weigh up the man. I wanted to assess how he reacted in unfamiliar circumstances, and to see if he had some hidden strengths I needed to be aware of. It struck me as odd that he already had a North Africa campaign medal and bars, as fighting had only been going on there for about three months. Although, we'd heard Hitler had ordered the decorations to be made even before troops had been sent, such was his confidence. What on earth was this colonel doing here, right now, in Normandy?

"I've had the honour of dining with the Führer on many occasions,"

I said. It wasn't a lie. I had done, but never at the same time as Hitler. It was usually after everyone else had eaten and in the kitchen with the staff ... and after I'd performed.

"I should die a happy man, if ever I were to be so lucky," the sergeant said, wistfully inspecting his empty glass.

I gave him what I hoped was my most charming smile and held the wine bottle out to him. He raised his glass and I filled it. He was welcome to another drink. If the colonel's driver was either dead or incapacitated, judging by the deadly-sounding thwack we'd heard, then the evening was rapidly heading towards only one outcome—the capture and return of the colonel for interrogation in England, and the unfortunate death of the man whose glass I was filling.

"I'm curious to know why you're here, Colonel?" I asked. "A man of your importance ...?"

"*Generalfeldmarschall* von Manstien has ordered me to travel to La Rochelle, where I'm to question three British pilots the Resistance have been hiding for several months. Men we have recently caught and imprisoned," Alberbach said.

From the corner of my eye, I noticed Édouard's quick glance at me. The colonel was an interrogator—that's why he'd been in North Africa.

"Perhaps they have information that might be helpful," he added, somewhat carelessly. "I have ways of getting them to 'volunteer' anything they might know."

"Well," I said, changing the subject abruptly, "I believe the countryside is wonderful around La Rochelle. I do hope you'll also have time to catch up with friends while you're there?"

"Oh, no," he said. "Apart from a few months in Libya, I've been in Poland since thirty-nine. I know no one, and no one there knows me ... yet." He patted his jacket pocket. "I have my letters of introduction here."

This was too good to be true. The circumstances were stacking up in my favour. "I don't know what could be keeping my idiot driver," I said. "Could I prevail upon your *Stabsunteroffizier* to come with me down to my car?"

The colonel nodded his permission, and I stopped him from rising with a touch on the shoulder. "You stay here, Colonel, your man can be my insurance should my driver need some encouragement."

"You look strong enough," Alberbach said.

"Yes, but there are some threats I can't carry out. You see, I have no pistol ..."

Édouard filled a kitchen bucket and handed it to the sergeant. I smiled sweetly, took my overcoat from Édouard, and then led the sergeant out into the darkness and through the orchard, towards where Luc and I'd stowed the bicycles. I placed myself so that we walked with a few metres between us, and he at my right-hand side.

"Is that a *Ruhrgebiets-Akzent* I hear, *Stabsunteroffizier* ... I'm sorry, I seem to have forgotten your name."

"I'd have been amazed had you remembered it, sir," he replied. "*Stabsunteroffizier* Helmut Wilhelm. I'm from Essen, and I've never been able to shake off my accent, no matter how hard I—"

It was now or never, I thought. I pretended to stumble in the dark, and he took a step towards me, in order to grab my hand to steady me. With one quick sideways step to my left, I swivelled on my hip, kicking my right foot up to connect under the man's chin. I felt the soft release of his thyroid cartilage as it ruptured under my instep, and at the same time heard an abrupt crack as his neck snapped.

He fell to the ground with a thud, the handle of the bucket clanging against its side, water splashing out over the ground.

Luc appeared out of the darkness. He'd seen what had happened and looked shaken. He'd heard me speak about Silat before, but had never seen it in action. It was only the second time I'd killed a man with a kick. I didn't have time to dwell upon it, except to note to myself, in a completely detached manner, how quickly and silently the man had died. With a crushed larynx and flattened trachea, he'd not even been able to grunt.

We grabbed him under the arms and then dragged him down to the gate at the bottom of the garden. "I have to go back to get the colonel," I said. "Where's his driver?"

"There," Luc said with a toss of his head. I saw a pair of feet protruding from under the hedge.

"You dragged him down here by yourself?"

All at once Luc turned his head and vomited. I'd noticed how shaky his voice had been and even in the dim light under the trees I could see the sheen of sweat on his face.

"Are you all right, Luc?"

"It's not as easy as you said," he mumbled.

"It never is, Coco."

"I came up behind him in the dark and then hit him across the back of the head with a fence post. Once he was down, I did what you trained me to do … only to make sure. But, I couldn't get the knife out." He gagged and turned aside once more, clutching his stomach, so I stood next to him and rubbed his back until he asked me to retrieve his knife. I went to see what he was talking about.

The dead German driver lay on his back, one eye open, staring at the sky. The handle of Luc's hunting knife protruded from the man's other eye socket. I pulled at the knife handle, but the backward facing barbs at the heel of the blade were caught in his orbital arch.

"Need a hand?" Luc asked.

"Turn your head," I said and then planted one foot on the driver's face and pulled the knife free, using both hands. When I straightened up, Luc was standing at my side, one hand outstretched for his knife.

"Are you sure?" I asked.

"I have to do this, *mon capitain*," he said. "My mother gave me this knife. It's all I have left of hers."

His eyes were full, and I could see from the trembling of his extended hand he was on the point of crying. I bent over and wiped the blade of his knife on the grass and then turned the handle towards him. He took it from me, kissed the hilt, and replaced the knife in its holster on his belt. "One down, a thousand to go," he said quietly. "That one is for *Maman* …"

It wasn't the right time to ask what he meant, so I waited a few seconds before speaking. Neither he nor his father had ever spoken of Luc's mother. Shorty and I had assumed something terrible had happened to her and had respected Luc's and his father's silence on the subject by not asking any of the locals either.

"Everything okay, Luc?" He nodded. "Work now, fall down later," I said. I gave him a quick hug and then headed back to the house. I picked up my Beretta from where I'd hidden it outside the back door.

"Place your hands behind your head and don't do anything stupid," I said, after kicking open the kitchen door. It slammed against the dresser so violently that a few plates crashed onto the ground. The German officer leaped to his feet involuntarily. "I'm sorry to do this, Colonel, but really, this wouldn't have happened had you kept your mouth shut."

He rushed at me clumsily, but I grabbed his arm and twisted it and then hit him heavily on the side of the head with the butt of my pistol. He fell to the floor.

"Help me tie him up, Édouard, and strip his insignia, I'm going to need them." The man was out cold.

"One day you're going to walk into my life with a bunch of flowers, instead of leaving a trail of dead people," he said, shaking his head. We laughed, as the times we'd been together in Spain had never been without some drama.

"Really, Édouard?" I replied. *"Eva, my brown cow?"*

He chortled. Eva Braun was the name of Hitler's mistress. "I thought we were dead men anyway, Tommy; couldn't help myself."

We tied up the unconscious man, stripped him of his epaulettes and emblems, gagged him, and then locked him in the priest hole. Once we'd done that, we sat at Édouard's kitchen table, about to have a glass of wine, when Luc burst into the room, dressed in the driver's uniform, which was two sizes too large for him.

"Lone Ranger to the rescue!" he shouted.

"Where the hell did you get this?" Édouard asked, in English, laughing loudly and indicating Luc with a toss of his head.

"Don't ask," I said, planting a quick, but playful kick to the young man's backside.

Édouard sighed and grabbed the back of my neck with one hand and squeezed it hard. "You were the last person in the world I expected to see, you son-of-a-bitch."

"What's that you said? 'Son-of-a-bitch'? What's that mean in French?" Luc asked.

"Salop!" I translated, trying to grab the half-full bottle of wine from which he'd begun to drink.

We continued in French for Luc's sake, and I explained to Édouard what I'd been doing in France.

★★★★★

I rifled through the papers in the colonel's jacket pocket.

I smiled. His photograph was loose on his *Soldbuch*—his military identification card. I knew there was a good opportunity here—I simply had to plan how to use it. One letter of introduction stated he was due to pick up a Gestapo captain from Granville, on the coast, which explained the rather roundabout way he was travelling from Trier, on the border with Luxembourg, to La Rochelle.

"I have something for you, Édouard," I said.

I gave him George's letter. "So this is the real reason you're here," he said. He stared at me for a moment, before asking, "What were the words he said when he gave you the letter?"

"He said he wrote this in September."

He tapped the letter against his chin once or twice and then said, "I'll be in the library. Give me ten minutes or so and then I'll help you bury the bodies."

I gave in to Luc's exaggerated eye-rolls, pointed stares at my glass, and exasperated sighs, so handed him the colonel's glass. He spat in it, rinsed it out, then held it out, waiting. I filled it with a heady-scented merlot. "Can you drink that in silence and give me ten minutes of peace, so I can sort out in my head what to do?"

"Sure thing, Pops!" he said in accented American English.

"Pops?"

"Yeah—I read it in *Dick Tracy*."

"Never heard of him," I said. I was rewarded with another magnificent eye-roll.

Luc sat in the corner slowly sipping his wine. The brief moment of cheekiness had passed. He'd begun, as fighting men in all wars had done, to think about the man he'd just killed and what it meant to him. I'd talk to him in a while, but for the time being, he needed to sort it out in his own head. My shoulder would be there for him when he was ready for it.

I sat at the kitchen table and drafted a coded message explaining our situation. We had a parcel to pick up. We also needed German-speakers to pose as a sergeant, a private, and the unknown captain in Granville. I realised we'd have to "deal" with the captain after we collected him. If Alberbach was expected, we couldn't afford not to pick the man up. Alarm bells might start ringing sooner than we needed.

I swore under my breath. We'd had no luck replacing the men in my Number One Kraut Squad, despite frequent lobbying at the MOD. I'd tracked down two Austrians and a Swiss who'd be perfect to train. But, as all three were pilots, my pleas had been in vain. There was no exchange rate for fly boys—nor was there a currency that could buy them. They were the most valuable commodity of the war.

In the message, I used the code-number requests for three men—Andrew, Andrzej, and Yves—one of the Frenchmen that was operation-ready, but inexperienced. Yves didn't speak good German, but we could pass him off as a *Hiwi*, or *Hilfswilliger*—a man from a conquered country who'd joined, or was coerced to join, the Wehrmacht. It meant "willing assistant". I didn't want Michael along on this one. If the captured airmen had some information about Rhys, I knew it would be really hard for my brother. His impulsiveness could make him too distracted to concentrate on the job at hand.

I'd salvaged the insignia from Alberbach, but needed my own officer's uniform, as there was no way I could fit into his. The other three would need to bring their own German uniforms. All of us who were field-ready kept six sets at Baker Street—that of a private, an NCO, and an officer, for both the SS and the Wehrmacht. I kept my fingers crossed Yves had already been outfitted as well.

I checked my watch. It was ten minutes short of nine o'clock. If my office was as well-oiled as I hoped, and Gladys could be found quickly, we could have everything in place by three or four in the morning. It was now only a matter of transmitting the message and then giving London an hour to see whether they could organise everything in time.

"All right, Luc," I said. "Time to loosen up those fingers. I have a message to send."

*****

By the time I joined Luc and Édouard, they'd finished laying both bodies at the bottom of a metre-deep trench. I'd been busy writing a few coded reports to go back to London with the pilot.

"Bit shallow, isn't it?" I asked as I gave Luc a cigarette. I started to help shovel earth into the wide grave.

"There's a *poire d'Anjou* in a small half-barrel near the cowshed," Édouard said to Luc. "Do you think you could bring it over here?"

"Legt mir eine Birne mit ins Grab," I said under my breath.

"Herr von Ribbeck auf Ribbeck im Havelland, Ein Birnbaum in seinem Garten stand ..."

Édouard had recognised my words and quoted the opening lines of the poem. It was by Theodore Fontane—the story of an old man who distributed fruit from his orchard to the village children. He knew his son wouldn't continue the tradition, so he asked for a pear tree to be planted over his grave so its fruit could be enjoyed by future generations.

"I'll plant it on a mound between the two of them," Édouard said, leaning on his shovel. "It'll be spring in about six weeks, and with this Kraut fertiliser no one will be any the wiser come midsummer."

I heard Luc mumbling as he looked for the sapling in the dark.

"Give me a moment alone with him when he returns, please, Édouard?"

"Just don't plant the tree. Wait till I get back."

I sighed. I was a farmer's son. I'd done my share of planting fruit trees. I knew what to do.

"You won't be here to look after it," he explained. "I need to be at its birth, during its adolescence, and at its first fruiting. I don't expect you to understand. A fruit tree is like the woman a man falls in love with—one must care for her, spoil her, and most importantly of all, be there when she is planted."

He gave me a broad grin and a wink and then disappeared into the house.

I found Luc struggling to move the wrong pot—a large, bare-branched peach, which was cordoned against the side of the shed. "Easy to tell you're the son of a fisherman," I said, while tousling his hair. "It's this one—here." I helped him carry the tree back to the grave.

"Come, Luc, sit here for a moment. Édouard's gone to get something from the house."

I leaped onto a chest-high stone wall, a few metres from where we'd been burying the bodies. I gave Luc my hand and pulled him up beside me and then took a swig from a half-full bottle of wine I'd jammed into my overcoat pocket. *"Salut,"* I said and then passed the bottle to him, noticing his hand was shaking as he held it to his lips.

I rested one hand on the nape of his neck and pointed up into the sky with the other. "Hey, *Coco*, look at the moon," I said. It sounded so much more gentle in French—*Tiens, Coco, regarde la lune.*

It was a new moon. Royal blue against the blackness of the sky, but due to the crispness of the late winter air, perfectly clear in its detail. It reminded me of a half-crown I'd once discovered while helping my mother wash the sheets. It had fallen to the bottom of the rinse tub, the water stained ultramarine by her Reckitt's Blue bag.

"Beautiful, isn't it …" he whispered.

"Yes, it is. We call it a new moon because it's the start of becoming something new."

"And it eventually becomes a full moon … so?"

"Men have been fighting wars for as long as there've been men on this earth, Luc, and for as long as there've been wars, there have been soldiers who've looked up at the moon for a special reason. It's because they know the moon's always going to be there, even if there are clouds in the sky. It's a certainty, like the sun rising every day. Men make promises to themselves that no matter what happens, they'll survive to see another moon or another sunrise. There'll always be another tomorrow, whether we're here to see it or not. Wars come and go, but there'll always be another new moon—a new beginning."

He took another swig from the bottle then handed it back to me.

"It's hard to believe it right now, because you and I are living through it. But I promise you this war will end. Whether we win or we lose, mankind will go on. The losing side will have to adjust to being ruled by the victor, much as it has had to for thousands and thousands of years. But you know what my dearest hope is, my friend? My dearest hope is that one evening, far off in the future, you'll be sitting on your porch with your grandchildren on your knee, looking up at the same moon in the sky and marvelling at how long ago tonight's events were, and what a small slice of your life this whole war took up in it—despite what you just did, and the horrible things that happened in this orchard."

His eyes filled with tears, and he swallowed deeply several times.

"That soldier," he mumbled, "he didn't even know …"

I put my arm around his shoulders and he fell against me, wrapping his arms tightly around my chest in a limpet-like embrace. In the space of two breaths he began to sob loudly, his body heaving with the effort.

I understood. It wasn't every day one killed one's first man. For me, the emotional cost still continued to be something I paid for at least once every day, ever since the morning in 1936 when I shot a young Spaniard who I'd found hiding in a barn. He'd lunged at me with a cutlass, of all things. I could still see the surprise in his eyes when he realised I'd shot him, and that the blood on his hands was his own.

I held Luc, with my head resting on top of his, until I felt him relax against my shoulder. "Will you be all right?" I asked, in an almost-whisper, once I was sure he'd stopped crying.

He nodded. "Please don't tell anyone I cried … *mon capitain.*"

He nearly called me *papa*. I'd heard the start of it on his tongue. I chewed on the corner of my lip for a moment and then spoke. "Call me Thomas, Luc," I said. "My real name is Thomas."

"Really? Thomas? Just like that? I thought you'd have some strange Aboriginal name—like Billabong or something."

I laughed and gave him a squeeze. He pulled away, searching my face, a slight smile on his lips, despite the tears on this face. "Truly … your name is Thomas?" I could hear the final "s" on the name felt odd. His eyes changed as he worked his lips around the unfamiliar, English version of the French name.

I nodded. I supposed he'd gone through some rite of passage and

I'd been there alongside him. I felt I owed him something—my real name, for a start.

"Thomas," he repeated, under his breath, and then chuckled softly, while shaking his head.

"Smoke?" I asked.

"Please."

I lit one and gave it to him. He studied it in silence for a moment, before taking a drag. "What is it with you, *mon capitain*? One minute you treat me like a child, and the next you're plying me with wine and cigarettes?"

"I merely want to know if you're all right after what you did, and what you saw me do."

"I'll live ... maybe the second time will be easier ..."

"I'll tell you one thing, you will never get used to it, Luc. Welcome to being a grown-up, my friend. It's fucking awful."

I stole his cigarette, took a few puffs, and then handed it back.

"You two? You done yet?" Édouard called from the distance.

"All clear," I called back.

Édouard had asked if Luc and I were finished. I, however, had a feeling our journey to becoming real pals was only just beginning.

*****

At nine thirty we received an answer from London. A Lockheed Hudson was to be dispatched, due to arrive at four thirty in the morning. It was a ten-man aircraft and the message said we'd be receiving four packages. Something had obviously developed in my three weeks away. The final word, at the end of message, was *Helga*.

Helga was a word we used at the end of messages that meant an important new development had arisen, and instructions would arrive with the aircraft. It indicated that either a monumental balls-up had happened in the field and an all-stops-out approach was now necessary or a desperate situation had arisen that need immediate action. All I could do was wait until the morning when the others arrived. The message had said four packages—why four? I'd only requested three. However, as it wasn't unusual to piggyback an agent onto an unrelated mission drop-off, I gave it no further thought.

Édouard made a phone call to a neighbouring farm and ordered *un lapin d'un kilo*—a one-kilo rabbit—it was a signal to round up the local leader of the Resistance, so he could be told to get the locals together to mark up the runway for the Lockheed. Once the man had arrived, had been given his instructions, and then had gone to organise some manpower, I decided to have a few hours of sleep, as I knew we'd have a lot to discuss once the plane landed. I fell asleep in a chair in front of the cooking range.

When I woke up, I checked my watch. It was two thirty. Luc was curled up in a ball at my feet in front of the stove, snoring softly, so I got up quietly and went looking for Édouard. The light was on in his study.

"So, old friend," I said, "I didn't think I'd meet you again under these circumstances."

He smiled at me and held up the duke's letter. "Nor I, under these." He handed me a note. "This is my reply. I'm sorry, but you'll have to deliver it personally. The instructions in his letter were explicit that it should not be passed on to anyone else for delivery. Only you can give it to him. You must say I was wearing a 'silver ring'."

"You have no other instructions for me?" I asked. I'd thought perhaps he might have word about my mission for George. "Anything from Berlin?"

He shook his head. "Instructions? No, Tommy. So, he told you about my connections in Berlin, did he? I was last there in early January, when the RAF bombed Bremen and Kiel. I heard about it at the American embassy, but there was nothing in the papers."

He'd purposely deflected my question. Perhaps his presence in Berlin was part of a greater secret. As it wasn't part of my brief, I thought it best to leave it alone. I knew Édouard well—he'd tell me only what I needed to know.

"Nothing about the bombing?" I said. "How could they keep that quiet?"

"Göring's promise," he said.

Ah! Herman Göring had promised the Führer and the German people not one English bomb would fall on German soil.

"What's on your mind, my old friend?" he asked. "I didn't spend two years fighting alongside you in Spain without knowing you a little."

He was right, of course. "There was something odd in the message from London," I said, sitting in a chair opposite him, at his desk.

"Go on."

"It was a pair of words."

"Go on ..."

I watched him carefully.

"Beacon Hill," I said.

The blood drained from his face. *Beacon Hill* was the codename of our long-lost mutual friend—his ex-lover, Elizabeth Petersen.

"It can only be her, Édouard, and therefore it has to mean Steve is somehow involved. He's the only one in London nowadays who'd know her code name. Have you heard from her since Spain?"

His vigorous headshake was accompanied by a very decisive "No."

Elizabeth Petersen had been Édouard's lover during the Spanish Civil War. Steve had introduced them. She was a tough, but very charismatic woman. One could never have described her as a traditional beauty, but she was exceedingly fascinating and always surrounded by a multitude of male admirers. She was an American, from Boston, like Steve and Shorty. She could ride and shoot, and was fluent in several languages. However, she was impulsive and often irresponsible, disregarding the possible consequences of her actions.

I'd missed her after we'd gone our different ways, despite her bravado and accompanying recklessness during our time together in Spain. She'd plunged headlong into situations to get a good story in a manner that at the time many had considered foolish, but which I thought were more "foolhardy"—there's a difference. After the Civil War, I'd heard she'd returned home, expecting accolades for her excellent journalism, only to learn her millionaire father had sabotaged those prospects, telling her she should forget her nonsense and instead find a man with money and start a family. He wanted grandchildren, not newspaper inches from his daughter.

I'd only received one letter from her, filled with bitterness and the distress of learning no matter what she'd done and how well she'd written, no one had considered her as a female version of Hemingway, an Amazonian "soldier of fortune", but as a spoiled rich girl who'd tried to muscle in on men's territory.

I'd never heard back after my letter of sympathy, asking how she thought I might be able to help, extending her the offer of my flat in Munich, which had a lovely spare room for guests, in case she wanted to get away for a while.

I didn't know what had happened between her and Édouard, or why they weren't still together, but somehow, out of the blue, it seemed as though she'd contacted Steve.

Édouard and I chatted about Spain for a while until I must have drifted off again, because the next thing I knew, he was shaking my shoulder a few minutes after four in the morning. We roused Luc, who was still in front of the kitchen range, snoring loudly, and then the three of us headed out into the field behind the château.

By the time I eventually heard the aircraft overhead, I'd become quite nervous. I'd been pacing up and down along the edge of the field chain-smoking for about twenty minutes. It was quarter past five when the aircraft flew low over us and then turned to make a landing. Although it wouldn't be getting light for a few hours yet, it wouldn't be long before farmers started waking up. Not all of them were anti-Nazi. We needed to turn the aircraft around quickly and get it back into the air.

The plane landed in Édouard's long wheat-field. No crops had been sown for two years and it was now covered in a cropped, even coating of grass.

Eventually, the Hudson shuddered to a halt. I pushed my protesting captive towards the aircraft, still bound and gagged. It was a morning of surprises. First to jump out was Steve, followed by Andrzej. Then my heart sank, for the next to appear in the fuselage doorway were Michael and Shorty. The last to jump down was Peter Farnsworth. As he wore his flying helmet, I could only assume he must have been the pilot.

"Holy Mother of God!" I swore. "Where's Yves and Andrew? Why didn't you just bring Gladys as well? We could have had a staff meeting."

"Yves broke his foot two days ago," Andrzej said. "Andrew couldn't make it tonight. He was on his way to Scotland when your message came through, but he's being dropped off tomorrow night outside Foligny. We have to pick him up there."

Shorty grabbed my hand, squeezed it hard, and then picked up Luc under his arm and began to run around in the dark, both of them trying not to laugh.

"Gladys wanted to come," Michael quipped, "but she told me to tell you she'd just lacquered her nails."

I laughed. Typical remark from Gladys. I could hear her saying it with her "Dorothy Parker" voice.

"Surprised to see me?" Peter Farnsworth asked.

"Not anymore, Peter, you seem to pop up everywhere."

He laughed. I handed him a sheaf of papers to pass on to Colin Gubbins, the head of SOE, and another longish coded note for Gladys. I was about to hug both Shorty and my brother when Peter pulled at my sleeve. "A word please, before I head off. I have something for you." He drew me to one side and handed me a thin tome. "I'm not sure whether you've already read these or not?"

It was a collection of Walt Whitman's essays and poems. Without answering, I opened the book and leafed through it cursorily. As I was about to snap it shut, my thumb touched a slight ridge under the endpaper of the back cover. I looked up at Peter.

"It's from the Duke. He said to tell you there have been recent developments."

A cold shiver ran up my legs and into the small of my back. It could only mean the blackmailer had finally surfaced, and I assumed that hidden under the endpaper of the book were the instructions from George for the retrieval of the letters and the stolen piece of jewellery.

Until that moment, I'd started to wonder whether things could possibly get more complicated. Now I knew that yes, indeed they could.

CHAPTER 11

Shorty and I stood hand in hand, watching the Hudson take off. I gave a half-hearted wave, even though I knew neither Peter nor his co-pilot could have seen me in the darkness.

He handed me a cigarette. "Miss me?"

I leaned against him, resting my head on his shoulder. "Yup."

"Even after one day?"

"You bet," I said.

"You aren't angry I'm here?"

"I know there must be a reason for you to come. Let's talk about it when we get inside."

As we walked through the orchard at the back of Édouard's house, he started to hum a random-sounding melody while staring into the clear, inky-black sky above us.

"Shorty?"

"Yes, babe?"

"You know, when you left on the plane—*the 'wo du bist ...'* Did you make that up?"

"I did. It was a spur-of-the-moment thing, Tommy. Why?"

I kissed him hard.

"What was that for?" he asked when we came up for air.

"Because I love you," I said, "and even though it might be dangerous, I want you by my side."

He wrapped his arms around me. The smell of his leather jacket and his cologne was so familiar and safe it made me feel all would be well.

"Funny, this is, babe," he said, "you and me here in France."

"How so?"

"For most of my life I dreamed of coming to Europe. Seeing where my parents' families come from, going to museums, checking out the Old World ..."

"And?"

"Well, I never imagined, not once in a million years, I'd be standing in a field in France, under the stars, with someone like you in my arms."

I didn't know what to say. Anything would have been trite at that moment. Instead, I squeezed him tighter. "I suppose we'd better go in, so I can bang a few heads."

"Head-banging time, is it, then?"

I chuckled. "Maybe. I was only thinking that once we get inside I probably won't want to hear what I'm going to be told."

"Well, I can't help you there, either. I've no idea what it's all about. All I know is, Uncle Steve's been frowning ever since we took off from Northolt. Anyway, whatever happens, I'm right here at your side. If it turns out to be a huge headache, we can work it out together."

"You and me versus the world?"

"Sure, Tommy, it's all part of the job."

"So, it's a job now, is it?"

"Yup. Permanent, full-time, and for life." He threw his arms around my neck and we kissed for a long time. An unsuppressed wolf-whistle came from somewhere in the dark near the house, but neither of us drew apart. I merely raised one arm and gave Luc my middle finger. I knew it had to be him.

Once we'd reached the terrace that ran along the back of the chateau, Shorty stopped for a moment to admire Diana the Huntress. "Tommy, about the head-banging thing ..." he said, stroking the foot of the statue absent-mindedly.

235

"Yeah, you're right, sweetheart, as usual. Being cranky won't help anything. Why don't you go inside and introduce yourself to Édouard? He and your uncle and I all fought together in Spain. I know you'll get on like a house on fire. And, while you're at it, send Steve out here and tell him to bring a glass for me and a bottle of Édouard's best. If there's going to be any head-banging, perhaps it's best if he and I do it in private."

"If I hear shooting, I'll come running," he said with a chuckle.

I grabbed the cigarette he'd just lit from his mouth then leaned against the plinth of the statue while I waited for Steve to come outside.

Édouard's orchard started only about ten paces from the terrace, separated from it by a broad swathe of lawn. The air was crisp, with not even the tiniest breeze. Only the wisps of early morning mist, weaving gently between the trunks of the trees, showed it wasn't frozen in time.

"Tommy."

As Steve joined me, he handed me a glass and held up a bottle of Édouard's wine. "Here you are," he said. He leaned next to me, our shoulders touching, while he fidgeted with the fringe on his scarf. He knew I'd be wondering why he'd brought Michael and Shorty with him. I still had no idea—all in good time, I thought—he'd tell me when he was ready.

I flicked my cigarette butt across the lawn, watching its red tip arc through the air and then suddenly wink out as it fell into the dew on the grass. "So, Steve," I said, "Elizabeth …"

He let out a long sigh. "Jesus, Tommy, I don't even know where to begin …" He rubbed his eyes and groaned loudly.

"Our friend the Duke of Kent once said exactly the same words to me, you know."

"What was your reply?"

"I quoted your nephew at him: 'the beginning is always a good place to start'."

"Tommy, this is so darned secret I'm going to get my butt kicked from here to up high for merely thinking about some of the stuff I'm going to have to tell you. But I reckon if you don't already know, you'll simply have to be let in on it, especially seeing we're going to be wading neck-deep in poop while we sort out Lizzie's spectacular mess."

"Then you'd better give me another smoke before you start," I said. I took one of his proffered cigarettes and began to pat my pockets looking for my lighter. Shorty had most probably stolen it, as usual. Steve flicked his Zippo and held it out to me.

Just as I leaned in to light up, he said, "Have you ever heard of Opération Rongeur?"

I could scarcely believe my ears. How the hell did Steve know about OR—one of our most closely guarded research projects? I took a slow breath, and then, after the briefest hesitation, accepted his light before answering.

"Opération Rongeur? What the hell, Steve? Of all the secrets in the war … Is it only you who knows, or the whole of US military intelligence?" Despite my promise to myself to stay calm, I heard the edge in my voice.

"Keep your shirt on, Tommy. I was merely testing the water to see what you knew. But I've gotta say that I'm pretty surprised you're even aware of it. As far as we know, everyone at the SOE has been kept out of the loop."

"I only know about it because I stumbled on it by accident and then had to be filled in because I already knew too much," I said.

In fact, it had been Stewart Menzies at MI6 who'd told me, after I'd inadvertently opened a package not meant for me, but which had been retrieved by one of my Paris agents and delivered to my desk in error. When I took it to Stewart and explained my mistake, he'd had no choice but to bring me up-to-date.

Opération Rongeur was the name for a collaborative fledgling nuclear research programme, run out of Cambridge University's Physics Department. The team was led by British scientists who worked alongside a group of French physicists—all members of Frédéric Joliot's laboratory in Paris—men and women we'd repatriated to England. No one was supposed to know about the project—the Americans least of all. I'd been informed Churchill wanted to use the results of the research as an incentive, to entice more concrete co-operation from across the Atlantic. To hear the Yanks already knew about it astounded me. However, right now there were more pressing issues to discuss.

"What has OR got to do with Elizabeth, Steve?"

He studied his hands for a moment and then let out another lengthy sigh. "You and Édouard both know what she's like."

"Too impulsive for her own good. What's she done now?"

"Well, it seems she's 'obtained' classified material from the Kaiser Wilhelm Gesellschaft—from Klaus Clusius, to be precise. She photographed nearly everything he had on the Germans' Uranprojekt."

"You've got to be joking!"

How would Elizabeth have managed to get access to paperwork about the Nazis' nuclear fission programme? She could have only broken into the building. The thought made my blood run cold. I guessed there was more.

"She also 'recovered' the rest of Joliot's missing papers from *Oberst* Petrus Jäger, in Paris."

"Jesus wept!" I said.

Frédéric Joliot was France's leading theoretic nuclear physicist. Just before the Nazi invasion, he'd managed to get most of his notes out of the country to England, but in his haste to flee he'd left part of the collection in his laboratory. It must have been those notes Elizabeth had got her hands on.

"When you say 'recovered', am I right in reading between the lines to assume she most probably seduced, then killed Jäger—a Wehrmacht colonel?"

"You know her as well as I do, Tommy. It's the way she operates."

"So, let me get this straight, Steve. We have an American citizen on the loose, stealing top-secret documents in the middle of a war, and then killing a high-ranking Nazi official while she goes about it?"

Steve shrugged. "Your guess is as good as mine, Tommy. But yeah, knowing Elizabeth, I wouldn't put it past her."

"Very well," I growled. "God knows how you Americans have access to one of the biggest British secrets of the war. And, what's worse, somehow a civilian gets to know the Nazis have a similar research programme, and then goes off into the field by herself? What the hell is *our* job at the SOE supposed to be, Steve? This is what our men are trained for ..."

My voice trailed off as I became aware of the way he was looking at me. *There's more to the story* was written across his forehead. I finally twigged why four packages had arrived instead of the three I'd asked for, and why Andrew was going to parachute in tomorrow night—a team of two was needed for another mission.

"She sent you a message through MI6, didn't she?" I said. "Let me guess—does it go something like this? The Resistance have hidden her, and she needs rescuing. She's using the documents as a carrot so we pull her out and then get her back to the safety of Old Blighty."

His grimace told me what I'd suggested was indeed the truth. "Tommy, the American embassy moved to Vichy last year. There's no bolt-hole for her in Paris. And, if she does have information we can use—"

"This is a joke, Steve."

"Well, I was thinking Henry and I could go to Paris and—"

I turned to face him, standing so close our knees were touching, and jabbed his chest with my forefinger. "No, Steve, there's no way that's going to happen. It's far too dangerous. Heinrich has had no experience dealing with the Wehrmacht as yet, and neither have you. You've forgotten that notwithstanding your perfect spoken German, neither of you even knows *basic* Nazi operating procedures, let alone what to do if you were stopped and questioned by the SS or the Gestapo. I'm sorry to remind you, but think it through. There are better options without exposing either of you to a situation that could easily get out of hand with one simple mistake."

"I'm sorry, you're right of course. My immediate thought was I needed to look after him … and please don't tell him I said that. He's a big boy. It's something his old uncle finds hard to admit."

I forced myself to relax. This was none of his doing. The whole mess was typical of Elizabeth. The way she treated, or should I say "used", people had always affected me the same way. She'd dumped us, her friends, years ago for greener pastures and disappeared from our lives. How typical it was of her to reappear when she was in trouble.

"I'm sorry, Steve. I overreacted," I said and then picked up my glass from the plinth of the statue where I'd placed it. I patted Steve's shoulder and smiled, to reassure him I wasn't angry with him.

"You're taking this better than I expected," he said. "I don't know I could be so self-contained if one of our guys pulled a stunt like this."

"It *is* one of your guys who pulled this stunt."

"Oh, yeah. I keep forgetting Lizzie's a girl."

We both chuckled and clinked our glasses.

His knowledge of our top-secret project piqued my curiosity. I couldn't let it lie. So, feigning indifference, I play-punched his shoulder, and said, "Say, Steve, how long have the Americans been aware of our nuclear project?"

"Really, Tommy? What makes you think we haven't got an Opération Rongeur of our own?"

I could scarcely believe my ears. "Do our people know about that?" My voice was calm, but my mind was racing.

"Tommy, as close as we are, you know darned well there's things I can't talk about. I've said enough already."

I took his statement as an admission that the Americans were indeed running a nuclear research programme of their own. I thought the whole idea of being allies was to share information, not to keep it from each other. Despite myself, I let out a soft harrumph.

"I recognise that sound," he said.

"Oh, yes? As what?"

"You know what. I heard myself letting out the same noise when I learned about your 'Range and Direction Finding' stations. Thanks for sharing, Britain!" he said to the air.

It was true, the Yanks had been furious when they'd finally learned of our "RADAR", as they now were calling it.

"Who was it who just said 'there's things I can't talk about'?"

He rubbed the back of my neck affectionately. "Well, it's not only our governments seem to be keeping secrets from each other. There's a lot they don't tell you at the SOE, my friend," he said.

"Meaning?"

"Meaning you should consider doing a private deal with MI6 on the Q.T., now you seem to be running your own show. There's a lot of important stuff going on you lot at the SOE know nothing about. Knowledge the other agencies have, but which you don't have access to."

"Like what?"

He stared at the ground for a moment while biting his lower lip. I did the same thing when deciding whether to disclose something or not. "Okay, you didn't hear this from me … there's Station X, for example."

"No such thing, Steve."

"So they tell you."

"Are you going to tell me differently?"

How come Steve knew about a secret facility and I was in the dark about it? If it was true, then it was another example of the left hand hiding what the right hand was doing. I'd been told when I'd first started at the SOE that the Roman numeral X was missing from the station list because it was a planned facility that had never eventuated, and then it had been too late to renumber all the others.

"No, I'm not going out on a limb to tell you I've heard differently," Steve said, sensing my exasperation. "I've been told to keep quiet about it. But, Stewart Menzies might tell you otherwise—if you let on you've heard rumours. He's taking a group of Americans through your non-existent Station X in March."

"I'll keep that to myself until I speak with him, shall I?"

"Might be best, Tommy. Now, had any ideas about how we go about the whole Elizabeth thing?"

Of course, I'd been sorting it out in the back of my mind ever since he'd said she needed rescuing—most musicians could concentrate on two things at the same time.

"Michael should go with you to Paris, Steve, not your nephew. He's had a lot of experience dealing with civilian and military matters in Germany and in occupied France. Besides, I have an ulterior motive. That Kraut we packed onto the plane to go back to England had been heading to La Rochelle to interrogate three captured English pilots. If any one of them knows anything about what might have happened to his Rhys, I can't have Michael with us. I know it's a long shot, but you know what he's like. He could go running off by himself on a wild goose chase and put us all in danger."

"I suppose you're right, Tommy, but … it's not that I didn't want Michael along, it's—"

"What is it with you and Michael, Steve? You pussyfoot around each other all the time. It's very confusing when my own brother and my best friend hide personal stuff from me."

He took a sip of his wine. "It's complicated," he said.

"Complicated as opposed to what?"

He stopped just as he was about to speak, as if someone had turned him off at the mains. I could see the struggle in his eyes as he searched for the right words. They came after what seemed like a very long time. "Michael and I had a ... a thing," he said, almost inaudibly. "It was only once, and long before he met Rhys. You were still in Munich."

This was something I hadn't expected to hear. Steve did stuff with other men?

"Why didn't you tell me, of all people, Steve? You're my best friend. Haven't we always shared our inner secrets? Didn't you trust me? You know I don't make judgements about what people do."

"I was ashamed."

"Ashamed of my brother?"

"No, not that. I was ashamed of the way I treated him, Tommy. It was the first time I'd even tried anything along those lines. It confused me, so I pushed him away. Finally, when I'd mustered enough courage to talk to him about it, he'd met his Welshman, and—"

"Enough, Steve. No more 'ands', okay?"

He nodded.

"It explains a lot, actually. I guess seeing Michael pining over Rhys must be hard on you."

"No, Tommy, you've got it all wrong—" I stopped whatever he was about to say by putting my arms around him.

"It's okay, Steve. I wish you could have been open with me. How long have we known each other? Six years?"

"This isn't just about that one time with Michael. It's harder for some people to accept these things than others, Tommy. We aren't all lucky like you and Henry. Besides, I asked Michael not to say anything about what had happened and told him I'd talk to you when I felt the time was right."

"You know, Steve, another Michael will come along some day, if that's what you really want," I said. Although I did my best to sound positive, this was something I hadn't really wanted to hear—my best friend carrying a torch for my brother, whose partner had gone missing.

"That's the part of the problem, Tommy. There will never be another Michael ..."

I couldn't quite make sense of the strange expression on his face, or the odd rhythm of the words. I was about to ask him what he meant when we were interrupted by a soft whistle. Shorty was leaning against the back door, holding up an empty glass and a bottle of wine. I motioned for him to come and join us. He stopped a few paces away with a quizzical look on his face.

"No black eyes or broken bones. It's quite safe," Steve said.

"I thought you guys could do with another bottle. Umm ... was I interrupting?" he asked, knowing full well he was.

"It was a timely interruption, Henry," his uncle replied.

"I hoped so—can't have my two favourite people in the world falling out, now, can I? So, what's the story, guys?"

"One of Édouard's old flames has unexpectedly turned up and is in a spot of bother. She needs rescuing," I explained to Shorty. "Once we're back inside, I'll fill everyone else in on what your uncle and I have been discussing."

"Should I take this bottle with me and go back inside and wait?" he asked.

I pulled him close to me by the belt on his trousers and shook my head. *"Wait a minute! Wait a minute! Cutter, you ain't leaving this village without my permission. Give me that bottle,"* I said.

It was a quote from one of his favourite movies.

"Sure thing. *Proceed with caution, Gunga Din!*" he replied, handing me the bottle, his face wreathed in a broad grin. The memory of him and Gladys discussing the movie made me smile—far more than our situation warranted. His cheerful nature and the joke about *Gunga Din* had cleared the air. Perhaps Steve and I had been more tense than I'd realised.

By the time we got back inside, I'd basically sorted out what I felt we should do, so explained my plan to my friends. I gave them only enough information to clarify our situation, without giving away anything above their pay grades, as we sometimes said. Seeing Michael was to go with Steve to find Elizabeth, he'd have to be told about the Nazi documents. The others could safely be kept in the dark, unless our situation warranted it.

I thought it best we get cracking as soon as possible, especially if the sound of the aircraft landing then taking off again caused inquisitive busy-bodies to come knocking on Édouard's door. I decided Steve and Michael should travel to Paris by train without delay. They were to pose as American businessmen and take a set of papers for Elizabeth, who'd masquerade as Steve's wife once they tracked her down. As finding refuge at the US embassy in Paris was no longer an option, I suggested that, once they'd found her, the three of them should travel directly to Berlin to meet with Leland Morris, the *chargé d'affaires* at the US embassy there. Morris could not only arrange new identity cards but also provide embassy staff travel papers, so they could take the train to Zürich. Once in Switzerland, it would be easy to get air tickets to Lisbon and then on to London.

Édouard informed us he already had a good undercover network set up in Paris. I sent him, Michael, and Steve into his study to start to work on the details of their trip, and to decide who to contact when they got to the capital, so they could start to look for Elizabeth. I followed them down the hallway, stopping Steve before he went into the office and quietly asked him to tell Michael and Édouard about the Nazi documents, without actually disclosing what they were. I felt it best to keep Opération Rongeur between the two of us, if possible.

"Well, Tommy," Shorty asked after I'd returned to the kitchen, "how are we going to handle the other situation—the airmen in La Rochelle?"

"It's going to be a bit tricky," I said, "but I do have an idea. Let's see what you think of it. How about we drop you off somewhere safe outside Granville before we pick up the captain Alberbach was due to collect? Once we've collected him, we'll get rid of him—and, once that's done, you can take his place."

"I don't understand," he replied. "Why won't I be coming with you and Andrzej? Andrew won't have arrived. I could stand in for Alberbach's sergeant."

"Not only does your German sound too posh for a sergeant with a strong regional accent, but we also need time to fill you in on how German military protocol works. Andrzej and Andrew have been training at it for years now. It's for your own protection. By the time we get to La Rochelle we'll have taught you the basics of what do to and say and when. I don't want you inadvertently giving away our covers by not knowing what the correct behaviour is between ranks in the Wehrmacht and in the SS. We'll have the captain's body in the boot by the time we arrive to collect you and Andrew."

"I'll have a grave ready and waiting," Shorty said.

I noticed Andrzej's small smile of approval. He liked Shorty's matter-of-fact soldier voice and attitude. It was something in him I admired too. He was as kind and gentle as the day was long, except when he was wearing his professional boots.

"Obviously, we can't make any plans about the airmen until we're actually in La Rochelle and get a chance to see the lie of the land," I added. "Other than that, does either of you have any other questions?"

"What are we going to do with the elephant in the room?" Shorty asked, in English. Luc was pretending nonchalantly to inspect his nails. I cursed myself. Ever since we'd returned to the kitchen we'd been speaking in French.

"Luc," I said, "perhaps you should stay here with Édouard until we get news that your father's been released."

Luc crossed his arms and scowled at me. "I speak Breton and Normand. None of you can do that," he said. "And I know who runs the Maquis in most places between here and La Rochelle. Most of them are relatives in some way or another."

"No way, Luc, you can't come with us. It's far too dangerous, and besides, you don't speak any German."

"And how much time do you think you're going to waste trying to convince the locals to help you?"

"We've managed before," I said.

He shook his head. "But not this time with so many of you—all travelling in German uniforms. If I were to go along, I could send warning to the people who matter, so some partisan with a flea in his arse doesn't blow your heads off on the open road."

Andrzej laughed.

"Besides, I'm the best and quickest radio operator you're ever going to find."

He had me there. He hadn't said it out of pride. It was a statement of fact. None of us, except Michael, was good enough at Morse code to converse at the speed needed for the quick reception and transmission of messages. The Germans were using interception vans to pinpoint Resistance radios, so it was of the utmost importance to keep outgoing messages brief and quick.

"I don't know ..."

"My father is still in jail. Are you sending me back like some kid, to be captured by the Boches?" He stared at me. It was a challenge. Not more than a few hours ago, I'd told him he was a man, and now here I was, treating him like a child.

"Tommy ..." Andrzej said softly. He gave me a barely perceptible nod.

"All right, Luc," I said, "but you travel hidden under a blanket. There is no way of explaining a fifteen-year-old French boy in a Waffen SS colonel's staff car."

"Oh, yes, there is," he said, pursing his lips and blowing me a blowsy kiss.

Once we all stopped laughing, I gave him a long lecture about how he'd be thrown over the nearest cliff if he put one foot wrong.

★★★★★

I rubbed the tips of my fingers slowly and softly across the broad expanse of Shorty's back, luxuriating in the sensuality of the situation. It was the first time we'd been in a proper bed for three weeks.

"You know, I love where we are at the moment," he said, his voice wistful and happy. He lay on his tummy, his head nestled in the crook of his elbow.

"In bed, in an empty French château, in the middle of a war?"

"No, you smart-ass. The comfort of 'us'. How I feel about you. The fact that you don't fight me anymore."

"I fought you?"

"You know you did," he replied with a small laugh.

"That's only because I wasn't used to letting anyone in."

"And I was?"

"You know what I mean. We're so lucky, Shorty. Think of the guys who spend their lives without someone special—or the men who feel compelled to get married, but who really want to be with another man. We're surrounded by a whole lot of people who respect our privacy and who couldn't care less about what we do."

"It's because you attract those sorts of people," he said, rolling onto his side. He pressed a forefinger on the tip of my nose and then smirked as I crossed my eyes to look at what he was doing.

"And you have nothing to do with it?"

He shook his head. "I was wondering about that on the flight over here, you know. I was thinking our life in London was a bit like the community in Boston's North End, where all the Italians hang out."

"Explain, please."

"People stick together in groups because they have something in common, right? You must have Italian, or German, or whatever, suburbs where you come from?"

"Of course we do," I said.

"Think what it'd be like to be the only Italian in the street. You'd go looking for other people in the town who shared your language and your culture—people you could feel comfortable with, people who didn't point at you because you were different. You could go about your business and be happy if you knew you could find time to be among your fellow countrymen—to have time to top up your batteries, so to speak."

"So, what you're saying is guys like you and me tend to cluster together for the same reason."

"Of course," he replied. "It's not about sex, it's about our sexuality. That's what we have in common."

I'd been thinking the same thing on the night we were dancing together at George's, before Christmas. All those military men having fun, being relaxed, and without having to think about looking over their shoulders every five minutes. "Maybe, after the war ..." I said hopefully.

"Maybe, Tommy, maybe. But, whatever happens, we'll make our own circle of pals who won't give a hoot about anything but who we are as people. In the meantime, as I said to you before, we just keep our heads down and go about our business. What happens between you and me is no one's affair but our own."

I laughed softly and then snuggled up against him. "No wonder I love you, Heinrich Reiter."

"You mean apart from my sparkling personality, devastating good looks, and manly physique?"

I raised myself onto my elbow and then tapped his nose with my forefinger. "Well, I'm happy to start with your manly physique ..."

"Again?" he protested playfully and then pulled me into his arms once more.

The next thirty minutes disappeared into a haze.

*****

I'd always dreamed of seeing Mont Saint-Michel close up.

Once, years before, I'd made out its shape from the beach at Genêts, near Avranche, but it was six kilometres from where I'd been standing. At the time, it had been so distant all it had done was make me feel empty and wanting more.

The five of us stood by the side of the road at La Caserne, leaning against the colonel's big black Mercedes, having a cigarette while looking out over the causeway at the island monastery.

Shorty had been beside himself when he'd first seen the car. Even I had to admit those bulky German staff-cars were impressive. We'd let him drive on the few long, straight stretches of road where we would be travelling too fast for anyone to really pick out the insignia of whoever was behind the wheel. Damn, we looked sinister, I thought, casting an eye over our collective SS, Gestapo, and Wehrmacht uniforms.

Captain Hans Hofschreiber had been picked up in Granville and then, once we were out into the countryside, despatched with no remorse. The man was a pompous moron, spouting propaganda-filled jargon at every opportunity, obviously trying to impress me. It got to a point when I could bear his odious ranting no longer, so asked Andrzej to stop the car, told the man I needed to talk to him privately, and asked him to accompany me while I'd a piss.

He, of course, had turned away while I'd pretended to relieve myself. I shot him through the back of the head.

Luc's presence had been a blessing. As he'd said, he had cousins all up and down this stretch of coast and knew which of them could be trusted. While we'd gone to pick up the ill-fated captain, we'd left him and Shorty south of Granville in an abandoned goatherder's cottage that belonged to one of Luc's "uncles". When we'd got back, with Hofschreiber's corpse in the boot of the car, we'd stripped it and then rolled it into the grave Shorty had prepared. Luc's "goatherd uncle" had appeared as we'd been covering the mound of earth with leaves and branches. He'd been somewhat disappointed to find we'd buried the man. He'd intended on feeding the body to his pigs. Not one of us had shown any revulsion, as we might have done during peacetime. We were at war and none of us could possibly have known what catastrophes might have happened to the goatherder, his village, or his family when the Germans had invaded his homeland.

"We'd best collect our 'parcel'," Luc had said. Our parcel was Andrew, who'd parachuted in late in the previous evening and was being hidden by a small group of local *maquisards*.

As we drove, Luc and Andrzej playfully exchanged insults, in Normand and Gascon. Andrzej's mother came from Bordeaux, halfway between La Rochelle and Bayonne. He knew the coastal area south of La Rochelle very well, having worked there on a fishing trawler in his university holidays. He told us that before the war, he and his mother had come to visit her parents every year.

Trying to smoke in a fast-moving touring car with the roof down was an exercise in futility. The airstream blew away more of the cigarette than we could smoke. That's why we'd stopped here, on the far end of the causeway at La Caserne, a mile from the ninth-century castle in the sea.

"Did you know the Archangel Michael was supposed to have appeared to Saint Aubert here in the eighth century?" I said to Shorty. "My brother would have loved to see Mont Saint-Michel."

"All the historical records were moved out late last year and stored near Édouard's house at Saint-Lô," Andrew said.

Andrzej looked at him oddly. "Why do you mention that? Is it important?"

"Of course it is. It's important we preserve Luc's heritage, Andrzej. The Germans won't win this war. We need to know where they've stored everything they've stolen and then get it back to where it belongs. Hitler and Göring have been 'appropriating' art works from all over France for their own offices and houses. Once this disgusting regime's over and they're dead, it will be the duty of the victors to return stolen art to the French people."

I felt much moved while my Scottish friend said this. I couldn't help but nod vigorously in agreement. It was my view that not only were most of the leading Nazis thugs but they were also vandals of the worst sort.

✶✶✶✶✶

We spent the night in Nantes, courtesy of Lieutenant-Colonel Karl Hotz—the *Feldkommandant* of the town. The British military hierarchy, many of them aristocrats themselves, had tried to be careful when appropriating some of the nicer stately homes in the English countryside. The Germans had not been nearly as subtle. The British requested them—the Nazis marched in and then threw everyone out into the street. Hotz had installed himself in the Château des ducs de Bretagne in the centre of town and entertained us in considerable style, even inviting Andrzej, our "driver".

Getting a room together had been simple. I merely mentioned that Shorty—posing as *Hauptmann* Hofschreiber—had been ordered to guard me during the night, mainly because the Resistance's favourite targets were SS interrogators. I felt the excuse was chancing my arm, but Hotz accepted it without question. They set up a camp stretcher for Shorty in the corner of the room I'd been assigned. We'd muss it up before we got into bed, in case we forgot in the morning.

Dinner was delightful. Hotz was a career soldier. As we chatted over dinner, it became clear he was operating under duress and in a position he didn't like. He told us he'd been working as a civil engineer in Nantes before Hitler invaded Poland. His posting, as its *Kommandant*, was ordered by the High Command, despite his wish not to accept it. He was very well educated, offering to play the piano for me when I spied a beautiful violin in a display case in the music room. The violin was a delight, only needing a little tuning. It felt so wonderful in my hands that I nearly cried. The time spent on my old QV instrument made this one impossibly delightful to play.

At first, I'd been extremely reluctant to pick it up, in case he'd ever attended any of my concerts in Germany, and might have made a connection and recognised me. However, earlier in the evening we'd done what any field operative would have done—teased out his past history. He'd told us he'd worked in Nantes since the 1920s, had returned to Germany in thirty-eight and then had been posted back here, due to his familiarity with the town. As I'd never performed in this part of France, and he'd returned to Germany after I'd left, I'd felt it safe to take up the instrument and play.

I'd been somewhat surprised when he'd returned from the library with pile of music, on top of which was a copy of Beethoven's Kreutzer sonata. I'd grabbed it with both hands, unable to stop myself kissing the cover with delight.

"Would you prefer something else? It's quite difficult for the violin," he'd asked.

I'd tried my hardest not to smirk, and although I'd memorised it years ago, I'd pretended to use the sheet music when I played it. It was a piece in my concert repertoire and I knew it back to front. I'd loved every note in the score for as long as I could remember.

His soft moan of pleasure as I played the opening four bars of the work was enough to tell me the man wasn't merely a piano player—he was a musician.

I experienced moments I'd never felt before when performing this work. Maybe it was the wonderful instrument, or Hotz's very skilled accompanying? However, I could have sworn I produced a new level of sophistication hitherto been beyond my reach. Could it be I was improving? It was more likely I was in love, and more in touch with my feelings, and therefore with the sound in my hands.

Hotz was genuinely moved and very excited after we finished the first movement. *"Das darf ich kaum glauben! Wunderbar! Bravo!"* he exclaimed from the piano stool, applauding loudly, his face wreathed in smiles and his eyes wet with unshed tears.

I politely refused to play anything else and reluctantly gave him back the violin. I shouldn't really have drawn attention to myself while undercover. But the magnetic draw of that wonderful instrument, together with the chance to make music, had been too much to resist.

"I was to go to the Wiener Volkskonservatorium, but my father insisted I study engineering instead," he explained, after I'd complimented him on his exceptionally fine playing. The piano part was extremely demanding.

He sighed and studied his hands while speaking. I recognised the gesture. It was one every professional performer knew only too well. We heard the accompanying phrase countless times—*"I could have been a ..."* but for some ignorant parent who didn't see the joy of music as a fitting livelihood. How much had been stolen from the world by the unfinished training of these embryonic performers? I felt quite sad for him.

To my surprise, Shorty sat down at the piano to play and sing some German popular songs and operetta. When he finished with *"Wien, Wien, nur Du allein"*, I nearly forgot the war for the second time that night. The terrible futility of conflict and the tragic madness that made sane, normal men kill one another in the most grotesque and cruel ways imaginable was evoked by the sudden, loud, and sustained applause from a small group of assembled officers and enlisted men who'd gathered outside the open door to listen to our impromptu performance. I loathed the moments when I saw the human face of the enemy. It was almost too much to bear. I could only do the things I did when I depersonalised them. Seeing their smiling faces, some with tears of homesickness in their eyes, was very hard to bear. I said my goodnights and headed off to bed.

I was genuinely sad to say farewell to *Obersturmbannführer* Hotz the next day. If people like him had been in command, instead of that manic Austrian, this stupid war would never have come about.

★★★★★

It took us about five hours to drive to La Rochelle.

We stopped outside town, at Les Grands Champs, to ask directions from an elderly woman with a handcart. Édouard had given us instructions to make contact with the priest of the abbey of Saint-Hilaire. The woman curtly told us where to go—both with directions and invective—then spat on the ground as we drove off.

I tipped my cap to her.

Père Christophe nearly had a heart attack when he saw us arrive in the Mercedes, dressed in our Nazi uniforms. It was only when Andrzej began to speak in Gascon dialect and Luc in Normand he relaxed and began to listen to our story.

We stowed the Mercedes in one of the barns of the abbey and then changed into civilian clothes. There was a lot to reconnoitre in the town and contacts to be made before we could approach the *Kommandantur*. Père Christophe invited us into the refectory of the abbey so we could talk about the German occupation of La Rochelle and its surrounding areas. Over a glass of decent local wine he explained things were very complicated. There were two opposing groups of local Resistance fighters. Neither had any formal contact with England as far as he knew, and there was a struggle for control between the two leaders—men who hated each other and had done for years. There was no chance they'd ever work together, and both groups would remain disparate as long as these two were in charge. However, Père Christophe said he'd make arrangements for me to meet with one of the leaders in La Rochelle in the early afternoon, offering us the use of his immaculate 1933 Citroën Coupe. He explained his parishioners each donated a litre of gasoline every so often so he could drive around the countryside attending to their needs—and to do a bit of spying while he was at it.

Some time later, I sat in a café near the church of the Saint-Saveur, waiting for my contact to arrive.

"Bonjour," said the man who sat down at my table.

"Bonjour," I replied, deciding to speak with my mother's Lorraine accent, rather than use cultivated French. I felt it would be friendlier. I introduced myself, substituting my mother's maiden name in place of my own surname. "My name is Thomas Thiriot," I said, holding out my hand.

He said his name was Martin. He didn't offer me his full name, which I accepted as being a precaution. He also didn't shake my hand, but tilted his head, albeit with a sad smile. I understood what he meant—*maybe later, when I know who you are.*

We strolled down to the harbour together, chatting about the weather, the fishing fleets, even which mushrooms were in season, but avoiding the reason for our meeting. Despite the cautious way he spoke, I couldn't help noticing he was naturally charming—every so often he let his defences down and unleashed a flashing, genuine smile.

"It's quite odd, Thomas," he said. "I have the strangest feeling I trust you already."

"You've no reason not to trust me," I replied, "and I have to confess I trust you too." I caught a glimpse of "almost-blond" hair beside one of the quayside stalls.

"This way," he said, indicating the narrow laneway beside a boarded-up *hostellerie*.

He knocked eleven times, in an irregular, complex rhythm, at the door of a small house, which lay hidden from the quayside behind the abandoned pub. I reckoned the knocks were to prevent anyone else who might be observing being able to repeat the sequence readily.

An old woman, probably in her eighties, opened the door and motioned us inside. The room in which we sat was bare, apart from a table and three chairs. Once we were seated, she leaned across the table and inspected me carefully before rattling off a series of questions about Strasbourg, first in Lorraine French and then in Alsace German. When I replied in Parisian French, instead of dialect, she slapped my hand, which made me grin.

"Very well, madame," I snapped. "It's obvious you're from Alsace too, but I have to tell you your German's as rusty as plough left in a barn!"

"Well, you certainly are from Strasbourg," she said, laughing at my use of such an old-fashioned saying, only ever heard in that city. "But, it doesn't necessarily mean you are who you say you are."

I knocked eleven times on the table, repeating the exact rhythm Martin had used—being a musician with a good memory proved quite handy. At that moment, a door behind her flew open, and a skinny, bespectacled young man burst into the room, pointing a Luger at me. I slowly stood from my chair, my hands above my head, while trying to assess vantage points around the room.

"Count backwards from one hundred as quickly as you can," he said, to my astonishment, in English.

I did what he said. He stopped me when I got to eighty with a gesture of his gun, and then shouted angrily, "Now the alphabet, backwards too!"

"All right," I muttered angrily, "don't do your lolly."

"Well, bugger me!" he said, and then laughed loudly while tucking the gun into his waistband. "Levi Samuels," he said, holding out his hand. "Ex-professor of English at Michel de Montaigne University of Bordeaux—originally from Collingwood in Melbourne—pleased to meet you."

"You're an Aussie?" I was past surprised.

"Too right!" he said, grinning as he shook my hand. "And I gather you telling me *not to do my lolly* means you are too."

I nodded. "That's as it may be, Levi," I said, "but, unless you let me open the door, my guess is a very tall, angry American is going to burst in here any moment and start shooting."

He looked startled, but I reassured him and the older woman. When I opened the door, of course Shorty was outside, tensed and waiting. I told him to come in and then introduced him to Martin and Levi.

"And whom do I have the honour of addressing," he asked in his perfect but strongly American-accented French.

The woman held out her hand, which he kissed. She looked as though she might swallow her dentures in surprise, but merely blushed and said, "You may call me Horloge."

"Clock?" Shorty asked.

"Yes, Clock," she replied, tapping the side of her nose with one forefinger, "because I know when it is the right time for everything."

As we talked, I noticed she couldn't take her eyes off Shorty. It was as if she was flirting with him, and he played right along. After a short time, I knew they trusted us completely. *"Mon dieu,"* she said, "how pleasant it is to talk in German to someone who is not a *Kartoffelbauer*."

"I don't speak like a potato farmer!" I protested. My German was perfect—maybe a bit of Bavarian slang every so often, but Berliner-correct.

"But he speaks beautiful, cultivated, *preußisches Deutsch*. True, he does speak French like a turnip ..." she said with wink.

I smirked, despite the grumpy look he gave me.

Levi had been telling me the Germans hadn't started rounding up the Jewish population yet, but he'd been dismissed from his post at the university with no notice.

"I left Munich in thirty-eight," I said. "On the seventh of December—and yes, it was because of Kristallnacht."

Once Levi produced a bottle and five glasses, the conversation became not only animated but also much more informative. After I'd explained our problem, Martin told me he'd be able to help, but—and there was a big but—there was a major obstacle. Jérôme, the leader of the other Resistance group, was both extremely narrow-minded and paranoid. It was his group who'd been hiding the three airmen now in captivity. They'd been smuggled through the country by the Resistance, all the way from the Belgian border to La Rochelle. The locals had planned to get them onto a fishing boat at Mimizan-Plage and then take them by sea to northern Spain. But someone had informed. And, while Jérôme had been at work in the local munitions factory, the Germans had raided the hiding place and carted off not only the three English pilots but Jérôme's wife and sister as well.

"Then we'll have to try to rescue them too, if we can manage it," I said.

"There's one more problem," Martin said. "Jérôme's father and his two brothers were killed at Mers-el-Khébir. He's not going to like talking to a load of Englishmen. He won't even look at Levi, and he's an Australian."

The sinking of the French Mediterranean fleet at anchor in North Africa remained the cause of a great deal of anti-British sentiment in France. Wounds were still fresh nine months later. If Jérôme had lost three of his family, then it would be difficult for him to look us in the face, even if Andrew was the only Briton among us.

"I found the whole sorry mess impossible to comprehend myself," I said. "Maybe when he hears we intend to try to rescue his wife and sister he might be more amenable?"

"Maybe," Martin mused. "He finishes work at around four thirty. I think you should wait somewhere nearby, and then, if he agrees to meet you, I can bring him to you."

"Did you get to meet the pilots?"

He nodded. "Two were Scottish, and the other was from Canada, I think."

My heart sank a little at this news. "I don't suppose you've heard of any other English pilots coming this way?"

Horloge answered. "There was one in, when was it? October, I think …"

That didn't rule Rhys out. He'd disappeared in September. But still, the chances were slim to impossible.

"He was in a terrible mess—shot in the leg. He was trying to get to Lesaka in Navarre, if I remember correctly. He stayed here until not long before Christmas when the other three arrived, and then he simply disappeared the same night, leaving a note to say he was grateful, but four were too many to hide safely."

My ears shot up at the mention of Lesaka, as I knew Michael and Rhys had spent a week in the Basque country at the end of April in thirty-nine. "Did anyone keep the note?" I asked. "Has anyone still got it?"

"Of course. Père Christophe has it."

"And there was another thing," Martin said.

"What was that?" I asked.

"He could speak Breton, although it was the strangest dialect I've ever heard."

My heart soared in my chest. Rhys Williams spoke Welsh. It was his mother tongue. Not many non-linguists knew Welsh and Breton were related. Migrating Celts had brought the language to Brittany from the west of England in the middle ages. Both languages were what we language specialists classified as being *Brittonic* languages. Oddly enough, if spoken Cornish still existed, a speaker would find it easier to understand Breton than a modern Welshman. Still, if needs be, each one could make the other understand. Rhys would often brag that if he ever came down in Brittany, he'd be able to converse with the natives.

*****

It was closer to five in the afternoon when I heard the agreed knock on the door of the barn where we'd been waiting.

It had been less than surprising to find Horloge already there when we arrived. I guessed she was there to be the peacekeeper. There was something about her that, despite her age, brooked no opposition.

The moment Jérôme spat on the floor as he entered the empty farm building, I knew the meeting was going to be difficult. His whole demeanour was aggressive. He'd neither meet my eyes nor take my proffered hand.

"I'm sorry for what happened to your father and your brothers," I said. "But, please be aware that neither of us is English."

"I'm only here because Martin said you might be able to free Simone and Nicole."

"Well, that will depend on whether you're able to help us or not."

"If I had my way I'd tell you to go fuck yourselves," he said.

Horloge smacked him across the shins with her walking stick. "You always were a nasty piece of work, Jérôme. If I had *my* way, your mother would have drowned you at birth. Never forget that, although you lost a father and two brothers, it was I who lost a son and the two better grandsons of the three of you."

"Sorry, Grandma," he muttered, managing to sound both contrite and angry at the same time.

"These men are going to risk their lives to try to save my grand-daughter and your wife. How did you ever get to be so mean and ugly in your soul?"

"Your son, my *father*, made me like it," he hissed. I moved between them.

"I think this is useless, Martin," I said. "I can't see this man could help us in any way. He has no self-control or discipline. It'd be like working with a thunderstorm. We'll manage by ourselves. I think we should go."

As Shorty and I turned to leave, the man gave a strangled cry. "No, please ..." He threw himself between us and the door and then grabbed the lapels of my jacket. "I'm sorry. My wife, my sister ..."

I carefully but forcefully pried his fingers from my coat.

"I'll let you know what I can do," I said. "But, at this point, until I get inside the *Kommandantur* and see the set-up, I can't promise anything."

Despite his continuing surliness and reluctance to talk about his own operations in La Rochelle, I questioned him about his group, mainly to assess how I thought he could help. It didn't take long to confirm our view the man was too unstable to trust with any primary attack, but could be useful as a backup. He became even more hostile towards us when Shorty pointed out he'd most likely be playing second fiddle to Martin's group of men.

"I don't know why we just don't storm the place," he said.

"And risk not only the death of your wife and sister but of your men? And then the Nazis' retribution on the citizens of La Rochelle?"

A direct attack on the Germans' headquarters would be suicidal. I'd walked past it earlier in the day. The *Kommandant* had commandeered the École Pratique de Commerce et d'Industrie, in the rue Albert. The building was protected by a high wall, in which sat a stout wrought-iron gate. Two sentries stood on guard outside, with another two behind the gate, patrolling the building's forecourt.

While I'd been strolling on the *quai* with Martin, Shorty had been busy, thinking of strategies. He'd come up with a well-thought-out plan that involved the transfer of the airmen back to Nantes. It was where the regional headquarters were, and he'd argued it could make sense for a high-ranking SS interrogator to take the prisoners there for refined questioning—torture in other words. It wouldn't be too hard to hijack the convoy on the way. Getting the women out of the prison was another problem, which couldn't be solved until we actually got inside and saw the layout of the German army building.

Irritated his suggestion to go in with all guns blazing had been dismissed, Jérôme left abruptly, and without bidding us goodbye. He growled his way out of the barn, without even saying goodbye to his grandmother, who merely shook her head sadly and appeared to lean more heavily on her walking stick for a moment or two.

"What are the chances of our pulling this off without him?" I asked Martin.

"If you don't include him, he's bound to find out, and then how will that leave us after you've gone?" Martin said, running his hand through his hair.

"From what I've seen of him, I'm surprised he hasn't already tried to storm the *capitainerie* and kill everyone."

"He's not stupid. He knows what the Boches would do. La Rochelle would be reduced to a pile of rubble. All of us either dead or in camps."

"It's the fear of my anger. That's the only thing that's stopped him," Horloge said, her face betraying hurt and some other, inner battle.

Every family had its secrets and struggles. This one seemed to be exceptionally fractured.

★★★★★

After the meeting, Shorty and I met up with Andrew in a tavern on the quayside, and the three of us wandered up to the tavern on Avenue de la Porte Royale, where we'd arranged to be collected.

Andrew had always been one of my best mates, right from the day when I'd first met him. It had been shortly after I'd returned to England and during my first weeks at MI6. As we'd both started at the same time, we'd quickly become friends. He was an irreverent, freckled, fair-haired Scot from Inverness, who could swear like a trooper in both English and French and who could shoot the eye of a pigeon at three hundred yards. His German was expressive, cultured, and used with great finesse, and, since July, he was truly one of the major assets at the Special Operations Executive.

I'd confessed my secret to him a few months after we'd first met. We'd taken some lunch and hiked to the top of Arthur's Seat in Edinburgh. It had been while we were lying in the sun he'd noticed my gaze roaming over the thick blond hair of his legs. He'd been very calm and non-judgemental over the whole thing. I'd been mortified, blaming my inspection of his calves on the fact he was wearing a kilt at the time. I'd never felt anything sexual towards him—it had been merely the appreciation of his masculinity. I'd explained it might be exactly the same for him, if he happened to throw a casual glance at a woman's legs, or notice the shape of her bust.

Andrew was married to Jean—Bonny Jean, as I liked to call her—and was the proud father of two little boys, the youngest and most recent of whom was my godson, Jamie. Andrew was like a brother to me. We'd always got on like a house on fire, and he'd warmed quickly to Shorty.

Andrzej and Luc arrived nearly an hour late to pick us up in Père Christophe's car, having been delayed by the search for a few litres of petrol to replace what we'd used, so it wasn't until around eight that evening we arrived back at the abbey. The most wonderful smell issued from the kitchen when we finally sat down. I wasn't at all surprised to find Levi there. It was he who'd been busy cooking.

"What's that magnificent smell?" Luc asked. Levi slapped his hand as he tried to sneak a look under the cover of the large *marmite* in the centre of the table.

"*Voilà, poule au pot!*" Levi announced, lifting the lid with a flourish. The aroma filled the room. I distinctly heard at least two stomachs rumble at the same time.

"Oh, my God," Shorty said, fanning the steam into his nostrils. "Chickens! My favourite!"

"Anything edible is your favourite," Andrew quipped and was rewarded with an elbow to his ribs.

"It's not exactly a chicken," Levi said, "it's a *pintade*."

"What the hell is that when it's at home?" Shorty asked and then apologised and crossed himself as he glanced at Père Christophe.

"It's a guinea fowl, you heathen," I said in English. "Ugly, stupid birds whose call sounds like a squeaky gate. But, my friend, they're the best eating bird on earth."

Père Christophe was obviously too hungry to wait and began to say grace while we were still squabbling. I only heard *"Benedictus, benedicat,"* before Shorty gabbled off, *"per Jesum Christum Dominum Nostrum. Amen,"* and then held out his plate.

I scowled at him, but Père Christophe laughed and then leaned over and ruffled his hair. What did I know about Roman Catholic boys?

★★★★★

Later that night, I lay curled around my big man, gently biting the back of his neck.

"Shorty, I need to tell you something," I said, trying to keep my voice low. We'd chosen to sleep in the hayloft, the others spread out in other parts of the abbey. Andrew was tucked up in the empty stables below us.

"I've been waiting," he said.

"Really?"

"After Peter dropped us off at Saint-Lô, I saw you and he were whispering—and the book he gave you."

"You aren't going to like it."

"Not if it means us being apart again."

I didn't answer.

"It's that business for the Duke of Kent then, I suppose."

I sighed. "Okay. I'm buggered if I'm going to hide anything from you anymore, even if it gets us both killed."

He laughed a little too loudly.

"Keep it down up there, you two," Andrew yelled from below.

"You could have stayed away for at least another half an hour," I called down at him.

"God, you two are like bloody rabbits. Now get to sleep, for Christ's sake."

"Shame on you, Andrew McGillivray," I yelled. "Blaspheming—in God's house too."

"You two weren't shy about fucking in it!"

"Goodnight," I replied, all three of us chortling.

"So," Shorty whispered, "how much can you tell me and still remain comfortable?"

"I have to go to Bayonne to recover some letters for George."

"Blackmail?" he asked.

"Someone has stolen correspondence between Hitler and the Duke of Windsor. The letters are pretty compromising, to say the least."

"How compromising?" he asked.

"Well, according to George, Hitler says that if Windsor helps him with the invasion of England he'll put him back on the throne—this time with Wallis Simpson as Queen."

"Holy cow!" Shorty said under his breath. "That's treason if he goes along with it!"

"If these letters came to light, they'd destroy the reputation of the Royal Family. The effects on morale in Britain alone are not worth thinking on, let alone on the other countries of the Empire."

"What a mess!" he said, and then, after a moment, added, "I guess your trip to Bayonne could involve more than merely recovering the letters."

"Yeah. It's not hard to work out how this could go down. No blackmailer who thinks they're going to make a million is going to hand over their ace card just like that."

"And?"

"And I'm not thrilled about it either. It's a woman."

Shorty turned onto his side and smiled at me. A sliver of moonlight shone through the hayloft window and slanted over the hay behind us, giving me enough light to see the love and care on his face.

"Shoot first, ask questions later," he said. Jimmy Cagney would have been proud of his gangster voice.

"That's going to be a great help if I haven't got the letters in my hot little hand," I replied, laughing at his playacting.

"There's more, though, isn't there?"

I sighed. "Yes, there is."

"You should have backup, Tommy," he said, his voice suddenly serious. "She might not be alone. There could be an accomplice, or even a whole gang."

"I know, sweetheart, don't worry, I'll be careful."

"Then what's the other problem?" he asked.

"She's taken something else that doesn't belong to her," I said. I fumbled in my canvas haversack to retrieve the book of Walt Whitman's prose.

"What's this?" he asked. I handed him my torch.

"Inside back cover," I replied. "This is the book you saw Peter hand to me when he dropped you off."

He disappeared under the blanket while I lay on my back and waited for him to read George's message.

"The Czarina's Necklace?" he asked, emerging a few moments later.

"Yep. It was a present to Queen Mary from her mother-in-law, Queen Alexandra."

"Ah … Queen Alexandra's sister was the Russian Czarina, that's right, I'd quite forgotten. That's how the necklace gets its name?"

"Hence the problem with Wallis Simpson," I replied.

"What? I didn't get that far …"

He disappeared once more, reappearing after several minutes. I could feel him rustling the two sheets of paper, reading and re-reading George's startling directive.

"Wow … what a bitch!" he eventually said, re-emerging once more.

"Yes, sweetheart, that's why there's such a strong reason to get the necklace back."

George's note, hidden under the back endpaper of the book, had informed me the blackmailer had made contact with a more substantial threat. She not only intended to sell the Duke of Windsor's correspondence to the *New York Times* but also, if there was no reply acknowledging receipt of her letter, she'd offer to sell the necklace to Wallis Simpson. George's note informed me he'd replied to her, saying he'd be sending a negotiator, giving the name of one of my French aliases as his go-between. Once I got to Bayonne, I'd be using a *nom de guerre* that hadn't seen the light of day for years—Jean-Loup Périgord.

"How did she get it?" Shorty asked.

"What, the necklace?" I asked.

"Look, Tommy," he said. "I see it one of two ways, either the security at Buckingham Palace is non-existent or it's an 'inside-job'—that's what we'd call it at home, anyway."

"To be honest, I haven't got an answer for that," I replied. "George was less than forthcoming when I asked him before we left. My guess is the Duke of Windsor is somehow to blame."

"That's what I was thinking too," Shorty said. "Anyway, about the necklace … Wallis Simpson isn't the type to break it up into individual stones, or leave it in her jewel box. She'd jump on the chance to buy that necklace. She'd flaunt it—to make it look as if the Royal Family had accepted her. What could they do once she wore it in public?"

"You have it in one, Shorty," I said. "You've no idea how much she wants to be called *Your Royal Highness*, which requires a curtsey or a bow, instead of *Your Grace*. The moment she wears it publicly for the first time the necklace will be recognised—it's too well-known for people to pretend they don't know what it is. Everyone knows the Queen Mother can't bear her. She won't even acknowledge her. They'll start to ask questions. How did she get it? Did the duke steal it from his mother to give to his new wife? The scandal would be terrific."

"What would be worse, Tommy, is that Queen Mary might have to concede to a lie. She might have to swallow her pride and say she'd actually given it to Wallis Simpson. It'd be humiliating beyond belief."

"And then there's George," I said.

"How does George come into it?"

"He doesn't, as far as I can discover. But there are people out there who think he's a complete degenerate and a disgrace to the Royal Family. If any of this gets out, then he's bound to be accused of being responsible for this whole nonsense—the Hitler connection as well."

"That's ridiculous," Shorty said.

"I agree. But let's hope this woman in Bayonne hasn't already started looking elsewhere for alternative buyers in case the Windsors decide not to buy the necklace. Otherwise, I might have to fight my way through a whole heap of villains who've heard she has it, and who are lining up to try to steal it from her."

"I can just see it," he said, drawing an imaginary screen in the air with a swipe of his hand. "Peter Lorre facing down Avery Kingston and the Bowery Boys, in the biggest heist of the century ..."

"Will you too either speak up so I can hear what you're saying or at least whisper so I can get some sleep?" Andrew yelled from below.

I chuckled and then pulled the blanket over both of our heads.

"This woman ... what's her name again? Lucretia Hollingsworth? I'm not totally convinced this whole thing could be operated by one person, working alone," Shorty whispered. "It's a fairly sophisticated and complicated scheme when you think about it—international blackmail isn't a run-of-the-mill thing."

"And I've already told you I won't do anything dangerous. I'll tread carefully, don't worry."

He was right to be concerned. If the woman worked alone, or was part of a small operation, then I knew I could manage it by myself. If, however, there turned out to be an extortion gang behind the undertaking, I might have to call for backup, or return at another time with more resources. In any case, there was nothing I could do right now. I'd simply have to wait until I got there to have a good look around.

"I sorta like parachuting, babe ... if you need someone to watch your back?"

I chuckled against the side of his neck and then thought it was time to change the subject. "After Bayonne, I need to go to Lesaka on the way to San Sebastian, if only to put my mind to rest. I could never forgive myself if the pilot who left the note here was Rhys, and by some miracle he'd made it all the way to Spain."

The scrap of paper Père Christoph had shown me had been written by someone whose French was basic. I didn't know Rhys's handwriting, so couldn't be sure. But, the fact Martin had told me the man who'd passed through La Rochelle could speak a form of Breton burned in my chest like a hot coal.

"So I'm going to risk my life at sea in a leaky fishing boat, braving grenade-tossing Nazi mermen, all the way to Spain and then travel on a flea-ridden donkey to Portugal, while you're sitting in the sun eating paella?"

As Shorty described this ludicrous scenario, his voice got louder, and we both roared with laughter. Andrew had had enough. "That's it, I'm going to sleep in the church," he yelled.

"Well, that worked," Shorty said, once we heard Andrew leave.

I laughed, even louder this time.

"Hey, you. I have something of yours," he said.

"Something of mine?"

He reached behind him, into his jacket pocket, and then retrieved a small, folded square of thin cardboard.

"What is it?"

He waved it slowly in the air, a few inches from my face. "It has words on it …"

I tried to snatch it from him, but he held it up away from me, out of reach. "Give me a clue," I said.

"Hmm … let's see. *'I am faithful, and being with you makes me happy and content'* …"

Oh, God! It was the card I'd sent him at the end of last year after we'd been caught in the bombing. I'd bought it with him in mind and had kept it in my desk drawer. It described, in the Language of Flowers, the meaning of the yellow roses I'd sent to him—the card had been tucked inside the bunch, nestled among the flowers.

I said nothing, but reached into my own pocket and withdrew the dried rosebud he'd given me before his first return flight to London. I kissed it and then pressed it to his lips. I'd memorised every word on that blasted card, and here I was in a barn in occupied France, with the very same card now in his hand, and over two months of our lives since gone by.

He whispered:

"In a romantic sense, yellow roses can also symbolise the comfort and enduring pleasure of a long-term relationship or marriage. Yellow roses are commonly seen as a symbol of steadfast and enduring devotion. They can mean, 'I am faithful, and being with you makes me happy and content.'"

The card remained between his fingers, still folded tightly.

"You memorised it, Shorty?"

"What do you think, Aussie? I didn't need to open it. I know Superman can use X-ray vision to read through anything, but I confess, I've read it so many times I've lost count of the number—"

He rolled on top of me and then gently kissed me.

"Hey, you, what do you think you're up to?" I asked, so profoundly moved I could barely get the words out. "This is a holy place—God is watching."

"I don't know about you, Tommy," he replied softly, "but my God up there is a God of love. I think in my heart He wouldn't care so much."

I ran my hands through his hair, thinking about how much he meant to me. I could deal with his God of love—after all, it was the same one we both shared.

I pulled his head to mine and kissed him hard.

CHAPTER 12

Thirty pairs of polished heels clicked together almost simultaneously and the room echoed with the same number of throats calling forth a snappy *Heil Hitler*!

Shorty and I stood in the entranceway to the dining room of the Hôtel Marin, on the waterfront of La Rochelle. The room was full of junior German officers, NCOs, and enlisted men who'd been eating their breakfast and were now standing to attention, waiting for me to say something. The room had exploded with the sound of clattering of plates, the clinking of silverware, and the scraping of chairs on the floor when a *Stabsunteroffizier* had first noticed us standing in the doorway. *"Achtung!"* he'd shouted, leaping to his feet.

Shorty meandered across the room until he came to the "high table", which was underneath the large window overlooking the harbour. "The *Obersturmbannführer* and I would like breakfast," he said to the lieutenant and the two sergeants who'd been sitting there moments beforehand.

After a few seconds, the lieutenant realised what he meant *"Jawohl, Herr Hauptmann!"* the man said, rallying the two sergeants to clear the table and move themselves out of the way.

Once the table was cleaned and reset, I strode between the two rows of perfectly aligned, and rigidly at-attention soldiers to one of the chairs, before turning and then saying, *"Rührt Euch, meine Herren!"* I sat. The room stood at ease and then waited for me to indicate they could also return to their seats. Although I hoped I'd pulled it off with the greatest aplomb, I had to admit I'd had my fingers crossed.

The lieutenant remained at attention at the end of the table, waiting for one of us to speak. Shorty said, "Please arrange two double rooms for the *Obersturmbannführer* and his staff. We can share beds—make sure the hotel employees go to no trouble."

The man went quite pale. "Here?"

"Yes, of course here!" I snapped. I didn't want to stay at the *Kommandantur*—we needed privacy. He tugged an imaginary forelock and gave me a *Heil* as he started to move away.

"My *Stabsunteroffizier* and driver are waiting at the reception outside. Please bring them in and find them space at a table near me," I said. "Once you have my rooms organised and my men fed, send word to *Hauptmann* Müller I'm here, and I'd like him to present himself once I've finished breakfast." I'd decided to summon the captain of the *Kommandantur* to visit me—a show of strength was in order, and if anything went wrong I could always jump through the window behind us.

"Here?"

Shorty rose from his chair; the room went very quiet. "Do you have a problem with your hearing, *Leutnant?*" he growled.

The officer seemed to have lost the ability to speak, so shook his head anxiously and then scurried away to attend to his tasks. Slowly, the hubbub started anew as the men settled down, all of them careful not to look in our direction.

"You're a tough bastard," I whispered to Shorty, in English, while hiding a smile.

"Not as bad as you," he said. "Two rooms, huh? You gonna bunk me up with Andrzej?"

"No, but I'm about to do some intelligence-gathering." Shorty looked at me oddly. I called a nervous-looking sergeant to the table. "Do any of your men come from Strasbourg?" He nodded and then saluted me, before scurrying away to the far end of the room, where he accosted a young, skinny corporal, who almost dropped his cutlery in fright.

"I'm from Strasbourg, Herr Obersturmbannführer," the youth said, after arriving at our table. His fingers were shaking as he saluted.

"Please draw up a chair," I said, smiling brightly at him. "You aren't in any trouble—I simply long to speak to someone from my own city. It's been such a long time."

About twenty minutes later, after a lengthy conversation in *Elsässerditsch*, the German dialect of Alsace, I'd found out everything I needed to know about the local German garrison—information I never would have obtained from the *Kommandant*, who was waiting patiently at the doorway for me to acknowledge his existence. I'd found out how many troops were stationed here, what level of armaments they had, who the major military personnel were, and what areas were patrolled—all under the guise of being a mild-natured, fellow Alsatian. For good measure, I even invented a family relation we might have had in common.

Eventually, I stood and indicated I was ready to speak with the captain of the *Kommandantur*.

Hauptmann Rittmeister Adam Müller, the commander of the garrison in La Rochelle, was a pleasant-looking, thin-faced man, who wore soft-yellow horn-rimmed spectacles. To my eyes, he seemed all of a colour—his pale, flaxen hair seemed to blend in with his complexion. He was all the hues of a shortbread biscuit.

"Obersturmbannführer," he said, and then gave me a *Heil*, after which he held out his hand.

"Hauptmann," I replied, with my own *Heil*, and then shook the man's proffered hand. I was somewhat surprised to see he not only held my gaze for the customary three seconds but also smiled. It wasn't the usual fawning greeting I'd been expecting—the captain seemed to be making an effort.

I watched him as he greeted Shorty and as they exchanged brief pleasantries. This was no fanatic. The man's face was genuinely affable. Like Hotz, in Nantes, I assumed he was another career officer. His behaviour was punctilious—correct to a fault in his treatment of a senior officer.

271

"Cavalry?" I asked, having noticed his insignia.

"Yes, I know," he said with a small chuckle. "It surprises most people that I'm an administrator. Motion sickness, I'm afraid—I can't do tanks."

It was then I realised he'd been focused on the bridge of my nose, rather than looking into my eyes. Even he, as pleasant as he seemed to be, was unable to make direct eye contact. It was something most people avoided when talking to SS officers.

"May I sit?" he asked. I gestured to the recently vacated chair my young friend from Strasbourg had used. "I knew you were arriving, but wasn't sure when …"

"Have the prisoners spoken?"

"No, Herr Obersturmbannführer. None of them speaks German, and their English is too heavily accented for our translator to understand."

"My sergeant was a staff member at the German embassy in London, under Von Ribbentrop. He speaks excellent English, don't you, Heribert?"

Andrew nodded.

I'd scrutinised the reports in Alberbach's briefcase and had noted one of the airmen had been captured while burning what was believed to be secret documents.

"May I ask, is anything remaining of the papers the airmen were trying to destroy when you captured them?"

"Sadly not. However, had we not caught them in the act, they'd certainly have been shipped off to an *Offlag* in the Eastern Reich …"

"And I wouldn't have had the pleasure of interrogating them."

"Quite so, Herr Obersturmbannführer."

From the way he replied, I had my first suspicions the man didn't approve of SS type interrogations. It reinforced my impression that he was indeed a career officer, in the army for the long haul, and not afraid to show disapproval of unacceptable behaviour—albeit in a cautious and veiled manner.

"Anyway, you've just arrived," he continued, braving a slight smile, while he smoothed down the fabric of his trouser leg. He didn't want to meet my eye. "There'll be plenty of time for you to visit the prisoners. Perhaps I can show you around the town?"

"I'd like my sergeant to visit them immediately, if that's no problem? He can report back to me on the most likely methods to yield the best results."

As he looked up, Müller's smile faded, and his mouth twitched slightly.

"Well, I for one would love to see the town," Shorty said, a little too brightly. But I trusted him. He had a precise sense of timing when it came to these things. "Perhaps after we've changed? I think it'd be rather nice to wander about incognito, in civilian clothing. What do you think, Obersturmbannführer?"

Of course, I agreed.

★★★★★

The porter in the hotel was excruciatingly apologetic about us having to share rooms, but space was at a premium. The officer in the room Shorty and I were to occupy had been quite miffed when asked to move elsewhere.

I made a fuss when I found Andrew and Andrzej had been allocated a room on the floor below, insisting they be in a room adjacent to Shorty's and mine. The porter looked ashen-faced at the prospect of asking the men in the adjoining room to move, so I volunteered, knocking on the door and politely "requesting" the men to change rooms.

"You're such a big, bad Nazi," Shorty said to me, once we were alone and sprawled out on the cover of the large bed in our room.

"How bad would you like me to be, eh?"

He laughed at me and then stroked my chin with his thumb. "Tell me something, Tommy. How come you aren't nervous about being recognised by someone? Surely, one day, someone is going to recognise you from your performing days in Germany?"

I snorted. "I'm constantly nervous about masquerading as a high-ranking German officer, but that's what our training's for. Learning how to hide the nerves and step into the role. But, as for recognising me? The next time we go anywhere while I'm wearing that SS uniform, check where people are looking. Everyone, even Wehrmacht officers of equal rank, are afraid of SS interrogators—they avoid eye contact. Didn't you notice Müller had a fixation on the space between my eyebrows? All they see is someone to be afraid of, to be nervous around—no one would possibly connect Thomas Haupner, the violinist, to Obersturmbannführer Leonard Alberbach. Besides, I haven't played in Germany since November in 1938."

He laughed. "Very well then, Mister Clever, what's our plan?"

"Well, let's wait until Andrew and Andrzej return from checking out the *Kommandantur*. I want to know the layout of the prison before I go making definite plans. That is, of course, unless you've come up with something else?"

He shook his head. "So, when do you think we might get the pilots out of there, if we can?" he asked.

"Perhaps Tuesday or Wednesday? It shouldn't seem like we're in too much of a hurry. I'll talk to the airmen and, if I really have to, see if we can't put on some sort of show—some pretend screaming and maybe a few real bruises, so it looks genuine. First of all though, before we resort to actual violence, I want to try a more subtle approach on Müller and attempt to convince him it would be better just to send them away with me."

"I did notice he looked a bit squeamish when you started talking about interrogation."

"Yes, and that's the reason I think I can convince him to let us take the men and women away to Nantes, as you suggested. We can meet either late tonight or tomorrow night with Martin, Jérôme, and Horloge to discuss exactly where we might stage an ambush."

"It'll seem odd if we don't take a few guards to Nantes with us, though," Shorty said, running his fingers through the hair on my chest.

"Well, why don't you keep an eye out for three or four who you think the world won't mind losing?"

*****

In the nearly four weeks we'd been in France, I thought I was past surprises. But, when Luc delivered our meal that night, dressed as a waiter, I nearly bit through the rim of my glass. "May I explain what our specials are for this evening, gentlemen?" he asked, in excellent, cultivated French. I'd only heard him speak in dialect. I'm sure my jaw dropped.

"I didn't think to bring my interpreter," the captain apologised, looking around the restaurant. Our table was an island in a sea of empty tables. The moment we were seated, the few other patrons of the restaurant had moved away from us.

"You don't speak French?" I asked, keeping my voice neutral.

"Only one or two words," he replied, looking a little uncomfortable. "*Merci; bonjour*—that sort of thing."

"That's no problem," I said. "Both the *Hauptmann* and I speak French. The waiter asked if we wanted to know what the specials were this evening." The captain of the *Kommandantur* gestured for me to proceed.

"Everyone in the town knows this *choucroute* you're sitting with hasn't bothered to learn a word of the greatest language in the world," Luc said, pointing at a blackboard on the wall behind me, his faux-smile and diversionary gesture covering any indication of what he'd said to me.

Shorty began to distract the *Kommandant* with small talk about the attractions of the town. His quick glance had told me he'd occupy the German officer while I found out why Luc had appeared.

"You're lucky this man doesn't speak French," I said to Luc, my face radiating false bonhomie. "What the damned hell are you doing here, and what's the special?"

"Looking out for you two, you *pousse-crotte*, and it's fish," he said.

"Looking out for us?" He'd called me a queer, using an extremely vulgar expression. It nearly made me burst out laughing, such was the effect of the word. It was all I could do to keep a straight face.

"Père Christophe told me he'd heard there was a collaborator working here as a waiter," he explained. "I borrowed the car, we bumped him off, and I'm taking his place for the night."

I waited for Shorty to finish what he'd been saying to Müller and then explained. "They have a delicious regional fish dish I think we might like."

"That was quite the explanation," the *Kommandant* said, puzzled at the length of my conversation with Luc.

"Oh, you know the French and their cooking," I explained with a smile, "a dollop of this, a splash of wine that comes from the northern side of the vineyard …"

He nodded in agreement, and then returned my smile, affirming the fish sounded delicious.

"We're all having fish," I said to Luc, "and make sure it's good, you little turd."

"I'd say we'd all pass the fish around in the kitchen and wipe our arses on it, if I didn't think you two shirt-lifters would like it." He bowed and then turned and left.

"Crumb in your throat, Captain?" Müller asked Shorty, who was choking, while trying not to laugh.

"Excuse me a moment," I said. *"Les toilettes?"* I asked of another waiter, who was passing by our table. He pointed to a sign on the wall, which indicated the direction of the facilities.

I caught Luc's eye and he followed me into the gentlemen's lavatory.

It was obvious the restaurant was somehow connected to the local *maquisards*. I asked Luc if he was all right, and he affirmed that he was, telling me Levi had come with him and had killed the interloper, silencing him first with a chop to the throat, using the edge of his hand. I made a note to myself to remember to ask Levi where he'd learned that.

As Shorty, Andrzej, Andrew, and I were staying overnight in the hotel, I told Luc we'd meet him and the others the following evening, in the same house in which we'd met Horloge, when we'd be able to give them news of the *capitainerie* after we'd visited it tomorrow morning, and I'd also explain the plan Shorty and I had worked out. On the way back to the table, I spotted Levi in the kitchen, who gave me a quick but subtle acknowledgement. There was no possible way Shorty and I couldn't protect ourselves if anything went wayward in the restaurant, but it gave me a tiny, warm glow to think friends were looking out for us.

The fish was actually quite delicious, although I had to stop myself thinking about what might have been done to Müller's in the kitchen.

Adam Müller was the second German officer we'd met who'd found himself in an impossible situation. Neither he nor Hotz, in Nantes, were what was perceived by the Allies to be an archetypal "bad" German. They were merely caught up in a war not of their own making, but one in which they were forced to follow orders imposed by irrational leaders. He was also, like Hotz, very well educated and charming—and a former athlete besides. I was both surprised and impressed when he told us he'd competed in the equestrian events at the 1936 Olympics in Berlin.

"So, do you ride, Leonard?" he asked me.

I hesitated before answering, as of course I did ride, as did every Aussie bush-kid where I grew up. But, I wondered about the type of riding Alberbach had learned. I knew he was from Dresden originally, home of the old-order Saxon aristocracy, so I imagined his riding would have been more like dressage, quite unlike my own "jump-on-and-gallop-like-buggery" style.

"I have done, but not for many years," I said.

"That's a shame," he said. "The countryside around here is excellent for riding."

"Well, I doubt I'll have time for any leisure activities. My sergeant reported back to me, and from what he said I think I'll question the prisoners tomorrow. He's very perceptive and can assess people's vulnerabilities easily and accurately. But I'd like to personally evaluate the Englishmen's resistance levels, to see how I'll proceed—there is quite an art to interrogation."

His small grimace signalled he didn't like what I'd said, so I decided to test the waters.

"I understand not everyone appreciates my line of work, nor agrees with it, Adam. However, for the security of the Reich, sometimes disagreeable things need to be done." He smiled and nodded, still looking unhappy. "Let's speak frankly. I see you're a man of some sensibility, and what I'll have to do might repulse you. So, to spare you any distress, I'll start by merely talking to the prisoners first."

"Sometimes fear of what might happen can loosen a man's tongue quicker than physical pain," Shorty explained.

The *Kommandant* blotted the corner of his mouth with his table napkin.

I continued, "I can see you're still uncomfortable with the idea. Let me make a suggestion. Perhaps I can do something that might possibly calm your misgivings? You know what they say—*Aus den Augen, aus dem Sinn.*"

Out of sight, out of mind had an equivalent in every European language.

"If I find I get nowhere with words, I'll move the prisoners to Nantes. The facilities in the Château des Ducs de Bretagne are far away from the residential and administrative areas. I appreciate anything I do at your *capitainerie* will probably resound through the building."

He blanched.

"I'll call Obersturmbannführer Hotz tomorrow and see whether it will be possible."

"Besides, the locals tend to get quite agitated when women are involved," Shorty added. "You wouldn't want to deal with civilian problems."

"You'd interrogate the women as well?" The sound in the word "interrogate" showed his disgust, even if his face didn't.

"But of course," Shorty said. "They were taken with the airmen; therefore they must have ties to the Resistance. Don't worry, we'll send back any information that could be useful."

"I suppose your returning with them to Nantes might suit both of us," Müller said, after a moment's reflection. "There's a squad of eight men I need to send back to Cholet."

"Cholet is on our way," Shorty said. "Do you have two *Lastwagen* we could use? One for the prisoners, and the other for the men who need to go back?"

My American was thinking sharply—a covered van, rather than an open one, would provide an extra element of surprise in an ambush.

"Yes, I have two Opels. One belongs to Cholet anyway."

I changed the subject. We'd spent enough time on it, and seeds had been planted. "Well, let's hope we don't need to go to all this trouble. The prisoners may simply decide to talk."

We raised our glasses in a toast.

*****

"You wore me out," Shorty said, snuggled up behind me.

We'd changed out of our uniforms and into pyjamas, waiting for Andrzej and Andrew to arrive, so we could discuss the events of the day. They hadn't returned from the *capitainerie* by the time we'd left to have dinner with Müller, so we had no idea what had happened at the jail.

"All those hours ago, and you're still worn out?"

He looked at his watch. "Well, nearly twelve hours ago."

"You're getting old, mister. I was getting all excited about showing you the stars and the moon again, right after the guys have gone."

"Damn, the things you put me through ..." He began to play with my forelock. "I was thinking ..."

"Yeah? Does it hurt?"

He thumped me.

"Your apartment and all ... it's bohemian and it's 'you'—it feels sorta like student digs."

"Go on," I said, wondering where this was leading.

"Well, when I was thinking, it came to me that I'd really like us to have a place of our own."

"Then why don't you move in? You practically live there as it is."

"No. What I meant is a place that's ours, as opposed to a place that's yours with me in it."

"I don't see the difference." I was teasing—I did understand what he meant.

"There's a huge difference. I mean somewhere we both chose. Somewhere we can entertain our friends, have room for a piano. A spare bedroom or two for visitors, somewhere that looks like we created it together."

"Monogrammed sheets and towels, huh?"

"Yeah ..." Little-kid voice on overdrive.

"Okay."

"What?"

"I said, okay."

"That easy?"

"Sure," I said.

He pulled me hard against him. "Man, I'm so happy you're so easy in every way."

I protested. "What do you mean in 'every way'? I hold out."

"When?" His laugh gave me goosebumps of happiness.

He didn't give me a chance to answer as he pressed his mouth to my own. "Are you sure you're fine with us living together?" he asked.

"Mm ..." I said.

"I heard the hesitation at the end of that 'mm'."

"There's nothing in the world I'd like more. I'm slightly worried about what people might think. You coming over and staying because of air raids is one thing. Moving out of the US embassy into a place with me is another ..."

He twirled a few strands of my chest hair between his fingers. I waited. I could tell he'd rehearsed what he was going to say. "Did you know I have to pay for board at the embassy? It's taken out of my salary. If I moved out, my pay packet would be bigger and there'd be an accommodation allowance I don't get right now."

"And ...?"

"You know Cary Grant and Randolph Scott live together?"

The underscore on "live" was unmissable. I'd made my own deductions. The tabloids and American movie magazines were full of descriptions of them being "Hollywood's most eligible bachelors". They even shared a house called Bachelor Hall.

"Uh huh ..."

"Well, their excuse is to save money. I'd be saving a lot, if the price was right on something we rented. If we got a place together with a bedroom for each of us, one of them merely for show, no one could say anything. After all, we're just buddies in the eyes of most people. Whaddyathink, Tommy?"

I lay on my back for a moment, thinking through the implications. Living together was something I already knew I secretly wanted, and the war had made many things expedient that before might have seemed improper or unusual. Therefore, I reasoned, it was quite acceptable for two pals to want to save some money by sharing costs. After all, a lot of men at my workplace shared digs. And, as our public life was conducted with discretion, I supposed we could move in somewhere together without anyone batting an eyelid.

When I saw the look of love and longing in his eyes, I knew I could only give one answer. "What do I think? As I said, sweetheart, let's do it."

"Won't you miss Coptic Street?"

"Well, to be honest, I will in many ways. But I can rent it out and that'll help a bit."

"Rent it out?"

"Haven't I told you? I own it. It had forty years left of a ninety-nine-year lease. I made an offer for a freehold purchase, and the owner shook on it. It took a bit of legal wrangling, but now I own it—no lease!"

"Leases! I'll never understand the way the Brits sell houses. Wait a second! That means you own the bookstore on the street level too?"

"Surely do," I said. "I thought it'd be a good business place for after the war and bring in some extra income for me, no matter where I was living."

"Wow! Not just a pretty face, Tommy."

"Well, it's been empty since thirty-nine, and I haven't looked for a tenant. I always thought it'd make a great delicatessen, but that's unlikely right now."

"Aren't you worried about finding a tenant for the flat, though?"

"Not really. The SOE is always looking for somewhere to put people up. I'll simply rent it out through work."

"How much do you think you might get for it?"

"About three quid a week, I reckon. I might be able to push it up to three guineas."

He mumbled. I knew something was up.

"You've already found somewhere, haven't you?"

"Who, me?"

"Yes, you, Heinrich Augustus Reiter!" I jumped on him and held him down by the arms. I'd known the discovery of his middle name would come in handy someday.

"Maybe," he said, his face split by a huge grin. I started to tickle him and he fought back until we fell on the floor with a thud, laughing. Someone in the room below banged on their ceiling for quiet. I lay on top of him, raising my upper body on my hands, which were holding his wrists. I wiggled my hips a little and waited. He smiled at me and said nothing. I wiggled a bit more sensuously, until he let out a small hum of pleasure. I raised a questioning eyebrow.

"Okay," he finally said. "Four main bedrooms, two reception rooms, library, enormous kitchen in the basement, and a maid's room in the attic." I raised the other eyebrow. "Manchester Square. Twenty-four guineas a month."

I whistled. "How the hell? A house that big in Manchester Square for six guineas a week?"

"I heard about it at work. It was leased by one of Joe Kennedy's hangers-on who decided to follow him back to the US. A couple who wants to keep the house for after the war who've been paying pepper-corn rent to keep their names on the rental agreement. There's more, though."

"Go on," I said.

"I spoke with the owner. If we decide we like the place and pay the full rent, she's happy to break their lease. But, Tommy, if we wanted to buy out the leasehold now, rather than paying monthly, she'd be happy with six hundred and fifty pounds. It's not like owning the building outright, but it means we own it for the rest of our lives … it can't be rented out to anyone else over our heads. It's a bargain-basement deal for a soldier and his pal."

Jokingly, I said, "So, I'm your *pal* now, am I?"

He rose onto his knees and then pulled me fiercely into his arms. "No, Tommy, you're more than a pal to me. I love you so hard it hurts me, babe. You are my everything. You are so much more than just a pal. That's *why* I want us to get our own place."

"That sounds like a marriage proposal," I said, smiling at him.

I found the wave of emotion running through me hard to contain. What my mind said was, *"If I could marry you, Shorty, I would, in the bat of an eye. But, that simply can't happen. So, yes, let's go look at this place you found, and let's plan to be together forever, but one day at a time, okay? This war is going no place in a hurry."*

He sat on his haunches, one hand on my shoulder, the palm of the other flat on my chest, and stared at me with wonder in his eyes. "I love you, Tommy," he said, with such simplicity that what I'd been going to say dried up in my mouth.

I kissed him on the forehead. "I love you too, Shorty; *und wo du bist ..."*

"... da bin ich auch," we finished together.

He kissed me.

We were interrupted by a soft tapping at the door to the room. It was Andrzej and Andrew.

*****

"Well, tell me all," I said, once they'd settled.

"One of them is Baen," Andrew said. "He said he knows you, Henry."

"Baen McFadyen?" Shorty asked. "He was on the same training course I did at Lochailort, last December."

Andrew nodded. "He nearly had a heart attack when he saw me in a Nazi uniform."

"Who were the others?" I asked.

"Two guys I don't know. RAF pilots from Inverness—Camdan Fitzgerald and Rory Beath. Camdan is the Canadian and he's not in good shape. I think he's got at least one broken rib, if not more."

"What about the women, Andrzej?" I asked.

"They're frightened, but holding themselves together as much as they can. Jérôme's wife is a tough nut, and as rude as hell with it, but the sister is on the ball. She's a bit like Horloge—doesn't get on well with her brother."

"Can we trust them enough to let them know the plan, or should we simply take them along for the ride and surprise them?"

"I think you should make up your own mind when you meet them ... and what plan?"

I ran through the proposal Shorty and I'd devised, which involved the transfer of the three airmen and the two women back to Nantes.

"You're quiet, Andrzej," Shorty said after we'd finished.

"Well, *Rudzielec*, I have a funny feeling about Jérôme's wife. I can't put my finger on it, but it's a *przeczucie*—a hunch. It's something about her manner. She's a little bit too cocky for someone who's been locked up by the Germans. Someone had to have tipped them off about the airmen. Maybe it was her?"

"But why? Surely she'd have been endangering the life of her husband and sister-in-law."

"Not if the Germans were to arrive while her husband was at work. She hates the English as much as Jérôme, I think."

Andrew laughed.

"What's up with you, caber-tosser?" I asked.

"I heard her asking what language I was speaking with Baen. Andrzej said it was Polish."

We all laughed because when Andrew was speaking in fully fledged Scots, none of us could understand a word.

"Well, it might be best if we kept to French and Gaelic tomorrow, just in case … what was her name, Jérôme's wife?"

"Simone."

"… just in case Simone is playing both sides of the field."

*****

The woman's temper was as brittle as her bleached-blonde, dry-looking flyaway hair.

Simone Pouilly, Jérôme's wife, smelled. I'd noticed it immediately. It wasn't the smell of unwashed body, or unsanitary personal habits, it was something else—a smoky, tar-like odour that was familiar, but not immediately recognisable.

"I'll only speak with *him*," she said, pointing at Andrzej, affronted because I hadn't succumbed to her pouts and powdered bosom. Andrzej was leaning on the bars of the cell the men were in, trying to keep an ear on both conversations while Andrew spoke softly to the pilots in his heavily accented Scots English.

"I'm trying to help you," I said, glancing at the yellowing remains of what, only a few weeks ago, would have been a spectacular bruise that ran up the side of her neck from her shoulder to her ear.

"I don't care. Your French is too foreign. I can't tell if you're really trying to help, or you're trying to lure us into a trap."

"My French is foreign?" I couldn't believe my ears.

"You speak with the same accent as *her*—you're from Lorraine. She hates me. And now here you are dressed up like a *Chleuh*, and probably in cahoots with her to do me some mischief."

I swapped out of dialect and began to speak in correct, scholarly French. "Your husband knows I'm trying to help, as does Horloge."

The woman spat on the floor at my feet. "Now you sound like some pompous *con* who's slumming it with the locals."

I was floored. I'd never heard a woman use such a vulgar word. It was the prude in me. I was a linguist—I knew it was merely two consonants on either side of a vowel. However, had I heard a woman use its four-letter English equivalent, I couldn't have been more shocked.

The basement prison of the *Kommandantur* was one long, rectangular room, with cells in each of its corners. A waist-high partition screened off a small area in each cell, in which was a covered bucket— otherwise the cells were bare. There wasn't even a palliasse on the floor for them to sleep on. I waved Andrzej over and asked him to try to speak sense to the woman in Gascon. The moment he spoke, she began to bat her eyelashes at him. Simone's cell companion, Jérôme's sister, shook her head and turned aside. She looked profoundly embarrassed at her sister-in-law's behaviour.

Andrew was still chatting softly to the two Scots, so I joined him and began to speak with Camdan, the Canadian airman. He was in a great deal of pain. I was no doctor, but the fact he told me he was in agony every time he breathed in, made me think his ribs might indeed have been broken. It was with some irony I learned the "secret documents" the men had been burning were merely pages from the aircraft flight manual. They'd been trying to keep warm.

"I'd only kept the blasted manual so we could use it to wipe our arses," Baen McFadyen told me.

"Well, it's a bit of luck you didn't," I said. "If you hadn't been burning it, you might have been shipped off straight away to the prisoner-of-war camp in Valençay and then we'd never have found you."

I gave each of the men a smoke and then moved to the cell wall, near the stairs that led down into the basement, while I watched the interaction between Andrzej and Simone.

Shorty returned from upstairs, where he'd been having a chat with the prison guards, who we'd asked to leave, so we could speak privately with the two women and the pilots. He whispered into my ear. "They call her *Trois Gitanes*."

"Three gypsies?"

"No, it's her price." He held up a cigarette. Gitanes was the name of a popular brand of smokes.

"Really?"

"Yup. It's a donation, so I was told."

Something clicked. I recognised the smell on her now—it was Lysol. I knew it to be known as "the poor woman's contraceptive".

"Don't tell me she does 'it' for only three smokes? That's ..."

"They said it was a donation. She does 'it' with the guards for nothing so she gets to see her boyfriend. The smokes are her 'bonus' if she does other tricks."

I found the thought of Simone's "tricks" more than disturbing. "Her boyfriend? You mean Jérôme?" I was really confused.

"Nope, Jérôme's her husband. She's got a lover on the side. His name's Fabrice, and guess what—he's one of Martin's men."

"Holy cow! That's playing with fire."

He nodded. "I also learned it was her who blabbed about the three pilots to get lover-boy out of the clink on the sly."

"Wait, she betrayed our men so she could have her lover freed from jail?"

He nodded.

"What the hell did Martin think when this Fabrice was released?" I asked. "Didn't he think it was suspicious?"

"I guess they made up some cover story—arrested by mistake, or something like that—it's the only thing that would make sense."

"She must really care for the man. Although, one thing's for sure, Shorty."

"What's that?"

"I bet she didn't think she'd get caught up in the raid too."

"You never know, Tommy. From what I was told upstairs, I wouldn't put anything past her. Maybe it's the only thing she could think of that would get her away from her husband. The guards told me it's well-known around town Jérôme uses her as a punching bag."

I felt sudden pity for the woman. The yellowing bruise also made sense now. To me, it was a shame she had to trade punches for Lysol in order to get away from her husband. But, then again, I wasn't her. I didn't know what her life was like, nor did I know what it might be like to be a woman, married to someone who abused her, and yet be in love with another man—one her husband most likely hated.

CHAPTER 13

Our Mercedes led the procession of three vehicles away from the Capitainerie and through the streets of La Rochelle, heading for Nantes.

It was raining heavily.

We'd planned the ambush for a short stretch of the road between two sharp bends, not far from the small hamlet of Les Longeards. Both sides of the road were heavily forested, offering plenty of cover for Martin and his men to lie in wait. Jérôme had been present in body only at the meeting we'd held the evening before. He hadn't really paid attention and had grunted in response at everything I'd asked him to do.

Just as we'd been about to leave La Rochelle, Luc had arrived on a bicycle. For a moment I'd thought something was amiss. He was supposed to stay behind, in case the hijack went wrong. He assured me he'd merely come to see us off and had then asked Andrzej for a cigarette. As he'd bent forward for a light, I'd heard him mumble something. The next time I'd turned around, he'd disappeared.

I still felt uneasy about Jérôme's involvement in the scheme. His team's role was to disarm the driver of the second covered van and hold the eight Germans who were returning to Cholet at gunpoint. I'd stressed several times he should capture them and disarm them only.

No shots were to be fired on the roadway. The plan was to take the men away from the road into the woods and dispose of them there. The bodies were then to be loaded into the two *Lastwagen*, which were to be driven into the large lake that had once been the local quarry.

Not far from where the ambush was to take place, I started to feel uneasy. It was a familiar feeling in my gut that told me something wasn't quite right. Premonitions had dogged me ever since I was a child. Michael called them my "feelings of impending doom". I was hardly ever wrong, and my apprehension made me feel very, very nervous. I looked over my shoulder at the road behind us to check on our convoy. Behind our Mercedes was the prisoners' van, which Andrzej was driving, and then, bringing up the rear, the truck with the guards from Cholet.

About a kilometre from the ambush point, the prisoners' truck burst a tyre. The convoy stopped while it was changed.

"You all right, Tommy?" Shorty asked. I'd begun to pace nervously in front of our Mercedes. I still couldn't shake the bad feeling, but nodded.

When we finally got under way again, the driver of the *Lastwagen* carrying the guards honked his horn and overtook the prisoner van, swapping places with it, while yahooing at Andrzej out of his window. It was a juvenile gesture. The driver appeared to be only in his teens, and probably thought he was having a bit of a lark. I was about to stop and order the convoy to regroup in the correct order, with the prisoners protected in the middle, but we'd passed the first bend and were already on the short, narrow stretch of road where the ambush was to take place.

"Damn," I said to Andrew, who was driving our Mercedes. "Bloody Nazis! What the hell do they think they're doing? I told that kid to stay in the agreed convoy order. Get ready to stop."

As I said these words, I heard the loud rattle of machine-gun fire from the woods behind us. Someone hadn't listened to what I'd said— no gunfire on the road.

I jumped out of the car and saw Jérôme blasting away at the sides of the rearmost van with his machine-gun. His face was red with rage, and he screamed wordlessly at the top of his voice as he held the trigger down on his antiquated *Maschinengewehr*. He didn't know the vans had swapped places and probably thought he was slaughtering the German guards from La Rochelle. Instead, he'd probably just killed his wife, his sister, and our airmen.

I pulled out my Beretta and fired into the air. "Stop!" I bellowed. As I ran towards him, two of the guards from Cholet ran into the road in front of me. I shot them as I ran.

The remaining German guards began to call out to each other in confusion, wondering why an SS colonel had gunned down two of their number. They already had their weapons drawn as they leaped from the back of the van. Not one of them managed to fire a single round. Martin and his men opened fire on them before their feet hit the ground.

By this time, I was only twenty yards away from Jérôme and his men.

He still hadn't realised his awful mistake and turned towards us, his upper lip curled with disgust, *"À bas les Anglais!"* he screamed.

His machine gun was aimed right at me.

Before he could pull the trigger, I heard the distinctive explosion of Shorty's Walther over my shoulder. Jérôme fell to the ground, the back of his head spraying over two men who were standing, open-mouthed, behind him. They'd heard what he had not—the abruptly terminated women's screams from the van he'd riddled with machine-gun fire.

I didn't stop to absorb what had happened. I raced to the driver's door of the *Lastwagen*. As I turned the handle of the door, it flew violently open and something heavy plummeted out of the cabin, knocking me to the ground.

It was Andrzej's body that had fallen on me. It had been leaning against the door. I didn't need to check; I could tell he was dead. For a split-second I was too shocked to move, and then began to call out his name, half-whispered, and yet almost shouted. It was all I could do not to howl with grief. It was only the glimpse of another arm, protruding from the cabin door, that made me move.

"Luc!" I shouted, at the top of my voice.

I pushed Andrzej's body off me and scrambled up into the cabin of the van. Luc was lying on his back on the cabin floor of the Lastwagen, one arm stretched above his head, hanging out of the doorway. I put my fingers to his neck to check his pulse. He was alive! I jumped to the ground and ran around to the other side of the van, calling to Martin to give me a hand.

Martin swore when he saw me trying to manhandle the young man's body from the floor-well. *"Il n'est pas mort,"* I said, to let him know Luc wasn't dead. "Heinrich!" I yelled over my shoulder, as loudly as I could.

Shorty was busy trying to restrain one of Martin's men, who was desperately trying to get into the back of the van. I guessed we now knew who Fabrice, Simone's lover, was. Shorty hadn't heard me over the man's loud wailing, so I screamed out again, this time feeling the tendons in my neck stand out with the effort.

"Shorty!"

He turned to look at me and saw Luc in my arms. "No! No!" He ran so fast towards me he slipped, falling heavily onto the packed gravel surface of the roadway. "No, no," he said again as he reached my side.

"He's all right," I said.

"What in God's name is he doing here?" he yelled at me, as if it were my fault.

"Take it easy," I said. "I've no idea. Now, get a grip, soldier!" I replied, in an attempt to settle him down. It was the first time I'd raised my voice to him since we'd met.

"I'm sorry ... I didn't mean to yell."

"Me neither. I'm sorry too. I didn't know Luc was here until now. But right now we have to sort out this mess, understood?"

He nodded.

Two men arrived beside us. I recognised one of them as Père Christophe's caretaker and factotum, Thierry.

"This is Pascal," Thierry said, introducing his companion. "He's our local doctor's assistant, he can have a look at your young man while I see what else I can do."

I asked Pascal to take care of Luc then told Shorty to come with me.

"Get these trucks off the road and get rid of the bodies right now!"

I called out to the *maquisards*, who were busy going through the pockets of the dead Germans.

"Tommy, there's a terrible mess in the back of the truck," Shorty said under his breath. He held up one finger. "Only one alive—Baen," he said. "He's been shot twice. Andrew is in there with him now."

"Jesus!" I said, clenching my jaw. "What a monumental disaster!"

"Your hands are shaking... what's wrong, Tommy? What's happened that you aren't telling me?"

I muttered something incoherent as I held out my hands to see what he was talking about. They were trembling violently.

"Oh, God!" I said and then rubbed my forehead, as if I could wipe what had happened from my mind. How was I going to tell him? I was barely holding myself together. "Shorty, it's Andrzej ..."

He didn't wait to hear what I was about to say, but tore off to the other side of the van, where Andrzej's body still lay, sprawled out on the ground where it had fallen. I heard him calling our friend's name, and then soft, muffled sobbing.

I rested my head against the side of the van. I lit a cigarette and smoked it, imagining I was taking my violin from its case, in preparation to play. The ritual, even when going through it in my mind, always seemed to settle me down. A few minutes later, cigarette finished, I found myself on my knees at Shorty's side in the rain with my arm around his shoulders. He had Andrzej's hand clasped between his own, pressed tightly against his chest.

"I'm glad it's raining," he murmured.

"Why?"

It was a rhetorical question. I knew he wouldn't want the other men to see him crying. War was a rotten business—everyone knew that. But in the space of a few minutes he'd shot his first man, and then, for the first time in this goddamn awful war, had lost a friend—and at the hand of someone who was supposedly on our side.

Simone, Nicole, Jérôme, and two airmen—one Scottish, the other Canadian—were dead, as were all the Germans we'd brought with us. I turned my face to the sky and allowed the rain to wash over my face.

"You okay?" Shorty asked.

"Yes, and I'm really sorry I yelled at you."

He gently pressed his cheek against Andrzej's forehead and began to whisper in Polish. I wiped the tears from the corner of his eye with my thumb—even in the rain, they still gathered on his long, almost-blond lashes.

"I need to go and sort out this mess," I said. "Will you be okay?"

"Sure thing, Tommy. You go. I'll be with you in a minute."

I gave his shoulder a quick squeeze then left him. I thought I should probably help Martin's men clean up the mess.

A voice came from behind me as I stood in the middle of the road, my fists on my hips, surveying the scene, trying to decide exactly what needed to be done.

"Tout va bien?" It was Levi. "It's not your fault, mate," he said, his Australian accent bright and twangy. He grabbed my bicep. "She'll be apples, Tommy—she'll have to be. Understand? Everyone needs a leader right now. Do whatever it is that you do. Sort this shit out. All right?"

I nodded and gave him the thumbs up. I'd been in charge here, and now two airmen, two innocent women, and one of my closest friends were dead. I should have planned this better. I hadn't realised the extent of Jérôme's hatred. We could all be lying dead on this road.

I felt as guilty as hell.

As I walked to the rearmost van, I passed Jérôme's body, spreadeagled on the road. Without thinking, I spat on it and angrily kicked the corpse in the ribs. I wasn't proud of what I did—I just did it. I knew it was wrong the moment my foot connected with the man's body. But my momentary spasm of uncontrolled anger served to remind me I was simply another human being—one who tried hard to be a good man, but one who had failings, like every other man who'd ever lived.

Andrzej was dead. A stupid, internecine war had killed innocent people, and my friend with it. Luc must have sneaked in next to Andrzej moments before we'd left La Rochelle—that was what the whispering had been about—no wonder he'd disappeared so quickly.

"There's another good thing about the rain," I said, when I finally went back to see how Shorty was getting along. "It'll wash the blood from the road."

He nodded then stood, Andrzej's body across his arms. I'd never seen him so tense. "Come on, Yankee," I said. "Business first—fall to pieces later. Andrzej would've been the first to say the same thing."

He smiled at me wanly and then took our friend's body to one of the German vans, asking the Frenchman who was driving it if he could take Andrzej to Père Christophe at the Abbey and then drive it back to meet us at the flooded quarry.

We watched as the van drove off the road, skirting the trees at its southern edge, before turning out of view to drive across the fields, in the direction of the Abbaye de Saint-Hilaire.

*****

An advisory sign was posted on the edge of the lake.

> *Attention.*
>
> *Bord étroit.*
>
> *Profondeur: 120 mètres.*

A ten-metre-long wharf jutted out from the foreshore. I'd been told the farthermost pile, which supported the end of the jetty, sat on the edge of the underwater precipice. Only bubbles marked the resting places of the Germans. The two *Lastwagen*, their driver's doors removed, and loaded with their weighted-down cargo of German bodies, had been driven at high speed down the jetty. At the last possible moment, the driver had leaped expertly from the cabin into the water and had swum ashore.

When it was time for the Mercedes to be sunk, Shorty, Andrew, Levi, and I stood in a line and watched as one of Martin's men revved the engine. After a second or two, he eased his foot off the clutch and the great, gleaming black car shot forward along the boardwalk, springing over its end, and then splashed onto the lake surface. It floated for a short while, giving the driver time to clamber onto the back of his seat and dive into the lake before it sank.

We'd taken the precaution of dressing four of the German guards in our uniforms. If the skeletons were ever found, perhaps the metal insignia might solve the mystery of the four missing German officers we'd impersonated. No one seemed to notice I'd pocketed the lieutenant-colonel's epaulettes and insignia. I thought they might come in handy at some time in the future.

"There goes five hundred smackers," Shorty said under his breath.

"And the rest, Yankee," Andrew replied. "More like close to a few thousand."

"Holy Toledo!" he said and then whistled softly. "Wait till I tell my mom about this. Two thousand bucks for a car? She'll never believe it."

Farewell, Obersturmbannführer Leonard Alberbach, I said to myself, as I watched the car and its dressed-up occupants disappear under the surface of the lake. We'd tied their legs to the seat braces, so the bodies wouldn't float to the surface. It gave me some satisfaction to know I'd be able to deliver the news of his demise to the very man himself in a prison camp, once I returned to England.

Surprisingly enough, Levi and I turned out to be the only two who weren't Roman Catholics. Père Christophe's caretaker took off his beret and led a short prayer, many of the men, including Shorty and Andrew, removing their caps and kneeling in the mud. They recited a prayer and then crossed themselves, before muttering, in unison, *"Resquiescat in pace. Amen."* In war, there was still honour for the fallen, even if they were the enemy.

Martin joined us for a cigarette. I asked him to promise me he'd keep his head down and stay quiet for a month or two.

"It's time we went," he said, when he'd finished his smoke. "I doubt the convoy will be missed until late tonight or tomorrow, but we need to get far away, right now."

I followed him to Père Christophe's Citroën, which was hidden in the trees, and the six of us squeezed into it and drove off, Shorty surreptitiously holding my hand in the back seat, and all of us very quiet.

I couldn't help but think of Horloge's sadness when she finally found out about the death of her granddaughter, and her remaining grandson and his wife.

*****

It was still only eleven thirty in the morning and we had perhaps twenty-four hours before the Germans were missed—there was a lot to organise.

Martin's men had disappeared shortly after we arrived back at the abbey. Père Christophe had promised them he'd drive to La Fromagère the next day to preside over the burials of Simone, Nicole, and Jérôme.

In the meantime, there was a sobering task to perform. We had to bury Andrzej and the dead airmen.

No matter what we said, the priest wouldn't allow us to bury the two Protestants in the abbey cemetery. Outside the abbey's walls, on the edge of the apple orchard, there was a small plot in which the unbaptised, murderers, heathens, and suicides were interred. It was only there he'd give us permission to lay the pilots to rest. The soil was soft, and we took turns digging the graves. I recited a prayer in English and another in French.

Andrzej's burial was a different story. Shorty and I were allowed to dig his grave among the headstones of former friars of the abbey. Andrew and Père Christophe took turns relieving us. Even then it took the best part of two hours to get down four feet, as the ground was compacted and very rocky. I knew the trench should be six feet deep at least, but we simply couldn't afford the time. Père Christophe gave a very short graveside service, and Shorty gave a eulogy in Polish, his words broken with emotion.

We were standing in prayer over Andrzej's grave when Thierry called out from behind us. "You'd better come. He's stirring."

Luc had been drifting in and out of consciousness since I'd pulled him out of the truck. He moaned fitfully and thrashed a little every so often, as if he was having a bad dream.

"I'll go," Shorty said.

"Not without me," I added. "Andrew, you coming too?"

"I'll give you some time with Luc," he replied. "I want a quiet moment by myself. I thought I might pick some wildflowers for the grave."

I squeezed his shoulder. I guessed he didn't want to be there when we told Luc that Andrzej was dead. He and Andrew had spent three weeks together in a small room in La Roche while we four had been training our separate Resistance groups in Normandy. They, too, had become close friends.

"Who's going to tell him? You or me?" Shorty asked, one hand on the door to the church's infirmary.

"I'll do it, if you don't want to."

"Tommy, I ..."

The words caught in his throat, so I squeezed his elbow and then pushed the door open. Luc and Baen were lying on miserable-looking mattresses on the floor. Thierry had told me the local German administrator had sequestered the infirmary's few iron bedframes for the platoon of soldiers stationed at Andilly.

I sat on the floor next to Luc, hopelessly struggling with my own feelings of guilt.

"Here, take this, and stop beating yourself up." Shorty handed me a cloth that smelled strongly of vinegar. I held it by one corner and then whirled it in the air over my head, before folding it and holding it gently against Luc's forehead.

"What's that do? Is it some secret Aboriginal healing ritual?"

"No, smart-arse, it's a secret white-fella healing ritual that cools the rag."

I smiled at him. He stroked the side of my face and returned my smile with a tender, concerned one of his own.

Without warning, Luc sat upright and began to scream, his eyes still closed. His movement was so violent it pushed my hand aside, wrenching my arm in my shoulder socket. My elbow hit Shorty on the bridge of his nose, and the vinegar-soaked rag flew across the room. The noise brought Père Christophe to the infirmary door, and he helped us to subdue Luc, who eventually fell back onto his mattress, panting and pushing his heels into the padding under his feet.

"*Freinez! Freinez! Arrêtez!*" he yelled at the top of his voice. I supposed he was reliving the last few moments before he'd lost consciousness. He was yelling instructions to brake and to stop the car.

"I'm sorry, my friends, there's only one way to stop this," Père Christophe growled, hoicking his soutane up over his trousers and then straddling Luc's hips. He slapped the boy hard across the cheek. The sound made me wince, but it made Luc sit up once more, struggling wildly. He struck out around him while we grappled with his flailing arms. Before I could catch his wrist, he landed a right-hook to Père Christophe's chin, knocking the priest onto his back.

"Holy Mother of Mercy!" The priest rose on his haunches and slapped Luc resoundingly once more across the face.

Luc gasped and his eyes flew open. He began to take in the room around him. *"Ou suis-je?"* he said, his voice threadbare, and then, *"Thomas? Mon Américain?"*

It was Shorty who moved first, pulling Luc into his arms. I wrapped mine around both of them, whispering soothing, wordless sounds—I cried on the inside.

It took perhaps five minutes or so for Luc to calm down and to let Pascal inspect the bump on the side of his head. Satisfied, and after a soft snort, he announced, "He's merely had a bad concussion. I don't think it's anything more. However, it would be best to get him to hospital."

I shook my head. He replied with the particular French tilt of the head and shrug of the shoulders that meant, *ah well, what will be will be—but it's a pity.*

"What's the last thing you remember, *mon brave?*" Père Christophe asked. I could see the beginnings of a spectacular black eye in the making—the bruise on his chin where Luc's fist had landed had already started to form.

"I saw Jérôme run out from the bushes at the side of the road before the convoy had stopped. It was too early—he hadn't followed orders. I could see he was about to do something stupid, so I called out to Andrzej to slam on the brakes. The last thing I remember was seeing Jérôme cocking his machine gun at us with a terrible look on his face and then Andrzej grabbing me by the jacket and pulling me towards him, telling me to get down …"

It was as we'd supposed. Andrzej had pulled Luc to him, in an effort to get the boy onto the truck's floor-well, to get the engine block between him and the machine gun. Luc must have hit his head either on the steering wheel or the dashboard.

Andrzej had given his life to save Luc.

Luc craned his neck over my shoulder and looked around the room. "Where is Andrzej?" he asked in a very small voice.

"Luc ..." Shorty said. He stopped to swallow a mouthful of saliva. The next words seemed to have stuck in his throat.

Baen groaned very loudly. Luc snapped his head in his direction. It was obvious he hadn't noticed the wounded man, lying on another thin mattress, not two metres from him.

"*Ce n'est pas possible.* "What happened? Tell me. Please don't say the plan didn't work."

I sighed and then leaned against the wall next to him, taking his hand into mine. I began to tell him exactly what had happened. During the telling of it, Luc remained immobile, only the sudden stream of tears that ran down his face when I told him of Andrzej falling out of the cab and knocking me to the ground hinted at any internal turmoil.

"*Alors, c'est Andrzej qui m'a sauvé la vie,*" he said in a whisper, after I'd finished recounting the events on the roadside.

"Yes, he saved your life, Luc," Père Christophe said from behind me. "*What the Lord takes away, he gives with the other hand.*"

Luc began to sob, quietly this time, not like his outpouring of grief with me in Édouard's orchard. "The Lord has spared you, Luc—that must mean something," the priest continued. "Turn your heart to forgiveness, as hard as that might be, and thank your friend for his sacrifice. He must have loved you very much."

Perhaps it was only me who saw the tightness at the corners of Luc's eyes. I knew forgiveness was the last thing on his mind. I could almost see the word "revenge" emblazoned across his forehead. It was at that moment I decided he needed to be out of harm's way. It would serve no one's interest if he were to grab a weapon and start shooting randomly at Germans. In his current state he was a loose cannon, one that could probably get us all killed.

Since returning from the massacre at Les Longeards, I'd been formulating plans. Weighing up alternative courses of action. Luc's quiet rage meant there was only one possible choice.

"Where is he?" Luc asked.

"I'll show you," Andrew said from the doorway. He'd returned from the orchard, a posy of daffodils and winter-flowering jasmine in his hand.

"That was an interesting paraphrase of Job, Father," I said after Luc and Andrew had gone. "We Protestants must have a different bible. Ours says *'Naked I came from my mother's womb, and naked I shall return there. The Lord gave and the Lord has taken away ... '*"

"Trust the heathens to know passages about nakedness, Thomas," he said with a glint in his eye.

"I was merely interested in the words of the Book, Father," I replied.

"Ah, *mon ami*, you didn't live through the last war, as I did. In times of conflict, it's intentions that count. One must learn to bend the Book to suit the reader."

He left me standing with my mouth open.

*****

Initially, when Shorty and I eventually made our way back from the monastery garden and into the graveyard, we couldn't see Luc. An empty hay-rick, in which we'd transported the bodies, had been returned from the orchard and was blocking our view of Andrzej's grave.

"Stop," Shorty whispered to me as we reached the tailgate of the wagon. He held one hand flat against my chest.

I could hear Luc talking under his breath. I peered around the edge of the cart. He was lying on his stomach, sprawled over the freshly dug dirt, repeatedly plunging his mother's dagger into the loose soil while murmuring, over and over, *"Dix pour chacun, dix pour chacun; je te promets, Andrzej ... "*

My blood ran cold. *Ten for one*, he was chanting. *Ten for one; I promise you, Andrzej ...*

Decimation was a word often used incorrectly. It didn't mean destroy or annihilate. It came from the Latin *decimatio*, which was an ancient Roman army punishment that involved killing one man in every ten in a cohort or a legion.

But, Luc's chant was the other way around. He was swearing, on

Andrzej's grave, ten men would be killed for every single one we had lost.

*****

I was greeted with stony silence when I ultimately revealed my plan.

I'd decided to send Shorty, Luc, and Baen back to London on a plane. Levi, Andrew, and I were to carry on to the south, as we'd originally planned.

Once the convoy didn't arrive in Nantes, as expected, German soldiers would be everywhere. It would be far too dangerous for us to remain in the area. I decided to contact London to arrange an emergency night-time pickup. I wanted Luc out of harm's way as soon as possible, and Baen needed immediate hospital attention. The calendula and lavender poultices prepared by the monastery's herbalist weren't going to fix two bullet wounds.

We'd never trained a Resistance cell in the area, so there were no pre-existing, surveyed landing sites near the abbey. Père Christophe suggested a remote field he thought would be perfect, and when he showed it to me on the map I agreed it would do. I had my own map with Cassini Grid coordinates that pinpointed the field. Those were all I'd need to send in my message to Gladys. The proposed landing site was south of La Rochelle on a headland near the small town of La Fumée. There was a lighthouse about a kilometre from the field. Père Christophe knew the area exceedingly well and told us that although the beam from the lighthouse was partially shielded, so it couldn't shine due north over the sea, it still shone over the headland to the west. The local fishing fleet needed to navigate between the mainland and the Île d'Aix. The lighthouse, with its westward-facing shaft of light, would be a conspicuous and handy landmark for the pilot.

With the small ruler of my penknife, I measured the field on the map. It was only big enough for a Lysander, so once more three men would have to squeeze themselves into the small passenger space meant for one.

Despite Luc's aching heart and foul mood, he and Andrew disappeared up into the bell tower of the abbey to set up the radio and to send the message I'd drafted.

"No, I'm not letting you go on without me," Shorty said, having almost dragged me by the collar out into the quadrangle of the abbey. "I was happy enough to go south with you and then to leave you to do your thing in Bayonne. But, this? This is another story altogether—"

"Shorty, listen to me. It's not about whether you can look after yourself or not. It's just that this operation has gone arse-up, and you being an American is now twice as problematical. They're going to be looking for us, and both Müller and Hotz, much as you liked them, will provide a very accurate description of you. You aren't exactly 'blend-into-the-crowd' material."

"Why not?" He genuinely looked perplexed.

"You are six-foot-bloody-three. Me? There are plenty of tall, blond Germans. But the colour of your hair and your height? It's not as if you could wander through the masses disguised as a peasant and not be noticed. They don't make them that tall over here, in case you didn't notice … and your French isn't good enough yet. It's bound to give you away the moment you open your mouth."

He started to protest, but then stopped. He knew what I'd said made good sense.

"You know I have to go to Bayonne for George, and then on to Lesaka. I promise you I really wanted to do it with you. But don't you see that's impossible now? When I get back home, I'll make sure we'll have some time off. It may be possible for me to wangle a week or two for us in North Africa, in the sun."

"Really?"

"Yeah, fingers crossed, though. I was asked to go shortly before we left to come here, and I think I could arrange for you to come with me. I'd have to interrogate some captured German officers while we're there, but I could argue it's part of your training. I'll get Gladys to send off the papers when I get back, okay?"

I tried to make it sound like something to really look forward to—sugar to disguise the bitter pill of disappointment.

"How are you going to get home, Tommy? We were going to travel in those German uniforms, and they're food for the fishes now."

"Andrew, Levi, and I will do as we originally planned. We'll go by train to Bayonne dressed as civilians. I'll get the two of them over the border into Spain. Once they're there, the British Consul in San Sebastian will arrange for them to get to Lisbon. After I've done the duke's work in Bayonne, I'll make a quick trip to see whether Rhys is in Lesaka or not. If he isn't there, I'll head to Lisbon and get on a plane back to London. There's no need to worry."

He snorted softly. He saw through my attempt to reassure him. Both of us knew it wasn't the time to thrash over "what ifs"—our current situation was too precarious.

"What'll I do with Luc when I get him home to London?" he asked.

"Look after him, I hope."

"I'm not going to be able to take time off work when I get back. Bill Donovan will want reports by the dozens about how we set up the cells, and how we recruited the locals and trained them. I'm going to be stuck in the office for weeks."

"No one expects you to babysit him. I've got an idea that will not only keep him busy, but I'm sure he'll be happy about it."

"Does it involve giving him a gun?"

We both chuckled.

"Tell Gladys to get Aimée Girole up from Bristol. She's about as ready as she could be. She and Luc can move into Coptic Street, he can have my bedroom, and she can live in the spare room on the floor above the bookshop."

"Why Aimée?"

"She's going to be his training officer. Tell Gladys to bill the SOE for the flat."

"Wait," he said, "you're going to train him?"

"Of course I am, Shorty," I said. "He's nearly sixteen. He can have some basic training at Baker Street. You and Aimée can be his support until I get back, and until we can arrange to send him back to Normandy. You'll have to ask Gladys to get FR Section to let his father know he's safe and he'll be away for a while. You know Luc, he'll jump at the chance—becoming a trained field agent to help his country is what he lives for. That, and annoying us."

"True, but you know we both love it," he said, rubbing the back of one of his hands against the top of my thigh. I slipped my hand into his. "Tommy, what about you?" he asked. "If Luc's in your flat in Bloomsbury, where are you going to live when you get back?"

I looked about, to see all was clear, and then wound my arms around him and pulled him behind one of the broad pillars in the arched courtyard. I kissed him. "Where am I going to live? In Manchester Square with you, Heinrich."

I felt compelled to make a promise for the future for the both of us. I was no fool. Anything could happen to me between here and Bayonne, or while trying to recover the blackmail items for George. I needed a goal—something to strive for—and Shorty needed to hear what I was about to say.

"Move into the house and make it ready for us. Steve and Andrew will give you a hand."

"You sure? Without even seeing it?"

"You know I'd do anything for you, sweetheart. I just want to be with you."

I wasn't sure whether the gentle trembling in his body was a reaction to the violence of what had happened earlier that day or to what I'd said. But his smile was as broad as the ocean and as bright as the sun on the sea.

A bell rang in the small tower above the chapel. It seemed like a signal for us to move apart.

"Three o'clock," he said.

"What?"

"It's *None*—mid-afternoon prayer. It must be three in the afternoon."

There was something I'd been worrying over, ever since returning to the abbey. Now was as good a time as any to ask.

"Shorty ..."

"I've been waiting. You have that look you get when you've been saving up something to say to me."

"I know today was the first time you killed a man. You all right with that?"

"Yeah, I suppose I am. I guess I have to be ... but I'm glad it was someone like Jérôme."

Every man dealt with killing in his own fashion.

*****

"I'm not sure I want my whole life to be standing somewhere in France in the dark, watching you disappear off into the night in an aircraft."

"How long will you be away do you think?"

"One week, maybe two. That'll give you a chance to start to get the house organised. I'll get word to you once I get to Lisbon, okay?"

Père Christophe had driven us. He knew the local priest and also knew he could be trusted. The man helped us by finding a few dependable locals to hold flashlights to guide down the Lysander. They'd gone over the field before dark, under pretence of measuring it out for ploughing in the spring, to check for stones or any other debris that could prove dangerous for the landing of the aircraft.

In the car, on our way to La Fumée, I briefed Shorty on everything he needed to pass on to Colin Gubbins. I also asked him to contact George and tell him I had a reply from Édouard, and I'd deliver it when I got back.

Despite his excitement at being told we were going to train him to be a professional, the hardest part of the farewell was prising Luc's arms from around my waist. He wasn't even trying to be a grown-up. I wiped the tears from his face with my thumbs and ruffled his hair.

"Don't get killed," he said.

"I'll try not to. You either."

He looked at the waiting aircraft. "Is that likely?" His eyes were very round.

"Not at all," I whispered. "By the way, Luc, please look after the big man for me, will you?"

He nodded solemnly. "So, when I'm in England, where will I stay?"

"You're a grown man, Luc. So, if you like the idea, you can live at my place. You'll have to share it, though."

"Share?"

"She's pretty …"

He chortled. "Is she ancient, like you?"

"No she's not ancient like me. But she is French."

"Ooh, la, la," he said, with a grin intended to make me smile.

"You'll get to meet all of our friends, get to go to the cinema, and the theatre—you're one of us now. I've even asked Andrew to take you to meet Général de Gaulle."

"Really?"

"Sure, if you want to," I said, "but if you go, we'll have to shoot you afterwards."

He kicked my shin.

Père Christophe called out to Luc to help turn the aircraft around for take-off. Shorty was standing behind me while I said my goodbyes to Luc. He was quiet for a change, his eyes glistening in the moonlight.

"Manchester Square," I said, aching to hug him.

"I'll have a bed in it at least." He saluted me, officer-style, with two fingers to the temple. "'Bye, Tommy," he whispered. And then he was gone.

For the second time in a week I watched a plane carrying my man disappear into the distance.

I reached into my overcoat pocket. After he'd landed, the pilot had passed me a sealed envelope with my name on it. I recognised Steve's writing. I waited until the sound of the plane had become inaudible and then opened the note and read it by flashlight inside my overcoat.

"So, onwards to Bayonne," Andrew said, once I'd finished reading and had put the letter back in my pocket.

"Yes," I said, "you two are. I'm going to Strasbourg."

"What …?"

"Steve and Elizabeth got home safely to London, but Michael and the stolen documents haven't returned. They've gone missing."

CHAPTER 14

I smiled at the man pointing a Luger at my chest.

"At least this time I brought flowers," I said, holding out a straggly, broken bunch of early daffodils and jonquils I'd picked from the roadside on my way from the station. The last time I'd turned up at Saint-Lô, I'd presented him with slaughter at his back door. Flowers made a nice change.

"Will you bloody well stop doing this?" Édouard said, the surprise on his face fading as he realised that if I'd returned, something must have gone seriously wrong.

The events of the last eight days had overshadowed the previous drama that had taken place in the kitchen at Saint-Lô. I was glad to see Édouard was at home when I got there. I'd been afraid he might have gone to Berlin.

I'd managed to get both Andrew and Levi onto the southbound train to Bayonne. It was fortunate Martin had a "tame" photographer at hand. He took new photos of Levi and attached them to both Shorty's travel papers and his Portuguese visa. Levi's fair hair wasn't as red as my American's, but the description stated *blondes Haar*, so he'd pass. It was his height that seemed to be the major stumbling block. Andrew solved the problem by carefully changing the 9 in 190cm to an 8 on both documents—one hundred and eighty centimetres was roughly five feet eleven. As Levi was a little over that height, we told him to slouch.

They were both travelling as salesmen from Minnesota. Levi, being a linguist, had no problems with a North American accent. Andrew's brogue was impossible to hide, but he'd invented a history to explain it. Neither of them had been happy about leaving me, especially as I didn't tell them why I was going to Strasbourg. I knew Andrew would insist on coming with me, and it was more important he got home safely to his wife and children.

Père Christophe had driven Andrew and Levi to Rochefort to catch the train to Bayonne. When he'd finally returned, quite late at night, he'd poured me a glass of wine and asked me what had happened at Les Longeards. I had been reluctant to tell him the details, but, as he'd insisted and was an accomplice of sorts, I felt I owed it to him. He'd sat silently, crossing himself and beating his chest gently with one fist as I'd told the story of Jérôme's treachery and the murder of his own wife and sister. He was a pragmatic person, having first been the harbourmaster in La Rochelle and coming to his calling late in life. He'd given me a spare cassock, saying it might come in handy some time and then he'd driven me to Poitiers in the dark so I could catch the early morning train to Caen. The connecting train had got me to Saint-Lô four and a half hours later.

Once Édouard had recovered from his surprise at my reappearance, I ran through the sequence of events since I'd left him, eight days before. I managed, despite my own feelings of guilt, to give an accurate description of the cock-up at Les Longeards, and the subsequent return of Baen, Luc, and Shorty to England.

"Phew," he said, after I'd finished telling him about putting Levi and Andrew on the train. "Tell me, Tommy, do I have to shoot you before you tell me why you're here?"

"It's simple. You and I are going to Strasbourg to find Michael."

He looked at me as if I'd grown two heads.

I opened my suitcase and took out a neat, brown-paper parcel. "I think Obersturmbannführer Leonard Alberbach, even though he's safely across the channel, might still be of service to us. I kept the colonel's epaulettes and insignia, and fortunately had the foresight to have this delivered when the Lysander came to pick up Shorty. It always pays to be prepared."

I opened the parcel and held up an SS officer's uniform "shell".

Édouard looked decidedly suspicious. "I'm getting a bad feeling about this ..."

"You still have the sergeant's uniform here?" I asked. "I can't travel as Alberbach unattended. An officer of his rank would always have an adjutant—and that would be you."

"But Tommy ..."

"We're going to travel as conspicuously as possible to Strasbourg by train. Once Alberbach's been declared missing, and an investigation launched, it'll be assumed he deserted his duty and is now a traitor to the Fatherland."

"*Oh, mon Dieu!* Remind me to never get on your wrong side."

"Yeah," I said, "the man was a pompous snob. I hate sycophants."

★★★★★

The train hurtled through the Meuse region on its five-hour journey to Strasbourg.

It was twelve thirty on Thursday, the sixth of March. Could it really be only just over two months since Shorty and I'd nearly been blown to bits on my birthday?

I felt a strange mixture of relaxation and anxiety. I still had no idea where I might find Michael, how he possibly could have got to Strasbourg, or what could have happened to the documents Elizabeth had stolen and killed for. All I knew was what Steve had written. There'd been a commotion on the train at Offenburg, southeast of Strasbourg. That was where I knew I'd to start to look for my brother.

I'd last been to my parents' home city in 1937 with Michael and Rhys. They'd come to visit me in Munich, and we'd made the short trip to see our Great-Aunt Berthilde—"Bibi" as she was called by our family. She was our grandmother's surviving twin sister and the only living member of our family who remained in Strasbourg. My *grand-mère* had died giving birth to our dad's younger brother, our Uncle Otto. If Michael was anywhere in Strasbourg, I hoped it was with her.

As the train sped past fields and then forests, I noticed a few of the trees were already dotted with bright-green buds. There was little snow on the ground at all, and although it was very early, spring was well and truly on its way. I distractedly practised the fingering of my scales on my right wrist while I looked out the window. I was anxious about my brother.

The ticket collector, to whom I showed the blank *Wehrmacht-fahrkarten* for both Édouard and me, had interrupted my reverie. "But, Colonel," the guard said, "there is neither departure station nor arrival station on your travel pass."

"Nor does there need to be for a colonel of the SS," Édouard snapped and snatched the document away before it could be inspected too closely.

A few moments later, after timid knocking, the compartment door slid open once more. The guard had obviously passed the word to the *Grenzkontrolle* that two cranky officers were inside, and that he should tread lightly.

"Yes?" I growled at the border control official.

He hesitated for a moment and then, seeing the look on my face, changed his mind, leaving us with a curt *Heil*.

"How do you do that?" Édouard asked me.

"What?"

"That intimidating look."

I smiled and curled up on the seat, my head resting against the window. "You wait until you meet Gladys, my personal assistant. She can frighten inanimate objects."

I was joking, of course. However, a year of dealing with German officers who were held at our prisoner-of-war camp in Stratford—nearly all of whom had an inflated opinion of their own self-worth—had given me plenty of models on which to base that "get-away-from-me-if-you-know-what's-best-for-you" look.

"If the look doesn't work, I've found the best way is to narrow my eyes and ask them where their families live."

"*Mon dieu*, did they give courses in 'scowls and growls' where you trained?" Édouard asked. "It's the sort of question that makes my flesh creep."

"And that's why it always works, *mon ami*. Wake me when we get to Saarbrücken please," I said, closing my eyes, and hoping to get at least an hour's rest.

*****

I woke to the smell of coffee.

"Excuse me please, Herr Obersturmbannführer," a young steward said, as he slipped a tabletop from its recess under the compartment window and folded it into an upright position. He covered it with a starched white tablecloth. His companion, a timid, pimply youth of about fourteen, stood behind him, carrying a large serving tray. Once the cloth was laid, the steward set the table with swastika-adorned *Reichsbahn* china. He then began to serve coffee. The assistant reappeared with a tiered silver cake-stand, laden with quartered sandwiches and small cakes. All of this in a first-class railway compartment during a major European conflict, I thought, comparing it to the "quaint" train Shorty had described in his letter from Scotland.

After they'd left, I looked at Édouard over my coffee cup and muttered, "And that's why they'll never win the war."

It couldn't have been more than an hour and a half later that Édouard and I were standing on the platform at Strasbourg. How unlike my last visit, nearly four years ago—the world at peace, and the threat of a demented dictator still a "maybe". I led the way to the far end of the platform and stood for a moment next to the locomotive in its swirling clouds of steam. I'd seen a familiar face near the main exit, someone whose name I couldn't place, but a person I vaguely recognised. I thought it best to avoid whoever it might be.

"Follow me," I said to Édouard and then skirted around the low picket fence that closed off the end of the platform.

He tagged along behind me around the perimeter of the parcel office and onto the street in front of the station building. The station itself I'd always thought quite ugly. It was tall and square, the pinkish-stoned construction only softened by half-star-shaped gardens, laid out symmetrically in its large forecourt. We made our way to the Boulevard de Metz, where we hailed a taxi. Several of the shabbier local types of cab moved out of the way for one of the official-looking limousines, reserved for the officers of the German Reich. There seemed to be no shortage of gasoline in Strasbourg.

"*Château de l'Ile im Ostwald, bitte,*" I said to the driver.

We didn't speak while the car headed south along the road that followed the Ile River. I asked the driver to drop us at the gate to the château, which was situated back from the road. As I thanked him with a generous tip, I casually mentioned we were here for a meeting, after which we were to be picked up by a staff car, which was to take us to Vogtsburg. It was the only nearby town I could think of without a train station. It was a fabrication. A precaution in case anything went wrong and our steps were retraced by the Gestapo.

"My great-aunt lives about a kilometre down the road from here," I told Édouard once the cab was out of sight.

It was nearly two in the afternoon, and although there was no traffic I thought it best we walk to her house through the woods and change in the bushes before attempting to knock on my aunt's door. I didn't want her to take fright at the sight of an SS colonel—she hadn't seen me in nearly four years, after all.

"*Jesus, Maria und Josef,*" she said, after her initial shock. "*Kann es denn wahr sein? Thomas?*"

I put out my hand to grab her elbow, as she looked as if she was about to faint. "Yes, Auntie Berthilde, it's me." She pressed her bunched-up handkerchief to her mouth. "Get a chair, Édouard," I said.

"*Und wer ist dieser Mann?*"

"This is our friend Édouard, from France."

"Michael ... you've come for Michael," she said suddenly and began to cry into her handkerchief, but then clutched the front of my jacket and pressed her cheek to my chest. It made me feel very anxious for my brother.

"Is he here, Auntie? Do you know where he is?"

She grabbed my face between her hands and kissed me hard on

both cheeks. *"Ach! Mein Gott,* Tommy! He is, how you say ... *'Verwundert'."*

I felt the hairs rise on the back of my neck. I knew she meant *verwundet*—wounded was something quite different from surprised. I'd simply forgotten for the moment that French was her first language, and we'd been speaking in German. Strasbourg was, for all intents and purposes, bilingual—to a point. It all depended on where you lived and who your antecedents were.

I tried to stay calm. "Where is he, Auntie? Please tell me where he is."

She pointed at the floor.

He was in the cellar. I kissed her hands and then ran around the back of the house, slipping on the icy grass as I raced around the corner. I fell, hitting my head hard on the stone corner-block. However, in my anxiety and haste to get to Michael, I didn't feel a thing. I flung the cellar doors open and jumped down the half-dozen steps, calling out loudly, "Michael, Michael!"

In the brief silence that followed, I heard a quiet, familiar snicker. "You took your fucking time."

He was lying on a camp stretcher in a corner of the cellar room, propped on one elbow, pointing his Webley service revolver at me. "Tommy, thank God you're here. I heard the clunking upstairs and thought the Gestapo had suddenly come a-calling."

He lowered the pistol then fell back against the wall behind his makeshift bed with a great sigh and a groan of pain. I threw myself onto his cot, not knowing what to do with my hands, wondering how I could pull him into my arms without hurting him.

"Watch my fucking side, you clumsy bastard!" he growled feebly. He began to cry and then pulled me down beside him on the cot.

"Mikey, my Mikey, what've they done to you?" I murmured.

"I thought you wouldn't find me, Tommy." His voice was barely a whisper.

I held him tightly, my heart pounding against his chest. I didn't need to look to know he was trying to force himself to stop crying in front of Édouard.

"Hello, Édouard," he said over my shoulder. He grimaced with pain as he raised his hand in greeting.

Édouard kneeled at my side, kissed Michael's forehead, and then gently whispered, *"Laisse ton frère regarder ta blessure."*

My brother returned a weak smile. I recognised it as one of my own. "Let's just do what Édouard says and have a look at your wound, eh, Mikey?" I passed his gun to Édouard and then gingerly lifted his shirt. There was a large, bloodstained bandage on his left side. "May I?"

He nodded. I removed the bandage and was relieved to find a clean bullet hole above his hip. Its edges were reddened, but it didn't look infected. I took a quick sniff; there was no hint of sepsis. Had the bullet hit a few centimetres lower, it would have probably shattered his pelvis. I rolled him gently over onto his right side and found a matching, but more ragged hole on his back.

"Thank God—the bullet went straight through," I said, happy not to see something worse.

"We need to get something on that," Édouard said.

"Have a quick look outside and check no one is about, Édouard, then ask Aunt Berthilde to put the kettle on. I won't be long. I want to bring him upstairs into the warmth; it's freezing down here." Michael was covered in a mountain of bedding, topped with one of her multi-coloured, crotched blankets.

"She wanted me to stay upstairs with her, Tommy," Michael said, once Édouard had gone. "But I wouldn't let her risk it. In case anyone official called by …"

I shushed him then told him to hold the bandage firmly over his wound while I lifted him into my arms. I kissed his forehead. "We really are twins, Mikey," I said. "Matching bullet scars." He started to laugh, but I could hear it hurt him.

I carried him up into the kitchen, placing him in a chair in front of the stove. My aunt was very nervous, but I reassured her it would be safe while Édouard and I were here. Besides, her house was right in the middle of a ten-hectare farm and there was no way of approaching it without being either heard or seen.

While I helped my aunt set the table for tea, Édouard went to get our things from where we'd left them in the woods. I placed my valise on one of the kitchen chairs and began to retrieve things from it.

314

First was my handkerchief—wrapped in it was the remainder of the cakes and sandwiches from the train. "It's nothing much, Auntie," I said. I didn't dare think of the last time she might have seen a pastry. "But I brought this especially for you, from France." I held up another compact, brown-paper package. My aunt nearly wept. It was half a kilo of sugar from La Rochelle.

Last of all, I produced my meagre medical pack. I rifled through it until I found a phial of sulphonamide and some clean gauze.

"Do you have any brandy, or schnapps, Auntie Bibi?" I asked.

At the sound of her nickname, she covered her face in her hands and began to cry. "Oh, Thomas," she said. "I was so frightened. Not for me, but for him."

I took her in my arms and rocked her from side to side. "It's good to see you, *ma tante*," I said.

She drew back, wiping her eyes, and then slapped my arm gently. "I didn't think I'd ever see either of you again, Thomas. It's good to see you too, *mon ange.*"

She pointed to a cupboard under her sink, where I found the schnapps.

"This might sting, Mikey," I said, as I pulled the cork from the stout stone bottle.

My brother grabbed it from me and took a long swig. "Don't want to waste all the grog on the outside," he said, grinning cheekily.

"Michael Haupner, you're very, very lucky. There's absolutely no sign of infection—Auntie Bibi has done a wonderful job."

"It was the Virgin, the last of my honey, and the *toile d'araignée*," she said.

"Les anciens remèdes sont les meilleurs!" Édouard added, tapping the side of his nose.

Michael and I looked at each other and smiled. When we were kids, and whenever he or I cut ourselves, my mother, my father, or my uncle Otto would ransack the barn, collecting spiders' webs to put on our cuts. As my friend had said, maybe there was something in these old remedies.

Michael took my hand and leaned back in his chair. His gaze held nothing but love and gratitude. "Shorty?" he asked, after searching my eyes for a few moments.

"He's good," I said in English. "More than good actually, we're moving into a house together."

"Wow, my bachelor brother is finally taking the plunge. Where?"

"Later, Michael, I'll tell you all the news later. First of all, I need to know what happened—how you came to be shot."

He glanced at our aunt, closed his eyes, and sighed.

"Aunt Berthilde, I'm sorry, but we're going to have to speak in English. I don't want you to hear things you shouldn't know."

She nodded and then reached into a large canvas bag on her kitchen table and drew out a skein of wool. She motioned for Édouard to hold out his hands, stretched the yarn over them, and then, while Michael recounted his story, proceeded to wind it into balls.

"Elizabeth Petersen happened. I'm sorry, Édouard, but it's the truth," Michael said. I held up one hand to stop Édouard from speaking. Michael hadn't forgotten she'd been Édouard's lover, even though he'd only met them once while they were together.

"I've known Elizabeth for as long as Édouard and Steve, Michael. This can't be right."

"She wants money, Tommy. She wants to sell what she stole to the Americans for dollars."

I couldn't believe my ears. I'd fought with this woman in the Spanish Civil War, had spent nights sitting around campfires talking and laughing with her ... I'd believed her to be a friend. The idea she'd sell information of such magnitude to her own country appalled me.

"Michael, she's not poor. Why would she want money?"

"So she can take her lover with her to live in Brazil." His voice was flat as he looked at Édouard.

"Lover?" I asked. "What lover?"

"Stanislaus von Willenbach."

The name fell like a stone in the room, even Aunt Berthilde glanced up from her wool-winding. Now I remembered who it was I'd seen at the station, whose name I couldn't remember—Stanislaus's father, Ludwig. Stanislaus von Willenbach was the only son of the wealthy German industrialist I'd nearly bumped into at the station that morning. Stan had come as a mercenary to fight with us in Spain. His immensely rich father loathed him and wouldn't give a penny to his son. The young von Willenbach had been a soldier of fortune of the worst sort—effete, useless, and invisible when needed. None of us, except for Elizabeth, had liked him.

"Are you sure, Michael? You'd better start at the beginning."

He settled back and began to tell us the story. "Steve and I finally found Elizabeth in a room above a café in La Muette in Paris. The Resistance got us as far as Meaux, where we got tickets on the Berlin express. Leland Morris at the US embassy in Berlin was surprised to see us, but, as he knew Steve, he rustled up diplomatic corps passes for him and Elizabeth to travel to Zürich. I thought it better if we didn't travel as a threesome, so I decided to go separately, on the same train, but as 'Herr Hoffmann'."

I knew this was one of Michael's established aliases, and he'd have brought appropriate papers with him from England.

"It was after we arrived in Berlin that Elizabeth started acting strangely," he said.

"What do you mean, 'strangely'?"

"Well, it really began on the second day … she went shopping for clothes and was gone for hours. When she came back, she said she hadn't found anything she liked. I found it odd, because she was still wearing clothes she'd borrowed in Paris—you know how much she liked to look fashionable. While she was away, Steve and I decided that, as I was travelling as a wealthy German banker, and they as Americans, it'd be better if I kept hold of the documents. It was simply a precaution. We didn't want there to be any problems in case she drew attention to herself or there was a fuss with their visas."

"Who? Elizabeth? Draw attention to herself?" The three of us laughed, causing my aunt to sigh and shake her head. I knew we were being impolite, but the less she knew the better. It was for her own safety.

"You should have seen the look she gave me when she came back empty-handed and when I informed her of our travel plans. At the time I put it down to injured pride. That we'd somehow decided between ourselves it would be best for a man to look after the documents. Anyway, as we were to travel to Zurich the next day, I put it right out of my mind. But I should have listened to the Tommy Haupner who lives in my brain—he was nagging at me and I had the oddest feeling all day."

"One of my feelings of impending doom?"

"When we got to Karlsruhe, I went to the dining car to get something to eat. Steve and Elizabeth had booked seats at the front of the train and I was right at the back. The dining car was smack-bang in the middle. Just after I'd started to look at the menu, I caught a glimpse of her. She was standing in front of the doorway that leads to the next carriage and was talking to someone whose back was towards me. I knew immediately it wasn't Steve. I thought it odd, because she kept leaning in close to the man and whispering in his ear. It looked as though she was kissing it."

"Stanislaus?"

"Yes, I recognised him the moment I saw his profile. He turned his head to one side to avoid blowing smoke in her face. I didn't think for one moment it could have been a chance meeting—they were far too pally. They were in their own little world, blocking the traffic between the carriages and seemingly oblivious to people who were trying to use the door. It was only when a guard spoke with them that she grabbed Stanislaus by the tie and drew him out of sight.

"I made my way down the dining car until I glimpsed the back of Stanislaus's jacket. They were standing near the external door to the carriage and had partially opened its window. I couldn't make out their words, but could hear them speaking loudly over the noise from outside.

"Unfortunately for them, but happily for me, the gentlemen's toilet wall runs alongside the small corridor in which they were standing. I slipped inside and stood on the seat. I could hear them clearly, even over the noise of the train, through the ventilation holes high up on the wall."

"Go on," I said.

"They were arguing. He was throwing a plan together ad hoc, and she was having none of it."

"Sounds like Elizabeth," Édouard said, a little too sarcastically.

318

"The fact Steve and I had turned up seemed to have put a spanner in the works. She hadn't reckoned on us being there. From what I gathered from their arguing, she'd thought Steve would pass the word from London, and local field agents would rescue her from Paris. She'd planned to make up some excuse then give them the slip, so she could meet up with Stanislaus."

Édouard spoke up. "I imagine the part of the rest of what you overheard was some ill-conceived plot to get the documents from you?"

"Ill-conceived?" Michael chortled. "Folly is the word I'd use. Stan's plan was to grab a guard just before they got to Emmendingen station then accuse me of stealing *his* briefcase."

I whistled. "That's a stupid idea," I said. "I bet Elizabeth wasn't happy. Your German is far more cultured than Stan's, even if he is a local. It'd be far too easy for you to bluff your way out of a situation like that."

"The part she really didn't like was that she was to stay with Steve. She was supposed to tell him she'd bumped into me in the dining car, and I'd told her I'd decided to change trains in Basel and then go on to Berne."

"Why would you do that?" I asked.

"To make a copy of the documents and post them to MI6 in case the plane crashed, or some other nonsense."

I almost laughed. "Stanislaus is deluded," I sneered. "Send the copies to England from Switzerland by mail? Why on earth would you do that? We have an embassy in Berne."

Steve would never have swallowed this codswallop. It was naïve of Stanislaus to even think he would. I was sure Elizabeth had another, more sinister plan of her own up her sleeve.

"Hold your horses, Tommy. I haven't finished. There's more yet," my brother said. "Stan told her when she and Steve got to London, she should say she'd developed some mysterious 'woman's trouble' during the trip and she needed to go to a gynaecologist immediately. That way, she'd give him the slip, get on the first plane back to Portugal, and then on to Zürich."

I clucked my tongue. It was a stupid, ill-thought-out plan. None of the pieces fitted together.

"Wait," Michael said. "You haven't heard the best bit. Stan said they should use his father's holiday house outside Mulhouse as their hideout."

"What?" I said, astounded at the stupidity of using that house. At some stage in the past, all of us who'd fought together in Spain had visited it for parties and country weekends at least half-a-dozen times. "The house in Adolf Hitler Strasse?"

Michael nodded.

"Holy cow!" I said, "and she went along with that?"

"Are you kidding? You know Elizabeth, she's no one's fool. She had plenty to say. She practically exploded!"

"I bet she did," I said. "Go on."

"She told Stan his plan was absurd. She asked him why he didn't merely get me off the wrong side of the train at gunpoint at Emmendingen, force me into the goods yard, shoot me in the head, and then simply take the documents."

"What?" I was outraged, but knew by the look on Michael's face he still hadn't finished.

"After I'd been taken care of, she said Stan should come back to the train, throw the gun up to her, and she'd shoot Steve. As they were the only two in the compartment, she'd pull the trigger before he even knew what had happened. We'd both be dead before the train left the station and they'd have the plans back. She ended by saying her solution would save a lot of *Firlefanz treiben*—fooling around."

When Michael had finished, Édouard's face was white, mine felt red hot—his with shock, mine with anger.

"But the sound of the gunshot in the train carriage—" Édouard started to say.

"Let me guess," I interrupted. "As there are rarely any passengers at Offenburg station, I suppose it was an 'Agatha Christie' solution—wait until the train sounded its first whistle for departure, she'd burst into the carriage, shoot him over the noise of the second *'toot'*, put the gun in his hand and then jump out of the compartment window as the train pulled out of the station."

"You got it in one, brother," Michael said. "A convenient suicide. Agatha Christie in spades."

"Remind me never to read that book," Édouard said. "What a ridiculous, implausible plan!"

"I tell you, they're both deluded. Stan really didn't like her idea at all. He tried to tell her I was a trained killer," Michael continued, "but she sneered, asking him if he'd forgotten he had balls ..."

"Well, then, brother," I said, "you'd better tell me how things panned out."

"The moment I heard an official-sounding voice and a commotion at the end of the corridor, I knew what was about to happen. I sneaked a look out of my compartment and saw von Willenbach and a German officer arguing near the carriage door. The train was drawing into Offenburg station, so I grabbed the attaché case, pushed the compartment window down, and jumped out. I rolled as I hit the ground then ran towards a little park near the railway line. I'd got right to the end of Rheinstrasse when Stan appeared out of the dark in front of me. He must have seen me scarper. I slammed the briefcase into his knee. But, as he stumbled, he grabbed it with one hand and shot me at the same time with the other. I screamed my head off. He went to shoot me again, but I grabbed his arm, so he kneed me where he'd shot me, and then, when I fell to the ground, slugged me behind the ear. It wasn't hard enough to knock me out, but it was enough to make me let go of him. I could see him tossing up what to do next. Guess he decided the documents were more important than I was. He probably thought I was dead meat, because he ran off like a rabbit. I could hear people shouting in the distance, running towards us."

"Jesus, Mikey, you were lucky."

"Nothing much more to it. I knew I had to hide, so, even though it hurt like buggery, I tore off in the other direction, hid in a doorway, and lay low until everything had calmed down. I found the nearest church, banged on the door, and asked the pastor for help. Of course, he didn't want to get involved, but he did bandage me up, and then, after I'd batted my eyelashes and sweet-talked him for a bit, he drove me to Ostwald. He prayed with me for a minute or two, and then left me down the road, outside the Château de l'Ile."

I decided another cup of tea was in order, so filled the kettle and put it back on the stove. I caught my aunt staring at my clenched fists. There was no hiding the fact I was in a white-hot rage. "I'll kill them both, I promise you, Michael," I murmured angrily. "No one touches one of mine without paying for it."

"Whoa! Settle down, Tommy," he said. "I can look after myself. I'll have my day."

"Neither of you is going to do anything right now," Édouard said. "You have no idea where Stanislaus is, Tommy, and we need to get Michael to a doctor."

"Steve and Elizabeth reached England as far as I know," I said, looking at the empty space where I remembered my aunt's biscuit tin used to be. She caught me searching and shook her head. I guessed rationing was as bad here as in England.

I pulled my Beretta out of my inside pocket, screwed on the silencer, and threw it to Édouard. "Dinner," I ordered. "Two rabbits should do us."

After he'd closed the door behind him, Aunt Berthilde spoke. "Stanislaus von Willenbach, eh?" She didn't look up from her knitting.

"I know you don't speak English," I said to her in French, "but your ears are as sharp as ever."

She smiled. "He lives in Freiburg."

Of course! That was why he'd planned to get off the train at Emmendingen. It wasn't where he lived, but it was close enough to get to Freiburg by taxi or bus.

She pulled herself out of her rocking chair and went to the wood basket near the sink, picked out a folded newspaper and brushed it off, before handing it to me. "I hated his father," she said. "He was an arrogant pig when he lived here in Strasbourg. That's why I remembered the photo."

On the front page, there was a picture of Stan standing outside a large house. The title read: *Hero of the Reich! Stanislaus von Willenbach, Glorious Son of the Fatherland!*

The article went on to describe how he'd offered to train members of the Hitler-Jugend in the fighting techniques *"he had learned in the Spanish Civil War"*. I felt myself getting even angrier over the lie and swore under my breath. Then, as I read further, I noticed they'd printed his street name. The number of the house, in front of which he was standing in the photo, was very clear.

The paper was yesterday's. I knew where I could find Stanislaus von Willenbach. He was less than a hundred kilometres away, waiting for Elizabeth to return from London, so he could join her at his father's holiday house.

★★★★★

Four days later, as I was preparing to leave for Freiburg, I sat for a moment with my brother. His colour had returned and he was able to walk without help.

"Are you sure you're going to be able to do this, Mikey?"

"Yeah, it'll be fine, Tommy, don't worry about me. It's only two hours on the train to Vichy ... and yes," he said, stopping me before I could interrupt, "I remember how to invoke an emergency procedure with the Yanks."

We'd decided Michael should go to the US embassy in Vichy, the capital of free France, to get looked at by an American doctor before making his way home. His subsequent return to London would mean a train trip to Marseilles and then being smuggled by fishing boat to Gibraltar. It was one of our planned escape routes, only viable while free France was actually free. It was roughly eight hundred nautical miles between the two ports, and even in a chugging trawler would only take about four or five days. We had everything in place for it to happen. Michael knew what to do and who to contact when he got to the south of France. Once in Gibraltar, it meant only a relatively quick flight home to London. He'd be there before I was. I'd stitched up his wounds as carefully as I could, using needles and thread from my aunt's sewing kit, boiling everything first. It would do until he could have the stitches replaced by a physician.

It was time for me to leave. I couldn't afford to wait around too much longer as Elizabeth would probably be back in Germany by now, tucked up and waiting for Stanislaus in his father's house in Mulhouse. I wondered whether she'd already sent a letter, using her pseudonym, Madame de Staël, to the US embassy in London or Berne, or to Whitehall, suggesting she had the Nazi nuclear programme documents for sale to the highest bidder. Knowing her as I did, I surmised it was already done.

"Now what's eating you?" my brother asked, twisting one of my nipples through my shirt.

"Ouch!" I yelled, brushing his hand away. "All right, can we be serious for a moment?"

He pulled me to him. "You miss him that much already?"

"For once it's not about Shorty ... I have to do a job I'm not particularly happy about."

He looked at me quietly for a moment before speaking. "So, brother, who do you have to kill, and where?"

"You know me far too well," I said, swallowing hard. "It's in Bayonne, and it's a woman."

"Oh!" my brother said softly and then ran his fingers through my hair. "Double agent?"

I shook my head and then took his hand in mine, kissing its palm, the way our mother always did when showing us she cared.

"I guess you wouldn't have been asked to do it if it wasn't important." The sadness was thick in his voice. "After the war, we're all going to have to live with the dreadful stuff we've done, Tommy."

"There's another thing ..."

As he looked at me, he slowly cocked his head to one side then smiled. "You want me to tell a lie."

That was the problem of being a twin—he did know me too well. "I only want you to save a situation, that's all. By the time you get home I'll have managed to get the documents back. There's no doubt about it, Michael, I *will* have them. You know what I'm like when I have a bone to pick."

"And I also know what you're like when you've got a bone to *point*, Tommy."

We both laughed with the same laugh we'd shared the whole of our lives. "Pointing the bone" was the Aboriginal way of planting a death curse, and neither of us was in doubt the bone was pointing firmly in Stanislaus's direction. No one could try to kill my brother and hope to get away scot-free.

"When you do get back to London, you must keep shtum about what went down here, okay?"

"Jeez, Tommy ..."

"Invoke the Official Secrets Act—that'll shut them up."

Michael didn't look too happy, but he knew where this was heading.

"I want you to say we agreed the documents would be safer with me, and that's why you didn't bring them back with you. If Steve asks why, say I pulled rank. But, as to where I went after I left you, you had no idea. All I'd say was I was on some secret mission for the government in the south of France. Shorty already knows what I'm up to in Bayonne and he's sworn to secrecy. You must get him alone and make him promise to say nothing to his uncle. Say it came from me. I don't want you to tell them anything about Stanislaus or Elizabeth's treachery, and certainly nothing about her plan to kill both you and Steve."

"Just in case either or both of them decide to hop in a plane and then parachute down to give you a hand?"

"Give me a hand? Get in the way, you mean."

"And how do I explain my gunshot wound?"

"Ah, come on, brother! You're an adventurer. You can think up some scenario that involves escaping the clutches of a handsome, leather-clad Nazi with designs on your virginity ..."

"Let's not get too carried away, Tommy." He guffawed until the pain made him clutch his side. "Okay, I do understand, and mum's the word. I'll make something up and then you can tell them the truth when you get back home—you hear me? I said *when*, not if. Understood?"

"I *will* be home. I have a date with a Yank, remember?"

"Very well, on your own head be it. But, Tommy, Mum would kill me if she knew I was lying for you."

"And we both know you've never, ever lied for me before ..."

"Nor you for me, either ..."

I chuckled then kissed his temple. "I love you, Michael."

"I know that, brother. Now, what are you going to do about Elizabeth?"

"It all depends on the results of my little visit to Stanislaus tonight. If he's got the documents and I get them back from him, I won't need to go to Mulhouse to pay my respects to Elizabeth. I'll write her a note telling her the game's up and she has until the end of the week to get out of the country. Then, I'll write a second letter and post it without a stamp—that'll delay delivery by about four or five days. I'll send it to the *Sicherheitspolizei*, telling them she's been a naughty girl."

"A naughty girl? Steve and I'd both be dead if she had her way—"

"Michael, what would you rather have? Either Elizabeth dead, or spending the rest of her life in hiding, looking over her shoulder and regretting her choices? I want her to agonise about her every move until her dying day. If things go according to plan, Stanislaus will be dead meat by morning. I'll have to confront him face to face, and I can't afford for word to get around I've been back in Germany. Once I'm holding the documents in my hot little hand, I'll get rid of the snivelling piece of shit and then I'll write my letter to Miss Peterson."

"Once she's out of the country, what's to stop Elizabeth calling in some favours, Tommy? Her father's a rich man."

"I don't care how rich he is, but he cut her off, remember? I'll make sure I spell it out in my letter to her she'll no longer be welcome anywhere in Britain, or the Empire, and will be considered 'undesirable' by both the SOE and MI6."

She'd understand these two agencies would circulate her name. It effectively meant she'd be fair game for any British agent who ran across her. They'd bring her in if they could. If not? Well, in the long run she'd be considered a traitor and therefore an open target.

"I'll also make it clear I'm letting Bill Donovan know about her plan to sell the documents to the US, which means she won't get a warm welcome at home either."

"What happens if she changes her mind and decides to donate the material once she knows you've spilled the beans?"

"I'm betting it will be already too late, Mikey," I said. "Knowing Elizabeth the way I do, I guarantee her first letter of negotiation has already been written and posted. Also, don't forget that you, Steve, and I can prove she and Stan were in this together. The fact he shot you puts them both on the hit list."

He nodded. "So ... South America, then?"

"That's where I'd go if I were her."

What I knew, but Michael and the others didn't, was Elizabeth was still on the payroll of the US Foreign Service. During her time in the Spanish Civil War, she'd reported on the movements of American civilians who'd gone there to fight. She'd been receiving a stipend from the Justice Department's Bureau of Investigation since 1935.

And, as a continuing employee of Uncle Sam, her letter, asking for money for information of this magnitude, could be easily construed as treason.

If I killed Stanislaus tonight and then wrote the letter straight away, it would give her perhaps two days to flee Germany. Otherwise, she'd disappear into the great Nazi mincing machine.

*****

"Check my soutane, please, Auntie."

"God will strike you down, Thomas," Aunt Berthilde replied, adjusting the rosary at my waist.

I'd decided to travel as a priest, using the robe Père Christophe had given me. "But I'm travelling as a *Huguenot* priest, Auntie Bibi." I winked at her.

"Then *my* God may forgive you," she said and then crossed herself. "And I really don't care what the other one thinks."

"Auntie, they're the same God," Michael protested.

She harrumphed loudly. "That's what you think, Michael Haupner!"

It was time for us to go and she was extremely upset. She was eighty-six years old and knew we'd probably never see each other again. I kissed her and then promised to give her love to her nephews—my father, and his brother, my Uncle Otto. This made her cry even harder. I'd tried to persuade her to allow herself to be smuggled to England, but she wouldn't hear of it, saying she was too old to learn a new language. We performed a ritual burning of Colonel Alberbach's uniform in her kitchen range and then we had to go.

We turned and waved goodbye to my elderly aunt from the gateway of the Haupner family farm, before the three of us walked north to the crossroads, to catch the tram to Strasbourg station. Even from the roadside, in front of the Château de l'Ile, I could see her tiny form in the distance, waving a small, white handkerchief.

CHAPTER 15

When I arrived at Stanislaus's address in Freiburg, I slipped over the fence in the dark and took off the cassock, hiding it in the bushes where I could find it again. I checked my Beretta and moved quickly and quietly across the yard to the living room windows. A slender young woman, wearing not much more than her black underwear, sat curled up in an armchair in front of the fire.

It took no effort to break into the house and confront her.

"I don't know who you are," she said, her eyes glued to my gun, and slowly raising her hands in the air, "but my name is Gretel Ilsenstein. My father is a general and my boyfriend is an important member of the Gestapo. This is a very big mistake." She started to move towards the door. I planted a bullet between her feet. She was acquiescent while I tied her up and gagged her.

The look on Stanislaus von Willenbach's face when he came home an hour later was something I'd never forget. For the fraction of an instant, it registered a pleased surprise—as if the young woman had somehow tied herself up to be used for his pleasure. That look soon changed as he glanced around the room and saw me sitting in the corner with my Beretta aimed at his forehead.

"I wouldn't do anything stupid, Stan," I said in English. "You know what a good shot I am."

His reply was blustering—pretend-astonishment tinged with half-laughter. "Tommy, what a surprise. But why the gun—why are you here?"

The general's daughter spat the gag from her mouth, coughed, and then began to shout curses at me.

"Shut up, Gretel," I said. The woman had not yet realised the seriousness of the situation in which she found herself.

Feigning a casual nonchalance, I sauntered across the room to the sideboard, not far from Stanislaus, and lit a cigarette, offering one to him, while the girl continued to yell. Her "hero" was invoked to save the day. Stanislaus seemed strangely attached to the doorframe behind him. He kept glancing at my feet. He knew not to get within two metres of me.

Without breaking eye contact with him, I stretched out my right hand and fired a shot over the girl's head, shattering the table lamp behind her. She instantly fell very quiet.

He clasped both hands over his mouth. "You could have killed her …"

"I still could," I said.

"Why are you here, Thomas?" he asked. "What do you want?"

His face told me he knew precisely why I was there.

"Give him whatever he wants, *Hasi*," the girl said hesitantly.

"She doesn't know, does she?" I asked.

He looked at her quickly from the corner of his eye and then shook his head. "So, she also doesn't know you're engaged to Elizabeth Petersen, who's waiting for you with bated breath in your father's house in Mulhouse?" I asked, this time in English.

Stanislaus von Willenbach turned ghostly pale. I could see the wheels turning in his head. How on earth could I possibly know this? But, before he could challenge me, Gretel spoke up.

"Elizabeth? Who is Elizabeth?" she asked loudly, in strongly accented English.

"Oops," I said.

"Wait ... I know you," she snarled. "You're that violinist who disappeared years ago. I remember you, now. Thomas ... Thomas Haupner! That's it."

"Shut up, Gretel," Stanislaus barked. "For heaven's sake, shut up!"

Of course, it was too late. It saddened me to think what must be done. Neither of them could leave the house alive.

"You wait until I tell my father!" the girl continued, oblivious to the fact she'd turned a corner and was now heading down the road of no return. "He'll hunt you down and skin you alive, you traitor!"

Stanislaus screamed at her, "For Christ's sake, shut your stupid mouth!"

"Do something, you fool!" she yelled back at him.

He simply shook his head slowly and then released a long, loud sigh.

"What's her life worth?" I asked him once silence fell in the room.

"Shoot the bitch. I don't care," he growled.

She began to hurl abuse at him, calling him every filthy thing she could think of. It was obvious I couldn't use her as a bargaining card.

"For fuck's sake, just shoot her!" he screamed.

So, I did. Then, or later—ultimately it didn't matter. I couldn't afford to have anyone know I'd come back to Germany undercover. It made me feel very uneasy, but I could also not afford to dwell on it. There was a job to be done.

"You know why I had to do that, Stan?" I asked after a minute or so. He nodded. "You next?" I asked.

He licked his lips and then said, "I have money."

I laughed softly then leaned against the sideboard, slowly shaking my head. "No, that's not true, Stanislaus. We both know Daddy hates your guts. You don't have money, but you do have something that doesn't belong to you."

"No I don't," he said.

Big mistake. I shot him through the fleshy part of his right thigh. He fell screaming to the floor. I pointed my gun at the other leg.

"Come on, Stan, you know that was only a graze. Now, let's have that conversation again. You don't have money, but you do have something that doesn't belong to you."

"You didn't have to fucking shoot me," he yelled, sobbing at the same time.

I crossed to where he lay on the floor, squatted down, and then grabbed the back of his hair, forcing him to look me straight in the face. "Maybe not, Stan. But, you see, I don't take kindly to people who put a bullet in my brother."

His look of fright told me things had clicked into place. He'd thought Michael had been taken into custody, or worse. The same look signalled he realised there was nothing he could say that could sway me. Typical of all cowards, who think themselves better men than they actually are, he tried a bit of bravado.

"I don't have whatever you're after," he said desperately.

"Now, Stan, I don't want to be difficult, but you're a terrible liar. Left leg, is it then?" I placed my gun barrel against his left thigh. I got no pleasure from this, but right from my early days of training, I'd been taught fear yields more results than pain—up to a point, after which most sane people will give up the truth if they think the agony will stop.

"No, no," he screamed. "It's in the desk under the window."

"Tsk, tsk, Stan—guess what? I already checked there."

I pulled the trigger. Then, as he lay on the ground, blubbing, I pushed the gun to his temple and ground my thumb into the bullet hole in the leg nearest me. Strangely enough, he had quite a high pain threshold. It took me about two minutes to get the combination for the safe I'd discovered earlier, hidden in the hallway behind a terrible Dürer print. I'd found it while searching the house, after I'd tied up Gretel Ilsenstein. When he eventually passed out, I tied his hands behind his back with his own necktie. I manhandled him onto the sofa next to the body of his girlfriend.

The documents were in the safe, as I'd suspected they would be. I sat at his desk, closed my eyes for a moment, and then slipped once more into the mindset of my favourite German alias, the Prinz von Plettenberg. Using Stanislaus's typewriter, I wrote a denunciation saying I'd been informed that Stanislaus had stolen important documents from Paris and had also photographed secret papers from Munich, both of which he'd intended to sell either to the British or the Americans. I'd

sent my agent to assassinate him, to avoid tainting the family name—
Ludwig von Willenbach was a major donor to the Nazi Party machine.
I added my agent had instructions to "convince" Stanislaus to hand over
his copies of the documents and then to offer the man the choice of an
honourable death by his own hand or a bullet in the back of the head.

When my agent arrived, he'd found von Willenbach entertaining
the daughter of General Ilsenstein—they were in the middle of dinner,
a large fondue on the table between them. While not important what
they were eating, it had relevance to the subsequent train of events.
There'd been a scuffle after Stanislaus had been escorted to his safe at
pistol point to retrieve the documents, and where, unbeknown to my
agent, he'd also stashed a revolver. In the commotion, Gretel Ilsenstein
had been unfortunately hit by a stray bullet.

With the situation eventually under control, and before his
execution, von Willenbach confessed he'd performed his traitorous acts
in tandem with his fiancée, Elizabeth Petersen, an American agent
who'd seduced and killed Oberst Petrus Jäger in Paris—I added the
address in Mulhouse where she could be found. Von Willenbach had
hoped sharing this information would allow some negotiation to spare
his life.

My agent reported he'd tried to call me, intending to put Stanislaus
on the line, but the operator had not answered. As he'd turned from the
phone, Stanislaus had picked up the fondue burner from the dinner
table, intending to throw it. My agent had fired, killing von Willenbach,
but the burner had landed on the pile of documents, saturating them in
oil and causing the room to catch fire. It had been so ferocious and
widespread he'd been unable to put it out and had been lucky to escape
with his life. He'd reported the house had been burning furiously by the
time he'd reached the corner of the street and had looked back.

I signed it: *Für das Vaterland! Ernst, Prinz von Plettenberg. Heil
Hitler!* and addressed it to *Kriminalrat* Reiner Hertel, the head of the
Munich secret police.

I added a postscript, saying I'd only heard of what had transpired a
day after the fire, when I'd called my agent in the evening at his home
to check on the operation. I also apologised for not presenting myself in

person with this information, but explained I'd only that morning heard news of a Dutch spy, masquerading as a party member and working in the red-light district of Ghent, which was something that needed my immediate personal attention. I was sorry I hadn't put a stamp on the envelope, but said I'd written in haste and had posted it at night—I was quite relieved von Willenbach's copies of the secrets of the Reich were now a pile of ashes in the smouldering remains of the house of a lifeless traitor.

I knew the letter read like a scene from a comic opera, but I also knew how Hertel's mind worked. I'd had the displeasure of meeting him socially several times before the war. He loved crime novels and attended performances at the Volksoper—light, frothy, mindless pieces that held a hint of melodrama. He'd find a missive full of high drama, written by a German prince, impossible to doubt. The veneration of the old aristocracy was absolute. A statement by someone of the upper classes was a *Diktat* to someone like Hertel. Despite Hitler's attempt to make his own henchmen the "new aristocracy", even he'd failed. He'd used members of the *ancien régime* to bolster his own authority and standing among those who'd once obeyed the nobility without question. "If it came from a prince, he must be telling the truth". I could almost hear the words in the *Kriminalrat's* thoughts.

Two birds with one stone—British and American hands would be clean, and the status of my favourite alias would rise in the eyes of the Nazis for his patriotism.

There was one task left to perform. I wrote a second letter to Elizabeth at the house in Mulhouse. I addressed it to the German alias she and I'd invented one night in Spain, as a joke. Gertrude Giftspieler— "Gertrude who plays with poison". There was no need to sign it; she'd know it came from me.

Our friend is dead, and so are you, if you don't leave immediately. There is a Schießen ohne Vorwarnung Befehl—*a shoot-without-warning order—issued for you. Run while you have a chance. The papers are now in friendly hands; you cannot negotiate. In case you think of*

denouncing your former friends, you know that this will
already have been covered. We were not there.
*   I hear that Buenos Aires is lovely at this time of year.*

Before leaving, I put everything in its place as I'd described in the letter to the *Kriminalrat*. I didn't intend to wait around to watch the house burn to the ground and the perfectionist in me wanted everything in its place. I shot Stanislaus through the forehead—I couldn't bring myself to burn him alive—and dragged his body to the dining table, the place in which he might have been standing to throw the fondue burner. I stashed the documents in my haversack and then scattered an impressive collection of pornographic photographs and books on the desk next to the telephone and across the carpet beneath it. I'd found the dirty pictures locked in the safe alongside the Uranprojekt and Joliot's research. Part of me rather hoped some remnants of the pornography would survive the fire and be found along with the remains of his body and that of his mistress. I drenched them in oil from the fondue burner then placed it on the floor next to the desk. With a final glance around the room, I took one of Stan's more alarming photographs and lit the corner with Shorty's Zippo, which I'd lifted from his pocket when I'd farewelled him at La Fumée. "This is for Michael," I whispered. I threw the burning photo onto the oil-soaked pile of papers on the desk.

"Ach mein Gott!" a woman exclaimed, as I passed her in the street a few minutes later. She pointed to the east. About a kilometre away, I could see the glow in the sky of Stanislaus von Willenbach's burning house.

I posted both letters in the post-box outside the railway station and then hurried down the street with my head down, the hem of my soutane flapping around my ankles.

CHAPTER 16

I'd reckoned on more than two weeks to get from Freiburg to Bayonne. But, with a little luck on my side, I'd made it in eleven days. For future reference, I needed to remember on the days I was dressed like a priest, even a Protestant one in a Catholic country, I could get to places and do things no one questioned.

There were many lonely and miserable nights spent sleeping in hedgerows, or hiding in barns, thinking about Shorty and how much I missed him. I often practised the fingering of my concert pieces on sticks held under my neck before I went to sleep. The music seemed to soar from leafless willow branches as I played soundlessly with my eyes closed and with his face sketched in my mind.

By the time I turned up at the Portuguese consulate, I was very tired, and very, very dishevelled.

Although my Spanish was reasonably fluent, I had no Portuguese. For the best part of half an hour, I speculated repeatedly on the idiocy of having a consulate receptionist in France who didn't speak French. Once I wrote down why I was there, in Spanish, she seemingly understood with a loud exclamation of, "Aah!"

I was so exhausted I could have hit her for that "aah!". She disappeared then came back a few moments later with a young man who addressed me at length, again in Portuguese.

I put my head in my hands, wanting to weep.

Eventually, an older woman appeared and apologised profusely. It seemed she was the receptionist, and the other woman was merely standing guard, so to speak. "So, Father, how can I help you?" she asked.

"Could you tell His Excellency I'd like to speak with him? I'm a personal friend of Conde João do Braga."

And that was how I got a new, genuine travel visa to Spain, a luxurious room overlooking the river in the Château Margot hotel, a good meal, and a bath. I slept for almost two days.

On Saturday morning, I asked the concierge of the hotel whether he could recommend a good gentleman's outfitter. I really had no idea of what to buy that would suit me, as Michael and Shorty had inherited the clothes-sense gene. So, when I arrived, I looked around the shop for the most handsome of the assistants and then asked for his help. At the time, I didn't think it odd he seemed to be hovering near the door when I arrived, as if waiting for me.

Although he was outwardly very masculine, he flirted with me subtly at first, something that grew to a not quite "slap-the-hands-away" ferocity as he kneeled on the floor to measure my inside leg. "The man who is my 'special friend' is a combat instructor," I growled, deciding that although I could easily look out for myself, I should come clean. He kept his hands to himself after that. But I did discover being a "member of the club" had its advantages. Not only did I get a discount but also the very best service imaginable, recommendations for the top restaurant in the city, and the packing and delivery of my goods to the railway station to be sent to San Sebastián to await my arrival. It amazed me such a thing was possible. People were scrutinised fastidiously crossing from France to Spain, but parcels by rail could go unimpeded.

I threw in a few cashmere sweaters and ties I thought might suit Shorty and asked the young man to add several silk scarves for Gladys from the ladies' couturier next door. I gave him an enormous tip to choose the items himself. The whole purchase was negligible—I had no qualms about using my money for things for myself or for those I loved.

337

The ambassador had been only too happy to advance me six hundred francs, roughly one hundred and fifty pounds, which he told me João would willing cover for me.

I went back to the hotel to sleep some more, because, later in the evening, I wanted to have a look around the area and check out the house in which Lucretia Hollingsworth lived. Surveillance was the key to success—something drilled into me from day one of my first class in covert operations.

Later that afternoon, after I'd picked up a map of the city from the *Conciergerie*, the hotel manager asked if he could speak with me privately. Once in his office, he shook my hand effusively, explaining he'd been contacted by the British consulate in San Sebastian. I didn't react, in case I was being set up, but he dialled a number and then handed me the phone. It was João.

"Don't worry," my friend said, "this line's totally secure. I only want to know when I can pick you up at Irún."

He told me that after I'd presented myself at the embassy, the Portuguese ambassador had called him to check my bona fides. He'd flown to San Sebastian immediately and had purchased a car, ready to be at my service. I was relieved. I wouldn't have to traipse through the mountains of Spain alone—João would drive me wherever I needed to go. He also told me the hotel manager, Monsieur de Crillon, would help me with anything I needed. So, after we hung up, I asked the manager if he could arrange for some surveillance on Lucretia Hollingsworth's flat and also to find out what he could about her comings and goings. He called for his assistant manager and rattled off instructions, assuring me he'd arrange for a small party, disguised as workmen, to start immediately.

As we chatted, he revealed he was very keen to set up some sort of escape route for pilots downed in northern France through to Spain. I thought it an excellent idea and said I'd see what could be done once I got back to England, wondering whether this might be exactly the sort of thing that might engross Luc, once he'd returned to Normandy.

I left the hotel around seven in the evening, feeling very dapper in my new, stylish wardrobe, and headed for the restaurant the young man at the outfitter's had recommended—La Caroche. The maître d'hôtel asked whether I had a booking. I told him I didn't. When he asked my name, I gave him the French alias I'd been using since arriving in Bayonne—Jean-Loup Périgord. His eyes lit up.

"But of course, Monsieur, I've been expecting you."

He gestured towards a table in the corner where, unsurprisingly, my young suitor from the gentlemen's outfitter was seated.

"Talleyrand Foucault," the shop assistant said, holding out his hand. He'd only introduced himself as "Talley" earlier that morning.

I shook his hand and raised an eyebrow. "Really?"

"*Vraiment,*" he replied, indicating the maître d'hôtel who stood by, waiting to seat me, holding menus. "My father here has a weird sense of humour."

"Perhaps he does," I replied, giving the older M. Foucault a slight bow, "but he's obviously a patriot."

"*Vive la France!*" they both said quietly under their breaths.

"Very well," I said, having sat and opened the menu, perusing an amazing choice of local specialities. "I imagine your shop wasn't recommended by chance?"

"*Non, pas du tout. Mais quand je vous contais fleurette, c'était sincère.*"

My smile was genuine and very broad. It was the first time I'd heard anyone use eighteenth-century French in conversation. "*The flirting was genuine*" sounded so gentle and poetic there was no way I couldn't accept it as anything but a sincere compliment.

"Thank you, Talleyrand, I'm most flattered, but alas, most definitely spoken for."

After a really excellent dinner, we went out onto the terrace to smoke, and his father joined us. They told me that together with Monsieur de Crillon at the Château Margot, they were part of a group of patriots who knew a structured Resistance existed in occupied France, but their own, local groups were unconnected and unorganised. The more I thought about it, the more exciting this opportunity seemed to be. I made a note that as soon as I got back home I'd get the SOE to set up one or two cells in the area. There also needed to be a regional co-ordinator—one of our people on the ground, who could arrange training, sabotage-missions, and infiltration into groups run by Vichy sympathisers.

Later that evening, as I was leaving, Talleyrand asked me, "Your man—you said those large sweaters were for him? He really is a combat instructor?"

"Yes, he is," I replied.

"Mon Dieu," he said, looking at me a little more than wistfully. *"Vous avez vraiment de la chance, vous!"*

Yes, indeed, Shorty and I were both very lucky to have each other.

*****

Lucretia Hollingsworth was a very foolish woman. She'd opened the door to me without question and had invited me into her sitting room and offered me a drink.

Even though she was surprised to see me, she'd accepted I'd come from Paris as George's negotiator to discuss how much the Royal Family was prepared to cough up. Her French was faultless. I could hear neither trace of an accent nor did she appear to be cautious. I was used to judging these things. No doubt she expected we'd haggle over a drink about a price and then negotiate a suitable meeting time and place to hand over the money in exchange for the letters. There were subtle signs she was weighing up whether she might gain advantage in our negotiations by a possible offer of intimacy—something not entirely unheard of in the world of the demi-monde. Fortunately, I was immune to her carefully crafted verbal and physical flirtations.

I jollied her along, using all of my skills to divert the conversation on to more mundane things, until I felt the time was right to ask to use the bathroom.

"I fell asleep on the train," I said, "and it was only when the conductor roused me I realised we were already at Bayonne. I came straight here," I lied. Of course, it was an excuse to quickly "case the joint", as Shorty would have put it.

She indicated the direction of the guest lavatory, which was in a small washroom off the hallway, just inside the front door. As I stood, she took a cigarette from her case and looked around for her lighter. I bent forward and used mine to light her cheroot. Her return smile of thanks was as false as her interest in our previous chitchat.

I used the moment to pretend I'd become distracted, as if I'd forgotten which way she'd told me I should go. Instead of heading towards the cloakroom, I moved to a curtained-off doorway in the wall behind where I'd been sitting. I'd noticed it immediately I'd come into the room. The chair she'd directed me to had placed me with my back to it.

"You remind me of Josephine Baker," I said, over my shoulder, my voice covering her attempt to tell me I'd gone the wrong way. "She's the only other woman I've ever met who smokes those *petits cigares.*"

I pulled back the curtain, saw the room behind it was the kitchen, and then apologised with an, "Oops."

"No, no! In the hallway, Monsieur," she said.

I thumped my forehead with my fist, feigning stupidity. This was the equivalent of "Diversion 101"—techniques designed to distract, drilled into us at the academy. In only a few seconds, I'd given the kitchen the once-over from the doorway and then the rest of the room in which we'd been sitting, all the while following her polite encouragement to go in the right direction. In those brief moments, and on my journey back from the cloakroom, I pinpointed all the reflective surfaces in the sitting room: the silver tray, propped on its edge on the credenza; an empty, shiny anodised aluminium wine bucket; the glass over the paintings around the walls—even the polished surface of the glazed ceramic lamp base that stood on her side table. All of these served to keep an eye on the room without having to move my head.

It was a precaution, part of my training—nothing so far had given me cause to be wary.

The locals who'd been sent to discover what they could about her had revealed nothing out of the ordinary. They'd told me she lived alone and had been in Bayonne for nearly a year. She'd made no friends anyone knew of and didn't seem to have had any regular visitors, apart from a local thug who visited her every so often. He sold drugs and worked a protection racket. I'd been reliably informed she wasn't involved in either business. Everyone presumed he was her casual lover, that was all. He had a mother in Biarritz who he visited regularly, sometimes for long periods, usually on his drug runs. He hadn't been around for days; it was supposed he was away right now.

"Now, Monsieur Périgord, perhaps we should get down to the purpose of your visit. I'm not an impatient woman, but we should talk business."

When I told her I'd come from the Duke of Kent to take the letters, and not to bargain for their return, she merely smiled at me. "So, you think the letters are George's?"

I'd merely said to her I'd been sent to collect the letters and the necklace. She raised an elegant eyebrow and denied having any jewellery belonging to the Duke of Kent. I wondered how well she knew George, to have used his first name with a stranger, or if she really knew him at all. It was probably an attempt to convince me she was a more important person than she thought I imagined her to be.

"I think nothing, Miss Hollingsworth," I replied. "I'm merely here to retrieve what is not yours."

"What makes you think I'm simply going to hand over these letters and some mythical necklace you seem to think I have?"

"How about I ask nicely? That's plan A," I said.

She laughed in my face.

"Well, asking nicely obviously didn't work," I said. "On to plan B." I casually let the left-hand side of my jacket open, revealing my Beretta in its holster.

She sneered at me. "Forgive me for mistaking you for a man with breeding, Monsieur Périgord. I thought you were here to negotiate. What sort of a man feels he needs to threaten a woman with a gun? Especially a woman who's never needed such a vulgar way of doing business."

I sensed she was telling the truth, and it surprised me. She looked genuinely annoyed I'd obviously thought her something other than a sophisticated Frenchwoman with a grace, charm, and wit.

"*Un Français* who works for le Royaume-Uni," I replied.

Her eyes narrowed. What I'd said was clear. Not that I worked for the Royal Family, but that I was a Frenchman who worked for the British Kingdom. No doubt she'd assume I'd been sent by MI6.

"I see," she replied, nodding slowly, weighing up the situation. It was only the whitening of the knuckles on her clasped hands that betrayed any anxiety. She was trying to formulate her next move.

But then, the look on her face altered ever so slightly. The thin line of her lips softened into a faint, almost imperceptible smile. We'd both felt it at the same time—the merest gush of air. It blew coolly against the back of my neck. I hadn't heard the back door to the kitchen open or close, but someone had come into the house. It had to be her gangster lover. An unwelcome and untimely return from his mother's house.

She stood, smoothed down her skirt, and then strode to the French doors of her balcony, throwing them open. Their frames banged loudly against the outside wall, such was her forcefulness. "I can't believe you'd threaten to shoot me in my own house," she said, projecting her voice, obviously for the man's benefit.

"Not before I got what I came for," I said, glancing at the silver tray on the credenza. In its reflection, I could see the curtained kitchen doorway behind me. "And shooting would be a last resort, don't you think?"

She gave me a crooked smile, pretending all was as it had been before her unseen visitor had arrived. "Whisky?" she asked, moving to her drinks cabinet. She held up a decanter and wiggled it in the air. "It's not poisoned, I promise you." Her laugh was silvery and light, despite her obvious unease and her furtive, repeated glances over my shoulder towards the kitchen doorway.

"Thank you," I said.

I tensed, waiting for what might happen next. The soft, metallic scrape of brass curtain rings as the curtain was gently drawn open alerted me to the man's first move.

"Tirer, cretin!"

Her shouted order to shoot came a second too late. I'd already made my move.

At the same time as I'd heard the sound behind me, I'd seen, in the tray's reflection, a glimpse of the curtain being carefully opened. I immediately pushed myself backwards in my chair, toppling it to the floor, and then drop-rolled across the room, landing at the man's feet.

He was so surprised at my sudden movement, and at Lucretia's shout, he hesitated for an instant—and it gave me the advantage.

He must have climbed across the balconies from one of the adjacent flats at the back of the building, or shimmied up a drainpipe. Perhaps he'd arrived and had noticed one of Talley's men outside, loitering a little too nonchalantly? All I knew was the back door of her apartment opened out onto a wrought-iron narrow veranda, on which was her washing line. The land fell away steeply at the block of flats. Although her front balcony was perhaps ten feet up from street level, the one at the back was some twenty feet from the ground.

When I glanced up, the man was standing in the doorway, his pistol pointing at where I'd been sitting only a split-second beforehand. Jumping to my feet, I grabbed both wrists and began to slam them repeatedly against the architrave of the doorway, trying to force him to drop his gun.

He roared, striving to push me away. I had, however, lodged my back against the doorframe, wedging us both in the opening. I'd also planted my feet on top of his shoes. He was a good six inches shorter and twenty pounds lighter than me—I had him pinned in place—he was going nowhere.

On the third or fourth violent thump of his hands against the wall, he fired his gun in a vain effort to unnerve me and to regain the advantage. I bared my teeth and growled, squeezing my fingers harder over his own, the gun firing each time his hands hit the architrave. The following four bullets shredded the lathe and plaster of the sitting room's walls. I knew we'd both counted the rounds, and, realising there was only one bullet left in the chamber, he screamed in frustration and then lunged, trying to bite my ear. I kicked him hard in the shins.

The last bullet ricocheted into a painting on the wall behind Lucretia, showering the floor with fragments of glass. She screamed from behind the couch, where she'd taken cover.

Once I knew the magazine was empty, I really gave him the toe of my shoe, hard in the shin, over and over, as an extra incentive to release the gun. I was only too aware that if I were him I'd want to whack me in the face with it—I couldn't allow that to happen. With a loud yell, he squirmed in a last, desperate effort to get me to release my grip, so he could either bite my face or knee me in the groin.

His high, keening whine told me he was in a great deal of pain, and he was losing his grip on the pistol. With one forceful thrust I slammed the weapon against the edge of the architrave so violently, the doorjamb came slightly away from the wall. At the same time, I felt his wrist crack. He screamed—his gun fell from his fingers and onto the floor. I kicked it across the room.

As I put my hand on his shoulder, to push him back into the kitchen, he spat in my face and then headbutted my chin. For one split-second I forgot my training and lost control. I grabbed him by the throat and shook him until he began to choke. However, a second later, once I realised what I was doing, the red mist cleared and I pushed him away. He fell in a heap to the floor, choking and clutching his wrist for a moment before losing consciousness. I bent down to check he was out to it, not pretending.

"Let him go. Get away from him. Just leave him be." Lucretia Hollingsworth had retrieved the gun I'd kicked across the floor and was pointing it at me. Her hands shook.

Her stupidity made me furious. I'd had enough of this nonsense. I was annoyed at the level of her boyfriend's forceful resistance and cross with my own momentary loss of self-control. "Give me that gun, or so help me God, I will kill you with my bare hands," I yelled at her.

"I'll shoot," she screamed, waving the gun in my face.

I strode across the room, wrenched the gun from her hands, and then slapped her face. "It's empty, Miss Hollingsworth. What are you going to shoot me with? Bad words?"

She proceeded to do just that, cursing me both in English and in French. I made the mistake of wiping the sweat from my brow with the back of my arm, and as I did so she launched herself at me, shrieking and clawing at my eyes with her nails.

"Stop it!" I yelled, grabbing both her wrists.

She kicked me and tried to push me against the wall. I'd had enough so I punched her hard on the shoulder, knocking her into the sofa.

"Shut up, Lucretia."

She smiled and glanced over my shoulder. I was about to turn to see what she'd been looking at when she leaped at me, wrapping her legs around my waist and trying to bite me. I pushed her away roughly and she fell back onto the couch.

"Allez vite, Jean! Allez chercher les autres!" she shrieked.

I wasn't intending to let Jean go find anyone, whether Lucretia's exhortation to get back up was a trick or not. But, before I could do anything, the man sprinted across the room, through the French doors, and jumped over her front balcony, still holding his injured wrist. I heard him hit the ground with a loud thump and an accompanying yell of pain.

"You'll never get him. He can run like a rabbit," Lucretia snarled.

I ran outside onto the balcony. Cars were parked along one side of the narrow street. The man was ducking and weaving between them, shouting over his shoulder at Talley's two men, hot on his heels, but several car lengths away.

Behind me, I heard Lucretia's loud, mocking laughter. "A running target? In the dark?"

I pulled my Beretta out of its holster. "Academy trophy prize in pistol marksmanship, three years in a row."

I fired. The distant figure skidded face-down on the paving stones of the laneway.

"You killed him!" she shrieked, trying to push past me.

"Not yet, Miss Hollingsworth—give me a moment." She tried to grab my arms, but I elbowed her to one side and then let off another, carefully aimed round. An accompanying spasm jolted the spreadeagled figure on the road.

"Now I did."

I pulled her back into the room. All of this nonsense had really irritated me, and, if I was honest, also quite shaken me. The man, despite his slender frame, had been stronger than I'd thought, and I'd been far too casual during my meeting with her before he'd arrived. I'd left myself open to injury or worse. I'd assumed she'd be harmless and I hadn't conducted a methodical surveillance when I'd passed by earlier that day, otherwise I'd have seen the rear kitchen door and would have placed someone there to keep watch while I was inside.

I pointed to the couch. "Sit," I said.

I wiped my chin with the back of my hand. Her hoodlum friend had split the corner of my lip with his headbutt. She sat, fiddling with the hem of her dress, muttering to herself angrily, tears welling in her eyes, while she waited for me to speak.

Loud voices filtered up from the street—men were yelling in Occitan.

"Don't move," I said. "I'm so angry, I might do something I later regret."

Her combative glare stirred something inside me—the knowledge I needed to put my professional hat back on. Too much anger made one reckless.

A voice called up at me from the darkness, *"Eh! Polit … ça va?"*

I returned to the balcony and glanced down into the street. Talleyrand stood below, barely recognisable in his Partisan guise—dirty clothing, a misshapen beret leaning at a perilous angle on this head, and a machine gun held loosely at his waist. He turned aside for a moment and then yelled at a few curious people, telling them to get back in their houses. He gave me a questioning gesture then asked once more if all was well. I replied with a thumbs up. He grinned and threw me a wave.

I lit a cigarette, took a few deep draws and then, when I felt calmer, finally spoke to her over my shoulder.

"Now, let's discuss what I came to retrieve."

"Get out! I have nothing for you."

"I still have four in the chamber," I said, after returning to the room. "Shots in the extremities can be quite persuasive."

Although she pretended not to be shaken, she leaned against the back of the sofa, white-faced, her breathing heavy. I looked around the room—it was a total mess. The floor covered in glass shards. The furniture dredged with a coating of plaster dust.

"But, if you find a gun too vulgar, Miss Hollingsworth, there are other persuasive ways that might leave you alive, but no longer … beautiful."

"When a man's down—kick him," my instructor in Duntroon was fond of saying. I hoped I'd done just that. In this situation, I had to show who was really in control.

If she'd semaphored her thoughts, they couldn't have been plainer. There was another weapon hidden somewhere in the house, and she intended to try to use it on me. She rubbed the side of her face, where I'd slapped her, before speaking.

"So then, if I give you what you want, will you leave me alone?"

"Scout's honour," I said, rather more cheekily than I'd intended. Although not literally, my fingers were firmly crossed behind my back.

"I'm not used to being told what to do," she snarled.

"Being born is the first of a long series of disappointments, Miss Hollingsworth," I replied. "Now, about the letters and the necklace ..."

She glared at me for a long while, obviously weighing up her choices, and then motioned for me to follow her upstairs to her bedroom, where she sat on the edge of her bed. After a long sigh, she removed the large, dark blue sapphire ring from her left hand and slid it onto the ring finger of her right hand. It was an unconscious gesture. I could tell by the distant look in her eyes.

"Very well," she said, the steel once more returning to her face.

I couldn't believe my eyes. She started to pull off her dress.

"Please, no, don't. Don't degrade yourself like this," I said.

I hadn't meant to sound disgusted, but it came out that way. How could she think she could change my mind by offering herself to me, or it was something I required of her?

Her cold, ferocious glare told me I'd offered her the ultimate insult. This was a woman who'd not only seduced a former king but also considered herself an arch manipulator and extortionist and was on the point of becoming extremely rich because of it. And I, an apparent French nobody, from nowhere, had not only killed her lover, but now turned down her proffered wares?

"Isn't that what all men want when they have a woman at their mercy?"

"Not this man," I said angrily.

"I thought as much," she scoffed. Her voice sounded weary.

"The letters," I said. Mine sounded cold.

She walked to the corner of the room, slowly refastening the buttons on the front of her dress. She opened a drawer in her dressing table, took out a sheaf of envelopes bound with a red ribbon, then thrust them at me.

"Untie the packet, and count the letters out so I can see them," I said. "If there are not sixteen, I'm going to be very unhappy."

I watched as she counted and opened each envelope to show me each one contained a letter.

"And now the necklace," I said.

"*What* necklace?"

By this time I was wholeheartedly sick of her. I pulled out my gun and put a bullet through one of the side-mirrors of her dressing table.

"Seven years' bad luck," she snapped.

"Only for you," I said. I waved my Beretta in her direction. "That leaves three in the clip."

She leaned over the table and fumbled behind it. I heard a soft click and then a small drawer in its front flew open. She took out a heavy, glittering strand of jewels and stared at the rope of diamonds for a moment before throwing it to me. I recognised it from the photograph George had shown me.

I held it in front of my face, dangling it from my fingers so it caught the light. It was truly magnificent. No one would have failed to recognise it if Mrs. Simpson were to have worn it to some gala function—something she'd undoubtedly have done the moment she got her hands on it.

"Beautiful, isn't it?" I said.

Lucretia didn't reply, but turned her head to one side, drumming her fingers on her dressing table, impatient to get on with things.

"How did you get your hands on it?" I was curious.

She snorted and then laughed softly. "It was a gift."

"A gift to you? Forgive me for doubting you, but I find that a bit hard to believe."

"You're half-right. It was a gift, but meant for someone else."

"For whom?"

"Oh, I think you've a pretty good idea already. You want to know how I got it? Believe it or not, it wasn't planned. I was in the right place at the right time. I'd always frisked his pockets to see if I could find anything that could be used at a later date. That's why I'd cultivated him in the first place."

"And he had no suspicion?"

She laughed lightly. "Perhaps you aren't like other men, Monsieur? Most men think of nothing but what's between their legs when the heat is in their ears. Besides, he always had several mistresses, and I knew he liked a curtain-raiser before the main act."

"I simply have no idea what you mean," I said, shaking my head.

She placed her forefinger in her mouth and rolled her tongue around it. I was revolted by her intimate revelation. She merely laughed at my reaction. "He was on his way to see *her*. I was an appetiser, something to 'get him going', a bit of fun in a private suite at the Connaught before visiting his American woman. He was quite open about the fact I was a time-filler. I didn't mind. We'd done it often enough before, and he always gave me a small souvenir of sorts. He'd brought two gift-wrapped packages with him, which he placed on the bureau near the door to the apartment before he got down to business. They weren't meant for me— I got a bunch of roses and some cigarettes."

"But you somehow 'rescued' what was in the packages meant for you-know-who."

"You'd be surprised how much he liked champagne, Monsieur … and a girl in my business always carries something to help her sleep at night."

"You slipped him a mickey and stole the presents."

"And I saved the nation."

"How do you figure that?"

"In one of the parcels was a beautiful full-length mink; in the other, the necklace. He was on his way to give it to her. Once she wore it in public, it would force the old Queen's hand. She'd have to acknowledge their relationship, otherwise it would have caused a tremendous scandal—that's what he thought, anyway."

"How could you possibly know that?"

"He told me, silly, while he was throwing back the Piper-Heidsieck. I found my moment, spiked his drink, and then swanned out of the joint wearing nothing but my high heels, the mink coat, and the necklace."

I could scarcely control my anger. Not at her, but at the stupidity of the Duke of Windsor. No wonder George had been tight-lipped about how the necklace had been stolen. The royal princes were terrified of their father. No doubt George's brother had simply feigned ignorance when his mother had reported the necklace was missing.

"Weren't you at all concerned they'd come looking for you?"

"They could look all their lives, but they'd search in vain. To arrange assignations, he'd always sent one of his footmen to the bar at the Ritz on a Thursday. I told him I was Mrs. Olivia Butler and I always drank there on a Thursday night while my husband was off doing Home Guard nonsense. He likes his women married, did you know that?"

She threw her head back and sighed loudly, as if to signal she was bored with the conversation. However, her stance, and the stiffness in her jaw, told me something else. She was tense, and not only because of the gun in my hand. And I thought I knew why.

"You're right-handed, Lucretia," I said. "I watched you while you were pouring drinks, and then when you pointed the gun at me downstairs."

"What of it?"

"You threw me the necklace with your left hand ... I wonder what's in your right." I was toying with her, with the faint hope I might goad her to be reckless. It would allow me to convince myself I'd shot her in self-defence.

She suddenly raised her right arm and pointed a small silver Derringer at a vague place near my shoulder. She'd palmed it when she'd pressed the release catch at the back of her dressing table. It was the second time she'd demonstrated she'd never used a gun before, and she was easy game. I took two steps forward while she was fumbling with it and smacked it out of her hand. "Really, Lucretia?" I asked. "That's twice now you thought you were going to shoot a trained assassin."

She picked up a powder compact from her dressing table and threw it at me—I ducked. It clattered against the *jalousies* behind me and then fell down into the street. I thought her action so juvenile, I laughed.

"I'd like you to move away from the table now, if you please," I said, switching to English.

She reacted as if I'd slapped her a second time across the face. "Of all the …" she growled, glaring at me. "You're not French!"

"No, I'm not. Took you longer to work that out than I'd imagined," I said. "Perhaps you now understand why I have a special interest in this whole sordid affair. It's not merely another job. I have a personal investment. Did you stop to think for one moment what effect these letters might have on the morale of the nation?"

"My only concern was the money, Monsieur Périgord."

She spat out my French alias as if it were something disgusting.

"You were only thinking of the money? In my opinion, you don't spend enough time thinking, *mademoiselle*. Perhaps you might hazard a guess at what's going through my mind right now?" I slowly drew up my arm and pointed my Beretta at her

"I'll give you everything I have," she said. "Just don't kill me … please."

"But you've already given me everything—everything I came for, that is. Do you think I'm going to rob you too? Take your valuables, or your money? Surely not."

I didn't miss the quick glance out of the corner of her eye at the fireplace opposite her bed. It was a nervous glance; something was there. She grimaced—she saw she'd given away her hiding place. Perhaps it was where she stored her valuables? But then the glint of panic in her eyes led me to believe there was something far more interesting stashed behind the register grate.

I sniffed. My nose took in the room. It was involuntary. A reflex action, triggered by the unexpected sight of a small vase of early lilacs on the mantel of the fireplace. I was storing a memory of the moment. Although I was standing perhaps two metres away from her, I could make out not only the faint, acrid odour of her sweat and fear but also her sweet, jasmine-like perfume, and the scent of her unmistakable, expensive washing soap.

I hesitated. My finger was taut on the trigger, but I had a gnawing need to tie up threads, to know why George had been pulled into this whole sorry mess.

"There's something that puzzles me," I said. "I do know what's in the letters. I know they were written by a madman from Austria and sent to a madman in exile in Paris. What I don't understand is why you'd try your blackmail attempt through the Duke of Kent? Why not try contacting the King directly?"

She snorted, as if I'd asked something stupid. "Everyone knows the King's letters are read by his secretary, and most probably a dozen other people, long before he gets to see them himself."

"What makes you think the Duke of Kent's mail is dealt with any differently?"

"The difference is one can't just get someone to drop a note to the King through the mail slot in his front door, marked private and confidential. He has no dark secrets to hide. But his brother, George—he does, doesn't he?"

I could see what she meant. George had a private life, one that had been rife with scandal. He wouldn't have wanted anyone else to read any truly personal correspondence before he did. The words "private and confidential" on any letter would likely have ensured a private reading.

"Pity the blackmail didn't work," I replied. "Instead of thousands of pounds, you got me."

"Yes, aren't I the lucky girl."

Her bravado had returned. It wasn't really bravado, in the sense of a false front to mask fear—her bravado was arrogance, and a misplaced confidence that she'd survive. And indeed I'd somehow hoped, deep in my heart, I could leave without killing her, that what had happened tonight might somehow have made her realise how stupid she'd been. But good sense hadn't prevailed—it had given way under the pressure of her conceit. It was as if she was daring me to shoot her.

I'd seen it before—people who believed their own lives were more important than those around them always also believed they were so special they'd survive any misfortune.

Faced with the fact it was now inevitable, I still felt reluctant. The killing of women was never pleasant, even when they'd attempted to take your own life first.

"Was this all really worth it?" I asked.

"It was worth a try," she snapped.

I held up the necklace. "And trying to sell Queen Mary's necklace to the Windsors—was that a wise move too?"

"If that American bitch wasn't prepared to buy it, I was going to break it down into individual stones and sell them."

"What made you think the Duchess of Windsor would want to buy such a well-known piece?"

She spat at my feet. "Don't play the fool with me. You may be an assassin, but I can see the cunning in your eyes. You know as well as I do just how much Mrs. Simpson wants to rub it in the face of the Royal Family."

"But, seriously, Miss Hollingsworth. Blackmailing the Royal Family? What on earth ever possessed you—?"

"A woman has to live, doesn't she?"

"Does she?" I asked, coolly.

Oddly enough, the anticipation of the deed was worse than its execution.

CHAPTER 17

Rhys Williams stirred quietly beside me, waking me from my half-sleep.

I checked his breathing, noting it had become laboured once more. I looked at my watch—it was quarter to eight in the morning. In an hour or so, we'd be landing at Northolt, and Rhys would be in the hands of an English doctor.

*****

The head abbot at Lesaka had been tight-lipped when João and I had arrived at the tiny monastery. He'd stared aggressively at João when he'd heard his Portuguese accent, but had then mellowed when I'd spoken in formal but broken Spanish. He'd been evasive when I'd asked him whether he knew if anyone was sheltering an injured foreigner, abruptly pretending he couldn't understand what I was saying.

All along the border with France, behind closed doors, Basques continued to protest against Spanish rule. They were especially resentful of the law requiring any Allied soldier or airman that might find his way into Spain to be handed over to the authorities to be incarcerated in a prisoner-of-war camp. This was the Pays Basque. The locals held no love for those in authority in Madrid. Memories were still fresh of Nazi

Junkers and Heinkels raining down destruction from the skies over Guernica.

Any enemy of Germany was a friend of theirs.

I'd had to convince the abbot I wasn't laying a trap. *"Luché en Badajoz. Me llamaban 'El Valiente',"* I'd said, somewhat reluctantly. I hadn't wanted to play my trump card—to use the nickname I'd been given after Badajoz. I'd been christened by the Spanish press as *The Brave One.*

The abbot had regarded me coolly and then whispered quietly to the monk who'd been at his side. The man nodded then left the room.

"Sit, please," he'd said to us, indicating two straight-backed wooden chairs.

I hadn't been sure why we'd been left waiting, but I'd returned the abbot's calm inspection with a friendly smile. Eventually, the monk had returned, accompanied by an older companion, who had been holding a large, leather-bound album. He'd opened it and handed it to the abbot.

"So, it is you," the man had said after a few minutes. He'd turned the book to face me. A newspaper clipping was pasted onto the page that he'd showed.

"December, 1937," I'd said quietly. "It was a long time ago."

"I think you'll find we Vascos have very long memories," the man had said, followed by nods from his two companions.

I hadn't believed the young, tousle-haired man in the photograph at the top of the newspaper article was the same one I saw in the mirror every morning. How could it have only been a little over three years ago I'd been awarded the Spanish Medal of Valour? The photograph had touched something else deep inside me. I'd been flanked on either side by Édouard and Elizabeth. Thankfully the Spanish press had never used my real name, only referring to me by my nickname.

The abbot had stood and taken our hands in his. He'd shaken them vigorously, at the same time calling for wine and food.

Forty-five minutes later, accompanied by the monastery herbalist, João and I had found ourselves standing outside a rickety-looking goat herder's shed in the woods at the far end of the town of Lesaka. It had taken me a moment to recognise the bedraggled, emaciated man was Rhys. He'd been in terrible shape, not knowing who I was, or where he was. His right leg had been so swollen the leg of his trousers had been cut open to mid-thigh. Once I'd removed the poultice on his leg, I could see the bullet wound, although passing through his calf, was very angry-looking. I'd leaned down close to his leg and sniffed, hoping I wouldn't catch a whiff of the recognisable "sweet smell of corruption", which would signal gangrene had set in.

He'd been far too unwell to move any great distance, so we'd carried him to the small local infirmary, which had been perhaps half a kilometre away. I couldn't understand why the herbalist hadn't taken him there in the first place, until I'd discovered he and the local doctor didn't get on. Not only did they hold diametrically opposite views on medical treatment but also something worse, had fought on different sides during the Civil War.

It had been one of the few times in my life I'd remembered actually losing my temper to such a degree I was on the brink of complete loss of self-control. Had not João held me back, I'm sure I'd have killed both men with my bare hands. It was precisely this type of jealousy and small-town rivalry that had led to the death of Andrzej a few weeks ago.

Later on, I'd laughed at João's description of me tearing my shirt open to show the room my bullet scar, and screaming, "I got this while saving the life of the Generalissimo's son, and all so you two could behave like schoolchildren?"

João had used the monastery's telephone to call San Sebastian to arrange to have large doses of Prontosil delivered. It was the most powerful of the sulphonamides available in Spain. There had been little to do but stand guard over Rhys and speak with him every time he was lucid enough to hold a conversation.

Over the following few days, João and I had played tennis, swum in the local river, sunbathed, and otherwise generally got to know each other. He was a genuine, intelligent man with a great sense of humour and forthright pride in his country. Portugal was supposed to be neutral, but the war hadn't stopped him from doing what he could to help the Allies under the table. By April Fool's Day we'd been in Lesaka for four days, and Rhys was only marginally better. I'd known his leg could still fester and end up killing him if something wasn't done very soon.

In his initial moments of clarity, when he'd first recognised me, Rhys had spoken desperately about how he might not see either his parents or Michael again. He'd begged me to get him back to England. If he was going to die, he wanted it to be in his homeland. I'd discussed it with João and made the agonising decision to drive Rhys to Lisbon, stretched out on the back seat of João's car. It had taken us two days of careful driving—the doctor from Lesaka "volunteering" to accompany us, with the offer of a bribe of seventy-five American dollars.

Once finally in Lisbon, I'd sent a coded telegram to Gladys—anxious to get a flight home as soon as possible. She'd cabled back within a few hours, confirming the pickup, which arrived later that same evening. I'd replied to acknowledge her message, adding the code word indicating I needed a medical team at the airport when I got back.

★★★★★

"How's he doing, Tommy?"

Frank Goyen had briefly abandoned the pilot's seat, leaving his young British co-pilot to fly the plane. He crouched next to the camp stretcher we'd set up in the rear section of the aircraft and gingerly ran his hand over Rhys's forehead.

I shrugged. Rhys's fever seemed to have abated, but he was very weak and constantly fell into deep sleeps, rousing himself every ten or fifteen minutes with a weary sigh. The sulphonamides had cleared the wound of its angry red margins, but he still moaned with pain when I bandaged it.

"What still amazes me is how he got from—where did you say? La Rochelle?—all the way to northern Spain with his leg in that condition."

"Sheer bloody-mindedness, Frank," I said. "From what I can gather, he managed to get a ride most of the way with a farmer who was taking his bull to Anglet, near the Spanish border."

Frank scratched his head, puzzled.

"Rhys speaks Welsh," I continued. "It's a close cousin of Breton. I imagine he bluffed his way. The farmer organised another lift to

Urrugne, just on the border. That's when the real problems with his leg started."

"How so?"

"Well, he told me it was on the mend until he started his hike to Lesaka."

"He walked?" Frank sounded astonished.

I nodded. "He sure did. It's only fifteen miles or so, but it was enough to knock his leg about so badly, he collapsed on the road. The last thing he remembered was standing in the middle of the main street of Zalain, calling out in Welsh, asking the air how far it was to Lesaka."

"Then someone must have picked him up and taken him to the monastery?"

"I reckon so, Frank. He's a lucky bugger, that's for sure."

The pilot reached over and pinched Rhys's earlobe between his thumb and forefinger. I recognised it as a "good luck" gesture—touching someone who'd survived something perilous and hoping their luck might rub off. A lot of the old cow-cockies still did it back home.

"And what about you, Tommy? You look bushed. You coping?"

I nodded and then broke eye contact, pretending to inspect my hands. Frank didn't need to know everything. Most of it came under the banner of top secret anyway. And I didn't really want to discuss my feelings right then either. Anyone who said taking another person's life, even in war, was somehow morally defensible had got it all wrong. During a war, lots of obscene things could be judged as inhuman, but then accepted as simply doing one's duty.

In the course of doing my duty for my friend, George, I'd left a trail of bodies behind me. Some I'd killed with neither hesitation nor regret. The likes of Gretel Ilsenstein, Stanislaus von Willenbach, and Lucretia Hollingsworth had been necessities. It had sickened me afterwards, but shooting them had been unavoidable. In time, I'd come to terms with what I'd done. It was the others that had left me struggling with my internal demons—the airmen who'd been killed in the ambush outside La Rochelle, Jérôme's wife and sister, even the man himself. These deaths lay heavily on my soul. Those people were, in many ways, victims of circumstance; accidental by-products of the factory that was war.

I'd have to find time to deal with Elizabeth's treachery. Betrayal was one human trait I found impossible to forgive. Maybe it was a failing in my character? In her case, I couldn't turn the other cheek and forgive her for what she'd done and what she'd planned to do—kill not only my brother but also Steve, my best friend. If the Nazis had got to her first and shot her, I'd have no feelings of sadness. I'd be left with only bitterness at what she'd become.

But there was one death over which I'd probably never find complete inner peace—that of my friend, Andrzej. I could argue to myself he'd died while trying to save Luc's life—that was the easy way to justify it to my conscience. However, whenever I thought of him, it was with terrible grief, responsibility, and guilt. Had I stopped the convoy and ordered the Germans to get back into the agreed order …

"You sure you're okay?" Frank asked.

"Yeah," I replied. "I'm fine, Frank. Really, I am."

He snorted. It was the type of snort that said both *I don't believe you,* and *have it your own way.*

I'd deal with what had happened in France and in Germany in my own time. Right now, I was tired, and anxious to get home. The Duke of Windsor's letters, Queen Mary's necklace, and Édouard's letter to George were safely stowed in my duffle bag. I'd fulfilled my mission and was sorely in need of a cup of tea, a hot shower, getting my hands on my second-hand steam-powered violin, and awakening in the morning with a sleepy head on my shoulder—not necessarily in that order.

I'd taken the opportunity of sending a telegram to the "sleepy head", the moment we'd arrived in Lisbon. I'd promised I'd send word once I'd finished my mission and was on my way home. I'd sent it to our new address—14 Manchester Square, London, W1.

"Smoke?" Frank asked, offering me his packet.

"Luckies?" I'd noticed the distinctive new white package with its jaunty slogan: *Lucky Strike Green has gone to war!*

"There's a Yankee PX at Northolt now," he replied with a grin.

We sat in silence, Frank glancing over his shoulder every few puffs to check all was well in the cockpit.

We were flying at about nine thousand feet, mainly because if we went any higher, we'd have needed oxygen masks and it would have been extremely cold. As it was, I was still freezing. I'd used my last five American dollar bills to buy a fleece-lined fly boy's jacket from a Portuguese pilot in Lisbon. It kept me warmer than I otherwise might have been at this altitude. Rhys's palliasse was heaped high with blankets to keep him warm.

"Do you miss home, Tommy?"

"What a question, Frank," I replied. "Don't you?"

I was aware my reply sounded downhearted and was about to explain, but my response had drawn the pilot away into a distant inner world. I could see my own visions of home reflected back at me from his eyes.

Of course I missed home—not only my family, and the house I grew up in, but the wide, brown land of my birth.

Frank eventually murmured, "Do I miss it? I asked you first."

I bit my lower lip before I replied. My own quick thoughts about home had left a pain almost too great to bear. It showed how damned exhausted I really was. "Yes, mate, I bloody do," I replied.

"Not to worry, me old cock, won't be long now. We'll soon have you and your brother's friend back Home to Blighty."

I smiled at his use of British expressions. It had been done to cheer me up. I laughed and pretend-punched his shoulder. He pulled the blankets up under Rhys's chin and then patted me on the top of the head before returning to the cockpit.

A few minutes later the plane tilted to starboard as it began its return to the English coast. *Back Home to Blighty,* he'd said. All members of the Empire called it Home—even spelled it with a capital H. Although we might be born in countries spread across the globe, we'd been taught Britain was our real home, our Motherland.

I sat on the cabin floor next to the stretcher and lit another cigarette, idly scratching my ankle. Home? I was going to a new home in England. A new life, more like it—a life quite unlike the one I'd led before parachuting into France a mere seven weeks ago. When I got back to London, I wouldn't be returning to my cosy house in Coptic Street. Instead, I'd committed myself to living in a large, Georgian house in Manchester Square; one I hadn't seen yet, but with a tall, handsome American, with whom I'd fallen in love.

So, what was I afraid of? For, to tell the truth, I was a little fearful. It wasn't real fear—a cross between trepidation and hesitation was closer to what I felt. I made a word up to describe it—*trepihesitance*—we needed a word like that in our language. It was something like the feeling I used to have when Michael and I went to the beach together in the winter. My fearless brother would throw himself into the waves, while I stood at the edge of the water, my arms crossed, listlessly rubbing my shoulders, while I gathered the courage to take the plunge. Michael would be in the water, calling out to me to join him. If I closed my eyes I could see him now—shouting and jumping around in the waves, his eyes sparkling, his face split by his big, toothy grin.

Trepihesitance was the split-second of indecision before gathering the courage to move. The moment of tension before I ultimately threw my arms in the air, yelled at the top of my voice, and then galloped through the shallows to dive into the breakers next to my brother.

And for a fleeting moment, I felt my familiar *trepihesitance* sneaking up on me in relation to my new life with Shorty. During the past few weeks, I hadn't allowed myself the joy of accepting my new future. I'd spent time worrying about what other people might think, rather than giving myself permission to embrace the type of nervousness I should have been feeling—nice nervousness: anticipation about the thing that really counted—my new life as a lover, and as half of a new whole.

No more hesitation, now was the time to let go. We would work it out. I knew we would. In fact, I'd bloody well make sure we did. "Bugger the world and what it thinks!" I said out loud to no one, my voice nearly drowned in any case by the sound of the plane's engines. I ran down to the cockpit, and, at the top of my voice, shouted at the two pilots, *"Cur ante tubam tremor occupant Artus?"*

"Wha ...?" Frank asked, lifting the earpiece of his flying helmet, looking at me as if I were off my rocker.

"Why should fear seize the limbs before the trumpet sounds?" I shouted, trying to be heard over the noise of the engines. "It's Virgil," I tried to explain.

The two men looked at each other and grinned, Frank twirling one finger around his ear, laughing. Crazy? I supposed I was. I'd done the job I came to do—it was over. I'd given myself a moment of joyous, uncontrolled madness. I'd realised I was finally on my way home, in love, and very soon would have my arms around my man. I had every intention of squeezing him so hard his ribs might break.

As I bounded down the short aisle towards the back of the aircraft, I nearly lost my balance. The plane shifted suddenly from side to side. I looked over my shoulder. Frank was grinning at me. He'd done a victory wave in the air, to salute my craziness and sudden bout of good humour.

I checked Rhys quickly and then lay on my back on the deck of the aircraft and stared at the ceiling of the fuselage above me. Slipping my hand into my pocket, I found what I'd been looking for—a pressed, dried yellow rose, folded inside a square of pocket-linen. I held the handkerchief in the air above my head, inspecting the now dark brown stain in its corner. I sniffed it quickly. His smell had long gone, but I felt myself smile.

In my mind's eye, the anticipation of the "perfume of Shorty" had conjured an image of my wonderful, six-foot-three, almost-blond man. He was standing in front of our new house—at least what I imagined our new house might look like.

In my daydream, I'd landed at Northolt, caught a cab to Manchester Square, and was jumping out of a taxi a few hours from now. As he saw me, his face would break into a grin and he'd open his arms. I'd drop my duffle bag and run into his embrace. I wouldn't care who was around to see.

"Tommy, Tommy ..." he'd murmur into my neck.

Home?

Home, Frank Goyen? Yes, please. Let's get home quickly. Home was where my heart was. And I couldn't wait.

THE END

AUTHOR BIO

 From the outback to the opera.

After a thirty year career as a professional opera singer, performing as a soloist in opera houses and in concert halls all over the world, I took up a position as lecturer in music in Australia in 1999, at the Central Queensland Conservatorium of Music, which is now part of CQUniversity.

Brought up in Australia, between the bush and the beaches of the Eastern suburbs, I retired in 2015 and now live in the tropics, writing, gardening, and finally finding time to enjoy life and to re–establish a connection with who I am after a very busy career on the stage and as an academic.

I write mostly historical gay fiction. The stories are always about relationships and the inner workings of men; sometimes my fellas get down to the nitty–gritty, sometimes it's up to you, the reader, to fill in the blanks.

Every book is story driven; spies, detectives, murders, epic dramas, there's something for everyone. I also love to write about my country and the things that make us Aussies and our history different from the rest of the world.

I'm research driven. I always try to do my best to give the reader a sense of what life was like for my main characters in the world they live in.

Website – https://garrickjones.com.au
Facebook – https://www.facebook.com/GarrickJonesAuthor

ALSO BY GARRICK JONES

The Boys of Bullaroo: Tales of War, Aussie Mateship and More (Nov 2018), MoshPit Publishing, Australia

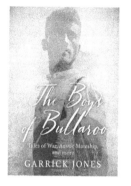

Six tales of men and war, spanning sixty years, and linked by a fictional outback town called Bullaroo. From the deserts of Egypt in 1919 to the American R&R in 1966, the stories follow the loves, losses and sexual awakenings of Australians both on the battlefield and in the bush.

The Cricketer's Arms (July 2019) MoshPit Publishing, Australia

Clyde Smith is brought into the investigation of the ritualised death of pin-up boy cricketer, Daley Morrison, by his former colleague, Sam Telford, after a note is found in the evidence bags with Clyde's initials on it. Someone wants ex-Detective Sergeant Smith to investigate the crime from outside the police force. It can only mean one thing—corruption at the highest levels.

The Cricketer's Arms is an old-fashioned, pulp fiction detective novel, set in beachside Sydney in 1956. It follows the intricacies of a complex murder case, involving a tight-knit group of queer men, sports match-fixing, and a criminal drug cartel.

Was Daley Morrison killed because of his sexual proclivities, or was his death a signal to others to tread carefully? Has Clyde Smith been fingered as the man for the case, or will the case be the end of the road for the war veteran detective?

Australia's Son (Nov 2019) MoshPit Publishing, Australia

A wrongly delivered letter sparks a chain of events that threaten the life of Edward Murray, "Australia's Son", the most renowned operatic baritone of his day.

It is 1902, and Edward has just returned to the Metropole Hotel after a performance of La Bohème at the Theatre Royal in Sydney, when the manager phones his apartment to tell him the police have arrived with bad news.

Edward, and his vaudeville performer brother, Theodore, are shocked to hear that Edward's dresser, the brothers' oldest friend from childhood, has been found dead, stabbed in the back, in Edward's recently vacated dressing room. Following a sequence of gruesome killings, Edward and the detective assigned to protect him, Chief Constable Andrew Bolton, are lured into a trap by a man whose agenda is not only personal, but driven by a deranged mind.

Set around the theatre world of early Edwardian Sydney, the story is steeped in the world of class divides, of music and the theatre. Its themes of murder, treachery and foul play, are ofttimes confronting, but the story is linked throughout by Edward Murray, the man with the golden voice, whose overarching belief is that even in the darkest of times, a sliver of light can mean that hope is at hand.

The House of a Thousand Stairs (March 2020) MoshPit Publishing, Australia

Warrambool
In Gamilaraay, the language of the Kamilaroi peoples of north-western New South Wales, it's the word for The Milky Way. It's also the name of Peter Dixon's homestead and sheep station, situated in the lee of the Liverpool Ranges.

In 1947, Peter returns from war, his parents and younger brother dead, the property de-stocked and his older brother, Ron, having emptied out the family bank account and nowhere to be found.

The House With a Thousand Stairs is the story of a young man, scarred both on the inside and the outside, trying to re-establish what once was a prosperous and thriving sheep station with the help of his neighbours and his childhood friend, Frank Hunter, the local Indigenous policeman.

Enveloped by the world of Indigenous spirituality, the Kamilaroi system of animal guides and totems, Peter and Frank discover the true nature of their predestined friendship, one defined by the stars, the ancestral spirits, and Baiame, the Creator God and Sky Father of The Dreaming.

Maliyan bandaarr, maliyan biliirr.

Wheelchair: Antarctica. Snow and Ice (Sept 2020) MoshPit Publishing, Australia

You can never judge an academic book by its cover. Simon Dyson, a quiet assistant professor, is a man of hidden depths. To the world he presents as a harmless, innocuous, shy and retiring intellectual. However, the man who lurks behind that public persona is far more interesting … and dangerous … and driven.

Wheelchair is a slow-burn contemporary psychological crime thriller about a man who suffers from both OCD and PTSD, a man who is unwittingly caught up in a cross-border war between rival crime gangs—a conflict that almost leads to his death, and more than once.

It's a study of compulsion and of disability, and of the many faces of emotional dependence and sexual compulsion. It's about how some men cannot just love or make love because their hearts or their bodies lead them to it, but who can only connect emotionally and physically through self-imposed rituals which involve struggle or self-abasement.

All available from your favourite on-line retailer

Printed in Australia
AUHW011132171120
337318AU00001B/15

9 781922 440747